Crooked Paths Straight

By

Elizabeth Wehman

Summit Street Publishing

Crooked Paths Straight
Published by Summit Street Publishing
131 West Grand River
Owosso, Michigan 48867

This book is a work of historical fiction based closely on real people and events. Details that cannot be historically verified are purely products of the author's imagination.

ISBN 978-1-7326522-8-6
ISBN 978-1-7326522-9-3   (ebook)

Publishing in the United States by Summit Street Publishing, Owosso, Michigan

Library of Congress Cataloging-in-Publication data
Wehman, Elizabeth
Crooked Paths Straight/Elizabeth Wehman-1st ed.   2021909434
The Newburg Chronicles - 2

Scripture quotations taken from The Holy Bible, New International Version®KJV® Copyright ©1973, 1978, 1984, 2011 by Biblica, Inc.™

Used by permission. All rights reserved worldwide.

Printed in the United States of America
2021
Cover Photo: Emily E. Lawson Photography
Cover Art: Emily E. Lawson

I would like to dedicate *Crooked Paths Straight* to my dear friend, Wanda Lamphere.

She's left us too soon but she leaves beautiful memories of her laughter, smile, love for everyone, and fondness of books.

Her absence just makes heaven that much sweeter.

Acknowledgements

The first time I saw the name, Hosea Baker, he was just another man in the history books of the Michigan Territory. Since 2019, he is now become one of my dearest friends. I love to hear him quote Scripture in a lyrical way—if just in my imagination. His mannerisms, his way of removing his hat to scratch his head, and his determination to tame a wild country—continues to spur me on to write more about his life and family. Just when I think I've exhausted all there is to know about him, someone brings me a newspaper excerpt, a history book paragraph, or I find a grave of someone who knew or loved him and can make a connection to his life.

He is in history books as one of the first farming settlers, but his attributes, habits, and character are of my imagination. I envision meeting him one day and having him tell me, "I'm excited to be famous long after I've lived but dear girl, that's not how any of my life happened." We will laugh and he'll probably tell me the truth of his adventures in the Michigan Territory but that will be okay.

The stories of the early settlement of Shiawassee County, Michigan seem to pour out of me like the spring by Hosea's house. Each one takes on the mystery, suspense, and intrigue of living in the early 19th century. I'm sure it was much more difficult than my attempts at entertaining stories, but I've done my best to capture the essence of early living in our beloved state of Michigan.

My thanks for *Crooked Paths Straight* production goes out to my beta readers, especially Brenda Stroub, Rebekah Szczygiel, and final proofreader Beth Hafer. Also to Emily Lawson Photography for her expertise in designing my book covers. And a special thanks to my faithful editor, Kathryn Frazier. Each one spurs me on to complete an intriguing book for my readers. I appreciate each one so much.

I'm excited for you to join me in celebrating the settlement of North Newburg through story. I'm eager to begin the third book in the series, but first—Crooked Paths Straight.

Enjoy!

Elizabeth

~ Psalm 34:8

Caroline Baker

Born: August 22, 1819

Died: November 16, 1893

"And I will bring the blind by the way that they knew not, I will lead them in paths that they have not known: I will make darkness light before them, and crooked things straight. These things will I do unto them, and not forsake them."   *Isaiah 42:16*

CHRISTMAS DAY, 1833

CHAPTER ONE

"Nothing brings me more joy than to follow this path we now have to Ma and Pa's." Betsey Swain took her husband, Aaron's hand, as they made their way down the trail. Aaron had created a new path for them to take to her parent's house during the winter months. He wanted it to be shorter than the first one he'd made for them, knowing that Betsey would now be carrying their baby, Julia, while traveling to and from their cabin on the ridge.

"It used to be just wide enough for two people; now it's large enough for a wagon." Aaron squeezed Betsey's mittened hand. "Perhaps we should name it."

"What?" Betsey giggled.

"How about the Swain Trail?" Aaron grinned.

"How about Crooked Trail?" Betsey winked. "This trail goes one way and then quickly shifts another way. Perhaps Zig-Zag Trail." Betsey adjusted the rope tightening on her shoulder from the baby board strapped to her back. Aaron dropped Betsey's hand to shift her load with a hand push under the tiny infant's rump. When he did, a slight grunt erupted from their baby tucked deep inside the tightly wrapped blankets. The noise made Betsey and Aaron laugh.

"Sounds like someone wants us to remember she's here." Aaron patted Betsey's back bump. "It's okay, Julia. We'll soon be at Grammy's house."

Trudging through the snow today was more efficient due to the snowshoes Aaron had made them. He'd surprised Betsey with a pair as a Christmas gift just that morning. Betsey was still getting used to how to walk properly in them.

"Hard to believe we've been in the territory for eight months."

"Longest eight months I've ever experienced." Again, Betsey clasped Aaron's hand.

"You should have allowed me to carry Julia. Are you okay?"

"I'm fine. I need to get used to the weight. This won't be the first time that I carry Julia this way, especially in snowshoes."

"It was nice of Waussinoodae to gift the baby carrying device to you."

"She's been nothing but a good friend. I care for her."

Aaron nodded. "I'm happy you aren't as afraid."

Betsey glanced upward to find the trail of smoke emitting from her parents' chimney. She'd looked forward to this day for a few weeks. Since moving to their cabin on the ridge, Betsey missed her ma, pa, and sisters. Every moment of her day seemed consumed with Julia's care and organizing a household which came with its own set of chores.

Aaron plodded forward through the deep snow, taking his time to help Betsey along the way. "This year hasn't been easy, but look how far we've come. We don't consider the Indians as threats. We have a couple of new neighbors settling close, Ambrose will soon be building his place, and we now have our cabin..." With that comment, Aaron again squeezed Betsey's hand. "And we're enduring our first winter in the new territory. Perhaps soon, we'll have a whole community here. Won't that be wonderful?"

Soon the path they followed took a turn to the east, heading directly for the Baker cabin. "Let's not get ahead of ourselves." Betsey felt the baby shift. Reaching around, she adjusted Julia back to where it was more comfortable. "Today, let's enjoy the holiday with the family."

Someone began waving, calling their names, from the back side of the barn. Betsey's brother, Ambrose, was doing his best to help forge a path from the barn to the cabin with Pa's shovel. His cheery greeting came just as the sun peeked out from behind a cloud in the bright blue sky, "Merry Christmas!"

"I hope this beautiful morning doesn't give way to a new storm. But by the darkness of the sky across the river, I have a feeling it won't last the entire day. We'll have to keep an eye to the sky."

Betsey let go of Aaron's hand. "I don't want anything to spoil this day."

Aaron had been right. Soon after the family ate their Christmas dinner and opened their gifts, a blast of winter's wind slammed into the cabin's eastern wall.

Aaron and Betsey were considering bundling themselves up to head home when the door to the cabin swung wide, and a man carrying a woman walked over the threshold. Gusts of wind combined with snow swirled around them. Betsey's pa, Hosea, stood up so abruptly that his chair slammed to the floor.

The stranger's snowy beard made it appear as if St. Nicholas himself were visiting them. The next word let everyone know that it wasn't the case. "Help!"

Aaron was the first to the door.

"Aaron."

He looked into the eyes of the man who called him by name.

"Who are you?" Without following through with the answer, the man dropped to his knees with the woman still in his arms.

Hosea jumped into action, rushing to take the woman from the arms of the frozen character who'd just entered.

Their clothes were crispy and stuck together with particles of ice. Aaron did his best to pry the woman's clothes away from the man who carried her.

Betsey's ma, Sally, handed blankets to Betsey and her sister Caroline, who gathered around the woman now lying on the floor of the cabin, shaking uncontrollably. The woman's mouth was clenched, her eyes wide, and her limbs stiff.

"Rub her down, girls. Help me strip these wet coats off of her." Sally began untying the woman's coat at her neck and worked her way down the front unhooking the button loops, using a gentle touch.

"Aaron." The man looked at him.

The stranger seemed to resemble his brother. "John Ferrar?"

The man forced a smile and then fainted in Aaron's arms.

Betsey turned as she continued to rub life into the hands of the woman on the floor, "Aaron, who is he?"

Aaron appeared to have not heard Betsey and now, with Ambrose's help, struggled to get the man to a nearby chair. Pa pulled a chair out from under the table. They began to strip off the man's outer clothing, the same as the womenfolk were doing to the woman on the floor.

"Once we get these wet outer garments off, we'll wrap them both in blankets." Ma motioned to Betsey's other sisters, Jillian and Etta. "Pull those chairs closer to the fire, Etta. Jillian, we need to get these folks warm."

Ambrose asked, "Who are they, Aaron? They seem to know you."

Aaron unwound the scarf from around the man's neck. "It's my brother, John Ferrar, and I believe the woman might be his wife. I haven't seen either of them in years."

"John Ferrar?"

"John is my brother's name, as well as my pa's. We'd often refer to him as John Ferrar so he and Father could be distinguished one from another. Ferrar is his middle name."

The family had placed the frozen guests close to the fire. Pa added more wood, and soon the blazing heat made everyone want to strip out of their winter clothing layers.

"I think he's coming around." Pa motioned to Aaron, who was on his knees by the man's chair.

"John Ferrar?"

The man's eyes opened, and he smiled. "Aaron. We've found you."

"Why are you out traveling on a day like today? How did you find me?"

"Well, that, my brother...is a long story."

"Don't make him talk." Betsey's ma interrupted the conversation between the brothers. "Here, John, drink some coffee. It will warm you on the inside as well."

John swallowed a large gulp from the cup Ma held. Some of the drink dribbled down into his beard, helping to melt icicles that had solidified there.

Caroline pulled Betsey aside from the commotion of reviving the frozen couple. "Did you know Aaron had a brother?"

Betsey whispered, "Yes. I believe he's from New York State."

Suddenly the woman gasped right out and took a deep, long breath. She began to moan. "My feet. Oh, my feet."

Ma bent down and gently began rubbing her feet with a bit of snow that Pa had brought from outside. Warming them too fast could cause frostbite. "Here, Jillian, gently rub her other foot with this warm cloth after I do a bit more rubbing with snow."

The woman grasped for her feet and gazed at Ma. "Who are you?"

"My name's Sally. I'm Betsey's ma."

The woman's eyes darted back and forth. "John?" She seemed to be searching for her husband but not able to see him.

"I'm here. We're safe now." John patted her shoulder as the woman fainted again.

"I've heard that frostbite can be painful. Your wife's fainting is probably for the best." Ma kept gently rubbing the woman's feet, which appeared waxy and white.

Aaron was doing the same to his brother's feet. "How did you find me?"

John took a cup of warm broth from Pa and took a long swig. "We've been on the trail for months. We started way back in August thinking we could be here before the snow fell." Taking another long swig, he swallowed. "I miscalculated a bit."

"It's December. Christmas Day, in fact!" Aaron told the man.

Pa's eyes twinkled. "Merry Christmas!"

The man did his best to smile, but his whole face lacked expression. Perhaps numb from cold. "We set off from Whitmore's post just yesterday morning. I believe we must have gotten a bit off the trail."

"Yesterday morning!" Ambrose held up their coats by the fire as the moisture dripped onto the hearth, each drop sizzling from the heat. "You've been out in this weather for almost twenty-four hours?"

John answered Ambrose, "We snuggled down in the wagon below blankets last night. Did fairly well, but with the storm today, we must have taken a wrong trail."

"That's not hard to do." Aaron picked up a nearby rag and began wiping down the floor around his family members.

Tears began to well in John's eyes. "I didn't realize how hard the trail was going to be. We've had quite the ordeal. From what Father told me..."

"You've seen Father?" Aaron reached out for John's cup, now empty, to fill it with coffee.

John suddenly stopped talking, glancing at Aaron with more tears. "I have. He called for me last summer."

"Last summer?" Aaron stooped to look into his brother's eyes. "What happened?"

"I'm sorry to have to tell you, Aaron. Father's passed on."

Aaron picked up Hosea's tipped chair and sat down. Betsey crossed the room and placed her hand on Aaron's shoulder. "When?"

"Just before we left him in Pennsylvania. He told me to follow you. Do my best to find out about this new land, like he had intended to do himself." John took another long swallow, gulping the warm drink. "The doctor believed he had an apoplexy of some kind. He never recovered from it."

"Hand me those warm towels, Jillian." Ma glanced at Betsey with sorrowful eyes. "We need to keep working on getting circulation back into her feet, or she'll lose them."

John rubbed his face, to bring feeling back into his cheeks. "Thank you for caring for us. Especially Abigail. We've had a tough time getting here." John looked at his wife with sadness. "She's young and fragile. I never imagined this would be such a hard experience for her. Traveling is hard on the sturdiest of us, but Abigail..." Aaron's brother stopped talking, as if sharing more about his wife would make him weep. He took another long swig of his coffee.

Betsey could see Aaron struggling to process the fact that his father was gone. She reached down, cupped his cheek in her hand. and whispered in his ear, "I'm so sorry, darling."

He glanced up at her with tears threatening to spill down his cheeks. She knew what he thought before he even said a word. They'd come with her family and left his relatives behind. He now probably felt as if he'd abandoned his father. Betsey hugged his shoulders to her.

"We've brought a few things for you folks. As soon as I get some more circulation in these toes and fingers, I'll go out to the wagon and retrieve them."

Betsey knew that everyone was wondering what Aaron's brother could have brought to them. But she regained her senses and asked, "Have you eaten? We have plenty left from our Christmas feast. Can I make you a plate?"

John handed Pa his cup. "I'd be grateful. We haven't had a good meal in weeks. Thank you."

Aaron's brother did eat as though it had been a long time since he'd been able to. As he finally got enough strength to talk more, he began telling the family of their ordeal and why it had taken four months for them to arrive.

Abigail continued to moan by the fire. Sally said her feet were beginning to turn red, which was a good sign.

"Let's move her to our bed, Hosea."

John stood to help them, but Aaron motioned for him to sit down. "I'll get her, John."

Aaron bent down, gently picking up his sister-in-law, carrying her to Hosea and Sally's bed. Sally pulled back the covers, and he placed her there.

"Jillian, get me two of those warming stones by the fire and put them under the covers here."

Jillian used a dry towel to carry the hot stones. Her mother placed them near the feet of the trembling woman.

"Her tremors are a good thing." Sally said as she tucked the stones at the foot of the bed and then pulled the blankets around them.

Hosea sat down at the table and handed another biscuit to John. "We're sorry to hear you had it rough."

"From thunderstorms on the Great Lake to weeks of recovering in Detroit. My poor Abigail was with child when we began our journey, but she lost the baby before arriving in Detroit. She's been having troubles ever since. Once we made it to Detroit, I allowed her to recover from the steamboat trip and the loss of our child. Toward the first of November, I knew if we didn't get moving into the territory, we'd never reach you before the snow fell."

Aaron sat down next to his brother. "Perhaps it would have been wise to stay in Detroit."

John sat back in his chair and folded his arms. "You're right, Aaron. But when you'd written Father and told him it was just a few weeks journey from Detroit, I thought we could make it. But things just got worse as we ventured farther. Abigail was so frightened by everything around her, from the wolves to the various Indians we encountered along the way. The trail was hard to find, especially when snow began to fall in the middle of November." John shook his head. "I kick myself now for not staying in Detroit, but I'm embarrassed to say...I began to run out of funds. There was a doctor there to treat Abigail, but we also had to eat meals at a local hotel. We did find a place to board but could only stay there ten weeks. I thought about staying, really I did, but it would have taken every penny we'd saved to get here. And even now—" John pulled on his beard, no longer covered in icicles. "We don't have much left."

Aaron patted his brother's shoulder. "You're here. We have plenty of food for a few months. We'll help you until you get on your feet in the spring."

Tears welled in his brother's eyes. "I hate to be a burden. I just didn't know what else to do." Scooting his chair back, John went to fetch his coat off the peg near the fireplace. "I have things for you. I need to see if I can find them."

Aaron stood. "Can I go get them? I hate for you to venture out again."

John shook his head. "It's okay. I'll find them quickly. I also need to use the outhouse. Point me in the right direction, and I'll be back soon."

Aaron led him outside, and pointed to the rope tied from the cabin to the outhouse. "This is so you don't get lost on the way."

John disappeared into the swirling snow.

Coming back into the house, Aaron could hear Sally talking to Abigail in the bed. "Is she awake?"

Betsey hugged her husband. "Are you okay?"

"I will be." Aaron went to the far side of the cabin, where his daughter was letting everyone know she was up from her nap and ready to be picked up. He lifted Julia from her cradle, kissing her cheek. She looked at him and gurgled. A heavy weight of sadness filled his chest. He'd longed to introduce his new daughter to her grandfather, and now that wouldn't happen. The opportunity of leaving family to head West often meant never seeing them again.

Betsey came toward him and Julia, placing her head on Aaron's shoulder. "Is someone finally awake?"

"Awake, and she seems ready to eat again."

The baby chewed her fist.

"She's about as hungry as my brother." Aaron looked into Betsey's eyes.

"When's the last time you saw John?"

Aaron shrugged. "After Ma died, he stayed with an uncle in New York instead of making the trip with Father and me. He liked

Abigail, way back when, and planned to marry her. He didn't want to leave her."

"So, you know her?"

"Yes, but not all that well." Aaron handed Julia to Betsey, who sat down in a rocking chair close by the bed to feed the demanding child.

"You don't sound fond of her."

Aaron sighed and sat on the edge of the bed. "I don't like saying unkind things about people, but she used to be—"

Betsey cocked her head.

"Difficult." Aaron leaned closer, so only Betsey could hear. "That's why he stayed in New York. She put up such a fuss about him leaving, he felt obligated to stay." Aaron shrugged. "Perhaps she's gained maturity since then." He swirled the coffee around in his cup. "I never thought I'd ever see John Ferrar again. All these months, I've been expecting my father. He's not who I expected to see. Let alone to travel all this way to be with us."

Aaron went back to the table. As much as he wanted his conversation to be with just Betsey, Sally and the others must have overheard.

"Sometimes what we plan doesn't always transpire." Ma took Aaron's cup and filled it with more coffee.

"For My thoughts are not your thoughts," Hosea quoted. "Neither are your ways My ways." Hosea lifted his cup for Sally, who filled it to the brim.

The door to the cabin opened, and in walked John. He carried a barrel.

Hosea got up from the table, taking the wooden drum so John could remove his coat. While he did, John held out an envelope to Aaron.

"This one's for you."

Aaron took the letter.

"And this one..." John held a smaller one.

Aaron grew skeptical.

"Is there someone here named Caroline?"

Caroline walked toward John. "I'm Caroline."

"This is from someone named Billie. Do you know him?"

John grinned at Caroline as she took the envelope from his hand.

Sally began prying the lid off the barrel that John Ferrar Swain had brought that afternoon. She'd recognized the barrel right away. She'd packed the container just before they left Pennsylvania for their journey to the Michigan Territory.

Hosea came into the kitchen area, where she struggled. "What have we here?"

"It's the barrel I thought we'd lost aboard the steamboat on our way here."

"I can't believe we left it in the wagon that Aaron's father returned home with." Hosea took over opening the barrel for his wife.

"I can't either. I thought for sure we'd gotten everything out of the wagon before Aaron's father left us in Erie."

As the lid lifted off, Sally reached in to find the extra blankets she'd packed last spring before coming to Michigan. They needed them, now that the weather had turned colder. At the bottom were the baby clothes and outfits her children had worn as infants. Sally shook out a dress and a bonnet she'd made in Pennsylvania that would fit Julia well now. "Look at this."

Hosea laughed. "I thought these things were long gone. I didn't realize you had saved them."

"Saved and kept them for our grandchildren. And look." Sally lifted her veil from the bottom of the barrel. It smelled a bit musty, but it was still intact and pretty. "Perhaps we'll have a bride to wear this soon."

Hosea laughed and stroked the soft veil. He seemed to recognize it right away. "Sally Mae, look how well this has held up."

Sally held it against her cheek. "I'm so thankful Aaron's father thought about sending these things to us with John." She carefully placed the veil back into the deep barrel. "I can't believe Aaron's father is gone."

"I feel for Aaron. It's hard losing your pa."

Sally agreed. "He has you now, too. You've been a father figure to him as well."

"I know. But it's always hard to lose your pa."

Sally glanced over at Caroline sitting close beside the fireplace hearth for enough light to read her letter. "Hard to believe that boy continues to pine for your daughter."

"What boy?"

"You can't be serious, Hosea."

"I'm completely mystified. Who?"

"Well, I'm not a bettin' woman, but if this veil doesn't get used this summer, I'll be as mystified as you."

CHAPTER TWO

Caroline did her best to shift the paper in her hand to make out, with just a faint light from the fire, the letter Billie had sent her. Watermarks blurred a few of the sentences. Tilting the page, she figured out the next word and inserted what she thought was correct. Billie was earning money to make his way to her.

She didn't realize she was holding her breath as she made out each word. A pop from the fire made Caroline press the letter to her chest and away from any sparks. She sighed. He was coming in the spring.

Closing her eyes, she clutched the letter. Could it be true? A boy, back in Pennsylvania, wanting to make his way to her, here in the new territory? Opening her eyes, she reopened the envelope and tucked the letter back inside. As she did, a movement across the room caught her attention. Caroline's sisters were looking at her with silly grins on their faces, hands pressed over their hearts as if mocking her. She glared back at them.

They came rushing toward her. "Oh, Caroline! Do you love me, or do you not?" Jillian looked upward in a dreamy fashion.

"Oh yes, my Billie. I do, I do!" crooned Etta.

"Oh, stop it!" Caroline stood up and made her way to the cabin's corner, where she could put Billie's letter in a safe place. Away from prying eyes and annoying sisters.

She peeked over her shoulder at her sisters, who were still mimicking her, behind her back. She couldn't take a chance on them seeing where she hid the precious letter. It would be a prominent hiding place to put the letter into a barrel that held her undergarments. They'd look there. So, she pretended to slip it into the barrel but instead tucked it into the waistband of her skirt. She knew the exact spot that it would be protected and safe. She'd put it there later.

She turned to come back to the table where the girls were whispering and giggling to themselves. She didn't care what they thought or what they were saying about her. Immaturity was the cause; Caroline ignored their taunts.

"Aaron? Do you think we need to head home soon? Do you think it's safe?" Betsey had just finished feeding the baby and was patting her on the back, awaiting a burp.

"Yes. Are you up to the climb?"

Betsey smiled. "Of course I am. Let me change Julia's diaper, and we'll be ready soon."

"Do you think it's safe, Hosea? It was snowing quite hard this afternoon." Ma came from the bed where she'd been caring for Abigail.

Alexander, the orphaned boy they had taken on last spring, began to pull on his boots, wrapping himself in the coat Ma had made him at the beginning of the summer. He'd wanted to spend the night with Aaron and Betsey for quite a time. Betsey had promised him he could join them for a week after Christmas.

"Aaron will know. Last time I looked, the snow had let up, and a bright moon was beginning to illuminate the forest."

Caroline loved to think of Betsey now living on the hill above their cabin. They'd moved into the almost-finished home last month. Aaron was determined to get the structure secure enough for them to stay during the winter. He would work on the inside during the secluded snowy season.

"It was a delightful Christmas Day," Aaron commented, and patted his brother on the back. "I'm not sure it would be a good walk for Abigail tonight. Why don't you and she stay here with Pa and Ma tonight, if that's okay with them?" Aaron gave Pa a fleeting look.

Ambrose piped up, "I can sleep in the barn tonight. Temperatures aren't that bad. I've slept in colder ones." He always seemed to be the one to concede to sleeping in the barn.

"Come stay in the loft with Alexander tonight, Ambrose. Betsey can make us popcorn to enjoy." It didn't take long for Ambrose to agree and pull on his coat.

"Stay as long as you need, John. We'll move Abigail to the girls' bed for the night, and you are more than welcome to stay here. I agree with Aaron. Sally has just now gotten her warm." Hosea pointed toward the bed.

Ma glanced his way. "They're more than welcome," she added.

"Why, thank you. I don't know what would have happened today if we hadn't found you all." John stood up and shook Pa's hand. "Thank you for your hospitality."

"Certainly. You'll soon find out, John, that everyone here wishes the new neighbors to be successful in their ventures to the territory. We need folks nearby. The more, the merrier." Pa patted John on the shoulder.

"If you stay here, we'll come back tomorrow and discuss plans for the coming weeks. Putting a house up in this weather will be impossible." Aaron sat down to pull warm socks up and to secure his high leather boots.

Betsey brought out the backboard that Waussinoodae, the Indian woman who'd brought Alexander to them, had given her a few weeks before. It had been an effective and easy way to tote the baby back and forth from her house to her parents. Julia was snug and warm in her cocoon-like papoose board on Betsey's back. Betsey had to regain much of her strength from the ague and childbirth, but Caroline could see she was stronger by carrying the baby as she did.

"Thanks for the celebration," Aaron added as he put his arms into his heavy coat and held Betsey's out to her to put on as well.

"You're so welcome, children. Thanks for coming and spending the day with us. I wish there could have been more presents and more sugary sweets to eat to celebrate the holiday, but at least we were together." Ma wiped her hands on her apron.

"It was a wonderful day, Ma. Look..." Betsey pointed to her brother-in-law, who stood beside Aaron. "We received a wonderful gift today. Aaron now has a relative to live close to."

Everyone seemed to agree.

"I hope Abigail continues to recuperate," Aaron told his brother. "I'm glad you're here and safe." He pulled his brother close and hugged him.

"I'm sorry that I couldn't bring better tidings on this holiday, but I am thankful we finally found family." John bowed his head.

Caroline was sure it was to prevent everyone from seeing his teary eyes as he wiped them.

"Can you help me, Caroline?" Betsey held out the backboard for Caroline to help strap onto her back. The baby shifted around, but her eyes were growing heavy, and soon the motion of the walk would put her to sleep. She was such a good baby.

Caroline waited for Betsey to put on her coat, and then she held the rope around the baby while Betsey tied it to her chest and waist. Betsey had wrapped Julia in a heavy blanket, and now all Ma had to do was place the blanket to cover her head.

"Wait a moment; I haven't kissed my grandchild goodbye yet." Ma rushed over and planted a kiss on Julia's forehead. "Sleep well, my sweet one."

Soon Caroline watched her sister and her husband, followed by Ambrose and Alexander, head outside into the evening twilight. If they hustled, they'd have just enough time to make it to their cabin before darkness settled over the property.

Pa called out after them, "Stay safe." He didn't keep the door open very long as snow from their footsteps swirled in. "Gotta keep the heat in." Closing the door, he placed the latch back into place.

"How about another cup of coffee?" Pa asked John, who now sat down at the table.

"I think I've had plenty. You've all been so kind. I am feeling a bit weary myself. Let's get Abigail moved to the other bed, and I think I may settle in soon myself. It's been a long day."

Pa patted his arm. "That it has."

Caroline wished they could still sing Christmas hymns into the evening as Pa had promised. But as Aaron lifted Abigail's frail body from Ma and Pa's bed to her own, she knew they'd need to be quiet so Abigail, and even John, could rest.

As Ma tucked the covers in tightly around Abigail, Caroline wondered what kind of person Abigail might be. Being Betsey's sister-in-law, certainly, they'd become good friends. Abigail appeared to be Betsey's age, and being married, they'd likely have many things in common. Perhaps Caroline could fit into their intimate circle soon, too. Lately, she'd felt too grown up for her younger sisters' conversations. All they could think about was how they looked or what kind of boy they hoped would court them. Those subjects seemed ridiculous to Caroline, especially since Billie was soon coming to find her.

Pa rigged up the blanket that separated the beds from each other as it had been when Betsey and Aaron were still living with them.

Caroline looked at her sisters, who had taken the new blankets from the barrel John had brought and begun making makeshift beds on the floor in front of the fire. She didn't look forward to the hard floor again. Caroline and her sisters had slept on the fireplace hearth enough that first summer. But somehow, she knew she didn't have a choice. Folks who were company always came first at the Baker cabin.

Thinking they would all sleep well after such an eventful day had been an illusion. Abigail had a fitful night. It wasn't an occasional loud moan; she once woke up screaming out in the darkness.

John seemed to do his best to quiet her. Caroline awoke with a start every time. It would then take her a long time to settle back to sleep. The moans and screams were frightening to hear in their otherwise quiet cabin. She thought Pa's snores were loud, but these outbursts from their guest seemed much worse.

As morning erupted, Pa left the cabin to start his day. Caroline heard his feet crunch in the snow outside as he rounded the house to head toward the barn. She tucked the corner of her blanket under her chin. It didn't feel as though she'd gotten any sleep. Her head hurt, and so did her hip against the hard wooden floor.

The fire licked the fresh wood Pa had added to it before he'd left the cabin. The room began to feel warm again. Caroline decided to get out from beneath the covers and start breakfast. As she reached for her clothes, Ma came from her own bed.

"What a night," Ma whispered to her as she held out her apron.

Caroline took the garment. "Did you hear Abigail, too?"

Ma tied on her apron. "It was a long night. I hope the dear woman can get relief from her pain today."

John soon joined them by the fire. "I'm so sorry. Abigail had a bit of a time last night." He added another log. "I'm sure it must have disturbed everyone's sleep."

Ma patted his shoulder. "It's fine, John. We understand how much she must be hurting. Frostbite is something many of us have suffered through, and it takes a body time to recover."

John rubbed his hands together over the now-crackling fire. "Good thing this cabin is as small as it is. The fire is warming it very well."

"Let's get breakfast started, Caroline." Ma nudged the slumbering bodies of her sisters. "Let's go, girls. Time to rise."

Betsey poured more coffee into Ambrose's cup. "Tell us a bit more about John, Aaron. What's he like?"

Aaron and Ambrose enjoyed their morning coffee together at the makeshift table Aaron had set up for them. He needed to make a proper table, but for now, this one served them well.

"John Ferrar is a lot like Father. We've always been fairly close. I think it's because he was my only sibling. When I moved to Pennsylvania to follow Betsey, John was determined to stay behind. Mostly because of Abigail." Aaron took another sip of his coffee. "To be honest, the rest of the family wasn't too keen on her. I mean," Aaron shrugged, "she's not mean-spirited, but she's just a bit—"

"Aaron, don't say anything. I want to make my own opinions of John's wife." Betsey joined them at the table.

Aaron sighed. "You're right. Forgive me. She was very young when John decided to stay back because of her."

"I can see why he'd stay back. Despite Abigail's appearance yesterday, she is a striking woman." Ambrose glanced over at Betsey and shrugged, too.

Betsey gave him a scolding look.

"What? She is."

Aaron laughed. "That she is. Father and I were pretty sure that after a year or so, John would figure out that looks aren't everything, but now..." Aaron sat back in his chair, folding his arms. "I'm afraid he never figured out how difficult it would be to have such a pretty wife."

"Difficult!" Ambrose chuckled. "I guess when you have such a pretty face, men overlook character flaws."

"That they do. But don't get me wrong, not all women who are strikingly beautiful are difficult to live with." Aaron winked at Betsey.

"So, what you're telling me, Aaron, is to find one that is not only beautiful but has a sweet spirit, too?"

Aaron grinned. "You'll find one, Ambrose. You're too good-natured not to."

"I hope so." Ambrose reached over and hugged Alexander, who now sat on the floor beside Ambrose's tree-stump chair. "How'd you sleep, boy? You snored enough to keep the critters awake last night."

Alexander had begun to use hand signals to communicate. It had taken them most of the first few months of winter to figure out the best ones to use, but Alexander caught on quickly. He seemed to communicate the best with Etta, but Ambrose did his best to make up motions for Alexander and him to converse. Alexander smiled up at him.

"Let's have some flapjacks for breakfast, boys." Betsey handed Julia to Aaron, then rose to fix breakfast.

"Where will John and Abigail stay? Pa and Ma have a houseful with just the girls."

Aaron knew Ambrose was right.

"They're coming here. Of course. We'll fix the other end of the loft for your family. At least through the winter." Betsey told them as she mixed flour into the bowl on the table.

Aaron tickled Julia under her arm. She grinned, spit drooling down her chin as she did. "John used to be a fairly good carpenter. Father always said he could build anything from a pile of wood. I'm sure they'll be comfortable here."

"Makes the most sense. Alexander can go back to Pa and Ma's house. On the warmer nights, I'll stay out in the barn, but when the temperatures are wicked, I'll make it into the house and cuddle up next to this snoring child myself. We'll make do."

Alexander seemed to still prefer the hard floor to any kind of makeshift bed Pa or even Ambrose made for him.

"We'll miss having you in the loft and being with us, Ambrose." Betsey began pouring out the batter onto the sizzling skillet near the fire. The smell of fresh pancakes filled the cabin.

"It will be somethin' to see how many newcomers we get into the territory this winter and spring. After talking to Whitmore this past fall, I think we'll be surprised how many neighbors we get soon."

Alexander stood up as Betsey held out plates for him to take to the table. Soon the men were eating the freshly made flapjacks Betsey flipped onto their plates from her hot skillet. It was pleasant how helpful Alexander was in the house and to Ambrose, Aaron, and Pa with the outside chores.

"I'll head down to the cabin today to check on John and Abigail. If Abigail is well enough, perhaps they could move up here today." Aaron shifted the baby to a sitting position on his lap as he started to eat his breakfast.

Betsey wondered what it would be like to have another woman in the house beside Ma and her sisters. It would be good to have help, especially with Julia now taking up so much of her time. What woman wouldn't want help with all the household chores? She hoped they could become not only close sisters but close friends. She tried hard not to allow Aaron's perspective of his sister-in-law dim her optimism.

CHAPTER THREE

"I need something to drink," commented a soft voice from behind the guests' makeshift wall.

"Just a moment, Abigail. I'll get you one," John answered his wife's plea.

Caroline looked to Ma for advice. She headed toward the water barrel, but Ma held up a finger, shaking her head.

Soon John reappeared. Ma pointed to a dipper hanging on a nail beside the barrel. Pa had just added to the water from the buckets of snow he'd brought in the night before. "Help yourself, John."

"Thank you." John filled a cup with the dipper, put his cupped palm under it, and delivered a mug to his wife behind the curtain.

"I think our patient is coming around." Ma smiled and turned a pancake sizzling on the skillet over the fire.

Caroline wondered about the woman named Abigail. She seemed not much older than her. Due to her condition the day before, Caroline imagined her to be shy and afraid. She could hear John coaxing the woman to take a sip from the cup he'd brought to her.

"Where are we?" Abigail mumbled.

"We've found my brother. The Baker family is his wife's family. They were gracious enough—"

"I'm hungry."

"Let's see how this water satisfies you for the time being."

"I don't think I'll ever forgive you for bringing me—"

"Abigail. Not now." John lowered his voice, but with a tiny cabin, conversations were rarely private.

"Why, John? Why couldn't we have just stayed in Pennsylvania?"

"We've talked about this." John lowered his voice even more.

"You hate me!" spouted the woman for all to hear.

Ma looked at Caroline and spoke loudly, "Caroline, bring me some more of that flour. These pancakes are a bit runny."

Ma's pancake batter was always perfect. Thick and ready to make into delicious, fluffy cakes. Caroline was sure that the batter did not need more flour.

Caroline brought her the flour anyway, and Ma added less than a spoonful to the ready mixture. She gave Caroline a look that spoke louder than any words: Mind your business.

"Etta, come over here and set the table."

Caroline and her sisters knew their place wasn't to overhear the conversation behind the curtain. Their job was to help Ma get breakfast ready for their guests. All three girls found a chore to do as Ma began to chat about their plans for the day. Her chatter didn't stop, but despite it, everyone could hear everything that Abigail was voicing.

Betsey and Aaron sat at their breakfast table discussing their plans to invite John and Abigail to stay in their new home with them. There was no question that it was their duty to help Aaron's family.

"We can set up a nice place in the north portion of the loft for them. It will give them a bit of privacy, too." Aaron placed another flapjack on his plate to go with the egg Betsey had fried for his breakfast.

"We had planned on just the two of us. With John and Abigail sharing meals with us, our food supplies will be stretched even further. How can I make it last longer?" Betsey knew that two extra mouths would add a burden to their already strained food resources for winter.

"I'll be more mindful of eating less." Aaron took a long swig of his coffee.

"But you are already eating less. We all are. It's almost January." Betsey topped off his mug and added a bit more to Ambrose's cup, too.

"We can head back to Ma and Pa's." Ambrose tousled the hair of the young boy seated beside him.

"That's silly. We'll figure it all out." Betsey hung the kettle back over the hearth and sat down.

"I never imagined my brother showing up like this. My father maybe, but not John and his wife." Aaron glanced down at his plate.

Betsey knew her husband had been mourning the news John and Abigail had brought with them. She knew the grief he now felt was still fresh as Aaron fought for composure.

"I am sorry you got news of your pa like that, Aaron." Ambrose took another long swig of his coffee. "But it isn't a horrible situation. We'll make do. I know deer have been scarce as of late, too, but we'll figure it out. We'll get out and hunt more."

Aaron set down his fork to wipe his mouth. "I wish there were easier ways for a man to earn a living here, besides farming. I'm anxious for a lawman position which would make me feel better able to provide for Betsey and the baby as well as John and Abigail now, too."

"Things will be better after winter is over. If I can make it on my own, like I did last year, that will alleviate me from being a burden to others, too."

Betsey sat down to pull Julia onto her lap. She wasn't intimidated to feed her in front of Ambrose and Alexander. She now knew how to do it discreetly without showing too much of herself in the process. The baby was an eager eater and didn't take long to settle in for her breakfast.

"It was nice to have this large cabin for the four of us, but we'll make do with the addition of John and Abigail, too." Betsey smiled at Aaron. "It will be nice to have another woman to share the load here." Even though Betsey had enjoyed having her kitchen and chores all to herself, it would be nice to have another woman in her home.

"Once we rig up a bed for them at the opposite end of the loft, you and Alexander can occupy the other end. Perhaps we can even make it two bedrooms instead of just one."

Ambrose rubbed the top of Alexander's head, causing the young boy's hair to stick up. "Thanks for that. We don't need much space, do we, Alexander?"

The young boy smiled up at Ambrose.

"I'll head out today and find some wood for another bed. We can make that our main job today and tomorrow; we'll scout around to see what game we can bring in that will help us get through the winter better." Aaron smiled over at Betsey. "We'll make it all work."

Betsey wondered how they'd make it through their first winter in the new territory with two more mouths to feed.

A fierce storm came upon the small cabin in the woods. The gusty winds felt like several strong men pushing against a wall with a team of oxen.

Over the past few days, Abigail had wandered from the bed. She flinched at every creak caused by the winter wind. "Can this house withstand such a storm?" she asked with a frightened voice.

Pa assured her that it would, but she continued to ask as the wind whistled through the slats around the door. During these storms, strong Michigan gusts caused snow to slip even beneath the door. It was hard to keep their home warm on days like this. The fire flickered with each burst of wind.

"I don't know why John thought it a good idea to bring us to such a wild country." Abigail moaned as if every breath she took reminded her of her plight and that it was all John's fault for her predicament.

Abigail had been a visitor for just over a week. Her rants became tiresome to endure. It was as if all she cared about were her own needs. She never helped with any daily chores, which included dirty dishes, endless mending, and gathering snow to clean and cook. Nothing stirred Abigail to help. She often took to her bed for relief of whatever ailment assailed her for the day. There was always a reason for her lament, everything from headaches to joint pain or frustrations with loud conversations. John did his best to appease her frustrations and often gave excuses for her behavior.

Due to tight quarters, Caroline and Ma didn't talk much about how Abigail acted more like a child than Jillian. The only pleasant conversations they would have with her were about how much she missed her folks and their well-to-do, stable, wooden-frame home back in Pennsylvania.

"It's a wonder any of you are surviving this. What made you come to this God-forsaken land?" She would shake her head and tsk-tsk anyone who tried to tell her differently. Her determination to make every second a hardship continued to be clear with each statement.

Caroline could only imagine the Bible verses streaming through Pa's head as they all sat and had to listen to the woman's tirades. As if she were the only one missing out on the comforts of "ordinary life," as she called it.

"My family just installed an indoor privy. Did I mention that?"

Caroline had heard it come out of her mouth at least twenty times since she'd begun to live under their roof. They'd never had the option of having an indoor privy, so Caroline had no clue what made such an extravagance a luxury. Before Abigail visited, she hadn't thought about trudging through deep snow to the outside facility. In weather like this, they all used the same chamber pot. Why couldn't Abigail just deal with it without having to make their home seem so inadequate?

Aaron had visited just once since Christmas, and he had asked that Abigail and John come to live with them. Abigail had come up with all kinds of reasons for not leaving where they were staying.

"Why do we need to move?" she would ask John, and he'd tell her they were overstaying their welcome. Abigail would shake her head and look at Ma. "We aren't in your way, are we, Sally?"

Caroline was sure Ma would want to tell her that it was time to move on, but because Ma had a kind heart, she wouldn't admit what they all were feeling. Leaving would bring needed relief to the entire family. Caroline knew that even she wished she didn't have to sleep on the floor each night.

They'd agreed to have Aaron and Betsey come to celebrate the New Year with them, but the winter storm had prevented that. So, they had done their best to bring in the year 1834, without any fanfare. Abigail had insisted she needed extra sleep due to the loud noises made from the storm, so they'd all headed to bed early.

One night, while lying together on the floor in front of the fire, trying hard to finish a letter to Billie, Caroline overheard Jillian and Etta whispering about the woman.

"I wish she'd hurry up and feel better, so she can go live with Aaron and Betsey soon. I'm tired of hearing her moans," Etta whispered to Jillian in the dark.

Caroline scolded them both with a—"Hush up!" It was hard to get the point across by whispering.

Jillian added, "Aren't you tired of hearing her?"

Caroline couldn't lie. "But it isn't kind to say such things. Go to sleep."

The two younger girls turned their heads from the fire and quieted while Caroline dipped her stylus into the ink well and finished up the last part of her letter. Billie would probably never get to read the letter until he arrived next spring, but it brought relief to write him at least one letter a week. She couldn't wait for him to arrive.

Placing the stopper back on the ink well, Caroline blew on her printed letters, so they'd dry. While the cabin grew quiet, Caroline only thought of Billie. The winter would grow long, now that she knew he was coming in the spring. She promised herself that she would try never to act like the spoiled young woman who was now taking up residence in their otherwise happy home.

Did Abigail know how much anxiety it brought others to hear her complaints? Did she realize the effect it had on others, especially in the confined spaces they shared? Caroline made a promise to God that if He would see fit to bring Billie safely to her, she'd never act that way around him. She was blessed to have a ma who did her best to keep a happy home. The thought made her wonder what type of wife she'd be.

Wife. The title brought Caroline as much joy as a chicken with a scrap of apple skin. She'd do her best to make him a good spouse. She felt she'd grown up so much since arriving in the territory this past summer. She'd managed to learn many new household chores. She could now make jam without Ma being close to give her guidance, she could get black dirt out of the dirtiest of Pa's trousers, and she didn't know any other woman who knew how to kill a wolf single-handedly. She smiled at the last bit of accomplishment. Did most girls back East act like Abigail? Spoiled and out-of-place in a world where she now lived with her family.

As she pulled her blanket closer to her chin and cuddled closer to Jillian on the hard, wooden floor, she began to dream of what kind of life she and Billie would have together. She'd make sure he would appreciate having her by his side.

CHAPTER FOUR

Betsey loved her window in her new home. It shared the wall beside their door. When a day didn't include snow, she'd open the window shutters and gaze out through the glass into the swirling snow. It was still impossible to see any storms approaching from the west, but it gave her an extraordinary glimpse of sunrises on a clear day. One thing was for sure, Michigan Territory didn't have many clear, cloudless days in January.

Aaron often scolded her for keeping the shutters open. A draft from the panes did send a chill into the room on windy days, but Betsey couldn't help allowing the morning sun to fill their home with light. It brightened her day not only to see it but also to feel it.

Their new living space resembled the one they'd shared back in Pennsylvania. Aaron had yet to finish constructing the walls inside, so their bedroom was open to the home's kitchen and living areas. Soon, he promised, he would seal off the walls to give their bedroom the privacy they desired in the evenings.

Ambrose worked outside most of the day, on less stormy days. Alexander traipsed behind him on his adventures. Often they'd return with a turkey for supper. Sometimes they'd even brave the cold water to catch a fish or two, but now the ice over the river didn't allow them any opportunities to fish.

Alexander was growing more and more communicative with his hand gestures and smiles. Everyone seemed to know what he was thinking without him having to answer with a motioned comment.

Betsey even taught him how to write a few letters on a slate she'd borrowed from Jillian. She would spell out his name and then have him write out each letter. It took much longer for Alexander to learn than it took to teach her younger sisters. Betsey would use sounds to help her sisters remember the letters they wrote. Even though she would sound out the letters to Alexander, he didn't repeat the sound but continued to grin at her whenever she tried to persuade him to say the sound. He still hadn't made any kind of vocal communication with her or with any of the rest of the family, but he was very good at copying his name and the letters that spelled it.

She had even taught him his numbers, and soon he was ciphering just like any other child his age. All of this made Betsey realize he was intelligent, but the language barrier just seemed to make teaching him...more difficult.

Julia grew. As she did, her smiles and giggles brought Betsey immense joy. Betsey had plenty of milk, and the child ate with gusto, often backing up from her breast with milk drizzling down her chin and a thankful grin. Those moments brought Betsey so much relief, knowing she was getting what she needed and would soon be toddling around the house in search of adventures.

Ma had assured Betsey that her efforts as a new mother would bring her great pleasure, but Betsey didn't know how much until she could place her sleeping child in her cradle each night and gaze on her with immense satisfaction.

Aaron loved his little girl. He'd taken over spoiling her from Pa as soon as they'd moved to the ridge above her parents' cabin. He'd rock her to sleep each night as Betsey finished up the dinner dishes. Betsey had watched Julia's early evening naps disappear within the last few weeks as she now interacted with Aaron during those times. The baby loved grasping Aaron's beard and chewing on his finger as he talked to her about his day.

Ambrose would look on for entertainment and would often take Julia while Betsey finished up cooking their meals. As much as she missed Ma and her sisters' company, she got great satisfaction from watching the men help her with the new baby.

"I talked to John today. He seemed to think that as soon as the weather gives way, he will be bringing up their wagon to unload some of their possessions. I think they'll be joining us soon." Aaron tickled Julia's chin.

"Is Abigail feeling any better?" Betsey asked as she stirred the meat, now filling the cabin with the aroma of a coming stew for supper.

"I think so. John continues to tell me that Abigail is in a delicate state."

"Is she with child?" Betsey didn't know any other way to ask about her sister-in-law's condition.

"Perhaps." Aaron twisted a ringlet of Julia's hair between his fingers. "He didn't say."

Betsey couldn't imagine the coldness Abigail had suffered on their trip lasting more than a few days. It had been two weeks since they arrived. Betsey was growing anxious to have them under their roof and have help from another woman, often missing her ma and sisters while cooking and cleaning.

Aaron handed his daughter to Ambrose. "I'm going out to fetch some firewood. Hold this precious bundle."

Ambrose took the tiny child into his arms and began to sing. Ambrose's voice was a deep bass, and somehow it seemed to lull the baby into a trance as she watched his face.

Aaron pulled on his coat and slipped his hands into gloves. "I'll be back."

Ambrose pulled Julia's blanket close around her face and tipped her toward his chest as the door opened and closed. "I didn't want to say this in front of Aaron, but Pa said Ma and the girls are having a hard time with Abigail."

Betsey had never heard gossip like this coming from Ambrose, but she asked anyway, "How so?"

"I guess she is a bit of a complainer."

Betsey didn't want to get the wrong impression of her new relative. "Well, we'll have to see when she arrives. I'm sure she's just not used to her new surroundings. It takes a while to get used to it here."

Ambrose smiled down at his niece. "I'm sure you're right."

"I can't imagine what it's like to be in such a tight living place with people who are strangers. It would make me uncomfortable."

Ambrose agreed. "Yeah, I'm sure that's all there is to it. I hope we can make her more comfortable."

Betsey finished chopping up chunks of potato and added them to the simmering meat and broth. "I'm sure it will be fine once she gets settled. But until then, we'll do our best."

It wasn't long before Caroline began telling Betsey about Abigail on a walk one afternoon. They'd met each other halfway on the trail to Betsey's cabin. Betsey scolded her for gossiping.

"But, Bit, you don't get it. Abigail doesn't lift even a finger to help. She sits in a chair and stares at the fire or falls asleep at the drop of a hat. Wouldn't you think she'd at least offer to help or even get some stitchin' done while she sits?"

"Those are our ways, Caroline. We know what will happen if we get behind in our mending or cooking if we aren't working on something every second of the day. Give her time. She'll catch on, too." Betsey shifted the papoose pack on her back to steady Julia as they made their way up the path that afternoon.

"So...what did the letter from Billie say?" Betsey had wanted to ask Caroline several times since the letter's arrival on Christmas Day, but there hadn't been a moment where she had the privacy to do so. It would also veer the conversation away from gossiping about Abigail.

Caroline blushed. "He's coming, Betsey."

Betsey stopped in her tracks. "He is? When?"

"In the spring." Caroline's face showed every bit of excitement in the sparkle of her eyes and a sheepish grin.

Betsey continued trudging up the path. The walk seemed extra burdensome as the snowdrifts from the previous storm were up to her knees. If she had known that the snow was this deep, she'd have remembered to wear her snowshoes. "That's exciting!" When Caroline didn't answer right away, Betsey added, "Do you think you'll marry soon?"

Caroline stopped. Betsey saw fear in her eyes. "I'm guessing that's the plan once he gets here."

Betsey asked, "Isn't that what you're hoping for?"

Caroline walked on without saying a word.

Betsey pulled on her arm. "Caroline. You do love him, don't you?"

"I don't know," Caroline said with resolution. "I mean. We've always been friends since way before I can even remember. But we've never talked about being..." Caroline looked away. "How did you know Aaron was the one for you?"

Caroline started again, and Betsey had to struggle to catch up. "I guess I just knew. From the first moment I laid eyes on Aaron, I hoped he felt the same way. Billie must have some feelings for you. He's comin' all this way to find you."

Caroline pushed strands of errant dark hair back beneath the confines of her knitted cap. "I guess. We just never talked about something as permanent as marriage." Her sister's face turned a crimson color. "I never quite saw him as someone to...you know...have more than a good friendship. We've not been of marrying age before now. But his letter seemed interested in pursuing things further."

"Well, there you go! Don't be intimidated by marriage. It's a beautiful, wonderful thing. You'll be a good wife and mother."

Caroline gazed up into the trees surrounding Betsey and Aaron's home. "I just continue to think of myself as too young to have what you have. There are so many things I'd like to do. I mean, being a wife and mother is on the list, but that seems as if it would restrict me. Did you ever feel that way?"

"I'm sorry, Caroline. No. Never."

Caroline sighed. "See! I'm so odd. I don't think as a normal girl should."

Betsey laughed. "That doesn't make you odd."

Caroline turned to face Betsey. "Don't get me wrong. I do like Billie. But I look at what you and Aaron share as a couple, and I hope someday that I can be as lucky as you. I do!"

Betsey grabbed her sister's wrist and continued walking. "I know. It's a confusing time."

"Maybe he isn't coming to marry me. Perhaps he's just coming because he knows our family well and wants to be part of the beginning of building in a new land. Just like Pa wanted to do."

"Perhaps, but wouldn't you be delighted to join him on the adventure?"

Caroline giggled. "I think so."

"Let's move on a bit quicker. I don't want Julia getting any more cold air than is necessary."

Caroline backed up a bit, and Betsey could feel her tug on the blanket that covered Julia's face. "She's fine. Just sleeping."

"The movement always puts her to sleep."

"Isn't it great that Waussinoodae brought you this?"

"It's been an efficient way to carry a child. Especially in all this snow."

The girls were nearing Betsey's cabin. "Have you seen Waussinoodae lately?"

Betsey shrugged. "Not since before Christmas when she brought me the baby carrier."

"I hope when spring comes, she'll come to visit more often." Caroline seemed as interested as Betsey to get to know their new friend.

"Me, too." Betsey reached the edge of the cabin. "If nothing else, the effort to carry Julia this way has increased my strength since my illness."

"I wish the same for Ma. She has yet to regain all her strength. It's taken her so much longer to recover than you."

Betsey pulled on the latch of the front door. "She'll get it back. I think her case was much harder than mine."

The warmth from the cabin spilled out as they hurried inside to rest from their walk up the hill.

A strong gust of wind made Betsey's house shudder. She woke in the middle of the night to the powerful winds battering their home. In the past few weeks, they'd been hearing a whistling in the cabin each time the winds picked up outside. Today, the sound seemed to pierce the night like a howl from a wolf in the darkness.

Julia was fussing in her cradle. She must have been disturbed by the sound, too. Betsey changed her diaper before she carried her toward the hearth to see if she was hungry.

Aaron stirred. "Is she okay?"

"She will be. In a moment."

Betsey went to a chair by the fire and slipped a log onto the glowing embers. Soon a small fire warmed the area. She snuggled Julia close as her daughter eagerly nursed. This next week, Julia would turn three months old. She'd begun to sleep well at six weeks. Now it was only occasionally that Betsey needed to rise in the middle of the night to feed her.

Unexpectedly, Aaron approached her from behind and whispered, "Here's another blanket. Sounds as if we're getting the brunt of another storm."

Betsey kissed his hand as he wrapped the blanket around her and Julia. "Thank you, love."

Aaron pulled up a chair close beside her.

"You don't have to get out of bed to join us," Betsey added, as he brushed a sliver of her hair off her face.

"I know. We don't get to spend much time alone these days."

Betsey shrugged, holding her shoulders in the position for a bit. "I know. As soon as John and Abigail move in, there will be even less."

Aaron placed another small log onto the fire. Growing flames licked the new piece of wood. "That's another thing I wanted to talk to you about."

Betsey finished feeding the baby and raised her to her shoulder for a burp. "What's wrong?"

Aaron sat forward and rested his elbows on his knees. "Betsey, Abigail can be difficult. I didn't understand how much until your pa began to tell me a few days ago."

Betsey shook her head, "Aaron, it will be fine. It's nothing to worry about."

"That's easy for you to say now. I don't know how long John and Abigail will be with us, but it could be until spring. Quite possibly, until John finds them a new place to live. We're in the wilderness. I can't imagine him finding an abandoned cabin anywhere close."

"Aaron, I'm truly serious when I say we'll manage. Whatever type of person she is, we'll make it work."

Aaron kissed her cheek. "You're wonderful."

Betsey looked into the dark eyes of her husband as another large gust of wind sideswiped their cabin. Both of them stared at the wall as if they weren't sure it would withstand the blast.

"I think this storm will bury us."

"We seem to get the brunt of the wind more here than what your parents receive in the clearing below us." Betsey shifted Julia to the other side to eat.

All Aaron could do was look on. His eyes were hard to see in the dim light from the fire's flame, but Betsey knew him well enough to know that only love showed there.

"What can we do to make Abigail feel more at home?"

Aaron shrugged. "You'd know about that better than I."

"Let me think about it. Perhaps all Abigail's missing is her place. I'll ask her if she needs any cooking utensils, or maybe I'll cook one night, and she could cook another. Maybe all she needs is something to make her feel important and needed. Sometimes that's all a woman wants."

Aaron smiled at her and again kissed her cheek. "I hope you're right."

"Oh, I forgot to tell you. John brought me money from the sale of our wagon and team. Father made sure to give it to him before he passed."

Betsey was surprised John hadn't needed it for necessities as they traveled but had been sure to deliver it to Aaron as instructed. "Have you been thinking of your Father?"

Aaron grimaced. "Hard to believe he's gone. I knew he wasn't well before we left, but I never imagined it would be the last time I saw him. I don't think John knew what the envelope held. John hadn't opened it."

Betsey placed her head on his shoulder. "I'm sorry, Aaron. I know how important he was to you."

"Now more than ever, the thought of not having any parents on the earth makes me feel like an adult, but something inside me also feels like I'm all alone. Like an orphan."

Betsey raised her head to check out Julia, who had stopped sucking and was fast asleep again. "Let's get this child back to her cradle. We've both changed since we've arrived here. In more ways than one." Betsey stood with the sleeping baby in her arms. "Now we're the parents. Are you sad about that?"

Aaron rose and put his arm around her. "Not in the least. It's just a new phase of life. For all of us." As they placed Julia into her cradle, Aaron added, "I just hope Abigail and John don't overstay their welcome."

CHAPTER FIVE

The winds howled through the early morning hours. The snowstorm made it difficult to sleep. Broken and flying tree limbs slammed against the walls, and the high-pitched whistle continued through the night. Alexander didn't seem the least bit disturbed as he climbed down from the loft and sat at the table to await his breakfast.

"Oh no, young man," Betsey called to him, "you can help set the table."

Head bowed in submission, Alexander approached Betsey and took the outstretched plates. As he looked up to see her response, Betsey smiled at him. "We need everyone to help, right?" She smoothed down his errant hair.

The young boy nodded. His English comprehension seemed fine. If only Betsey could figure out what would make him speak. What would keep a child from speaking?

Aaron and Ambrose entered the cabin in a swirl of winter white. Stomping their feet made snow skitter across the wooden floor. The door pushed shut against a large bank at the threshold.

Soon coats and mittens deposited more snow on Betsey's floor. "What am I going to do when this baby starts to crawl? You men need to leave more snow outside than inside!"

Aaron removed his coat and carefully placed it on the wooden peg by the door. "Honey, I'm not so sure that is possible today."

"Impossible!" Ambrose retorted as he sat down to pull off a boot. "There is at least three feet or more of it piled outside."

"And the sky is filled with heavy, dark clouds. It won't let up anytime soon."

Betsey took Ambrose's coat and hung it beside Aaron's.

"Come sit down for breakfast. I'll pour some coffee to warm your insides back up."

Both men grinned as they sat down. Ambrose watched Alexander set the table with plates and a fork by each one. "You're lucky to be a little boy, Alexander. I'd give anything to set the table again instead of working hard to put food on it."

Alexander smiled as Ambrose ruffled his hair.

The snow continued throughout the entire day. Each time Aaron opened the door, a fresh new layer of the dusty white powder dampened Betsey's floor. She knew it was impossible to keep it dry on a day like today.

"Don't think we'll have company for a bit yet. I can't imagine Abigail eager to get out in this today. They'd lose themselves in the swirls of white just trying to get up the hill," Aaron said, wiping off his gun before placing it back over the mantle on the wooden pegs.

A man's gun was rarely dirty in the winter months. Each night Aaron would take it down from its place and polish it until it gleamed against the fire's light.

Late that evening, the winds began to die down. To get an idea of how much snow had fallen, Aaron opened the front door to find about three feet covering the entrance, the etches of the wooden door indented in the hard snow wall.

"I've never seen so much in one storm. Unless spring comes tomorrow, we'll be stuck alone for a few more days."

Ambrose assured them both that this was what happened in a Michigan Territory snowstorm. "It got so bad last winter that one morning I couldn't see past the wall of snow at the door. Just you wait."

"It's not much different than Pennsylvania, is it?"

"Meadville had its moments of snow, but snow here comes and never goes away. For months you wonder if the dips in temperature or the winds will ever die down." Ambrose lit his pipe and sat back to enjoy a few puffs.

"Remember when Ma used to make us snow ice cream?" Betsey added, as she gazed out at the now quietness of the night.

"I do. That was a great treat on a winter night." Ambrose added, "Too bad we don't have a milk cow."

"Hosea? Can I speak to you in private?" John stood after the family finished their supper and motioned to Hosea to follow him outside.

As the men headed out into the cold, Hosea wasn't sure why their conversation couldn't have been inside the warm cabin. At least the snow had stopped falling, and the winds had died down.

The men's steps crunched in the fresh snow. The dark sky, filled with bright stars, blanketed the earth.

John made his way to the barn. Hosea held up the lantern he was carrying to illuminate the path for both of them.

"What can I do for you, John?" Hosea placed the light at his feet. Both men leaned against the fence that now kept the oxen close to the barn during the day.

John folded his arms and then unfolded them. He scuffed the snowbank close to the barn as if trying to see if it would speak to Hosea so that he wouldn't have to. "I needed to bring you out here to discuss something a bit uncomfortable."

Hosea became agitated. *What did this man need to discuss?*

"My wife." John sighed heavily.

"John." Hosea uncrossed his arms. "You don't need to—"

John held up his hand. "No. I know what you will say. She's a fragile being. She needs care. She's weary and frustrated."

Hosea fought his urge to share with John what he thought of his inconsiderate wife. She'd been staying with them for almost a month now, and Hosea felt they'd given her ample time to recuperate from her frozen trip north. Sally continued to struggle with having enough strength to get through a long day of work, yet this woman hadn't lifted a single finger to help. She couldn't even sit in a chair and mend a piece of clothing.

"I think moving her to Betsey's cabin will be tragic. She'll not make the walk. It might kill her."

Hosea had to turn away and face the river for a moment. He didn't want John to see his expression, which often revealed much more than he was comfortable showing. When he regained his control, he turned back. "Again, I understand your concern for your wife, as I care for my family. Aaron and Betsey have a warm, comfortable home. It is larger, and you'll have almost a separate area to relax and have a bit of privacy. We aren't pushing you out for our benefit but want you to be comfortable." He then wondered if he could go along with this calamity anymore. He'd never felt such contempt for a woman. He even felt sorry that it would now be Aaron and Betsey's burden.

"So, you're pushing us out."

Hosea couldn't help himself. He laughed. "Um, if that's how you feel, but that is not our intention."

"I see. Well, thank you for all you've done for us so far. We'll get packed and leave tomorrow." Without another word, the man turned on his heel and headed back toward the cabin.

That's when Hosea glanced over the fence and talked to the only One who would listen and understand his intentions clearly. "God...am I missing something here?" The only word to come to his mind, at that moment, was *contentious*. "Please grant wisdom to Aaron and Betsey," he murmured.

Both John and Abigail were silent the next day at the morning table. Hosea did his best to draw out a conversation with both of them. They ignored him. The silence was deafening. He didn't enjoy his home with such a dark cloud shadowing out the ordinary joy.

As John opened the door to allow the couple to leave, Hosea asked if there was any way to help them as they made the trek to Aaron and Betsey's cabin. John just shook his head. "I think you've done enough."

The sun pierced through the clouds as he watched the couple walk off his property and head for the hill leading to his daughter's cabin. They walked as if the world were upon their shoulders.

As he turned to shut the door, Sally stood by the hearth with her arms crossed. "What in tarnation was that about? I've never before felt such an ominous feeling that we'd done something wrong. What did you possibly say to John last night?"

Hosea went back to his chair, holding his cup up for a refill; Sally filled it from the kettle. "I did nothing. I didn't even really say anything. He spoke. Not me." He stopped then. There was nothing he could even tell Sally that would appease her. He only had unkind thoughts that didn't need uttering.

Hosea turned to his daughters, who were doing their best to do their chores quietly. They'd had to do this since their guests arrived at Christmas. Abigail's head couldn't handle the singing or their chatter. He smiled at them and said, "How about you girls singing a praise song this morning?"

Silence followed for a bit until Caroline burst into laughter. The other women chuckled. Without any more prodding, Jillian began to sing "Come Thou Fount of Every Blessing."

Hosea caught Sally Mae giving the young girl a sideways stern look, but all Hosea could do was laugh. Songs were again a part of the Baker family home.

A knock sounded loud at the front door. Betsey nearly dropped Julia as she rose from her chair to open the door. Her family would usually knock lightly and then open the door with friendly greetings. Who else would wait for her to greet them? They didn't have close neighbors yet, and the Indians never knocked.

As she opened the door, she drew Julia closer to her bosom to keep her warm from the outside air. "John. Abigail."

Abigail swooned as she crossed the threshold. John picked her up and carried her to the closest chair. "She's had a trying time walking uphill."

Betsey ran to Julia's cradle to place the baby there, so she could get back to assist her sister-in-law.

John fawned over his wife. "Oh, Abigail. I'm sorry that walk was so hard for you. We're here now. At Aaron's house. The walk is over."

Betsey was a bit confused. She'd known for the last few days that John and Abigail would be arriving to stay with them, but seeing her sister-in-law so exhausted from the mere walk from her parents' cabin puzzled her. Perhaps she was more ill than anyone knew.

"Oh, John. I can't take another step. I'm so glad we made it. With all those wild animals and such out there."

Betsey had heard the stories from Caroline about Abigail's strange behavior. Perhaps she wasn't exaggerating when she told her that she was faint of spirit. Betsey often took the hill at a quick speed when a storm was fast approaching, even with a baby on her back, but this woman looked like she had just walked from Whitmore's trading post in knee-deep snow.

"Betsey, can you get Abigail something warm to drink?"

Betsey went for a cup. "Certainly."

"Where's Aaron?"

"He and Ambrose went to the river to see if they could dig a hole through the ice to catch us a few fish for supper."

"I know that your father means well, and they have been gracious to us since arriving at Christmas, but I'm sorry to tell you...they kicked us out of their home last night. We slept fitfully through the night and left as soon as we could this morning."

Betsey knew this couldn't be true. Neither her parents nor her sisters would purposely kick someone out of their home. Betsey also knew how long John and Abigail had already overstayed their welcome at the Baker home. Either John was lying to her or trying hard to lure Betsey to believe something ill of her family. Either way, she did her best to calm her angry heart.

"I'm sorry to hear that you feel this way." Betsey didn't know what else to say.

"Oh, believe me. It's hard to tell you. I know you care for your family, but it's true. We had no choice but to come to you this morning, even with Abigail's fragile nature."

Betsey eyed the woman now swooning as if she'd just undergone twelve hours of labor to bring a child into the world. "We'll do our best to make you feel at home. Have you eaten?"

"Yes. Your mother was gracious enough to feed us before we left."

So many thoughts flew through Betsey's mind as she handed a cup of warm tea to Abigail, who just looked at her as if she wanted Betsey to spoon feed it to her. Betsey decided that if the woman wanted it bad enough, she'd have to pick it up herself. Betsey placed the cup on the table beside her.

"Where will we be staying?" John went to the packs he'd brought with them and picked them up again.

"We've made room for you both in the loft." Betsey pointed up the ladder.

"The loft?" Abigail seemed to regain some vigor again. She glanced back and must have seen the ladder. "I will not tromp up and down a ladder to get to my sleeping quarters!"

John knelt by Abigail and again shushed her. "It's okay, dear. We'll make it work."

"We will not. There is a perfectly fine bedroom arrangement down here." Abigail pointed to Betsey and Aaron's bed against the wall. "That will do us just fine."

Betsey stood and, without realizing it, placed her hands on her hips. Was this woman demanding she move her bedroom to the loft? In her own home?

Just then, the door opened, and in walked Aaron in time to see Abigail again moan as if she'd been through the most tragic of ordeals.

"John. Abigail. So good to see you both."

John stood, dropping the packs on the floor. "We've come to stay with you now, Aaron. I hope you are fine with that?"

Aaron removed his coat. "Of course. Yes. We've been planning on you joining us."

John thanked him for the hospitality. It seemed to Betsey as if his attitude had taken a turn, and a pleasant demeanor replaced the demanding one from just moments before.

Betsey couldn't believe her ears.

"Aaron, we were wondering if it would be okay for us to take the downstairs area for our bedroom? Abigail is delicate, and it will be hard for her to go up and down the ladder to have privacy. Would that work for you and Betsey?"

Aaron seemed a bit taken back by the suggestion, and he looked to Betsey. He did seem to notice the fiery look Betsey was giving him, but timidly said, "That will be fine, won't it, Betsey?"

What could she say? She was caught off guard, but her manners got the best of her. "Yes. They're welcome to stay anywhere that makes them feel the most comfortable. I'll move our things today."

But then she had to leave the area. She only wished there were bedroom walls and a door to slam as she went back to check on Julia.

Ambrose noticed the chill in the air from even the warm cabin as he arrived later. Alexander trudged in behind him. Both stamped their feet free of snow.

John, who now sat in Betsey's rocking chair, scowled at them but didn't say a word. Abigail moaned at the commotion.

"Bit. We didn't get a fish, but perhaps these few potatoes from Pa's barn will help with tonight's supper. The ice is too deep for us to fish."

Aaron moved closer to Ambrose and Alexander at the door. "Um, boys. We have visitors now. Perhaps you can be a bit quieter. Abigail seems to have some kind of headache or something from their walk here."

Ambrose apologized, but as he glanced at Betsey, he knew the problem was more significant than a mere headache. He watched as she purposely went up the ladder with clothing and blankets in tow. It seemed as though she were moving their possessions to the loft to join Alexander and his belongings.

Ambrose could hear Julia fussing in the corner where her cradle sat.

As Ambrose removed his outer clothing, he watched Alexander scramble up the ladder behind Betsey. He appeared shy of their new guests.

Ambrose put another log on the fire and poured himself something warm to drink from the kettle. Skeptical about the scene he found, he settled at the table and did his best to make conversation with Aaron's brother.

"What do you think of Michigan Territory so far, John? Quite different than the civilized communities back East, don't you think?"

"Different indeed."

Ambrose laughed. "You'll see a better territory in the spring. Now all the best parts are covered in white. It's pretty now, but it's completely different with leaves on the trees and new fields to plant.

You'll see." Ambrose did his best to encourage the couple, who had been through quite the tumultuous time since their arrival.

"Yes, Ambrose is right. It's hard to see the best part of the land now." Aaron scratched his head, looking to Ambrose with a smile.

"We'll pray so." John leaned his head on the back of the chair.

Betsey descended the ladder and spoke to Aaron. "Let me get Julia's things, and then Abigail can settle into her living area."

Betsey's tone wasn't all that hospitable. Nothing like the normal Betsey that Ambrose knew. He wondered what could have happened so soon to cause the crackle of tension between Betsey and their new guests.

Abigail moaned again, and then he realized. She hadn't said a kind word to anyone.

John stood up and moved toward her. "Thank you, Aaron, for allowing us your bedroom area. We appreciate that."

The look Betsey then sent Aaron said about all Ambrose needed to know about the situation. He hoped he was wrong, but it seemed as if a new matriarch had entered Betsey's home.

CHAPTER SIX

Betsey settled into the loft as best she could. It would mean feeding the baby in her bed instead of getting up each night. The bed in the roof space was comfortable, and they'd done their best to make it that way for John and Abigail, but if Julia were to need comfort in the middle of the night, walking the floor would be almost impossible. The pitch of the roof was too steep to stand completely erect.

She also worried about disturbing Alexander and Ambrose, who slept at the opposite end of the loft. They were sound sleepers, though, and being winter, they could sleep during the day if need be.

She scolded herself for not believing Caroline when she told her about Abigail the first time. How was she to know that one woman could control a whole houseful of men, as she now did?

John seemed mannerly while Aaron was around, but as soon as he would walk out the door to do a chore or go hunting, his demeanor changed toward Betsey. How could she justify this or explain it to Aaron? Surely, he'd believe her, but Betsey also knew to keep quiet until it was necessary. She didn't want to speak ill of his family. They were all he had left.

During the daytime hours, Abigail seemed to become an invalid. She would sit in a chair and gaze at the fire as Betsey cleaned or did her cooking. Nodding off to sleep was a regular part of her early afternoon hours. If she didn't do it in the chair by the table, she'd go to bed and sleep.

Betsey soon began to worry. Perhaps the woman had some kind of melancholia. She'd heard of this, and next time she was with her mother, she would ask her about it.

Abigail never asked to hold Julia. She would gaze at the child as she cried in her cradle but never touch her. Betsey heard her sigh in frustration every time Julia had a crying spell. The anxiety that it would bring to Betsey probably caused Julia to cry even more. As soon as Aaron would enter the room, Betsey would hand the baby to him, and she would immediately begin cooing and smiling as if she sensed the anxiousness in Betsey.

Time would tell how long Betsey could handle the frustrations. However, what could change? Abigail was here. At least until the spring thaw and the robins returned to their property.

Each night, Aaron and John would pull out Hosea's maps of the local area, and John would try and decide on a substantial place to build a cabin. Ambrose and Aaron offered to girdle a few trees for him, but he denied the help. John would go out hunting with them, but he rarely shot anything. Aaron told Betsey it was because

John wasn't as accurate as he. Betsey tended to believe that, but how would he learn if he never tried?

Life for Betsey, Aaron, Alexander, and Ambrose hadn't changed all that much from before their guests arrived. There were more mouths to feed and a bit more work, but they each carried the same load as they'd done before.

It wasn't two weeks since their arrival when Abigail began to complain to John, always in front of Betsey, that her bed needed fresh linens. Betsey didn't have other linens for her own bed, let alone John and Abigail's. They had to wait until spring to be able to gather more grasses down by the river to renew and refill the bedticks, but trying to explain that to Abigail seemed futile.

"I hate the smell of our bed. It is musty and dingy-looking." Abigail whined to John after Aaron had left one morning. "I would think an efficient housewife would change the bedding once in a while."

Betsey hadn't slept well the night before. She was tired, and Julia was cranky that morning. Teething had begun early, and Julia chewed vigorously on her fist or a tiny edge of her blanket. She fussed or went into a full-blown cry whenever Betsey placed her in her cradle to get some housework done.

"I'm sure Betsey understands the need to have a fresh bed. Perhaps she'll manage it today." John patted the top of his wife's hand.

"She shouldn't need to be told that," Abigail spat out.

Betsey had heard many complaints from the woman, but this morning seemed even more juvenile than before. She was being scolded about her housekeeping skills by a woman who did nothing to help.

Sweat trickled down her cheekbones as she adjusted the cooking pot over the stove. She'd decided to steam a turkey bone over the fire that morning to glean whatever leftover meat she could for the evening's soup. They were running short of potatoes, and it was still winter.

"How can I make it feel fresh for you, Abigail?" She had to ask. She wanted Abigail to know that it was impossible to provide fresh linens without having to fill a multitude of buckets with snow to thaw for water in the dead of winter.

"It needs fresh straw. Or even feathers. My mother had feathers in our bedsteads."

"We have no feathers. Maybe come spring, we can retrieve some and start saving them for your bedtick at your new home." Betsey wanted to sound cheerful, but Julia had cried enough for both of them that day.

"It's atrocious how horrifying it is to live in a land like this," Abigail moaned. "I can't believe you brought me to this godforsaken land, John." Abigail stomped off to bed.

John's face flushed bright red, as if his wife had just slapped him across a cheek.

Silence penetrated the cabin as Julia finally succumbed to her afternoon nap, and Betsey decided to pick up on some mending while she slept.

John looked over at her and said, "I'm sorry, Betsey."

It was the first apology the man had offered in the last four weeks since being at Betsey's cabin.

"I should never have brought her here. Father said it would be difficult, but I never imagined it would be this hard for her."

Betsey wanted to tell him that it wasn't his fault, but there were moments when someone needed to stand up to Abigail. Make her see her childish behavior for what it was—unfair to everyone around her. Wasn't that John's responsibility?

Betsey also knew how hard it was for a woman to be in the new territory. She remembered the past summer when she'd been alone with a sick mother and her younger sisters. The only male help she'd had was a little boy who had done his best to help with whatever situation came about. Alexander was a godsend. But Betsey had to learn not to be childish and grow up. Being a woman in the early nineteenth century was hard, but by doing her best and learning, each woman could make it joyful. Abigail didn't appear to even desire to try.

"It's a rough life we live here. There are no women's teas to attend in town. A place to purchase needed supplies is miles away. We don't have sewing clubs or even other women to discuss the latest fashions. But if Abigail believes the winter months to be hard, it will be even harder when the snow melts, and we need to work hard to keep our homes clean and well-stocked with food, and the mending will stack up until we can look to it again in the winter." Betsey used her teeth to pinch off the end of her thread. "Perhaps..." she wanted to say something encouraging. She prayed a quick prayer that what she was about to say would help. "Perhaps Abigail will see that if she participates a little in the daily chores, or finds something productive to do, it will allow her less time to..." Betsey wanted to say *complain*, but then she added, "Feel miserable about her circumstances."

"I hope so. I want you to know I'm thankful for all you've done for us. You've been very kind. So has your family."

From that point on, John seemed a bit less frustrated with Betsey as the winter moved closer to spring.

The next afternoon, the sun shone brightly in the eastern sky. With the absence of clouds, Betsey decided she and Julia needed some fresh air for a change. Without saying anything to John or Abigail, she gathered up some clothing and a few items for Julia and began packing to head down the hill to see her family. It had been weeks since she'd ventured outside alone, but she needed to see friendly faces for a change.

"Where are you headed?" John asked as she began to put her coat on.

"I think we'll go and see my parents today. Maybe spend the night with them." Betsey placed the baby board on the table and wrapped Julia up to put her in it to walk down the ridge.

"How long will you be gone?" Abigail asked.

"I don't know. Perhaps a day or two." Betsey fitted the ropes to the board and asked John to help her as she lifted it into place on her back.

"What will Aaron do while you are gone? Who will prepare his meals?" Abigail chewed on a fingernail as she watched Betsey prepare to leave.

"He knows I'm leaving. He and Ambrose have plenty to fix themselves while I'm gone. I've left them things to cook up for their supper." Betsey tied a knot in the bag of clothing and shifted Julia on her back for better comfort.

"But what will we do?" Abigail asked.

Betsey shrugged. "I'm sure there will be plenty for all to eat. It will give you and John a bit of time to yourselves. I know I could use a bit of different conversation." Betsey smiled. She hoped that didn't sound anything like what she meant to say. "Can you throw the blanket over Julia's face before I head out, John?"

John did as she asked.

She then opened the door. "Have a good day, and I'll see you soon."

As Betsey closed the door behind her, she heard Abigail say, "Well, of all things!"

She smiled even more.

Making her way down the hill didn't take long. The morning was a bright one. The sun reflected off the bright-white snow, blinding Betsey at first. As soon as her eyes adjusted, Betsey reveled in her walk. She couldn't wait to see her parents or her sisters. It had been way too long.

As she walked, she marveled at the trees. Clumps of snow glistened on each of the branches. The pine trees were the most magical looking with each bow weighed down by the heavy snow. She had put on her new snowshoes to make walking more manageable. Aaron had modeled them after a set that Whitmore wore, making them during the late evening hours. The snow crunched with each step she made, but she didn't sink to the ground. She managed to stay on top of the drifts formed by the February winds.

A snowy owl hooted from a nearby tree branch. Even a few squirrels chased each other in the warm sun. It would be a while yet, but she looked forward to when winter would disappear, and the spring rain would bring out the wildlife from hibernation.

As she walked, she could hear Julia cooing from beneath her blankets. She seemed almost as happy to leave the confines of their winter home as Betsey.

Betsey breathed in deep the coolness of the day. She could see the tiny trail of smoke filter out of her parents' chimney as she drew near to the cabin.

Aaron was outside looking at a hoof of one of the oxen. He stopped as she drew near. "Look who has ventured outside. Isn't it a beautiful day?"

Betsey smiled back at him and stopped to chat at the fence. "It's so wonderful! I'm so glad it stopped snowing long enough for me to venture out."

"How long do you plan on staying?" Aaron asked her as she continued trudging toward her parents' cabin.

"I think until May." Betsey turned to see Aaron tip his head back and laugh. He knew perfectly well what she meant.

Knocking on the door, Betsey didn't wait for an answer before she pushed the door open to her first home in the Michigan Territory.

Jillian was the first to jump up from the floor and run to meet her at the door. "Betsey!"

Everyone stood up from a quilt they were sewing on to greet her with hugs and kisses.

Ma hugged her and then turned her around to remove the blanket covering Julia's head. She laughed. "Baby Julia. How Grammy has missed you."

Betsey could feel the baby squirm to be set free from the tight pack. "Hold on, child. Let me undo a few of these ties first."

Soon the women placed Julia on a blanket on the floor and admired how much she'd grown since they last saw her. She jabbered baby talk and smiled at each one, proceeding to blow bubbles in excitement to see other faces besides Betsey's and Aaron's. "You all make her happy. She does the same thing when Alexander, Aaron, or Ambrose plays with her, too. She's her own little communicator these days."

Everyone laughed at her antics. "Wait until your pa sees her and how much she's grown."

"Where is Pa?" Betsey asked, as she unwound her scarf from her neck.

He and Ambrose went to see Whitmore today. We needed a few things, and they were getting antsy from being inside all the time. It is a fine day to take a walk," Ma said. "You picked a good day to come for a visit. They may spend the night at the post tonight, and hopefully, the weather will be good to head back in the morning."

"How are your house guests?" Caroline looked to Betsey for an answer.

"I'm sure they'll be enjoying a little quiet themselves. I just hope they don't starve to death before I get back." Betsey eyed her mother for a scolding expression, but instead, she giggled.

"She hasn't regained much of her strength yet?" Caroline asked, as she picked up Julia's foot and kissed the bottom of it.

"No. Not at all. Ma, have you ever known anyone that has melancholy like her?"

Ma picked up Julia, placing loud kisses on the baby's cheek. Julia laughed at each one. "That poor woman doesn't have melancholy. She's just plain lazy."

Everyone stopped what they were doing and looked at Ma. The sisters all looked at each other. They'd never heard their ma say anything so harsh, even though they all knew it to be true.

"What's wrong with her, then?" Jillian asked next.

"She's a very immature woman. Wait until she doesn't have us to help her anymore. She'll have to begin taking care of her household just as we have to do, every single day." Ma smoothed down the soft hair on Julia's head. "Look at this child's hair. She'll need a haircut sooner than later."

The baby put both her hands on the side of Ma's face and laughed right out loud.

"Oh, my baby Julia! How you've been missed around here." Ma planted another kiss on the baby's forehead.

"We have missed you, Betsey." Jillian stood up and hugged Betsey tight.

Betsey hugged right back.

"Not as much as I have missed all of you."

CHAPTER SEVEN

"So good to see you all again." Whitmore shook Pa's hand, Ambrose's hand, and even Alexander's, when he put out his hand, too. "How has your winter gone so far?"

Pa removed his heavy mittens and took a seat on an upturned log by Whitmore Bragg's fire hearth. "We've done well. Michigan winters are sure somethin'. Nothing to laugh at."

"That, my friend, is indeed true. After all these years, I long for April much more every year. My bones do, too." Whitmore poured coffee in mugs and added a bit of rum to all the cups except Alexander's.

"We were noticing all the Indians camped near the trading post. Is that odd for them to be surrounding your place?" Ambrose lifted the mug and took a long swig.

"Has happened every winter for as long as I can remember. They store their canoes in the mud close to the shore, then they just bring their families and settle here until the weather clears some. But this year," Whitmore pulled up a log and sat down, "it's been a rough one."

"How so?" Hosea asked.

"Sickness. Seems to be some kind of cholera. I've treated as many children as I care to admit, but many have been lost. As soon as the ground thaws, we'll need to be burying a few. Hard to see the young'uns dying like they are. Even a few squaws." Whitmore's eyes grew misty talking about it.

"That's probably hard for anyone to see." Pa took a long swig of his drink. The added rum warmed his throat.

"It's inevitable. As soon as more civilized people come filtering into the territory, you'll see more disease in the Indians. Sorry to say. I've been here too long. The white man has become immune to the disease. Perhaps we had it as children. That's why we don't get it so much, but I guess the Indians haven't been around it before. They seem to get sick much easier than we do. You don't see the settlers getting the same disease. Odd as it sounds."

Ambrose unwound his scarf and placed his gloves close to Whitmore's hearth. He took Alexander's scarf and mittens and did the same.

Whitmore pulled on Alexander's ear. "Are you talking yet, boy?"

Alexander looked up at the man and smiled.

Pa answered, "Not a word. We've learned to communicate using hand gestures, but he hasn't said a word to us yet."

"That's just odd. When you talked to me about him last year, Ambrose, I did a little investigatin'. Sounds as if the Indians have done this to the child on purpose."

Pa sat back. "How so, Whitmore?"

"The Indians are private people. Always have been. They find it hard to have strangers entering into their territories. Knowing their ways. And because of that, they fear the white man will figure out how to take over their lands, hunt all their food, remove their traditions. You can see how they feel that way, can't you?"

Pa and Ambrose both nodded.

"Well. How do they stop it? The only way they know. They vow the others to secrecy."

"Secrecy? But how does that have anything to do with Alexander?" Ambrose looked over at the little boy eyeing Whitmore with interest.

"I think Alexander can speak. I think he can speak just fine, but he's been told not to speak. They've either threatened him with taking his life or the life of someone he loves if he is to utter any word to a white man."

Pa gazed at Alexander. "Are you sure?"

Whitmore took a drink from his mug. Swallowing, he added, "I'm fairly sure that's what's happened to the boy. The Indians don't want him sharing information that could bring harm to them. Or even worse, used against them."

Alexander stood. He looked at Whitmore with suspicion in his eyes.

Without blinking, Whitmore gazed back. "That's right, son, isn't it?"

Alexander shook his head in defiance, but soon he looked back at them and lowered his head.

"Now I know I'm right. He won't speak. He fears their warning. Whatever it might be."

Ambrose pulled on the arm of the child and urged him to sit back down beside him. He wrapped his arm around him and hugged him close. "It's okay, Alexander. We won't let anyone harm you."

"If I'm wrong, I'll eat my hat. But never was much on chewin' animal fur."

"Can we change his mind? Let him know his secrets are safe with us?" Pa smiled at the young boy. He knew for a fact that Alexander knew he loved him.

"Probably not! Indians teach their young'uns to listen, obey well. They will not defy the law. Can you imagine being a little guy like this and having someone either threaten your life or the life of someone you love and not believing it?" Whitmore added, "But there is one thing that might fix it."

Hosea, and it seemed as if Ambrose also, hung on to Whitmore's words because he knew whatever Whitmore said was inevitably true. Whitmore knew the Indian ways. He'd been with the tribe long enough to know them well.

"Ya gotta convince him that speaking English wouldn't reveal anything that could harm the Indians. The problem is, I don't have a clue how to get that across to the child. The only way would be to convince an Indian to explain that to him, but an Indian would feel that it would harm the child if he knew. As hard as they are on enforcing their rules, they love children. Perhaps I can do some convincin' to one of them that speaking English to other English people won't reveal any Indian secrets. If I can do that and the Indian can permit the boy only to speak English, it might work." Whitmore rose and went to the pot simmering over the fire. He stirred it with an iron bar.

"I know one Indian that might be up to the task. He lives close. Just outside the post and back down the river a bit. He's learning that the settlers aren't all interested in the Indian ways as much as just finding new places to live. If I can convince him, perhaps we can urge him to talk to the boy. It might even end his silence for good."

"That would be wonderful to communicate with Alexander," Hosea added.

"Not sure it will work. If the boy has been this silent for this long, he must be awful determined or afraid to speak for fear of what the Indians might do to him. Never seen a child so determined to obey so well." Whitmore looked over at Alexander, who seemed awful intent on staring at the fire. "He does know what we're saying by this time. He's been with you long enough to learn English. Let me see what I can do." Whitmore then added, "I hope you'll stay for dinner tonight. Havin' turnips and potatoes for supper."

"We'll thank you for supper. And if we can settle right here by your fire for the night, we'd be much obliged."

"You're always welcome at Whitmore's Trading Post. You're good people. You've been good to this child. Not many people would take a young boy like him and adopt him as one of their own without some kind of money exchanged."

"He's a good boy. He's brought us nothing but joy." Hosea desired nothing more than to have Whitmore understand that.

"He is a good boy. That's why I'm determined to see him do well. He needs to speak. I'll talk to the Indian tonight, or maybe in the morning, see if I can convince him to speak to Alexander."

The next morning, Whitmore took Alexander by the hand and led him down a path just north of the post. Whitmore suggested that Hosea and Ambrose stay behind. He wasn't sure of the Indian's reaction to seeing Alexander, now dressed as a white child. Whitmore assured Hosea that Alexander was safe with him.

It wasn't a few minutes later that Whitmore and Alexander came back up the trail. The only change: Alexander had a scowl on his face. As he approached Hosea, he stood straight and jutted his chin out.

"Well?" Hosea pulled the boy in for a hug. The child seemed eager to see Hosea and wrapped his arms around his waist.

"No luck," Whitmore told them. "This particular Indian didn't recognize the boy. Whoever gave this demand of Alexander is the only one who can remove it." Whitmore raised his hands in surrender. "Sorry. I did the best I could."

"So, you're saying we need to find the Indian who scared the child into muteness?" Hosea put his hand on the child's head.

"That's about it. I'm sorry." Whitmore stood and eyed the boy. "I'm pretty sure he can speak. Whatever edict put on the boy will be permanent unless we can assure the Indian who enforced it that Alexander's communication won't pose a danger to the tribe. I'll keep asking around."

Hosea shook Whitmore's hand. "Thank you for trying. Perhaps a little more persuasion from us will help the boy learn to speak."

Whitmore then shook his head, "I doubt it. For whatever reason, the mandate has put more than fear into this little guy's head. Whatever demand they made, he truly believes."

"Thanks again, Whitmore." Ambrose shook Whitmore's hand.

"I wish I could have done more for the boy. If nothing else, he is faithful to whoever's life is in danger." Whitmore turned toward his trading post. "It's a noble trait, but especially in a boy as young as this one."

Betsey loved to watch her ma play with Julia. They talked and smiled as if they couldn't live without one another. She'd never seen her mother so enamored. She also loved the help she'd received from her ma and sisters during the last afternoon, evening, and morning.

"I better be heading home before we get another storm." Betsey felt horrible to have to leave. She missed her own home, but her hesitation in returning home had much to do with her guests. She desperately wanted to be hospitable, especially to the only family Aaron had left. Perhaps the visit with her kin would spur her to continue to have patience with her sister-in-law.

"Please come and visit me soon. Even if it's for an afternoon of tea and chatter." Betsey pulled on her mittens while her ma tightened the ropes of the baby's backboard.

"We'll try. But like you, we need to keep an eye out for the weather." Ma kissed her grandchild's forehead. Tears welled in her eyes. "We'll miss you both and will be prayin' your circumstances get a bit better."

Betsey pulled all three of her sisters in for a hug and then kissed her ma's cheek.

As she headed out into the cold wind, she knew her reason for heading home. She could feel the dampness in the air. A storm could soon trap them inside again for a few days or maybe longer. Betsey followed the trail of steps she'd made just the day before up to the ridge, her crunching footsteps the only sound in the snowy landscape as the wind made her cheeks feel as if they were on fire.

"Betsey!"

Betsey looked up from concentrating on her steps to see Aaron venturing down the hill toward her. "Aaron! I'm so happy to see you."

Aaron pulled her into a hug. "How was your visit with your ma and the sisters?"

Betsey smiled up at him. "Good. I enjoyed the break. They came in handy helping me care for Julia."

"I missed you."

"I was only gone one night, silly man." Betsey knew how cold their home felt with their new guests. She could only imagine having to endure it alone.

"It was a bit of a night. But I wanted to speak with you alone before you got back to the cabin. I thought I might find you here or just preparing to leave your ma's house."

"You timed it just right." Betsey stopped. "Is something wrong?"

"I just want you to know that I know Abigail has been a real chore. I know you are doing the best you can with her."

"Aaron, it's..."

"No. Let me speak. It's not fair that you care for them all alone. If they were strangers, I wouldn't have a right to say what I did this morning."

Betsey froze and not from the cold of the winter day. "What did you say to them, Aaron? Please don't make matters worse."

Aaron shrugged. "I don't think I made it worse. I just want you to know that it isn't your responsibility to be the only cook, housekeeper, and also now a mother...all by yourself. It isn't fair for John or Abigail to expect you to wait on them. I told John so this morning. Either Abigail needs to help, or John does. We can't put them out in the cold, but I told him that if you don't get help, I'll start charging them like an innkeeper would a tenant."

Betsey couldn't believe what Aaron was telling her. "You told him that?"

Aaron grimaced.

Betsey couldn't help herself but soon tipped her head back and laughed right out loud.

"What?" Aaron seemed puzzled by her laughter.

"Thank you," was all Betsey could say. "I'm tired, Aaron. I didn't quite know how to tell you that."

"You didn't need to. Now let's go home and see what my talk will produce." Aaron took Betsey by the hand. "I think another winter storm is a-brewin'."

CHAPTER EIGHT

"I think you should use this skillet," Abigail handed Betsey a tinier pan than she'd planned to use.

"That one is a bit too small." Betsey held up the larger one.

"It would be less for us to have to wash."

"That's silly," Betsey did her best not to show a scowl or use a frustrating voice. "We have men to feed, not a home full of children." It didn't work.

"You're making us work too hard."

"Here, Abigail, why don't you set the table, and I'll whip up a few biscuits with this larger pan." Betsey handed the stack of plates to Abigail.

"Suit yourself."

Betsey had just spent the last six weeks dealing with the contrary woman and her attempt at trying to help. She was growing close to having Aaron have another talk with John. The first week her sister-in-law had changed. Now she got out of bed each morning. She attempted to help with the meals and housekeeping. But what replaced the complacency was criticism. Most were opinions as to how awful Betsey accomplished tasks in her home. She seemed extra critical while John was away. More winter storms descended on the property, making it impossible to go outside. Betsey longed for her ma and sisters. She missed them horribly.

Aaron now noticed Betsey's predicament and assured Betsey it wouldn't be long before he found another place for John and his wife to live.

This morning, Betsey didn't feel all that well. She'd found herself exhausted trying to care for Julia and supervise the household duties. She fell into bed each night with nothing but a longing that Julia would sleep through the night. Lectures on how to better care for her child accompanied every effort Betsey made to calm, soothe, or placate fussy Julia. Her normal, happy baby had turned into a cranky one as one after another tooth came through the baby's sore gums.

Ambrose seemed to understand the torment the woman had brought to the home. Many evenings he offered to walk Julia across the floor as she fought to fall asleep. Betsey was thankful for his help. If nothing else, it brought her relief from the prattling woman who shared her home.

Today, she'd felt exhausted even before rising from her bed. Was it the frustrating days awaiting her each morning, or was it just because she longed for spring and the ability to spend time alone with her family again? Whatever it was, she hoped it disappeared soon.

"Sit down, Betsey." Aaron took a plate from a pile that Betsey struggled to place on the table. She'd been afraid she'd drop one. All Abigail did was watch. "You look tired today."

As Aaron finished grace, Ambrose seemed eager to share something with those at the table. "John."

John looked up from opening his biscuit.

"I've been chatting with Whitmore. That's who I went to see yesterday. He has told me there are two rooms open at his post, and he's looking for a carpenter to come and help him this spring. I wondered if you'd be interested in applying for the position?"

"Carpenter, huh. I have training in that line of work. Remember, Aaron. Pa helped us both learn carpentry skills as teens."

"Sounds like a good possibility for you, brother."

"Yes. How do I go about looking into this position?"

"Oh, darling. We can't possibly move yet. I'd hate to get our things out in the weather we've been having. We'll surely be caught up in a storm." Abigail dabbed her napkin around her mouth.

"The weather is looking up, getting warmer every day. The only major thing you'd have to fight is the muddy roads from here to Whitmore's post. We'll figure out a way to transport your things. Won't we, Aaron?" Ambrose nodded to his brother-in-law.

Betsey held back the 'amen' at the tip of her tongue. If Ambrose were to get this cantankerous woman out of her home, she'd feed him well for as long as he wanted to be a house guest.

"What do you say? I'll take you down this next week and introduce you to Whitmore. He said he'd hire you as soon as you could arrive." Ambrose encouraged John with a pat on the back.

"Okay. It sounds like a good opportunity. Thank you, Ambrose." John smiled at Abigail, who looked at her husband with an indignant face.

Betsey wanted to cheer. She wanted to stand up and sing with all her might, but the way her belly roiled at the food she just ate curbed even her ability to thank her brother. She swallowed hard.

It wasn't a week later that Aaron and Alexander came in from an afternoon of being outside. They held up a fish they'd caught in the river. The Shiawassee was accessible and flowing again.

"Look what we caught!"

Alexander held up the tiny fish that would probably be just enough of a meal for Alexander, but he smiled brightly. His two front teeth were missing. He'd lost them almost at the same time as Julia had gained hers.

Betsey put her hands on her hips. "Fresh fish. It's been a long time..." Suddenly, a slight breeze from the open door flooded Betsey's nostrils with the smell of the tiny fish. She looked at Aaron and covered her mouth with her apron.

"Betsey? What's wrong?"

Before she could run outside, Betsey vomited into the bucket by the fireplace.

"Honey." Aaron shooed Alexander and the fish out the front door and shut it tight. "What in the world?"

Betsey had done her best to keep her morning sickness in check, but today, there seemed to be no control.

"I didn't know you were still feeling poorly. You said you thought you were getting over what was causing you to be so tired and sick the past few weeks. I think I need to get your ma up here to take a look at you." Aaron bent down and patted her on the shoulder.

Betsey wiped her mouth off with a nearby towel. "It won't be going away for a time."

"How do you know that?"

"I'll be feeling a bit better in a few weeks. But Aaron..."

Aaron looked at her with concern that almost made her weep.

"I don't think this will be over until at least the end of the year."

CHAPTER NINE

Betsey woke the next morning to a warmer cabin. It was the end of March, and April would soon be upon them. They'd made it through their first winter. Food was growing scarce, due to their additional guests. On Ambrose's last trip to see Whitmore, he'd been able to pick up a few items. They were now out of potatoes. Thankfully, the chickens were still producing at Pa's house.

As awful as she felt in the morning, there could be nothing on this day to cause Betsey to fret. Today, John and Abigail were leaving their home for his new job at Whitmore's trading post. Betsey rose and even opened the door to allow the bright spring sun to flicker across the wooden floor, illuminating a few dirty areas she needed to clean. She couldn't wait to bring their things from the loft and be able to have their bedroom back. John had helped Aaron build a permanent wall to separate their bedroom from the main room.

Abigail had fussed greatly upon learning that they would be moving. She'd moaned about how long the trip would take, which possessions to pack, and how to bundle them for the journey. Betsey did her best to calm the woman, but soon realized it was better to keep herself busy caring for Julia. She knew whatever she did would be criticized.

Aaron seemed as eager for them to leave as Betsey. He'd brought John's wagon up from Pa's farm and was waiting at the door to load their things into it.

"I'm sure you're happy we're finally leaving you today."

Betsey turned on her heel to see Abigail standing near the hearth.

"Abigail! You frightened me. I thought you were outside."

Abigail stared back at her, arms crossed, with a stern look on her face. "I'd love to thank you for allowing us to stay these past few weeks, but..."

Betsey wasn't sure what the woman was going to say. It hadn't been weeks, but months. Not that Betsey was counting or anything, she thought sarcastically. Betsey thought about the morning. Had she said anything to offend Abigail? Had Aaron, perhaps? But what?

"You're just one of those. You're a perfect wife, mother, housekeeper. It's clear to me that—"

Before Abigail said another word, John walked through the front door. "Abigail, honey, you ready to go?"

Betsey watched as Abigail dropped her arms and put a fake smile on her face. "Oh yes, John. I was just telling Betsey here how thankful we are to them for allowing us to spend the last couple of months here." Abigail's sudden attitude change made her words flow over Betsey like a bucket of sap from a nearby tree. Sticky and far from sweet.

Aaron had followed John in through the front door. He pointed to the trunk at the foot of the borrowed bed, "Can I help you load that?"

John went for the trunk, "Yes, Aaron, thank you. You folks have been so generous in allowing us to stay these long months. We're grateful."

Aaron had left the front door open, and a chill washed over Betsey as Abigail's smile turn into a smirk as she stared back at her. The relief of the couple moving out was replaced with something Betsey couldn't imagine. What was the woman going to say? Why did she now feel anxious, almost intimidated, by the expression on Abigail's face?

The one thing Betsey wanted to do once their winter guests had left was to return her home to its original state. Despite her churning stomach, she put Julia on a blanket by the window allowing the light of the spring day to warm her there. Julia seemed to be enamored with her fingers, as though she had never seen anything so magnificent. She held them up to the light and then inserted them into her mouth for an additional inspection.

Betsey pulled all of the blankets from their bed. She wondered if it was too early in the season to put new grasses from the riverbank into their bedtick. A fresh smell would bring a good night's sleep.

Going to the front door, Betsey opened it and looked out toward the ridge above the river. She decided to venture out to the edge to gaze down at the mighty Shiawassee as it rippled northward. Picking up Julia, Betsey left the musty cabin and took in a large breath. As much as she would have liked to see the view from her cabin window, it was much too far back into the woods to get a good glimpse. As soon as Julia's toddling legs learned to walk, the distance would be a blessing.

The wind still whistled through the bare trees of the forest behind her. She gazed out to the south of their cabin and could see the trail of smoke rising from her parent's chimney off in the distance. Perhaps after she cleaned and rearranged the house today, she and Julia could go down tomorrow to see her ma and sisters.

As she reached the edge of the precipice, Betsey gazed down at the roaring Shiawassee below. The heavy snows had made the river higher than they'd found it on their arrival last spring. Snow still lingered on the grassy banks that never caught the rays of the sun. That meant that the grasses to freshen up her bed would have to wait. She'd wash their blankets today—anything to drown out the effects of the long winter.

Julia squealed and sneezed at the fresh air outside. Her expression from the sneeze made Betsey laugh out loud. As she placed a kiss on the top of Julia's head, a flash of white drew her attention to the forest edge. There stood Waussinoodae. Her bright-white leather clothing made her appear like a ghost standing against the darkened forest wall beyond.

At first, the sight caught Betsey's breath, but she knew that the Indian woman was now a friend. Betsey shifted Julia to her left elbow to wave. Waussinoodae waved back and started toward her. The woman's face appeared gaunt and tired. Her body frail and skinny.

Aaron, or Ambrose, had been around during their past visits, but today, Betsey and Julia were the only ones at home. Betsey scanned the edges of the woods, and it appeared that Waussinoodae was alone. She felt a bit timid but not as afraid as she'd been on their first arrival to the territory. Some Indians, such as Waussinoodae, were friends, yet Betsey still felt hesitant.

As they drew close, Waussinoodae reached out her hand to Betsey and patted Julia. Smiling, she smoothed down the tuft of growing hair now shooting out from the back of the baby's head. It brought smiles from each of the women.

Pulling out a small leather pouch from beneath the cloth wrapped around her waist, Waussinoodae opened it and held out her hand to Betsey. She motioned for Betsey to do the same. Betsey did as the woman suggested, and a smattering of herbs filled her palm. Waussinoodae pointed to Julia and then to her mouth.

Betsey wasn't sure what the herbs were for until the woman pointed to her teeth. "Is this for teething?"

Waussinoodae pretended she was crying with her nails against her cheek. Betsey felt embarrassed that perhaps Julia's cries had even disturbed their Indian neighbors.

"Thank you." Betsey closed her hand around the precious herbs. She wished they could communicate better than pointing and motions, but Betsey did the same with Alexander. She wished there was something she could do for the woman who'd been so kind to Julia, Alexander, her family, and her.

"Would you come in?" Betsey motioned to the cabin, but Waussinoodae shook her head and pointed back to the forest. She tucked the pouch back under the cloth wrapped around her waist and smiled at Betsey.

Betsey smiled back. Before the woman dashed into the woods, she reached down and patted Betsey's stomach. She pointed to Julia and then to Betsey's middle. Waussinoodae knew before Betsey had told anyone else but Aaron. Waussinoodae smiled back, then turned and dashed into the forest.

Betsey turned to walk back. It seemed much too early for her to be with child again. Julia just five months old. But she knew that, without a doubt, the familiar morning sickness and the fatigue could only mean one thing. If her calculations were correct, Julia would be a big sister near the last month of the year.

But how did the Indian woman know?

CHAPTER TEN

Pa came into the cabin that morning as disgusted as Caroline and her sisters had ever seen him since moving to the new territory. He plunked his rifle down onto the kitchen table.

"Hosea. Can you kindly put away your rifle?" Ma was doing her best to place a skillet of hot scrambled eggs on the table.

Pa gave her "the look." She stepped back a bit but then held out the hot skillet. "Would you like to hold this? Or perhaps you could finish setting the table for us."

Pa's stern looks never lasted very long. "Confounded wolves. They got two chickens last night." He picked up his rifle and placed it in its pegs over the mantle.

"Chickens!" Jillian sat down with a thump. It wouldn't be long before tears would flow.

"Can't be helped. They are extra fierce these past few weeks. Probably have pups to feed." Pa sat and pulled his plate closer to him. "Sorry, girls."

Caroline placed the rest of the eating utensils close to each plate and sighed. "Guess we better take turns watching the pen again, Pa?"

"Probably right! Ambrose said they prowl more in the spring than any other time."

Ma placed the biscuits on the table and put a cloth over them to keep them warm. "Perhaps Henry has some more pullets to divide with us. They were so good to us last summer to share part of their flock. Do you have anything you could trade them for?"

"Don't know. I'll think on that a bit." Pa spooned a large scoop of eggs onto his plate.

Etta reacted first, clasping her hands together. "I love new pullets. We often get double yolks."

"We won't get any yolks if we don't get the wolves under control. I wish I knew what else we could do to keep those nasty animals from digging under the fence." Pa motioned for everyone to hold hands as he said grace.

Betsey drew near to her parents' cabin. She'd decided to carry Julia instead of wedging her in the papoose board this trip. Julia chattered on until the breeze caught her breath. When it did, she'd gulp and shiver. The day was sunshiny and warm. April would soon be upon them.

Betsey approached her pa, who was digging into the soil behind the cabin. "Hey, Pa!"

She'd startled him. "Betsey! My land sakes, daughter, give a man notice that you're a-comin'."

Betsey laughed. As she did, so did Julia.

Pa leaned against the pole of his shovel. "And what are you laughing about, sweet girl?" Pa lifted Julia's chin with his dirty finger. The child looked at him and turned her head toward Betsey.

"Are you bein' shy? It's just your Grandpappy!" Betsey laughed at the little girl who was now reacting more to others around her.

"What are you doing out and about this warm spring day?" Pa asked, removing his hat and wiping the sweat from his brow.

"We decided we needed to get out today and see if Ma needed help with spring cleaning. I finished most of mine yesterday, and I'm sure it wouldn't hurt to have some extra hands down here. More people to care for than I have."

Pa spat on the ground. "That there is. More and more comin' each day. Henry and Claire stopped in last night and said they have two new neighbors now up on the hill south a-here."

"That sounds wonderful. New neighbors. Perhaps soon we'll have enough children to start a school." Betsey switched Julia to the other arm. "My arms are gettin' a bit weary, Pa, from carrying this squirming baby down from the ridge. I'm going to head into the house."

Pa waved. "See you at lunch."

As Betsey came around the edge of the cabin, she nearly ran right into Caroline, who carried a bucket of scraps for the chickens.

"Caroline! Watch where you're going." Betsey laughed, and again, Julia imitated her. Both the girls laughed.

"Someone is a happy girl today." Caroline smiled at her niece, shifting the bucket to her other hand. "I gotta feed the chickens. See you back at the house."

Betsey let her sister pass.

Ma had come out of the cabin and was shaking a rug. "Betsey. Just the person I longed to visit with this morning."

Betsey laughed. "Is it because you needed a distraction from your spring cleaning, or you're happy to see help arrive?" Julia began to wriggle in her arms when she saw Betsey's ma.

"Both!" Ma handed Betsey the rug and took Julia from her arms. "Come with Grammy, my sweet baby. I've missed you." Ma planted a kiss on Julia's cheek.

Soon the women were busy scrubbing floors, with the cabin door wide open for the first time that year. The fresh breeze from outside seemed to suck the winter-musty smell right out of the house. The breeze carried the singing voices of Betsey's sisters as they polished the stones around the hearth and stirred the pot of boiling water washing bedding.

Jillian's voice filled the air with a joyful sound.

> "We sing the mighty power of God
> that made the mountains rise,
> that spread the flowing seas abroad
> and built the lofty skies.
> We sing the wisdom that ordained
> the sun to rule the day;
> the moon shines full at His command,

and all the stars obey."

Betsey added to Jillian's voice by asking, "Remember that shooting star display we got to see last fall before the first snowfall?"

"You and Pa only told us about it, remember?"

Betsey smiled. "You're right. You were still sleeping. Betsey stirred in a bit more lye soap as her sister twirled a blanket in the scorching water over the fire on the hearth. Sweat dripped from her forehead. Soon they'd build an outdoor fire, and this job would be a bit easier. "It was a magnificent thing to see."

"Just like all the new plants growing now. Winter seems to kill so much, yet in the spring, up the growing shoots come, pointing toward the heavens to start another season." Ma handed Betsey another blanket to wash as she removed the now-dripping-wet one that she'd take outside to dry.

"Did you hear, Betsey? Pa said we have new neighbors located close to Henry and Claire Leach."

Betsey looked at her youngest sister, who was jabbing a broom into the corners to clean them. "I heard. Perhaps they'll have some nice girls to play with."

"Or boys to admire." Etta put her hand to her brow as if in a swoon.

Caroline shook her head. "Etta, is that all you ever think about, boys?"

"You would, too, if you didn't have a beau coming for you from back East."

"Oh Billie boy, Billie!" Jillian called out, in a pleading voice.

"I don't talk like that," Caroline scolded her younger sister.

"Have you gotten any more letters from him?" Betsey asked Caroline, who shook her head. "They'll come. Perhaps he'll personally deliver one."

"I won't believe he is coming until I see that shock of blonde hair comin' toward me," Caroline said, in a skeptical voice.

Betsey heard a voice from outside. "Shh, listen. I hear someone."

All the girls stopped their cleaning to listen.

Ma called to them from outside the cabin. "Girls, we have a visitor."

Caroline was the first to the door, followed by Betsey's other two sisters. Betsey glanced toward Julia, sleeping on the floor, and then headed to the door to see who was outside.

Pa was walking toward them with a young man walking beside him. Ma wiped her wet hands down her apron, "I wonder who that could be."

Caroline went to stand beside Ma as her two younger sisters and Betsey crowded close together. The last visitors to their property had been Abigail and John. It was quite momentous to have a newcomer arrive.

"Sally Mae, girls, this is Horace. Horace Knapp. He's a newcomer to these parts and wanted to stop by and say hello."

Ma was the first to hold out her hand. "Horace, it's so nice to meet you."

The young man removed his hat and shook Ma's hand. "Nice to meet you, ma'am."

"I'm Sally, and these are my girls." Ma pointed to each of them. "This is Jillian, Etta, Caroline."

"And I'm Betsey." Betsey also held out her hand to greet the newcomer.

"Horace has been staying at the trading post all winter. We met him last time we were there. These are all my daughters and my wife."

Horace nodded to each one, gripping his hat so hard that it seemed to be losing its shape. "Nice to meet you all. I heard singing from off in the woods back there." He pointed to the back section of the property. "I had to see where it was coming from."

Pa laughed. "You could say that if you hear singing, it's more n' likely the Baker sisters."

Horace blushed. "It sounded beautiful."

Caroline looked the man up and down. He was taller than Pa but much skinnier, and with his hat off, his brown hair stuck up in several places. It looked like a month of Sundays since it had seen any water.

"Won't you stay for supper tonight?" Ma asked.

"I'd like that." Horace grinned wide, as if the invitation offered him something he hadn't done in a while.

"What we having, Sally?"

Squash, some turnips, and I hoped we'd have Aaron and Ambrose bring us some fish, too."

Horace seemed as though he hadn't eaten that good in a month or two, by his reaction to the menu's recitation.

"You're more than welcome to stay." Ma then turned. "If you don't mind, we have a bit more things to wrap up this afternoon. Excuse us."

Caroline wanted to move. She should be following Ma and her sisters, but for some reason, she couldn't take her eyes off the man standing beside Pa. He looked to be about her age or maybe a year or two older. If he was, this young man was courageous to come to the new territory all alone.

"Carrie girl, Horace is about your age. He just turned nineteen."

Caroline smiled. "I turned sixteen. Last August."

Horace tipped his head. "Nice to meet you. I'm Horace."

"I know," Caroline laughed. "I heard."

Pa patted the younger man on the shoulder. "Why don't you and I head down to the river? We'll see if the men in the family are having any luck with catchin' us a few fish for supper."

Horace placed his now-misshapen hat back on his head and looked toward Caroline. "Nice to meet you."

Caroline watched as he and Pa made their way down the bank toward the river.

"Caroline!" Ma called for her.

"I'm coming."

It had been a long time since Caroline had seen someone her age.

"I'm twelve." Jillian smiled at their visitor that night at the supper table.

"And I'm fourteen," added Etta.

Caroline laughed at her sisters. Each one had taken a bit of extra time primping themselves for supper. Their hair was freshly combed and tied up in neat buns. Jillian had even washed her face until it shone from the dim lamp on the table.

"I'm not going to tell you how old I am, Horace, but I am the oldest girl of the family." Betsey winked at their guest as she dished some squash onto Aaron's plate.

"So, what's brought you to these parts, Horace?" Ambrose asked the visitor.

"It's a bit of a complicated story." Horace had seemed preoccupied scooping forkful after forkful of food into his mouth. He often commented about how good everything tasted. It seemed their guest hadn't eaten like this in a good while.

"How is it that you're all alone? Where's your pa? Ma?"

Horace stopped eating. Wiping his mouth off with his sleeve, he swallowed. "Um." He pushed the extra food around his plate with his fork. Silence was his answer. He didn't glance up.

"I'm sorry," Ambrose commented. "I didn't mean to pry."

The young man finally looked at everyone. His eyes watery, he wiped his nose on a sleeve. "My parents were both killed coming here from Pennsylvania." He looked down at his plate, shifting his food from one side to the other with his utensil.

Ma gasped, "Oh, Horace! We're so sorry."

"I have no brothers nor sisters. I'm alone now."

No one moved. Caroline gulped. *How awful. What would I do without any family?*

Ambrose placed his hand on the man's shoulder. "We're truly sorry for your loss."

Alexander seemed to understand, as he pointed to himself. Jillian interpreted, "Alexander said he had the same thing happen to him."

Horace kept his focus on his plate. He coughed as if something was in his throat.

"What are your plans now, Horace? Is there anything we can do to help you?"

Horace wiped his eyes. "Um, maybe. Whitmore Knaggs said you folks might be willing to give me some direction. I'd like to stay in these parts. Settle maybe. But I'm not sure. He told me you're one of the first settlers to come to this part of the territory, and you'd be good folk to chat with about where I could maybe settle. Maybe even build a place."

Pa pulled a tiny fish bone from his mouth and placed it on the side of his plate. "We'd be more than happy to help you, Horace."

Caroline saw Betsey and Aaron look at one another, and Aaron nod.

"Horace, you'd be more than welcome to stay with us for a bit. We have a nice loft where Alexander and Ambrose stay."

Aaron added, "Yes, Horace. You're more than welcome."

"I'd hate to intrude. I just need a place for a bit until I get my bearings. Figure out what I can do."

Pa picked up the bowl of turnips and motioned for Ma to pass it along to Horace. "You're more than welcome to help me here on the farm for a bit. I'm working the ground up now, preparin' for plantin'. I could use the help."

Horace glanced up at Pa as if he'd just received a prize for a winning steer.

"We can't pay you, but we'll feed you, and as Betsey and Aaron said, you'll have a roof over your head for a while." Pa sighed. "What do you say?"

"Um, I don't know what to say."

Ambrose patted the young man on the back. "Just say yes. We'd like nothing more than to help you. I'm building a house south of here. I could use help from time to time, too. Once my place has been built, I can help you. That's how we manage to pay each other back. What do you say?"

Horace looked down at his plate and then up again. Tears were escaping his eyes. He seemed embarrassed as he wiped at them with his sleeve. "That's awful nice. Thank you. Yes. Yes, I'll stay."

For some reason, Caroline had been holding her breath. She wasn't sure why. She exhaled and took another bite of her bread as a howl outside filled the air.

"Doggone wolves!" Pa slammed his fork on the table.

Caroline didn't hesitate. The men had been working awful hard that day, and she stood and went to the mantle for the rifle. "I'll check on it, Pa."

"Caroline, you don't need to go." Pa turned toward her.

"It's fine. I need some air. I'll go check the barn."

She looked back at Horace as she slipped into her coat.

The look on his face made her almost laugh right out loud.

"Well, Horace, you're probably wondering why we allowed my sister to go out and check on the barn?" Ambrose smirked.

"Um, now that you mention it."

"She's experienced when it comes to wolves. Last year she shot three."

Horace took in the news by nearly choking on the water he'd been drinking. "She killed three wolves?"

"Yup. But even so, I'm going to head out with her as soon as I finish this last bite—"

"Let me. Let me go and help her. I'm no expert shot, but I can keep her company." Horace picked up his plate and handed it to Mrs. Baker.

He went for the door and slipped into his coat. "I gotta see this!" He went out the door, shutting it behind him. As he did, he could hear the roar of laughter coming from the table he'd just left.

CHAPTER ELEVEN

Caroline was surprised to watch Horace fit right into the family just as Alexander had. She caught herself watching Pa and Horace plant crops. He appeared attentive and to take instructions well, following Pa's actions as if his very livelihood depended on it.

His help came in handy to Pa, leaving Ambrose and Aaron able to concentrate on finishing up Ambrose's house. Spring brought with it the strenuous work they'd experienced the previous year in preparing the fields, planting corn, potatoes, and now keeping up with the outside chores. Repair work needed to be finished on the roofs, and the cabins needed to be aired out and cleaned.

With Horace on the farm, Caroline found her sisters enamored with his attention. In turn, Horace took notice of their flirting with winks and smiles. Caroline made every effort to not swoon over him or have to fix her hair before dinner each night, like her sisters.

Jillian and Etta hid behind outbuildings to catch a glimpse of Horace working. They also insisted on baking him treats and presenting them to him after dinner each night. Caroline thought it was futile and childish to act silly over a boy.

Horace was a kind young man and often offered to carry their buckets of water or stand at one end to help fold a freshly laundered quilt. Caroline knew it wouldn't be long before he chose one of her sisters to court. Jillian was pretty young, but Etta, at fourteen, was all about getting his attention.

"Like you don't want his attention?" Etta murmured to her one night when she'd told her how immature she was acting toward the boy.

"I assure you...I don't care what he's up to." Caroline sat on the edge of the bed, scolding her sister for even assuming she was interested.

"Then why are you waiting longer at the spring to see if he shows up to help us with the buckets each morning?"

"Estelle Baker! You take that back. I do no such thing!" Caroline crawled into bed and pulled the blankets up to her chin. "Now stop prattling and go to sleep. I'm exhausted."

As the weeks passed, Ma's cooking began to fill out Horace's stature. His lean body slowly turned into a man with broad shoulders and muscular arms. The scrawny teen soon turned into a full-fledged grown man.

Caroline turned her head away one afternoon and scolded herself for her second looks.

As she went to fetch the eggs one morning, Horace met her on the path from the house. "Morning, Caroline."

Caroline always felt embarrassed to talk to the boy. She knew how much Etta had taken a liking to him and thought it her duty to bow out of the way of their growing friendship. "Morning, Horace."

"Getting eggs?" Horace held out his hand to take her basket. "Can I help you?"

Caroline scooted around him as he stood in the path. She called over her shoulder. "No, I'm fine. Ma's got breakfast going. I'm sure you're hungry."

Horace's nature had turned into a pleasant, happier one since staying with them. "I'm always hungry, but I don't mind helping you."

Caroline headed toward the barn, with Horace following close behind her.

"I'm awful grateful to your family for helping me out so much." He opened the nesting box near the coop to allow Caroline to reach in and gather eggs.

"I'm sure Pa appreciates all your help, too."

"I hope so. I wish I could do more."

Caroline reached in for another egg. She felt almost too close to Horace as he held the door up for her. She didn't dare look at his face, which was just inches away. The morning was far from warm yet, their breath visible and now mixed in the morning's coolness. Caroline felt her face grow warm.

"I've gotten to know your sisters well over the past month or so, but I guess I still don't know you very well yet."

What was she supposed to say to that? She placed the last egg into her basket.

"I was hoping...maybe we could go on a walk some afternoon."

Caroline stopped moving and looked directly into Horace's face. "A walk?"

Horace grinned.

For the first time, Caroline noticed his long eyelashes as they blinked against his bright blue eyes. It was as if his eyes mirrored the sky on a clear, spring morning. His cheeks were now tan from the sun, and recently Betsey had given him a haircut that made him look even older than the young man who'd shown up at their doorstep.

Neither one of them moved.

"You have the prettiest smile."

With that, Caroline turned on her heel and headed back toward the cabin.

"Caroline!" Horace called after her.

She ignored his call.

Betsey had brought Julia down for the day, and Ma was bathing her in a wash barrel. She was sitting up now and using her hands to splash in the water. Caroline wasn't sure who was getting wetter, Julia or Ma.

"Oh, you sweet baby! I can't believe how much you've grown this winter." Ma picked up the infant and wrapped her in a shawl that had been warming beside the fire.

"She has grown some. I think I may start her off on some solid food soon. Do you think she can handle that now, Ma?" Betsey smoothed down the unruly hair at the top of her daughter's head. Despite it being wet, as Ma toweled her off, it still stood straight up on top.

"Are you having problems with your milk?" Ma asked, as she handed off the baby to Betsey so she could dress her.

"No. I just think it's time. I am a bit sore these days."

Ma stood to place the now-wet shawl on a peg above the fireplace to dry. "You shouldn't be sore." Ma looked concerned.

Betsey smiled. "Well, if your body is changing, perhaps being sore is just another season of your life."

Ma pushed Julia's arm through a dress sleeve. "Why should you be—?" Ma stopped mid-sentence and gave Betsey a funny look.

Betsey just smiled. "Aren't we all just a bit sore at the beginning of another pregnancy?"

"Betsey! No!"

Betsey grinned. "I'm afraid so."

"But you're nursing. You shouldn't be able to..."

"Whether I'm nursing or not, I'm expecting again." Betsey handed Julia's socks to Ma to put on the baby. Ma didn't even appear to notice, as she looked back at her daughter with questioning eyes.

"When?"

Betsey shook the socks to distract her ma's thoughts. It felt funny even to tell Ma she was pregnant again. She had a hard time believing it herself, with it being just months since she'd had Julia. But even last October seemed a long way off. She glanced at Caroline, who appeared as shocked as everyone else.

Ma finally burst into a smile while she continued to wrestle with the squirmy, now fussy baby. "Well, that's some mighty wonderful news. When do you think?"

Betsey took her fully dressed baby from Ma. "Christmas. Maybe it will be a boy, and we can have a real baby to play Jesus for our celebration."

Caroline placed her sewing project on the table and stood to hug Betsey. "Another baby. How wonderful."

Betsey took Caroline's seat. "I need to feed this fussy baby, and perhaps she'll sleep a bit so I can help you this afternoon with some chores."

"Caroline, why don't you start sweeping now? We'll bring in a kettle of water and give this floor a good scrubbin'." Ma handed the broom to her. "Start over there in that corner so the dust won't bother Julia while she nurses."

As Caroline began shifting dirt into the center of the floor from all the corners and crevices of the room, she wondered when it would be her time to start a family. She adored Betsey. She longed to have a healthy marriage like her and Aaron and to add more grandchildren to the family. Wasn't it a given that Julia and Betsey's new baby would need cousins?

She'd been lying in bed each night dreaming of the moment that Billie would come for her. Would Pa allow them to marry right away? Would they have a place to stay if they did marry so soon? That thought made her blush as she pushed more dirt into the center of the room with her broom. Married! Having children. She'd planned her whole life since getting the letter from Billie at Christmas time. And even though she'd known Billie her entire life, they'd never been romantic with each other. Was she ready for that? He'd always been one of her best friends, but the thought of being intimate with him made her blush.

Interrupting her thoughts were her sisters as they burst through the front door with sloshing buckets in each hand. "Ma, where do you want this water?"

Ma stood in the middle of the floor with both hands on her hips. "Girls! You're getting water all over the floor, and Caroline hasn't finished sweeping yet." Ma's scolding didn't stop her sisters from heading for the hearth with buckets ready to boil. They had a floor to clean.

Spring was here. There was a baby on the way. The days were getting brighter, and the birds were heralding each morning with chirps, trills, and tweets that the family hadn't heard in months. Life was continuing in the new territory. Despite her fears, Caroline knew it was time she began a life of her own. For now, she was content to scrub a floor.

Each week, new families came scouting out the area for a place to settle. Henry Leach came on horseback one day to discuss the situation with Hosea. They sat down after supper to have a cup of coffee before Henry headed home to the property just south of the Baker farm.

"I'm astounded. I knew we'd have neighbors before long, but Hosea, one a week? I can't believe it." Henry took a long swig of his coffee. "I think I may head to the land office to purchase the land to the left of me before it's snatched up by someone else."

"The folks that came last week were from New York State. With the canal open and more steamboats heading into Detroit, more folks are coming from the East. Don't you think?" Pa took the last bite of cake.

"The ones who stopped at our house last week are from Ohio, just like us." Henry tapped the table with his fork after finishing his cake.

"Whitmore said he plans to add additional space to the post soon. He needs rooms for those just needing a place to stay. It's only May. I wonder who will wander in during the summer months?" Ambrose added.

"Henry, I agree. You need to get to the land office soon. I'd hate to see you have to give up the land where you've built your barn. Can you manage the trip alone?" Hosea pushed back his plate, sat back in his chair.

Henry took another swig. "I think so. I'd be mighty obliged though if you or Ambrose could check on my family while I'm gone."

Ambrose answered, "I'd be happy to. Once the weather gets warm, I plan to be finishing up my house, and with us being so close, I could ride over to check on Claire and the children."

"Much obliged, Ambrose. You folks have been good to us. I'll never forget your kindness."

"After last summer, I'm happy to help you out. What would Betsey, Sally, and the girls have done without you here to repair their roof after the bad storm? " Hosea lifted his mug to swallow the last of his coffee. "I am might happy that we decided to get our property sooner than later. We're going to have a village, if not a town, here soon." Hosea smiled. "It will be fine to see the place settled by neighbors as nice as you and Claire."

The Baker family was not the only one to begin the arduous task of spring cleaning and harvesting. Caroline watched as robins, finches, and red-winged blackbirds set to finding tiny branches and tufts of long grasses with which to build nests and lay their eggs. Their chirps and trillings filled each morning with musical tones. As the leaves began to burst from the buds on the trees, hidden nests could be found among the bright green leaves of new growth. The forest around the cabin took on the hues of sage and emerald.

The family couldn't get enough of the fish the menfolk were now bringing up to the cabin for supper. Pa had taught each daughter to till the ground in preparation for new seeds, and had expanded his crops to another twenty acres.

Caroline did her best to take over the chores Betsey had been doing before moving to the ridge. She helped with the heavier chores while her younger sisters did the rest. And as had happened the previous year, night didn't come fast enough to lie down again to rest from each weary day.

Ma seemed to be suffering the worst. Last year's illness had just sapped the strength she once had. Caroline knew she needed to take up the slack. She also urged Etta to do the same, much to Etta's dismay.

"You've gotten so bossy lately. What's the matter with you?" Etta turned the dough she'd been kneading and patted it.

"We just need to work harder. That's all."

"But why? Things seem to be going fine." Etta sliced through the rising dough to make separate loaves for baking. "Can you hand me those two tins?"

"I'm worried about Ma."

Etta stopped patting the dough and looked up. "Ma?"

Caroline would often find Ma napping in a nearby chair just after lunch each day. If she didn't try and sleep for at least a few minutes, by night, her face grew pale, and she struggled to stay awake to finish up the supper dishes.

"What's wrong with Ma?"

"I think last year's illness has made her weak. Doesn't she look old to you?"

Etta winced. "Old? She's always been old."

Caroline handed her sister the tins.

"Can you grease them? I'll be able to place this dough in them. They'll be rising to bake early this afternoon. We can have fresh bread for supper."

"Betsey doesn't seem to have been as affected by the illness last year, but Ma..."

"I'm sure she's fine. But yes, work harder. These longer days make me wish for a winter storm again."

"Bite your tongue!" Caroline didn't want anything to do with winter for a bit. She'd rather be outside in the fresh air doing chores.

Caroline decided to ask Etta about her impressions of Horace.

"He's a nice boy. I like him." Etta smiled. "What do you think of him?"

Caroline shrugged. "I don't know. He seems very nice to me, too. I think he'd make some girl a very nice husband."

Etta gave her a skeptic look. "Someone?"

"Yes. Don't you think so?"

Again, Etta smiled back at her with a smirk on her face.

"What? Why are you looking at me like that?"

Etta wiped her floured hands down the front of her apron. "I don't think I'm all that interested. I mean, I want a husband, don't get me wrong, but Caroline, I don't think he's smitten with Jillian or me."

Caroline lowered the tins to allow the dough to rise over the warm glow of coals on the hearth. "What are you talking about?" When she stood up and turned around, Etta had stopped working to face her with crossed arms.

"What I'm trying to say, sister. Horace isn't interested in your younger sisters. He's interested in you!" Etta pointed her finger, covered in flour, right to Caroline's chest.

Caroline shook her head. "He is not! Take that back!"

Etta laughed. "I can't believe you haven't noticed it yet."

Caroline stood back and looked at her sister. "I don't...I can't believe..." and as if she hadn't thought about it at all, she slowly shook her head. "I do believe this spring weather and the newness of life has done something to your brain."

Etta tipped her head back and laughed. "Caroline, I think you better make up your mind. Do you like Horace, or will you wait for Billie to arrive?"

"There's no question in my mind about that. It's all settled. Billie is coming, and I don't want to hear another thing about Horace and me!" Caroline gave her sister a glare that made her go silent.

The warm spring days turned sharply cold again. It was near the end of May. Pa had just planted the first of the crops, and rain began one day and continued each day for a week. At first, Pa was pleased with having a good spring rain on his fresh planting, but then—the wind changed.

The Baker family awoke one morning to a cabin almost as cold as it was in the middle of February. Pa was up early stoking the fire as if it were a winter morning. Sparks flew as he placed several logs on the embers from last night's fire.

Caroline's face was about the only thing not covered by blankets on the bed, and it was cold. She quickly pulled the covers over her head to breathe warmth into her face before getting out of bed. She whispered to Etta, who was still sleeping beside her. "Etta?"

Etta stirred, and as she thrust her arm out to roll over in bed, she immediately pulled it back under the warmth of the covers. "It's freezing in here."

"We'd better get up. Ma will need us."

Etta moaned as she rolled over. "You first."

Caroline bravely pulled the cover off her body and then her feet. The cold air from the room took her breath away. "Oh my!"

Etta pulled the covers back over her backside. "I'm not getting up yet. Not until the fire warms the air more."

Caroline slipped into her dress and then grabbed a shawl from a hook above their bed. She bent down to pull on her winter wool socks she hadn't worn since March. She called out to Ma, "I'll get the buckets filled, Ma. You stay by the fire."

"Thank you, Caroline," Ma called out from in front of the fire.

Caroline knew that if she stopped to warm herself, she'd never get outside. So, she opened the door and then picked up the bucket handles.

What caught her sight made her gasp. A thick, white frost covered the ground. It was everywhere. As she stepped out of the cabin, her feet crunched on the grass. She could see her breath as she made her way down to the spring at the edge of the river. A frost this late in spring was unusual. Specks of green grass seemed to cry out from the heavy white layer of dew on the ground. Even the spring birds were quiet. It was as if it had snowed the night before, but Caroline knew it was nothing but a heavy frost.

As she made her way to the river's edge, she could only think of one thing. Pa's crops!

CHAPTER TWELVE

"This frost was unexpected."

Pa leaned on the hoe he was using to dig up the now-dead plants. "Things were just starting to spike from the ground. I didn't think the deep frost would hurt them, but now, almost all are dead."

Ambrose sighed. "I'm sorry, Pa. You and Horace worked so hard this spring."

"The Lord giveth and the Lord taketh away! He doesn't purposely create bad things to discourage us but, hopefully, give us more strength to endure the world's frustrations. We'll have to replant this year." Pa bent over and dug up a few more plant shoots.

Ambrose had stayed back to help Pa remove the dead plants. There was nothing he could do to remedy the situation for his pa. They'd lost so many seedlings in the heavy frost just days before. Now the sun beat down on his back, and he removed the shirt he'd used to keep warm that morning, tying it around his waist. He looked up and pointed to Horace at the other end of the field, "Horace sure is a help to you, isn't he?"

Pa stopped, pulled out a handkerchief from his back pocket, and wiped off his forehead. "He sure is. He's a good boy." He began digging again. "He's gonna be a big help when we have to plant this field all over again."

Pa sat down along the row of dead plants and whistled out a breath. "My winter body is sure havin' a hard time gettin' strength this season. Been feeling awful weary as of late."

"Let me dig this row. Horace and I will have it done in no time."

"I've been thinking," Pa handed Ambrose his hoe without much hesitation. "With all these new folks comin' into the territory, I wonder if we should plant just a few crops and then get busy on building something everyone will soon need?"

Ambrose smiled. "And what would that be, Pa?" He wasn't quite sure what his pa was suggesting.

"A sawmill."

Ambrose stopped digging. "What?"

"You know. A place that harvests trees and makes them into usable lumber pieces."

Ambrose laughed. "I know what a sawmill is, Pa." He began digging again. "What made you think of that?"

"We have at least one family a week head into the territory. What do they need?" Hosea picked up a leaf that was on the ground at his feet. He began picking it apart as if to examine it. "Lumber! And lots of it. If we had it sawn and ready, they'd have enough to get their homes up quick." Hosea smiled. "We'd make a killin'."

Ambrose stopped hoeing and wiped off his forehead. "Pa, out of all the ideas you've ever had, I think this one is the best yet."

"Yup, I agree. A sawmill, perhaps even a gristmill later on. With bein' right close to the river, we can use our property to build it on. We can girdle trees now and be cutting wood by next spring. Will you help me?"

Ambrose put down the hoe and headed toward his pa. He held out his hand to help Hosea up off the ground. As his pa rose, he couldn't help but agree. "Sure. As long as I get half the profits."

"Half!" Hosea slapped his knee and laughed. "You certainly are my son."

Hosea picked up the hoe. "But first, let's replant this field. Perhaps Horace will want in on the idea, too. Three partners will be just enough to get this little village right off the ground and buildin'. What d'you think?"

"We wouldn't have to just depend on crops to feed us. We'll get plenty of money from the trees right on our land. Pa, this is a great idea."

"Why not take advantage of the best crop we have around here? The trees." Hosea stooped over and took out a couple more dead plants, rubbing them to flakes that fell to the ground. "And the best thing, trees don't succumb to a frost."

Caroline was spreading heavy blankets over the bushes one afternoon to dry in the fresh spring air. They were heavy, and both her sisters were busy helping Pa with replanting. Washing the blankets had been enough for her ma to need to sit for a bit.

She'd managed to spread one out on the weeds, but the second quilt was longer and required her to adjust it many times to get it out over the reeds by the river.

A voice from behind her made her jump. "Need some help, Caroline?"

"Oh, Horace." Caroline placed her hand over her heart.

"I'm sorry." Horace, with a smile on his face, reached out his hand to steady her. "I didn't mean to scare you."

"Sure you didn't." Even though boys weren't all that plentiful in the Michigan Territory, she was still accustomed to their ways to frighten a girl, but not their reasons to do so.

"No. Everyone needs some water, and as I walked out here, I saw you struggling to get these blankets out to dry and thought I'd come and offer you a hand."

"I have them. I don't need your help—" Before Caroline could get out the entire sentence, the first quilt she'd placed across the reeds fell into the dust beneath it. Caroline placed her hands on her hips. "I give up."

Horace ran to pick up the quilt. "You'll have to rewash these blankets if this keeps happening."

Caroline folded her arms. "Do you have a better solution?"

Horace wadded up the still damp, heavy quilt. "I believe I do."

Caroline tilted her head as if to permit him to tell her. Her look made Horace laugh. She pushed her hair away from her eyes and off her forehead.

"My ma used to hang these up on a line. You know, a clothesline. Why don't I rig one up for ya?" Horace placed the quilt back into the basket by the river.

"That would be great, but where are we gonna get any extra rope?" Caroline pointed down the trail toward Whitmore's trading post. "Better yet, why don't you head to the trading post and see if they sell it?"

"There's gotta be something around here we could use for rope." Horace looked around the property. "Wait a minute; I have an idea."

As he ran to the barn, Caroline stood, trying to decide if she should continue struggling with placing the quilts out to dry or wait to see if this young man could come up with a better solution.

She grabbed up the last quilt she'd spread and placed it back in the basket, too. Horace was right. The quilt was getting dirtier doing it this way. The spring reeds weren't yet strong enough to hold up under the heavy bedding.

As Caroline placed the last blanket in the basket, she saw Horace climbing a nearby tree on the edge of the woods. Stopping to watch him, she shielded her eyes from the late morning sun to see him pulling what looked to be a vine from a nearby tree.

The vine tumbled to the ground at the foot of the tree. Lifting the heavy basket of quilts, she headed toward him, calling out to him when she was just a few feet away. "Horace. What are you doing?"

The young man turned. "Virginia creeper would make a great line for hanging clothes. Let's try it."

Caroline placed the basket on the ground. "Are you sure that's what that is? Pa said we need to be careful of the vines around here. They can give you a bad rash."

"I'm sure. Look!" Horace held up a shoot of the vine. "Five leaves, not three."

Caroline looked on. "How do you know so much about plants?"

Horace scrambled down from the tree, began gathering the vines he'd pulled off the tree, and then headed toward Caroline. "My father loved plants. He would often take me on walks through the woods, naming and pointing out the plants to me." Horace came closer. "Let's string this vine up from the edge of the barn to that small tree over there." Horace pointed out the tree.

"It just might work, Horace."

Horace smiled again. "Of course it will. Wait and see."

Horace raced off for the barn. Caroline scolded herself as she thought of his smile. Something about it made her smile herself, as though it was contagious.

Soon the two had rigged up quite the clothes-airing solution. They were proud of their efforts. The blankets were now flapping in the breeze.

"See, we did it." Horace placed the last edge of a quilt out to dry. He then began to scratch his arms that had grown red.

Caroline watched as he raised the bottom of his shirt up to scratch his chest. "Um, Horace, are you sure about that plant?" Caroline blushed at the sight of his bare chest.

"Course I am!"

Caroline turned to head back into the cabin. Ma was probably wondering what had happened to her. She'd been gone way longer than she'd anticipated.

Looking over her shoulder, Caroline watched as Horace scratched his other arm, now growing red, too.

He smiled her way. "See you at dinner," he yelled, as he scampered off toward the field.

Turning back, Caroline laughed at the thought of the others wondering what had happened to their bucket of refreshing water.

Caroline entered Betsey and Aaron's cabin the next morning to find Betsey kneeling beside a bucket. Julia was crying from her cradle by Betsey's bed.

"Oh, Caroline!" Betsey's face was as white as paste, and she motioned for her sister to come in. "Get the baby, please."

Betsey heaved into the bucket beside her. "Oh my. This morning sickness is just getting worse. That was all of my breakfast. I can't keep anything down."

Caroline shushed her niece as big droplets slipped down the baby's cheeks. She wiped them off her face with the back of her hand, "Oh Julia! Auntie's here."

"I just couldn't stop this morning. Poor Julia," Betsey leaned back against the stones in the hearth.

Caroline bounced the baby, and the crying changed to hiccups. "Shh, it's okay."

"I'm sure glad to see you."

Caroline smiled, "I'm glad I came. Ma made extra bread this morning and wanted to be sure you got a loaf."

Her sister's eyes grew wide as she went for the bucket again. Caroline decided to take Julia outside into the morning's fresh air. She left the door ajar to hear if Betsey called for her.

Bouncing the baby on her hip, she looked out over the landscape around her sister's house. The lush green from new leaves made the trees come aglow with spring. Soon the baby had her finger in her mouth, and the shudders of crying gave way to smiles amid tears. "That's my girl!"

Caroline wondered what it would be like to have a baby of her own. She loved fussing over Julia. They knew the new baby would take away attention from Julia, so giving her extra love wasn't hard. Caroline kissed her cheek, "There...you feel better now?"

Betsey appeared at the door. Her face was still white, but she wiped off her mouth and took a long drink of water from the barrel beside the door. "I'm sorry, Caroline. I just couldn't seem to keep anything down this morning. How's Julia?"

Caroline smiled, "She's fine. See." She lifted the baby to see her momma.

The baby burst into giggles upon seeing Betsey.

"She's all better now."

She held her chubby arms out to her momma.

"Betsey, can I ask you a question?"

"Of course, Caroline. As long as you don't mention food."

Caroline agreed. She'd wanted to get up to talk to Betsey for weeks, but she'd been so busy, she was grateful when Ma asked her to take the loaf up to her sister. "Do you think Billie will ask me to be his wife as soon as he arrives?"

"Um," Betsey hesitated.

Caroline wasn't sure if she hesitated because she didn't know how to answer or she needed to relieve her churning stomach again.

"What would you say if he did?"

"Well, of course," Caroline shifted the baby to her other hip so she'd not want to go back to Betsey. "I'd have to say yes."

Betsey gave her a quizzical look but reached out for the baby, who again lifted her arms for her momma. "Have to?"

"Well, I mean...what else would I say?"

"Are you having second thoughts about Billie?" Betsey cuddled Julia close. Julia popped her finger into her mouth and leaned her head on Betsey's shoulder. "I'm so happy babies are quick to forgive mommas who have morning sickness."

Caroline patted Julia's back. "I've always just thought that Billie would be the one I'd marry. For the longest time."

"But...?" Betsey tilted her head in question.

"I will say yes, if he asks me."

"Caroline. Are you having different thoughts?"

Caroline turned her back to her sister. She crossed her arms. She knew she'd have to answer, but saying it out loud made her question her motives.

"Caroline, what's wrong?"

Caroline turned around. "Oh Betsey, I'm a mess. I've thought long and hard about Billie. He's traveling all the way from Pennsylvania, for me! I think I love him. I've known him my whole life. But..."

Betsey looked at her sister with sympathetic eyes. "Caroline Baker! I've never seen you doubt your relationship with Billie like this."

"I will say yes. It just seems so long ago that I left Billie to travel here with the family. We've been friends since we were six years old. It's just that..." Caroline wiped off her forehead. "I'm not sure how he feels about me. He's always been someone to talk to, fish with, take a walk with, but he never made me nervous when I saw him."

"Well, you've not had another man to challenge that yet. Have you?"

"No. Of course not. I'm marrying Billie." Caroline patted the back of her now- sleeping niece on Betsey's shoulder. "I can't wait for him to arrive."

CHAPTER THIRTEEN

The letter she held grew moist from her tears. Abigail had finally received a letter from home. She'd read the letter with abandon, each word jumping off the page as if her mother were in the room talking to her. Oh, how she missed her family.

Thumbing the edge of the page, she read again how they'd just had a coming-out party for her youngest sister. It was hard to believe that Marguerite would be old enough to start entertaining beaus. Abigail could almost taste the tiny lemon tarts her mother would request from the kitchen for such a special occasion. She could practically feel the square crumble as she took a bite. At one party held at her family's home, Abigail had taken a whole plate back to her bedroom and consumed at least ten in one sitting. The next day, she could barely lace up her corset.

When was the last time she'd eaten something so sweet, let alone delicious? That thought drug her back to her two-room home in the desolate Michigan Territory. Glancing around the room in disdain, Abigail shivered at what she saw. Her maid back in New England had larger quarters than the tiny space Abigail occupied with John. The narrow bed, the sitting room with only one window, her chair the only place to sit to read her mother's letter...what had her life become?

Closing her eyes from the sight, Abigail leaned her head back against the rocking chair. This life wasn't what she'd thought it would be when John had asked for her hand. Before marriage, it had been decided that he would accept a position as an established pastor at her parents' church. Father had been sure to speak with the diocese to get their permission. It had been all settled just after the wedding until the letter arrived from John's stepmother.

They'd had to rush to Pennsylvania to be with John's father. If Aaron hadn't left to come here, John would have been able to stay in New York with her. They'd just begun their lives together. They deserved at least a year-long honeymoon to do so. But instead, they'd hurried to John's father's side.

If that hadn't been enough, John's father had asked him to head to Michigan Territory to deliver not only the barrel to Betsey's family but also the money he'd set aside for Aaron.

John had assured her that it would be a short trip, and as soon as the items were delivered to their rightful owners, they'd return to New York. Still, their trip had been delayed by the storms while on the steamboat, and then the loss of their first child in Detroit. Tears threatened to spill as Abigail recalled the horrific moment. The pain. The heartache of losing a child. She'd been so frightened, yet frustrated at the same time. She hadn't known what to do. The amount of blood she lost had sent John to seek a doctor. The experience made her feel empty inside.

It had been a dreadful journey to Aaron's homestead. She wanted to forget all of it. But now, here they were. John seemed determined to make a go of it in this godforsaken land, but this was no life for a lady of her standing.

Opening her eyes, she sighed. She'd cried for days. John had insisted she give it a try. He liked the land here and wanted to be a part of the creation of a new state. Yet now, John had stopped listening to her. Her influence floundered. She needed a new plan.

Abigail stood. Creaks from the floor echoed in the tiny space as she went to the window and then to the door amid their small living area. Back and forth. Each clomp of her shoes giving her more determination to figure out a way to draw her new husband back to the life she'd left in New York.

She wished Marguerite was with her right now. They often solidified schemes together. How to get food from the kitchen? How to convince another girl in school to lie about her best friend? How to get a young man to turn his eye from one girl and set his sights on them? They'd done it all and quite successfully. But without Marguerite's help, Abigail found herself weak and at a loss for a ruse. Ideas fluttered through her thoughts only to end up as a jumbled mess of unfulfilled concocted plots.

What would be one thing to pull John away from here and back to the life she knew? The life she loved. There had to be some way to change his mind.

Abigail stopped pacing and held the letter up for another glance at her mother's familiar handwriting. Perhaps a tiny idea would come from the page. Studying it hard, the only lines that stood out were these—

MARGUERITE WANTS TO MARRY PHILLIP RENNER, BUT HE REJECTED HER FOR ANGELINA MINNOW. TOMORROW SHE HAS HER FIRST OUTING WITH TRUMAN LEVERING. I PRAY IT GOES WELL. HE'S A WEALTHY NEW LAWYER IN TOWN.

If only Abigail were still home. She and Marguerite would come up with something great to pin on Angelina. Something terrible enough that Phillip would see how perfect Marguerite would be as a wife. But alas, she was here.

Abigail placed the letter on a small table by the window. She'd probably read it several times more that afternoon, for what else did she have to do in her miserable chamber? Coming up with a way to live here would be impossible; she needed somehow to convince John Ferrar Swain to take her back home.

Sitting back in the rocking chair, she realized some of the pull for John and her to settle in this wilderness was so he could be close to his brother. What if that relationship fell apart? She thought back to the winter living with Betsey and her husband. They'd been kind to them. Too kind. It is hard to pull up disgusting facts about people like them, but how could she influence others to doubt their kindness? If others started to challenge their goodness, perhaps John would follow.

In some way, she'd have to spread misinformation about the family. There had to be some kind of dirt she could scrounge up on the Swains, including Betsey's family. Desperation made many a proper woman turn to unscrupulous ways.

If she could tear the brothers apart, in some way, surely John would head back to New York to fulfill his purpose there. Not here. Not as long as she had breath.

But first, she'd do what every well-bred woman does while in desperate circumstances; she'd beg with something that always worked. Tears.

Two more families came upon their property within two weeks. Both were from New York State. The Wilkersons and a family named Pierce. Settlers seemed intent on finding land close to the river and establishing nearby communities.

Ambrose had built a small lean-to at the back of the house that helped provide shelter for a night or two if the weather was bad, but most families camped in their wagons. Ma became an expert at stretching what meager food they had to feed the weary travelers. She and the girls greeted all who entered their home with as much hospitality as they were able to offer. Caroline assisted in preparing more food each time to accommodate the unexpected guests, and fell into her bed every night exhausted beyond imagination.

"We're much obliged to your family for the vittles," commented Megan Pierce. She had just two small children, so feeding the Pierce family wasn't all that hard. The youngest child was a few months older than Julia.

"We're so happy to help all who come along," Ma assured Megan.

"We weren't sure what to expect. A woman at the post said that some of the settlers weren't all that welcome to newcomers."

Ma scowled. "Who said that? There isn't anyone I know here yet that isn't hospitable to all who find their way here."

"Not sure of her name. She's a small thing. Her husband is a worker at the post, I believe."

Caroline looked at her ma. Who would say such a thing?

"She also said that most of the folks north of the post hoarded food, too. But you have been nothing but kind and generous." The woman spooned some pureed squash into the mouth of the child on her lap.

"So, you don't know her name?" Ma asked as she spooned more squash chunks on the woman's plate.

"No. I think her husband's name was John."

Ma gave Caroline a look of disgust behind Megan's back.

"Why would Abigail say such a thing?"

Hosea snuggled close to Sally that night in bed. "You can't be sure that's who it was."

"I know." Sally pulled the covers over them both. "But who else would have a husband named John who works at the post?"

Hosea rubbed his beard on her neck. "Well, let's not suspect anything just yet."

Sally didn't have to wait long before Hosea began his nightly snoring regimen. The man worked himself to exhaustion every day planting new crops and tilling up more of the ground behind the barn. Whatever snippet of conversation she could get with Hosea, Sally took advantage of it. Although sleep always replaced her worries.

She stared into the darkness of night. Like Hosea had said, why would Abigail tell anyone they were stingy? They'd given up so much of their lives that past winter to make Abigail feel at home. So had Betsey and Aaron. As Sally drifted off to sleep, she hoped it wasn't Abigail who was spreading the false information. She hoped their hospitable efforts were enough to help others know the truth.

Pa relayed to the rest of the family his idea for a sawmill after their Sunday dinner.

"I think it's a great idea, Pa." Caroline stood to gather plates to wash. "It's like we're starting one of the first of the businesses in these parts. Who wouldn't be happy to have lumber prepared and sawn to build their homes?"

"That's the way I have it figured." Pa used his finger to nudge the last of his fish onto his fork.

"I do think you're on to something, Hosea, but I think I should be looking more to find marshaling work first. I hate to be the one to bow out on your idea." Aaron patted Julia on the back. He'd taken her from Betsey so his wife could eat.

"I understand." Hosea pointed his now-empty fork to Aaron. "I had a feeling that would be your answer. Please don't feel obligated to join us. I completely understand, and we do need law enforcement, too."

Aaron smiled. "But I am a bit jealous. I think you're taking on a great venture. It should only bring you success in your efforts. The settlers will have an easier time getting settled if they could get a shelter up faster."

Ambrose handed his plate to Caroline. "I think it's a great idea, Pa. When can we start?"

A knock interrupted their planning. Caroline went to the door. Standing outside was Whitmore and a few of his closest friends.

Caroline backed away from the door seeing the look on the faces of the Indians surrounding the fur trader. "Pa!"

Pa made his way to the door, pulling out his handkerchief to wipe his mouth. "Whitmore! Come in, come in."

Whitmore shook his head. "We came to talk to the boy. I think my friends here can help him."

It took a minute for Pa to register why Whitmore wanted to see Alexander. Before he could turn to the boy, Alexander was already at the door and headed outside. Pa followed as Aaron handed Julia back to Betsey and walked outside, too. As the women gathered at the door, Caroline noticed that Alexander was standing directly in front of Waussinoodae. Caroline pointed the Indian woman out to Betsey, who nodded her acknowledgment.

The Indians began chattering to each other. There was an exchange of translation between Whitmore and the four Indian males surrounding Waussinoodae and Alexander. The only non-Indian who understood the conversation was Whitmore.

The largest man in the group pointed to Alexander and then to Whitmore. They sounded like the squirrels often did in the trees, bantering back and forth. Often Caroline would think birds had invaded the forest around the cabin, but it wasn't too long ago that Horace had told her the chatter from the woods wasn't birds but squirrels. This conversation reminded her of that.

Whitmore put his hand on Alexander's shoulder and pointed to his mouth. Alexander didn't speak, even though he acted as though he wanted to say something.

His slight hesitation mesmerized the family. He'd never even opened his mouth to speak when encouraged by the Bakers. Caroline fixed her eyes on the young boy. He seemed to be the main focus of the conversation between their fur trading friend and the tall, strong males standing with them. Soon Waussinoodae took Alexander by the hand and pulled him close to her. He tucked himself under her arm that now circled his chest.

Whitmore would say a few words and then point to Pa. The Indian would then wave his hand over the rest of the family, standing inside the doorway.

"What are they saying, Pa?" Jillian nudged closer to Pa and asked in a quiet voice.

Pa shook his head and folded his arms as if trying to make out what was happening.

After a few minutes, Whitmore turned to Pa. "Hosea. Maemaeketchewunk wants to ask you if you have been good to Alexander. I assured him that you have. I pointed out that he is strong, healthy. And that you've cared for the child well."

Pa let his arms fall to his side. "We love him like a son."

"I know you do. One moment." Whitmore went back to exchanging words with the Indian man. Soon he turned back to Pa. "I want to introduce you to Maemaeketchewunk." Whitmore pointed to the large man.

Pa placed his hat, which he'd been twisting in his hands, back on his head, then held out his hand. "Nice to meet you."

The Indian looked at his hand and slapped his fist to his chest.

Whitmore smiled. "He's also happy to meet you." Whitmore then placed his hand on Pa's outstretched hand and pushed it down. "They don't shake hands."

Pa pulled his hand back. "Whitmore, what is this about?"

Whitmore slapped his fist to his chest and said a few more things to the Indian. The Indian pointed to Waussinoodae.

Their Indian friend turned Alexander to face her. She placed her hands on both sides of his face and kissed the top of his head. She said a few words to him, and Alexander smiled up at her.

Whitmore leaned back toward Pa and whispered, "I'm doing my best to get this whole language thing fixed. For Alexander's sake."

"What language thing?" Ma asked Pa quietly.

Pa put his finger to his lips.

Waussinoodae said a few more words and then turned Alexander to face the large Indian who'd been communicating with Whitmore. She said a few words, bowed her head then backed away from Alexander.

Alexander's eyes were wide as tears threatened to spill down his cheeks.

Caroline looked to Betsey, who gave her an odd look, but Caroline could see by her sister's stern face that she seemed to question why Alexander was so afraid.

"Is Alexander her child?" Ma whispered to Pa.

When she did, Whitmore turned to Ma and Pa and whispered, "Trust me."

The Indian man named Maemaeketchewunk then placed his hand on Alexander's head and chanted a few words and again pounded his chest three times with his fist. Alexander nodded as if in agreement regarding something he said.

Whitmore said a few more words to the Indians, and then Alexander came back toward Pa. Pa knelt on one knee as the boy circled his neck with his arm and drew in close.

The whole conversation seemed finished until, without any hesitation, Alexander pulled back from Pa and uttered his first words, "I will speak now." It was just a whisper, but the words were English.

Without realizing they'd been doing it, the whole group sighed as if they'd all been holding their breath.

Ma exclaimed, "Alexander! Praise God. You spoke." Soon she was dabbing her eyes with her apron. She reached out and squeezed Pa's shoulder.

The two men and Waussinoodae turned away and headed back into the woods.

Whitmore stood beside Pa and patted Alexander on the back. "He has been given permission now to speak. Maemaeketchewunk had told the boy that he would kill his mother if he spoke to you. I think he meant in Ojibwa, but the boy must have misunderstood and thought he shouldn't speak at all."

Ma gasped and pulled Alexander to her apron, stroking his hair.

"The Indians are afraid. New settlers coming into their land has frightened them. They are afraid of us and our ways. They believe that if you hear or know of their customs and beliefs, that we might use it against them. They've been watching Alexander and how you've been caring for him. They see that you love the boy and will take good care of him." Whitmore sat down on a stump and wiped the sweat off his brow. "I wasn't sure if it would work, but I did manage to ask through the other Indians about Alexander. Most told me they didn't know the boy, but then I realized they seem to be keeping something a secret about him. Excuse me, ladies,"

Whitmore tipped his hat, "but I had to get a few of them drunk so they'd tell me the story of the boy."

"Before long, a young brave told the whole story about Alexander. It sounds as if the boy became a part of the tribe after some of his braves killed his parents. Maemaeketchwunk gave the child, who was then a baby, to his wife as a gift."

"Waussinoodae is Alexander's mother, and she's the chief's wife?"

"In the Indian way, yes," Whitmore added. "She took care of the boy until...they brought him to you."

"That makes sense," Betsey added. "That's why she was always at the edge of the woods watching him."

"Did you see her doing that?" Whitmore brushed his brow with his sleeve.

"Yes, we often found her there once he began staying with us." Ma hugged the young boy.

"She was there to watch out for him, but also another reason. Maemaeketchewunk had threatened Alexander to silence. If he were to utter any Indian words to you, they told him they would kill his mother."

Pa took hold of the boy's hand. "Oh my. What a burden to put on a child."

"I'm okay." Alexander looked up at Pa and smiled.

Pa pulled him closer and hugged him. "So, why is he able to speak now, without worry?"

"I convinced the chief that the boy misunderstood him. He would still honor the Indian by not speaking Ojibwa or tell you any of the Indian legends or secrets, but I asked if it would be all right for him to speak English words. Communicate with all of you. That satisfied Maemaeketchewunk. He also warned the boy not to say anything that would harm his mother or their ways. Alexander agreed."

"So, you're telling us that Alexander thought the chief would kill his Indian mother if he were to speak?" Ambrose repeated what Whitmore had just told them.

Whitmore nodded. "It's a typical threat. What astonishes me though, is Alexander's been with you for almost a year now. He is quite the brave boy for not uttering one word. When they threatened him, he not only listened, but he obeyed very well."

"It's clear that he loves Waussinoodae." Betsey kissed the top of Julia's head, who she now cuddled.

"True. I'm sure Alexander does. But he also loves you folks. I can see how much now. He was so scared to say anything that he even vowed to himself not to speak English to any of you. That says quite a lot about this young lad. He's loyal and trustworthy." Whitmore reached out and tousled Alexander's hair.

"He might just surprise you now with how much he will speak. He's been around you long enough to pick up on your English. It won't be long before he is speaking just like any other normal boy."

Whitmore stood and put his rifle over his shoulder. "Well, I'm off."

As Whitmore turned to leave, Ma called out to him.

"Whitmore? Why did the Indians allow Alexander to even come to us?"

"They wanted him to be with his people. He is young enough to adapt to your ways instead of theirs. It will also appease their gods that they've allowed him to live after some of their braves killed his parents." Whitmore turned and pointed to Betsey, "Waussinoodae also told her husband that he could trust you. You have been good to her."

"We didn't know that Waussinoodae is the Indian chief's wife. That tells us so much," Betsey added.

"She's important to the tribe. Yes." Whitmore turned again. "I'm going to head back before dark. You folks have a good day, now."

Pa called after the fur trader, "Thank you, Whitmore."

A small voice echoed Pa's, "Thank you, Whitmore." Everyone looked to the boy who now had a voice.

CHAPTER FOURTEEN

John found Abigail pacing the room. He'd been gone most of the day, only home for a quick lunch.

"Abigail. How was your day?"

Abigail went to the table, sat down, and began to weep.

Sliding out of his coat, John knelt beside her on the floor. "Abigail sweetheart, what's wrong?"

His wife looked up at him with red-rimmed eyes. Had she been crying for hours? Her face was blotchy and pink.

"Darling, please tell me what's wrong."

Abigail blew her nose into a wadded-up ball of a handkerchief. It appeared wet and useless as Abigail wiped at her nose, which was as red as her eyes.

"I can't, John."

"You can't what, love?" John placed his hand on his wife's shuddering shoulder.

"This place," Abigail waved her hand as if to take in the whole room, "is awful. I can't bear to be in this room another second longer."

John knew for weeks that his wife was unhappy. Her emotions went from anger to sappy sweet with a snap of a finger. He knew it was a matter of time before this conversation would evolve.

"How could you possibly have thought that I'd be happy here?"

"I didn't know. I barely knew what to expect myself." John pulled out a chair from the table and sat down. "I'm sorry you're so unhappy."

His wife looked up at him. "Unhappy! I'm not just unhappy. I've never been this miserable in all my life." She eyed him as though he should know her thoughts before she had to tell him. "I am not one to mince words, but this is no place for a woman of my..." Abigail hiccupped, "my upbringing. I shouldn't have to live a life like this."

John sighed. He knew it was true. At least he could go out of the room every day and work. Abigail was all alone. No other women were around other than a few Indian squaws roaming around Whitmore's trading post. "Abigail, you're right. I'm sorry."

Abigail stood up, knocking the lantern off the table. It crashed to the floor.

The flame from the lantern burst into a bright blaze as it hit the spilled oil now seeping out onto the room's floor. Abigail screamed.

John grabbed a nearby cloth and began beating the floor with it. Flames quickly settled down as John nearly burnt his hands with getting the fire under control. "Abigail! You might not even have this room as a home. Settle down."

Abigail wailed, "John! Why do you torment me so? It was an accident."

John put out a bit more of the lantern fire with the tip of his shoe, stomping at the last of it. Waving his hands, he tried his best to clear the room of the smoke now wafting in the air. "I don't know what you expect me to do, Abigail. I know you aren't happy here. I've been doing my best to keep us going. I'm paying Whitmore for this room, our food, and it's hard to save any money for even a trip home."

"Well," Abigail covered her mouth with her handkerchief. "You had better make it soon enough. If you don't, I'll just up and leave you."

A knock at the door interrupted the problematic situation.

"John, everything okay? We can smell smoke out here."

John went to the door and opened it to another worker who lived across the hall. "It's okay. Just a bit of an accident with a lantern." The smoke in the room drifted out into the hallway.

"Need some water?" The man fanned away the smoke from his face.

"Yes. Can you get me some?" John opened the door to allow some fresh air from the hallway into the room.

Abigail ran to the bed and threw herself across it, sobbing into a blanket.

"We'll do our best to get you home soon, Abigail." But as the words left his mouth, John was sure, at least for now, this would be impossible. Even if it was, Abigail was in no way ready to travel as far as New York.

After cleaning the floor of the dark soot and picking up the shards of glass, John settled back into a chair at the kitchen table. His hunger from late that afternoon was now gnawing at his belly.

Glancing over at Abigail, he noticed she'd fallen asleep. What had he been thinking? She was too delicate of a woman to be out here. She needed a fine home, pretty dresses to wear, jeweled combs to draw back her hair, and fancy parties to attend each night, not this godforsaken unsettled territory where they now found themselves. But what could he do?

John enjoyed the work that Whitmore had provided for him. He loved working with his hands, being outdoors in the spring air, and viewing the new Michigan Territory. Yet as much as he liked it, Abigail hated it even more.

Perhaps she needed company. Womenfolk. The only place he knew to find other women was back at Aaron and Betsey's house. Sunday was just two days away. Maybe it was time to take her for a short visit.

Summer was close at hand. Bright green leaves ushered in some shade from the warming sun. Blades of grass now peeked through the muddy areas around the farm, but more evidence of the season change was the chance to see baby ducks and geese trailing behind their parents along the river's banks. Occasionally, a family of skunks skirted through the yard behind the house. During the past few nights, baby raccoons were making messes in the piles of food scraps Ma had started behind the barn. Pa used mounds of eggshells, animal bones that were long since boiled clean, and squash shells to put into the soil to make his fields richer.

Betsey leaned back on the blanket and watched Julia playing with her bare toes, now free from her winter socks. She cooed at everyone who got close, smiling wide grins that made everyone stop what they were doing to give her attention. She'd stolen the hearts of everyone who stopped long enough to smile back. Even Horace loved to chat with her. Betsey patted her belly, now revealing new life growing inside; her heavy winter skirts shed for thinner ones.

Aaron bent down to kiss Julia's forehead as the baby reached up to grab a fistful of his beard. Laughing, Aaron took her hand and lovingly scolded her after a firm tug made him flinch. "Hey, young lady! Easy on your father."

Betsey laughed. "She's got quite the grip, don't you think?"

"That she has." Aaron tickled the baby's foot, and she laughed right out loud.

Everyone else had brought out a blanket to place on the warmer ground surrounding the cabin. They'd just finished up the dishes from dinner and now could enjoy the Sunday afternoon warming sun. It felt good to have it seep into their bones.

"It's hard to believe it's been just over a year since we arrived, isn't it?" Ma leaned back and pulled Alexander into a hug with her right arm. He leaned up to look into her face, and she planted a kiss on his cheek.

"Love you, Ma."

"Oh, young man, I love you more."

Alexander had no trouble now communicating with the family. Each day they were amazed at the young man's conversations. He'd been asking so many questions. When there was a word he couldn't pronounce, he'd ask for help. And now, as much as they enjoyed hearing the boy learn, there were moments when family members would shake their heads at his inquisitive mind. His questions were often endless.

"Why don't you run out there to the creek and throw some rocks?" Ma tousled the dark hair of her youngest child.

"Want fish for supper?" Alexander smiled. "C'mon Pa."

"No more fish, Alexander." Pa stood up to take the hand of the boy. "Today's the Lord's day. I'll go down and skip a few rocks with you, though."

As the two walked away, Ma just laughed. "That boy! How did God know we needed him in our lives?"

"I'm heading up to my cabin tomorrow," Ambrose announced. He'd been daily working on his home now. It was on Hosea's property, but farther away from the Baker cabin, near a cluster of houses rising south of their location. "Horace has been such a great help in getting the finishing touches on my roof. I think I'll be able to move in by the end of summer."

"Ambrose, that's wonderful!" Betsey reached down to pick up the baby, who began to fuss for her afternoon snack.

"We'll need to be building a table, some chairs, and find a few rocks for the hearth soon." Horace leaned against the cabin logs. "Won't be long now." Horace glanced over at Caroline.

Caroline's eyes averted from watching Horace as soon as he looked at her. Betsey wondered how long this game would go on. She could see a mutual attraction but knew Caroline still had her heart set on Billie.

A horse carrying two people caught Betsey's attention. It broke through the trees at the southern edge of the property. "People coming." Betsey pointed out the horse to the others.

Pa must have seen the visitors as well and began walking toward the horse from the river.

Aaron shielded his eyes from the sun, "Looks to be..." He waited a moment or two and then added, "It's John. And Abigail." He stood and followed Hosea toward the approaching riders.

As he left the family near the cabin, Betsey leaned over to her ma. "Are you going to say anything to Abigail?"

The womenfolk had been hearing a few more rumors of things Abigail had been propagating to others about their family. It was disturbing and hurtful.

"No need. Abigail knows what she's doing. The truth will win. It always does." Ma stood, wiping off the back of her skirt and adjusting her apron from being on the ground. She began to head out with Pa to greet their guests.

Caroline came over and sat down on the blanket with Betsey. "I wish she wouldn't come for a visit."

"Ma's right, Caroline. We need to be kind. Nothing is gained by fighting rumors with anger. She's unkind, but we can outshine her unkindness with love." Betsey adjusted the now sleeping Julia and fixed the front of her dress to be presentable to the guests.

"How can you say that? She's been saying so many mean things about us." Caroline almost hissed out the comment.

"Caroline!" Betsey scolded her. "It's hard to take, but God knows our hearts. We only answer to Him."

Caroline sighed, then snuggled the baby to her as Betsey stood.

They couldn't hear the conversation of the group gathered around John Swain's horse, but Betsey finished buttoning up her blouse and headed over to greet her in-laws.

Abigail was all smiles and laughter. It seemed the young woman had changed her demeanor as she greeted each member of the Baker and Swain family with kisses on their cheeks, followed by hugs.

"It's so good to see you all." John smiled and shook hands with the members of the Baker family and gave Aaron a good hug. "Enjoying the warm day."

Everyone voiced their affirmation. Ma motioned toward the cabin, "Please come in and have some tea. Have you eaten yet?"

John shook his head. "We are hungry. We set out this morning."

"Well, come, come in and have a bite to eat." Hosea urged the group toward the cabin. "We have plenty left from lunch."

As Betsey drew near, she was as welcoming as the rest of the family.

"Betsey, so nice to see you." John opened his arms and hugged his sister-in-law as he'd done with Aaron. "How are you? The baby?"

"Julia's just settled down for her nap. But please, come. We'll round up something for you to have for lunch."

Abigail took Betsey's hands in her own. "Betsey, it's so good to see you."

Betsey hesitated, then asked, "What brings you around on such a beautiful day?"

John quickly answered before he took Abigail's hand. "It's such a nice day. We thought it would be time to escape the small confines of our tiny room to venture outdoors." John pointed up to the tree. "So good to see new leaves on the trees and the territory erupting into a new season."

"Before you know it, these spring days will bring forth the heat of summer and, unfortunately, a few of those pesky critters again." Pa laughed. "But before mosquitoes hatch, we're getting a bit of time outdoors. Let's get you some food and bring it outside to enjoy. How does that sound?"

"We won't be eating it at the table inside?" Abigail began to fuss.

"Well..." Pa was caught a bit off guard.

Ma put her hand at the back of Abigail's waist. "If you feel more comfortable inside, we can arrange that as well."

Abigail tipped her head back and stood erect. "I might live in a godforsaken country, but I'm still a lady."

Betsey lingered back by Aaron, who followed behind the others. Aaron gave her a look but sighed. They all knew that, despite the frustrating comments, they needed to be hospitable.

The afternoon dragged on. Caroline attempted a happy demeanor despite the fact of being dragged back into the cabin from one of their first warm days of the season. Still, she could feel angst increasing as Abigail prattled on about how awful her life is and how she only wants John to take her back to New York where the civilized and mannerly people live. Caroline knew their life here in the territory was new, different, and from the rituals of a progressive home, it was far from perfect. They loved their new farm. Why did it seem as if this woman thought living in a remote part of the country reflected a lower social status?

"I don't know how you put up with this substandard way of life. Don't any of you miss the social events? The concerts? The sophisticated way of the country's eastern states?" Abigail didn't stop, even when John touched her arm in response to her last statement. It was as if they all had lowered themselves to live in a way that deemed the Baker and Swain family as primitive as the "savages," as Abigail called them, that lived around them.

"We don't mind the Indians. They have been nothing but good to us." Betsey sat up straighter on the bench at the table. "They've done more for us than we've done for them."

"Well." Abigail looked down her nose at Betsey. "You have to say that. You have one at the table with you."

Caroline could see her sister's eyebrows arch and knew that if someone didn't say something soon, Betsey would react as Caroline had wanted to at the discovery that their guests were John and Abigail.

"Well, darling. I think it's about time for us to leave." John lifted Abigail's elbow from the table. "It's a long way back to the trading post."

Thankfully, John's attempt to go back to the post made it easier for Caroline to swallow Abigail's last comment, and by the way it looked from the other faces, for the others as well.

"But John, we've just gotten here. I hate to have to get back up and mount that horse again for the long trip home." Abigail began to pout. Caroline was astonished when Abigail's bottom lip began to look like Julia's when she wasn't getting fed as fast as she desired.

"I know, sweetie. I hate to be the bearer of such sad tidings, but yes. I have to be back to work in the morning." John put his arm around his wife's waist and lifted her from her chair.

"You may join us again soon. Now that the weather is letting up and warm weather is coming, we'll have you out again to enjoy another Sunday afternoon with us." Ma could always make an uncomfortable situation easier.

Caroline wasn't sure, but she wondered if anyone else was cringing at the thought of the Swains' next visit.

"We need a buggy for this part of the country. John, you need to provide one of those as soon as we can afford one. I will not be coming out to visit on a horse each time we come." Abigail pulled on her fancy gloves.

Caroline hadn't seen gloves like that since attending the small church in Meadville.

"Thank you so much, everyone, for a wonderful afternoon visit." John stood, seemingly waiting patiently for his wife to pull herself together.

Everyone did their best to offer the couple their best wishes for the journey back to the post. As the couple left the cabin, Aaron and Betsey ushered the couple back to the horse, ready for them. Ambrose must have given the horse a good brushing, evident in the now shiny coat.

As John mounted, Aaron gave Abigail help in getting on the horse behind John. The conversation seemed short as the horse began to head into the woods while Aaron and Betsey waved to the couple.

"My, oh my! What an afternoon!" Pa looked at Ma like he'd never heard anything like it. Ma wiped off her hands as if she'd been knee-deep into rolling out pastry dough for a pie. Although there wasn't anything on her hands, wiping them off seemed appropriate to everyone watching her.

"She doesn't like me." Alexander sat down after helping to wash the dishes.

Sally pulled the young boy into her side. "Alexander, we love you. That is all that is important."

"But why doesn't she like me?"

Sally felt at a loss as to how to tell Alexander that it wasn't him. Abigail wasn't keen on anyone, let alone a young boy who appeared Indian to the rich, eastern woman.

"It doesn't matter what she thinks of you, Alexander. God and all of us love you. That's all that is important," Pa added with a wink.

Anger boiled up in Sally's heart. How dare this woman make this child think that he wasn't special? Resentment began to fill her heart. How could one woman spew such hatred? After all they'd done for her.

Abigail pulled off her gloves in haste as soon as they returned to their room at the trading post. "John, I need to talk to you about something that happened at the Bakers' today."

John sat down on the bed and was removing his riding boots. "What is it?"

"I could see that Betsey is expecting again. Did you notice?"

"How would you know that?"

"It was showing. Betsey didn't have on proper skirts to cover herself."

John rubbed his feet. His old boots were making his feet sore. He could feel a hole starting to form over his right big toe. "Well, if she is, it's not that far along. I didn't notice."

"She loves to flaunt it in front of me!"

John was skeptical of why Abigail was so concerned about something that was none of their business. "I didn't see anything like that."

Abigail turned her back to him. "I figured that's what you'd say. Men don't see what women see. Ever!"

"I've never seen Betsey do anything to upset you, Abigail. I'm sure you're imagining it."

"Is that what Aaron told you while you were outside together?"

"He never mentioned anything about Betsey. Men don't talk about things as intimate as that. You should know that."

"Well, there's one thing I do know." Abigail turned on her heel and faced him. "That Baker family does not like me. They've shown that to me when they kicked us out, and Betsey wasn't the same to me whenever you and Aaron were out and about leaving us alone. She's never liked me, either. You'd think that a husband would understand and see the unkindness shown to his wife. I will not be subjected to this kind of hatred. Perhaps we need to keep our distance from now on. Now get off the bed. I have a headache and need to lie down."

John got up from the bed and made some kind of excuse to leave her alone. He began to wonder what Betsey or the other Baker women could have said to his wife to upset her so.

CHAPTER FIFTEEN

Horace took the splashing bucket before Caroline had time to acknowledge to him that she could handle it. As he shifted the bucket to his right hand, he smiled. "Let me help you."

Caroline tried her best to wipe the droplets of water off her skirt. She'd filled the bucket too full at the flowing well, and it must have appeared to Horace that she was struggling to carry it back home. "It's fine, Horace. I've carried many a bucket before you came along."

Caroline watched in horror as Etta looked over her shoulder at the two now on her way to the cabin with a bucket equally as full as Caroline's. Without seeing her face, Caroline knew a smirk was on Etta's face.

"Isn't this a nice day?" Horace looked around the property as they made their way to the cabin early that summer morning.

Caroline wiped the sweat off her brow with her apron, "It's getting warmer." Although she wasn't sure if the perspiration was from the warm July day or the uncomfortable feeling descending on her from having Horace help her.

"If this is how summer will be, we're in for a hot one."

Caroline had been doing her best to keep Horace at bay. She knew that sooner than later, she'd have to tell him that Billie was coming for her, and that her life was all planned. Billie would arrive, and they'd be married, raising a family in the place she now called home with her family. "Horace." Caroline needed to say it soon. She knew Etta was listening for it as she was only a few feet in front of them, but she needed to build up her courage.

"Yes?"

Caroline's courage disintegrated from just the mere look of his eyes.

"Did you want to talk about something?"

Etta seemed to understand the problem because she took off down another path. As Caroline watched her hurry down the longer route, Etta glanced back and winked at her.

Caroline felt her face grow warm, but she forged ahead.

"Why is your sister going that way? It's farther away from the cabin." Horace pointed to Etta disappearing into the woods at their right.

"I don't know." Caroline took a deep breath. "Horace, we need to talk."

Horace stopped in his tracks. He placed the bucket on the ground, "About?"

Caroline picked up her apron, twisting it in her hands. "Um, I need to tell you something."

Horace stepped a bit closer to her.

Caroline never felt so intimidated by a man. She'd been around men her entire life, but somehow when she was around Horace, everything around her melted into oblivion.

He crossed his arms. "Yes."

"I know this might seem a bit odd for me to tell you this. I mean..." Caroline backed up a step, but there was nowhere to turn. Her back now came into contact with a tall tree. She couldn't think straight with Horace in her face like he was.

"If it's about my forwardness..." Horace stepped closer again, narrowing the space between them.

Caroline let her apron fall and pressed her hand to her chest.

"Well, that's what I wanted to talk to you about."

Horace took a tiny step closer. "I like you, Caroline."

Caroline felt her shoulders droop as she looked into the eyes of the man in front of her. She'd dreamt of this encounter with Billie. Not this man. She had to escape. Avoiding Horace and his looks had kept her busy in the past month. Her sisters had told her how Horace felt before he'd even had a chance to say a word.

"Horace! I'm afraid that I can't reciprocate your feelings." Caroline felt her whole body exhale air.

Horace picked up her hand. "I know you feel something for me. Why would you be avoiding me if you didn't?"

"What?" Caroline looked down at her bare feet. "I've been trying to tell you..."

Before she could utter one more word, Horace took the opportunity to kiss her cheek.

"I like you, Caroline. I like you a lot."

Caroline could stand up to a scary wolf in the backyard. She could hold her ground when an Indian drew near. She could muster up enough courage to help Pa attach the oxen to their yoke. But as Horace's lips went toward her mouth, she couldn't stop him. He kissed her softly and long. Then abruptly, he stepped back and picked up the bucket again.

"We best be getting back to the house." Then he walked off.

Caroline's legs felt weak. She felt like she was melting into a puddle at her feet. What had she just allowed to happen? Tears sprang to her eyes. She choked down a sob.

Her bucket sat outside the door. Picking it up by the handle, Caroline opened the door and walked over the threshold. Everyone was busy. Pa had announced that morning that they would be celebrating the Fourth of July. Chores needed finishing. Ma was busy baking a fruit pie. Etta and Jillian were singing patriotic songs—one right after the other.

"Caroline, can you put a few more logs on the fire outside? I need it extra hot to cook this pie before supper," Ma called out to her.

"Yes." Caroline headed back outside to find her sister already stoking the fire as she sang a line from "Yankee Doodle Dandy." Etta shot her a glance and winked.

Mortified, Caroline swallowed hard. Did her sister know what had just happened? Had she pretended to go the longer route but had glanced back to see Horace take advantage of her? What was she going to do? Would Etta tell Pa or even Ma?

Dropping a few extra logs near the fire just outside the door, Caroline felt guilt penetrate her soul. Why had she allowed Horace to kiss her? She loved Billie. Didn't she?

Etta soon joined her as she went back for another few logs of wood. "Well?"

Caroline did her best to pretend that everything was fine. Nothing had happened. It was a single kiss, for goodness' sake. Yet why did she still feel the softness of Horace's lips on her own? She'd never kissed Billie. He'd kissed her cheek before she left Pennsylvania, but even that didn't compare to how it felt to be kissed by Horace. "Well, what?" Caroline forced herself to remain calm.

"What did Horace do?"

Caroline smirked. "What are you talking about? He carried my bucket."

Etta laughed loud. "He wasn't on a mission to *just* carry your bucket, my dear sister."

"Well, whatever it appeared, it was just a kind gesture to carry a woman's bucket. That is all."

Etta crossed her arms and winked. "Okay, so let's say that's all it was. I'm the younger of us. If he wanted to help, why would he carry *your* bucket when I'm much younger, smaller, and not as strong as you?"

"Are you jealous?" Caroline knew she was right, but there was no way she'd allow her the opportunity to know that.

Etta laughed right out loud. "Yes!"

In one second, Caroline went from practical, nothing-is-wrong to a melted mess. She felt her legs give way, and she sat on the ground and buried her face in her hands. "What have I done?"

There's a thing about sisters. The minute you are sure they will mock and tease you is the very moment that something changes in them, and the real bond of sisters gives way to precisely what Etta did next. She knelt beside Caroline, put her arms around her, stroking her hair away from her face as she attempted to cry away her guilt.

That night, every settler they'd previously met came to the Baker cabin to celebrate the birthday of the nation. The Leaches came with their three children, joined by Josiah and Megan Pierce and their two children. Also attending the festivities were Aaron and Betsey, baby Julia, and Ambrose, as well as Horace. John and Abigail brought with them a new family who'd arrived just the week before. Jacob Wilkerson and his wife, Susan. They hadn't had a celebration like this since Pennsylvania.

They managed to get the table outside, and it was laden with all kinds of goodies. Fresh-snipped beans from the garden, fruit pies and cobbler, white sauce over potatoes, and fresh peas, and Pa had managed to shoot a turkey that now sat brown and roasted in a pan for all to enjoy. Megan Pierce had made fresh biscuits and gravy with sausage, and Claire had prepared delicious rolls with slices of fresh bread.

Caroline was serving pie and cobbler to the men off to the side. The men, eager to hear about the political news that Wilkerson had brought with him, gathered down by the river.

"The new territorial governor is Mason. Stevens T. Mason. He seems to be a good fit," commented Wilkerson, pulling on his long beard. "But he's just twenty-two years old."

Pa seemed more intrigued by the conversation than all of them. "Twenty-two! Who in tarnation makes a child that age a governor?"

"His father is John. John Mason. Secretary of Michigan Territory. They hail from Kentucky. Mason and Michigan Territory Governor Lewis Cass have been appointed by President Jackson to other parts of the United States. From all I hear, his son was a perfect fit for the position. Stevens has often filled in for Governor George Porter, who everyone says has passed away. Everyone is hoping that he takes us on to statehood." With that comment, the entire group gave a whoop.

"How could a boy that young take us anywhere?" Pa shot a disgruntled statement to the men around him.

"President Jackson appointed him. He wouldn't do something so ludicrous without good reason," shouted Wilkerson.

"Probably not. But that is definitely what this new territory needs. We need to be a state. There are beginning to be too many people here to ignore or leave us out of the Union." Everyone around acknowledged an agreement.

Caroline had just turned seventeen. It was hard to believe that someone Betsey's age could be running the territory for them. She picked up a few cups around the men and headed back to the women. They needed to keep cups clean for all in attendance. She could wash up a few left by the men.

As she turned to pick up Horace's cup, he reached for it and winked at her as she took it from his hand. She felt her face warm as she looked at him. Why had she allowed him to kiss her? She needed to share her heart with him. Etta had even encouraged it after her meltdown that morning by the fire. She knew Etta was right, but something inside her wanted to keep Billie a secret from Horace for just a bit longer.

Julia squealed out a cry of delight as Aaron lifted her high into the air over the food table. She'd pulled herself to a standing position, and as the make-shift table shifted under her grasp, Aaron had scooped her up to prevent her from tipping all the table contents onto the dirt. Betsey reached out to steady the table.

"You need to leave your momma alone, little one." Aaron kissed the fat, almost wanting-to-walk baby and pressed her to his cheek. "Momma's busy."

"She's just hungry again," Betsey sighed, as she took the squealing baby away from her husband. Aaron left the two, grabbed a freshly washed cup from Caroline's drying towel, filled it with water, and left to sit by the men talking politics.

"Isn't it about time you weaned that child?" Claire patted Betsey on the arm. "I know it's hard, but she's eating regular food now, isn't she?"

Tears filled Betsey's eyes. "I just hate to think of not nursing anymore. I've enjoyed it so much, and now with another baby coming..." Betsey stopped talking.

"I had a feeling you were expecting again." Claire pulled her close, giving her a sideways hug.

Betsey covered her mouth with her hand. "I know it's probably not ladylike to be talking about such intimate things, but as you can see," Betsey smoothed her dress down over her bulging bump, "it's getting hard to hide."

Claire winked. "It's natural. We need to relish the moments of pregnancy. God created it to be wonderful and beautiful. Right now, He is knitting that baby into something unique and amazing. It isn't wrong to be thankful and rejoice in the news."

Caroline glanced at Abigail for a reaction. It didn't take long for the woman to respond to Betsey's openness. It would have been easier to have her announce right then her thoughts, but instead, she turned away and headed toward Megan Pierce. She pulled her aside. "I think a real lady should be farther along to announce to the world that she is in a motherly way."

Caroline could easily overhear Abigail, and she glared at her. The woman was starting to get on her nerves.

Ma must have heard the conversation, too. "I don't think Betsey meant to announce her womanly way to the world just yet, but sometimes, as Claire says, this kind of news is hard to keep quiet." Ma winked at Betsey.

"How old is Julia?" Abigail fanned herself with a decorative fan she'd brought with her. Everyone was astonished that something so "back East" had been brought to a picnic. Not many women owned such frivolous items.

Betsey cringed as she answered Abigail, "She's just nine months."

"Awful close together to have babies." Abigail called out to John, "Shouldn't we be getting back to the post soon, John? John turned and waved her way but didn't get up or move from the political conference by the river.

"We'll be eaten alive by the panthers that roam these parts." Abigail waved her fan. "I do declare."

Caroline snickered as she turned her back on the woman.

Ma shifted the conversation away from Betsey's womanly way. "I love the sweetness of these rolls, Claire. Did you add something sweet to the batter?"

Claire held up her thumb and index finger to emphasize. "Just a bit of honey. Seems to give them a sweeter flavor than just a normal roll."

Ma took another large bite. "I agree. I'll have to try that."

"We've got a hive close behind our house. I harvested quite a bit of honey last fall." Claire opened her arms and took the now-sleeping Julia away from Betsey, cuddling her close. "I do miss having little ones around."

Betsey smiled at their friend. They'd all enjoyed the Leach family as neighbors and were thankful for them. Betsey got up to get another fresh roll.

Caroline went to the fire to put another log on it. She felt a bit out of it. Not a man to talk politics, not a housewife or mother to talk over subjects about babies or cooking, and she felt way too old to join the other children in their games down by the river.

She went into the idle cabin to sit down and enjoy some quiet.

"Where's Caroline?" Etta asked Ma, who was bundling up a bit of extra food for John and Abigail to take back to their home with them.

Ma shook her head. "I don't know, Etta."

Etta gazed around at the separate groups of people now scattered throughout their property. Claire and Betsey were looking at Pa's crops and the garden. Jillian and the other children were chasing chickens around the barn. But where was Caroline?

Ma asked her to fetch an old basket from under her bed to pack up Abigail and John's food. As Etta opened the door, she found Caroline sound asleep in Ma's rocking chair. The squeak of the door startled Caroline, and her eyes blinked open.

"Caroline. What are you doing in here?"

Caroline rubbed her eyes and sat up straight in the chair. "I must have fallen asleep."

Reaching under her ma's bed, Etta pulled out a few baskets her ma had stored there. "Ma needs a basket for Abigail's food."

Caroline stood. "I can't believe I fell asleep. I'm sure everyone thinks it very rude of me to do that on a fun day like today."

Etta started back outside. "No worries, Caroline. There are so many people here today. I don't think anyone noticed." Etta let out a giggle. "Well, maybe Horace did." And she hurried out the door.

Etta handed the basket to Ma and then looked off to see if John was even preparing to leave. Abigail seemed in a rush to make it back to the trading post before darkness descended. As she looked toward the men, she saw past them a horse, being led by a man, approaching the group from the edge of their property.

Putting her hand over her eyes to shield them from the late afternoon sun, she saw a body lying across the horse. Before she could call out to the others, Caroline came up from behind her. She nudged past Etta.

"Is that Whitmore?" Caroline poked Etta.

"It looks like Whitmore, but who do you think is on the horse?"

Caroline put her hand to her mouth, "I don't know, but he doesn't look like he's well."

"Do you think he's alive?"

Caroline stepped away from the cabin and headed toward the men. Etta watched her walk out to Pa and put her hand on his shoulder. She pointed to Whitmore.

Pa and Ambrose rushed toward Whitmore and the horse he was leading to them.

Ma tapped Etta on the shoulder. "Honey, go get my medicine pouch."

Etta obeyed. As she rummaged through the barrel beside Ma's bed, she heard Caroline scream. It was all she could do to dig out Ma's tiny pouch and head outside.

As she reached the door, she looked out to see Caroline kneeling beside the man who now lay on the ground beside the horse.

Etta looked at Betsey, who was wide-eyed and tearful. "Who is it?"

"By the look of Caroline's reaction, I think Billie has arrived."

CHAPTER SIXTEEN

Whitmore commented that Billie was burning up as Pa placed his limp body on Caroline and Etta's bed.

"He passed out on the way here. I don't know how long he's had this fever. He arrived last night, pretty worn out. He told me he wanted to make his way to the Baker home, and I told him I'd help him get here today," Whitmore told everyone. "Do you know him?"

Pa put his hands on his hips. "He's a friend of Caroline's. I know his family back in Pennsylvania."

"He's got the fever pretty bad. He seemed pretty exhausted from his trip. I can't imagine having this fever and having to travel alone. Would he have come with his family?" Whitmore kept prying for more information.

"He told me he would be coming alone," Caroline spoke up, as she wrung out a rag she'd dipped in cool water to place over the young man's forehead.

"Seems pretty young to make a trip like that by himself."

"He's eighteen," Caroline told the trader.

"Well, I've seen younger venture into the territory. Can't hurt to have the Baker family women care for him. I think I'll be heading back now." Whitmore turned to walk back outside.

Ma hurried after him. "Let me pack you up some food to take back with you, Whitmore."

Whitmore took off his hat. His matted hair clung tight to his temples with sweat. "I'd be much obliged."

"Will he be okay, Pa?" Caroline placed the cool cloth over her friend's forehead. Tears wetting her cheeks.

"I don't know, Carrie. But we do know now how to better care for those who have this nasty ague. We'll do everything we can to nurse him back to health." Pa patted Caroline on the back and went outside to tell their visitors his goodbyes.

Caroline turned the cool rag on Billie's forehead over, hoping the opposite side would cool him. He did look older, but the sickness made dark circles under his eyes, and it looked as if he'd lost weight since she last saw him.

His sudden arrival made her feel anxious. She thought she'd be so happy upon seeing him again. But there was one thing that threatened her to shed more tears. She felt the guilt of that morning's kiss weigh upon her soul. What had she been thinking?

Horace watched the Baker's cabin door. Would she emerge today? Since the holiday, he'd been helping Ambrose build his house and hadn't been around the Baker farm. He did his best to keep busy. Helping Ambrose would soon give him the know-how to erect his own cabin. If he didn't pay close attention, he'd later regret it. He'd be building his own home soon and didn't want to miss a single step. But it did nothing to take away his thoughts of Caroline and the young man who'd made his way to be with her from Pennsylvania.

Why hadn't Caroline said anything about him? Had she known he was coming? He appeared to be her age, not quite a man. Who would allow such a young man to set off on his own from Pennsylvania?

If wishes could make doors open... He concentrated on his desire. The only ones who came out were Caroline's sister and their ma.

He walked to the barn to fetch a chisel from Hosea's tools. Ambrose needed it to fine-tune a few logs by his hearth, and he'd sent him to find it. As Horace rummaged through the barn, he saw Etta headed toward the woods. With a bucket in hand, she ventured toward the north of the homestead.

Horace went back to searching for the tool Ambrose needed, but as soon as he'd found it and put it in his pocket, he looked out to find Etta just at the edge of the woods. She was kneeling as if picking berries.

If he were casual enough, Horace could get more information about the young man who'd arrived at the Baker home, but he didn't want Etta to get the wrong impression.

Looking both ways, he meandered out to her. He could hear her humming as he drew near.

"Hey, Etta!"

Etta nearly fell backward onto the ground as she shifted around to see him. As she stood, she put her hand over her chest. "Oh Horace, you frightened me."

"I'm sorry. Whatcha pickin'?"

Etta sighed, "Berries. Ma wanted me to check and see if there were enough ripe ones leftover from after the picnic."

She stooped again and pushed back the bushes around her.

"Have you found any?"

"Not yet. I think Caroline probably picked so many for the pies we made that day that it will be a few days before they are ripe again." Etta looked back at him, "What are you doing here?"

Horace dug into his pocket for the chisel and held it out. "Ambrose sent me to get this from your pa's barn. Do you know where he is?" Horace glanced around the property and quickly spotted Hosea out in his garden. "Oh!" He pointed to where he was. "I should have looked a bit harder."

Etta smirked and then went back to her picking.

"So..."

Sitting back on her heels, Etta asked, "Horace, did you just come for a tool?"

Horace placed the chisel back into his pocket. "Course. Why else would I be here?"

"You weren't trying to see someone while you were here, were you?" Etta found a few berries and placed them in the bucket beside her.

"Um..." Horace folded his arms and scuffed his boot into the dirt, "Not really. Who would I be here to see?" Horace looked at Etta to see if she knew of his eagerness to be on the Baker property. "I mean..."

Etta turned on her toe, giving him a questioning look. "Caroline?"

Horace coughed. "Why would I be here...I mean, why would I be here to see Caroline? I told you, I needed a chisel."

Etta winked at him. "Of course." She went back to pushing back the bushes.

"Well, now that you mention her, where is she?"

"In the house."

"Oh." Horace scratched his head. He wasn't getting far. His coy spirit gave way to a bit more courage. It could be days before he'd be able to be back to the Baker property. "Is she okay?"

Etta turned again. "She's fine."

Horace gave up. He wished Etta well in her berry picking and headed over to let Hosea know that he had borrowed a chisel.

Scuffing his feet, he ambled around the back part of the cabin. If he walked slowly enough, perhaps he'd still get a glimpse of Caroline heading outside.

As he approached Hosea, he knew enough to announce himself before scaring him like he had Etta. "Hosea," he called out.

Hosea stopped his work, looked up, and waved. "Horace. What finds you here on such a nice day as this?"

Horace drew near. "Ambrose sent me. He wanted me to fetch him a tool."

"Did ya find it?" Hosea took off his cap, scratching his head.

"Yes, sir." Horace again pulled the chisel from his pocket and showed it to Hosea.

"How's the house comin'?" Hosea placed his hat back on and went about digging the hole now opened fresh near him.

"It's goin' well. Ambrose can sure build a cabin." Horace sighed, "He's teaching me a lot."

"It's good you can help him. Make your cabin go up easier."

"Um, Hosea. Can I ask you something?" Horace glanced back at the cabin to see if any life stirred yet. The only movement he saw was the smoke dancing into the sky from the fire out front.

"Sure, son." Hosea stopped his work and leaned on his shovel.

"Do you know the young man that came onto the property last week?"

"Yes. His name is Billie. He's from our place back in Pennsylvania."

"He seems a bit young to come all that way alone."

"I agree. Surprised me, too. Only—there is a reason why he came all this way." Hosea winked and then shifted his hat on his head once more.

"Why's that?" Horace held his breath.

"I think he's fond of one of the girls."

"Caroline?"

"Yes, son. I do believe so." Hosea stuck his foot on the shovel, thrusting it into the ground. "They've known each other since they were young'uns."

"Must be pretty serious if he would come all this way to see her." Horace grimaced as his shoulders sagged.

"I'd say...that *is* the case." Hosea stopped what he was doing and looked at Horace. "Is there a reason you ask?"

Horace felt defeated. All he wanted now was to get back to Ambrose and dig into the work there. "No..." Horace stuttered. "No reason. Thanks for the chisel."

"You bet." Hosea bent down and began sifting the dirt through his fingers.

Horace walked off to the south of the property. Ambrose had made a trail from the Baker property to his own, and now, after hauling loads of wood back and forth, the route was easy to find.

Horace's heart began to ache. He glanced up into the trees above him. That young man had come all this way to be with Caroline. Despite his efforts to prove to Caroline that he liked her, he realized that now he probably didn't have a chance in the world to win her heart. A deep sadness penetrated his soul, for he loved that girl something fierce.

Etta did her best to pick enough berries for Ma. She'd only found enough to fill the bottom quarter of her bucket, but it might be enough for some of Ma's blackberry cobbler.

As she placed the bucket on the table, she could hear Billie moan from the bed in the corner of the room.

Caroline came out from behind the curtain they'd put up again, carrying a small bowl of water. She was concentrating hard not to spill it as she transported it to the table. Her hands were shaking.

"How is he?" Etta asked, as she took the bowl from her sister. "Let me rinse this out for you and get you some fresh water."

Caroline sat down and wiped the sweat off her forehead. "It's so hot in here, and Billie is burning up with fever. I can't seem to cool him off. Ma needs to hurry back with the quinine from Betsey's house."

"Has he come around enough to know where he is?" Etta flung the used water out the front door and then filled the bowl again with cooler water from the barrel.

Caroline shook her head. Etta could see tears forming in her sister's eyes as she placed the bowl in front of Caroline on the table. "Sit down and rest for a bit. You've been up at all hours of the night caring for him."

Caroline sighed as she pulled out a chair and sat down. "I can't help it. It's all my fault that he's here, and now he's..." Caroline covered her face with her hands.

Etta sat down beside her sister. Jillian must have gone up to see Betsey with their ma because they were alone in the house. "He'll be fine. He's young and strong. Almost all of us have gotten through the ague while we've been here. Ma was the only one who had it worse. The rest of us are just fine."

Caroline lowered her hands and stared at them. "I hope so."

Etta wasn't sure if she should mention that Horace was outside. She knew Caroline and Horace were becoming more than friends. She'd seen Horace kiss Caroline on their walk before the picnic. "What about Horace?"

Caroline shot Etta a frustrated glance then looked back at the curtain separating the room. "Shhh! What if he hears you?"

Etta lowered her voice. "I don't think he's awake enough to hear us, but what about Horace?"

Caroline stood, picked up the bowl of cooler water. "Billie has come all this way to find me. There is nothing to stop me from becoming his wife, especially Horace."

CHAPTER SEVENTEEN

August was a week away, descending on the territory with oppressive heat and blue, cloudless skies. Trying to remain cool, while performing the duties at hand, seemed impossible. The girls squabbled over who would do the washing each week so they could put their feet in the river to stay cool while working.

Caroline went from helping outside to nursing Billie through the worst part of the sickness. Ma had said that having the young man in their house, with a houseful of young girls, was quite improper. They had neighbors and a reputation to protect. Two more families had entered the area around Ambrose's cabin in the past two weeks.

One evening, they were sitting around outside, keeping cool, and struggling to fight off the torment of evening mosquitoes, at the same time.

Caroline left them and went inside to check on her patient. She needed to try to get him to eat something. She carried some broth from their leftover vegetable soup, perhaps if only to spoon a bit into him.

As she approached the bed, he startled, and his eyes opened wide.

"Billie?" Caroline kneeled to get closer to him. The cabin had grown dark with the fast-approaching night.

"Caroline, is that you?"

Without hesitation, Caroline reached out and stroked the side of his face. "Yes, it's me, Billie. How do you feel?"

Taking in a deep breath and seeming to size up how he was feeling, Billie grimaced. "Like I've been drug behind a mule." He tried to raise himself onto his elbows but to no avail. "All the way from Pennsylvania."

Caroline gently stroked a shock of blonde hair off his forehead. His hair had grown so long, he almost looked like a teenage girl lying on the bed. "Do you think you can swallow some of this broth?" She took the cup and filled a spoonful.

"I don't know."

"Let's try. You need some nourishment."

It wasn't easy trying to help a man, lying on his back, to drink a bit of broth. Billie worked to swallow, but broth dribbled from his mouth and onto the blanket under his head. "I'm sorry." Caroline picked up his head and wiped off his neck.

Caroline put down the cup and again stroked the side of his face. "It's okay. We've all struggled at this point."

"What does," Billie swallowed, "that mean?"

"We've all had what you're having. It seems to be the first disastrous thing to hit a settler here. We've been calling it *ague*."

Billie shivered and then looked up into Caroline's eyes. "I'm so happy I made it to you."

Caroline smiled and pulled the blankets up under his chin. "Me, too. Now get some more rest."

As if on command, Billie closed his eyes and fell asleep. Caroline breathed a sigh of relief. He was coming out of the worst of it. She'd seen it with Jillian, Ma, Betsey, and even as she began to feel better. Once they became more alert and awake, they could start to eat and gain strength.

Leaving Billie, she walked outside.

"How's our patient tonight?" Pa asked her, as she went to wash the cup and spoon she'd used to feed Billie.

"Better. I think the worst is over."

"Praise God from whom all blessings flow," Pa added.

Everyone seated around whispered their own "amens."

Caroline was thankful he was doing better. As she took his cup and spoon and put it into the boiling water by the fire, she couldn't help but be thankful the worst was over. Yet even as she did, she hated to think of the conversation she'd have to have with Horace. He'd haunted her every thought since Billie arrived.

The next day, Pa finished up his breakfast and asked Ma for a bit of paper, a quill, and the tiny inkwell they'd brought with them from Pennsylvania.

"Who are you writing to, Pa?" Jillian asked, as she took away his breakfast plate.

"I believe it's high time we get us a doctor here. Back in New York, one of my best friends was named Nicholas Harder. He was a doctor and a darn good one. I think I'll tell him about our need for a doctor here. Perhaps he knows of a doctor willing to make this area his home."

"Nicholas?" Ma placed a thin sheet of paper and a quill down on the table in front of Pa. "Hosea, that's such a good idea."

"It doesn't hurt to ask," Hosea said, as he dipped the quill into the inkwell.

As he began to write, it took the quill a bit of dipping before he got it working just right. "Sally Mae, bring me those fresh turkey feathers from the mantle there. This one has seen better days."

Ma looked through a few of the carved feathers now drying and then brought Pa one. Again, Pa had to dip the quill a few times, growing frustrated with the effort, before he finally got it to work the way he needed it to.

"Etta, perhaps it's high time you get some penmanship skills rekindled. Come here." Pa pointed to the chair beside him. "Let's have you finish this."

Etta loved to write. "It's been so long since I wrote anything, Pa. Do you think I can still do it?" Etta began dipping the quill to finish the letter Pa had started.

Ma looked over her shoulder. "Pen well-formed letters, Estelle. I'd hate for Dr. Harder to think that we've become so uncivilized here that we don't know how to form our letters anymore."

Caroline watched Etta dip the tip and then start to write the message Pa was now reciting to her.

"Dear Nicholas." Pa held the top of the paper for Etta. "Hope this letter finds you well. We've arrived in Michigan Territory..."

"Pa," Etta exclaimed, "I can't write that fast. Slow down."

Pa laughed. "Sorry, Etta."

Soon Pa was reciting everything slowly so Etta could take down the letter he wanted to send to his doctor friend in New York. "We'd be mighty obliged..."

"Okay, wait." Etta held up her hand to Pa. "Caroline, how do you spell *obliged?*"

Caroline spelled out the word for her sister.

"All right, Pa, keep going."

"We'd be mighty obliged to have you..." Pa watched Etta dip her quill and start again. "...a part of our community here."

Painstakingly, Etta wrote the letters in perfect form. Caroline always thought she did have the best penmanship of all of the sisters.

Pa asked Dr. Harder to send another doctor if he wasn't interested in the position. He told him a little about the new territory. He then finished with, "Sincerely yours, Hosea Baker."

Etta scrawled out the letters with precision. "You do mighty fine at that, Etta girl. It looks much better than what your pa would have scrawled out."

Etta finished the *sincerely yours* part and then handed Pa the quill. "You write your name, Pa. Then he'll know it came from you."

Pa took the quill. "Good idea, Etta. Good idea."

As Pa finished up his signature, Ma asked Caroline, "Do you have an extra envelope from your letters from Billie?"

"Yes, Ma." Caroline left the table.

"We'll just use one of her envelopes. We can scratch out the address on one side and use the other for the new address to Dr. Harder."

Caroline brought back an envelope and handed it to Ma. "This one has just my name on it. It was the envelope John Swain delivered to me. It was my first letter from Billie.

Ma acknowledged, "This is perfect. Thank you, honey."

Caroline thought back to that first letter that had been delivered to her by John and Abigail. Oh, how she'd loved it. That's why the envelope was still in such good condition. She'd read it over and over.

"I don't have an address for Nicholas, but I'm sure if we address it Dr. Nicholas Harder, Newburgh-on-Hudson, New York, it should be enough information for the person delivering it. How many Dr. Harders can there be in one city?"

"Newburgh-on-Hudson is an odd name for a city, Pa." Caroline laughed when she heard the name. "Why not just Newburgh?"

Pa shrugged. "Don't know, but that's the place where Dr. Harder lived when we left New York so many years ago. We've had various letters from him but not since we arrived here. So, we'll see if this one reaches him."

"I hope so, Hosea," Ma said, as she folded the letter after it dried for a bit. "It will be so nice to have a doctor close by again."

Pa sat back in his chair, folding his arms. "I agree, Sally. We've got an Almighty Father who heals all, but having a doctor close helps gives peace of mind. And in my opinion, it's never too early to get one."

CHAPTER EIGHTEEN

The next morning, Caroline woke before the rest of the family. She'd been nursing Billie almost non-stop, and she grew tired of being in the cabin. She needed some time away from him to settle her anxious heart and figure out what she'd be telling Horace the next time she saw him.

Fastening her skirts and buttoning up her blouse, she decided she'd fetch the water for the day. Most days, this was Etta and Jillian's job, but today, Caroline needed fresh air.

Opening the door to the bright morning, Caroline picked up both buckets and headed toward the flowing well down by the river. Rain overnight had taken the edge off the humidity of the July day. A fresh breeze rippled through Caroline's hair. Placing the buckets at her feet, Caroline twirled her hair at her neck, winding it into a bun at the back of her head. It felt good to get her hair off her sweaty neck. She slipped her bonnet on and tied the strings under her chin.

As she knelt to pick up the bucket handles, a deer skittered away from the water and bounced, white tail in the air, into the woods across the river. A stirring by the edge of the river caught her eye. She stopped moving as a spotted fawn stretched to life and bolted into the woods behind its momma.

The stream shimmered rainbow colors as the sun cast its morning light onto the waters. Caroline took in a deep breath. Looking toward the heavens, she whispered a prayer for direction. Could she love two men at the same time? The whole ordeal was unfair not only to Billie but also Horace.

As she lifted the buckets to the dribbling of water from the artesian well, Caroline struggled to think of which man she should love for the rest of her life. Counting off all of their admirable qualities wasn't any help in making her decision. Both men were honorable, fair, and hard-working.

Was it dishonorable to look at their physical features? Caroline could feel her face blush thinking of Billie's handsome face and soft brown eyes, but he was short, and probably due to the illness, his frame was thin. Then she thought of Horace and his deep blue eyes. They made her swoon every time he looked at her. He stood almost a foot taller than her. Indeed, a man's height didn't determine his loyalty or trust.

Caroline lifted the next bucket to fill, splashing water on her feet as she did. Billie made her feel comfortable and secure. Horace made her heart race, and she couldn't wait to see him each day. Yet Billie hadn't been here to test the pace of her heart, so how was that fair?

Back and forth, her heart wavered, like the pendulum at the schoolhouse back in Pennsylvania. She'd watched that pendulum swing to and fro whenever she had to sit and wait for the bell to ring for school to be out each day, ticking off the seconds until she could head home.

As she picked up both buckets, she realized her thoughts distracted her from how much water she'd put into each one. Both sloshed her now as she crept up the bank of the river, her skirt growing soaked with each step.

That's when she saw him striding toward her across the back of Pa's field. He seemed determined, especially when their eyes met. He picked up speed, running toward her. What was he doing here so early? She'd gone over what she'd say to him over a zillion times, but she was not any more prepared than she was the day before.

"Caroline, let me help you." Horace took a bucket from her, easing the ache in her hand from carrying it.

"Thank you, Horace." She caught her breath. "What are you doing here so early?"

"Your Pa wanted to head into the trading post today. I told Ambrose I'd head up here this morning to give him a list of the things we need."

Caroline stopped and placed her bucket on the ground. Wiping her hands down her skirt, she looked up at the tall man, now brown from the summer sun. Her heart raced in time to her thoughts. "Horace, I think we need to talk."

Horace placed the other bucket on the ground. "Do you love him?"

Caroline folded her arms. Horace deserved an answer, and she knew it, but she didn't have one to give him. What would she say?

"From what I've overheard, he's come all this way to be with you. Do you plan to marry him?" Horace folded his arms and then shifted his weight from one foot to the other.

Caroline looked down. "Horace, I've known Billie my whole life. We've made plans, yes. He did come all this way for me..."

"But Caroline, do you love him?"

Caroline looked off to the edge of the forest. She wanted to tell him what she thought of him. How much his friendship meant to her since spring. But she owed Billie much more. He'd traveled from Pennsylvania to be with her.

Horace took her chin and turned her head to look at him. "But do you love him? That's all I need to know."

Tears welled up as she looked into the blue eyes of the man who had entered her life at the wrong time. "I do love him."

Horace sighed. "Okay then. Let me help you get these to the door, and I'll deliver my list to your pa."

Horace picked up both buckets and headed toward the cabin. With his back to her, she knew he didn't see the tears now falling down her cheeks. She wiped them with the back of her hand and turned her back to him. She wanted to be alone.

Jillian heard the knock on the door as Pa went to answer it, pulling up the straps of his suspenders as he walked across the floor.

"Who could this be, at this hour?"

As the door opened, a fresh breeze slipped into the warm, musty room. Jillian flipped the blanket off her warm legs, standing to see who could be at the door. It seemed they'd all slept later than usual.

"Horace!" Pa announced. "What brings you here so early, boy?"

Ma would never forgive Pa if he allowed a young man into their home at such an early hour. She pulled the blanket up to her neck, but soon Pa slipped out the door to speak with Horace.

From her spot, Jillian heard moaning from Billie behind the curtain. Ma was stirring in bed, but Etta was still sound asleep beside her. "Etta, wake up. Horace is here."

Etta pushed Jillian's hand away and pulled the blanket up over her shoulder. "Go away. Let me sleep a bit longer."

Jillian heard Ma call for her from her side of the bed, "Jillian, get up and dress. Sounds like Billie needs someone. I'll get busy and get breakfast started."

Billie moaned again. Jillian stood to fasten on her skirts. "I'm coming, Billie."

"Where's Caroline?" Ma said, as she pulled her apron around her waist and tied the strings behind her. "What brought that young man to our house so early?"

Jillian shrugged. "I don't know, Ma. Maybe he needed a tool from Pa."

Jillian went to look for a dipper to retrieve Billie some water. Once she found it, she scooped a dripping share out of the barrel from yesterday and took it to the bedside for Billie. "Are you thirsty, Billie?"

Billie grimaced. "Yes. My mouth feels like dust."

Jillian raised the young man's head to help him drink from the dipper. He sucked down the water. "Can I have more?"

"Of course. Just a moment. I'll run down to the well soon. Then it will be fresh, colder water."

"It doesn't matter. I like it warm. Easier to swallow."

"All right, just a moment. I'll be right back."

Hurrying to get some more water, Jillian watched Etta sit up and stretch her arms. "I hate mornings."

Ma scolded her from the kitchen. "You're gonna hate mornings even more if you don't get a move on!"

Etta stood and folded blankets as Jillian carefully carried another ladle of water back to Billie's bedside. "Hurry up and get up, Etta. We need water."

"I'm coming. I'm coming." Etta snarled at her sister.

As Jillian raised Billie's head again, she saw him looking at her as she held the scoop for him to drink. "You sure have gotten older, Jillian. How old are you now?"

"I'll be thirteen next month."

Billie smiled. His lips were now moist. "That's crazy. You're turning out to be a very pretty young lady."

Jillian giggled. Standing up, she added, "I'll be back with your breakfast soon. Do you think you can eat?"

Billie pushed a lock of his long, blonde hair off his forehead. "I'm starving."

"That's a good sign." She adjusted his covers and pushed his pillow up better for him. "Have you seen Caroline yet this morning?"

He shook his head. "No, I haven't. Where is she?"

Jillian turned to help her ma. "I'm wondering that myself."

Pa thanked Horace for hefting the water buckets to the house. "How did you know we need water this morning, Horace?

"I didn't." Horace handed the list Ambrose sent him to deliver to Hosea. "Caroline was hauling them up from the river this morning and I went to help her."

"Caroline?"

"Yeah, I think she's down by the river. I need to be getting back."

Hosea watched the young man, shoulders slumped, head off toward the back of his property and Ambrose's cabin. He looked dejected and sad.

Hosea peered off toward the river and saw Caroline's shoulders just over a ridge. She appeared to be at the river's edge. Why would she have Horace haul the buckets back up to the cabin?

Hosea looked toward the sky. An urging prompted him to head down to the river to check on his daughter. He called out to her as he drew near. "Caroline?" He didn't want to startle her.

She was crouching low, close to the flowing river. Her shoulders were shaking, and her hands covered her face.

"Carrie, sweetheart? Are you okay?" He knelt beside the girl who seemed to be crying as hard as the river flowed.

Caroline jumped as he placed his arm around her shoulders. "Baby girl, what's wrong? Did someone harm you?"

Caroline wiped her face with her hands and then used her apron to dry off her face as best as she could. "Oh, Pa. I'm miserable."

Hosea choked back his own emotions. He never did very well seeing his daughters so emotional. "Carrie girl, tell your pa all about it." He hugged her close and let her cry a bit more.

She struggled to gain her composure. "I'm a horrible person."

Hosea wiped the tendrils of hair off her forehead and stroked her damp cheeks. "What have you done to feel that way?"

Caroline let out a deep sigh. "I told Horace I love Billie."

Hosea was taken aback. "Well, isn't that the truth?"

"Yes." Caroline's tears started again.

"Telling the truth is important. Don't you think?"

"Yes."

"Then, what's wrong?"

Caroline looked up at him. "Pa, I don't know it for sure."

His daughter's words caught Hosea off guard. This girl had a decision to make, and she was fighting for the right one. "Carrie, don't you love Billie?"

"Yes."

"But you love Horace, too?"

Sobs again shook his daughter's body. "Yes."

Hosea pulled his daughter close. "Oh baby girl. This decision happens to many women. You're not alone in deciding between two fellas after your heart."

"I'm not?"

"No, ma'am. Girls as pretty as you have a hard time when more than one man is pining for them."

"Tell me what to do, Pa. Tell me which one you think would be a good husband for me."

He pulled her closer, took his handkerchief out of his pocket, and wiped her face, "Carrie, I can't do that. Only you will know which man is the one you want to spend the rest of your life with."

"But that's the problem, Pa. I don't know. I like them both."

Hosea stifled back a chuckle. He knew laughing at his daughter now would only make her problem worse. "Well, they are both fine men. Horace is hard-working and loyal. He seems to like you fine. But Billie has come all this way to be with you, too. We know his family. He comes from good stock."

Caroline gave him a look that made him feel as if he'd just sorted through her thoughts and spit them right back at her, but he knew he couldn't make this life-changing decision for her. "Perhaps you need to think about this? Who do you see spending the rest of your life with?"

Caroline looked at him with questioning eyes.

"All right. How about this? Choose the one whom you can't live without."

He seemed to have struck sound wisdom. A hiccup replaced Caroline's heavy sobs. "I think I know which one that is."

"There you go!" Hosea pulled her to her feet as he stood. "Now you know your answer. Sometimes God has to help make our crooked paths straight."

"And boy, are my paths crooked right now. But Pa, how do I tell them?"

Hosea wiped the remaining tears from her face and kissed her forehead. "That's a good question for your ma." He then pulled her toward him for a long embrace.

CHAPTER NINETEEN

Megan Pierce had decided to travel with her husband that morning to Whitmore's post. It was a beautiful day to be out for a wagon ride. She clung to his arm. It had been a long time since they'd had the opportunity to spend a bit of time together without the distractions of chores and tending to the needs of their children.

Her neighbor, Claire, had agreed to allow their children to spend a few hours with her that morning, giving Megan the privilege of heading to the post with Josiah. They needed to exchange a few beaver pelts her husband had skinned the day before.

"What a glorious morning!" Megan inhaled the fresh air. "I can smell honeysuckle."

Josiah tried to smell the aroma but shook his head. "You're better at smelling flower scents than I." He grinned at her.

"How much do you think Whitmore will give you for the pelts, Josiah? Maybe we can get a few hens from Claire. I'd love to be getting eggs soon. I could make cake and eggs for breakfast."

Josiah smiled. "I'll see what I can do. First, I need to pay Ambrose for the work he did on our cabin."

Soon they were at the post. Megan saw Abigail Swain out fanning herself on a nearby stump. "I think I'll stay out here and talk to Abigail. Would that be okay?"

Josiah pulled back on the wagon brake. "Of course. I'll be a few minutes."

Megan approached Abigail, waving to her. "Abigail!"

Abigail looked up, startled to see her. "Megan. Where did you come from?"

Megan explained that she'd accompanied Josiah to the post that morning and that she'd been able to leave her two children with Claire.

"Sit with me. It's good to see another white woman for a change." Abigail used her foot to scoot another stump close to her.

Megan sat down. "It's nice to see you out this morning, getting a bit of fresh air. Isn't it a wonderful day?"

Abigail didn't stop fanning herself. "If you can stand this oppressive heat and the bugs." As she said this, she slapped her neck. "Pesky things. I don't know how you folk handle being outside all the time."

"We use the lotion the Bakers gave us. You know, the Indian salve."

"That disgusting-smelling stuff! How can you even stand it on your skin?"

"It's better than allowing those insects to leave giant, itchy welts on your skin."

Abigail slapped her ankle. "I will not wear it. I refuse."

Megan giggled. "I'd rather smell bad than have welts."

"I'd rather itch!"

Megan had done her best to befriend Abigail. They were close in age, and she longed for friends out here in the new territory where womenfolk were hard to find. She cherished her friendship with Claire.

"Did you hear about the young man staying at the Baker house?"

"The one whom Whitmore brought to the picnic?" Claire nodded.

"The young man is staying in the same house with them. How preposterous! What father would allow his daughters to be subject to such an atrocity? It's not fitting for young girls to live with a young man who isn't a relative. Don't you think?"

"Well, I—"

"I mean, truly. He's sweet on Caroline Baker, and they're living under the same roof, from what I hear. It's just not right, I say. Not at all."

"I heard the young man is quite sick. What else could they do?"

"Send him off. Perhaps he could stay with Betsey."

"Betsey is with child. Ague is dangerous around women in that condition."

"And there's that. What's the matter with Betsey? Doesn't she know that having babies so close together is dangerous? That first baby of hers isn't even a year old yet. I'd say that's taking too many risks."

"Abigail. I don't believe Betsey expecting so soon was on purpose."

"Well, she's married and old enough to know how it all works, isn't she?"

Megan felt her face blush. "Yes, of course."

"It's too soon. Children need nurturing. How will she even be able to take care of two, so close together?"

Megan wanted to ask Abigail why she hadn't had children yet, but it wasn't any of her business. Just like them discussing Betsey's childbearing issues wasn't any of their business either. Megan stood. "I better be seeing to Josiah. He might need me. Have a good day, Abigail."

Abigail looked at her as if she were judging her harshly. She looked away without saying anything more, her fan fluttering like a butterfly wing.

Betsey stopped by the cabin to drop Julia off for her sisters and ma to watch while she took lunch to Ambrose, Aaron, and Horace. Aaron had decided to help Ambrose finish off his house, and soon they'd start the foundation for Horace's house. The late morning brought sunshine accompanied by a cool breeze. Betsey decided a walk to Ambrose's house would be healthy for her. She'd packed a good lunch to serve the men.

She'd never left Julia for long, but she knew a strenuous walk alone would calm her heart. Julia would enjoy being with her aunts and grandmother.

The walk through the woods that bright day brought a flood of thankfulness to Betsey's soul. She'd been feeling baby flutters for a few days now, and as she walked, she began to feel more movement from the growing child inside her womb. What a blessing it was to grow a new life within her body. A woman is a treasured being to help nourish new life. Betsey sighed from contentment and joy.

Birds flittered above her head from tree to tree along the now well-worn path to Ambrose's cabin, each one seeming to chirp a greeting to her as she ambled along the trail. She switched the heavy basket of food to her other hand.

She was eager to see Ambrose again. She hadn't seen him since the picnic at her parents' cabin. The trail was quiet except for an occasional scuttle in the woods from the scampering squirrels.

It was hard to believe that this time last year, they'd been all alone in this part of the territory. Now neighboring farms were popping up all around them. Ambrose's cabin would soon be finished, with Horace building just as close. Two other neighbors had farms started, too. Through the trees, she caught a slight glimpse of the Leach farm. Perhaps she'd see Claire and the new neighbors, Megan and Josiah.

The heat of the summer day warmed her shoulders. Despite her manners, Betsey removed her bonnet so the wind could blow through her hair. If she were alone, on her ridge by her farm, she'd also take out the bun at the back of her head and let her braids fall. It felt glorious to be outside.

Before long, she caught sight of the house in the distance. She could make out verbal requests for tools, whistles, and a brief chuckle from the men perched on ladders assembling the last part of Ambrose's chimney. Aaron was perched at the top of the ladder, as Horace carried rocks from a nearby pile up the rungs to him. Ambrose appeared to be mixing up the mortar used to fuse stones onto the forming chimney. He carried a rock in one hand and what seemed to be a bucket filled with mortar on a finger in the same hand. Ambrose and Aaron worked well together. There seemed always to be laughter and teasing accompanying their work. It caused Betsey to smile as she approached them.

She admired the house from afar. It wasn't like her parents' primitive log cabin, but more like their house back in Pennsylvania. Ambrose had used lumber for the walls, and he'd even put in two windows at the front with a porch attached. Betsey thought it would warmly welcome a young woman when Ambrose found an available one to court.

Horace had agreed to work with Ambrose on his house, and soon they'd be putting up another home just off of Pa's designated property. Betsey admired Horace. He had a good nature and a helpful demeanor. Betsey prayed that more young women would soon enter the territory, so some of these men could find suitable wives.

As Betsey drew closer, she called out, "Hey boys! Anyone hungry?"

Being high enough to see her clearly down the path, Aaron called out to the others. "Betsey's here with our lunch!"

Heads turned, and hoots and hollers erupted from the team.

Ambrose continued stirring the mixture as Horace stopped at the bottom of the ladder. Aaron came down to greet her.

"Hey Bit, you're a welcome sight." Aaron took the heavy basket from her and swung it up on a table by the front door. "I'm starving."

"Me, too." Ambrose leaned the heavy paddle he used to stir the mixture against the cabin wall.

Horace grinned and wiped the sweat off his forehead with the bottom of his shirt.

"Hello Horace," Betsey added.

He nodded to her. "Ma'am."

"Are you hungry?"

"We wouldn't know." Aaron pushed on the shoulder of the young guy. "He's been awful quiet today."

"You feeling all right, Horace?" Betsey knew a quiet Horace wasn't the usual.

"I'll be fine, ma'am." Horace sat down and guzzled a large scoop of water.

"How about some fried chicken, a baked potato, and greens?" Betsey smiled at the grins it brought the men. "And for dessert, some jam on bread."

Betsey placed a cloth under their meal and handed each worker a plate of food.

As they sat down to start the meal, someone yelled to them from down the road. John Swain sat aboard a new wagon he'd recently purchased from Whitmore. Abigail sat on the seat beside him. She held tight to an elegant hat, complete with a bright-purple feather, under an umbrella trimmed with lace. She looked like she was going calling in downtown Meadville, not in the backwoods of Michigan Territory.

She gave Betsey a side glance as John helped her down from the wagon. Her fluffy skirts edging the ground. Betsey looked down at her dress, which barely brushed the tops of her shoes.

"Betsey." Abigail looked out from beneath the brim of her hat.

"Abigail. You look beautiful today." Betsey knew it was probably a waste of a good compliment, but perhaps it would be a good day to spend with her sister-in-law.

"Why, thank you. John said we were going to come out and see Ambrose and Aaron today, so I wanted to be sure I looked my best."

John grinned at his lovely wife, pride gleaming in his eyes. "I knew you'd need my help around the base of that chimney today. I thought it would be good for Abigail to get out for a bit."

Betsey stood up. "We have plenty to share. Would you join us?"

"We ate before we came, Betsey, but we can sit and enjoy the conversation with you all." John motioned for Abigail to swish herself over to the others seated around the table.

"Here, Mrs. Swain. Sit at my place." Horace rose from the table, taking his food with him. He found another place to sit, leaning his back against Ambrose's front porch.

"We were just about to say grace." Aaron looked to John. "Join us."

Each person sat down and bowed their head to thank the Lord for their food. Betsey felt joy as Aaron thanked God for Betsey's safety as she walked to bring them a good lunch.

"Can I get you some jam with bread?" Betsey asked John and then motioned to Abigail. "It's not an extravagant dessert, but it will give us something sweet to enjoy."

Abigail turned her head away from the table. "No, thank you."

"I'd love some," John admitted eagerly.

Betsey spooned jam on a thick slice of bread she'd made that morning. The bread was still warm.

"Do you have time to help us today, John?" Aaron took another large bite of his sandwich.

"Of course. That's why I'm here. It can get tricky sometimes getting that mortar just right around a chimney like yours, Ambrose."

Ambrose scooped a bit of greens into his mouth. "I have done chimneys before, but I was hoping you'd brought some tin that Whitmore said he had available at the post."

John caught a portion of jam slipping off his bread with his finger. He licked it clean. "It's in the wagon. It works pretty well, keeping the rain and snow out from around the chimney. I think you'll be pleased with it."

"How are you feeling, Abigail?" Betsey knew Abigail had been under the weather after hearing about it at the picnic. Betsey wondered if Abigail would soon be in the family way again.

"Other than being deathly bored, I'm well."

Betsey slipped another piece of chicken onto Aaron's plate. As he looked for a reaction to Abigail's comment, Betsey raised an eyebrow. Aaron smiled.

"I'm happy to hear about your news." Abigail glanced down at Betsey's waist.

Betsey blushed. It wasn't something she wanted to discuss, especially in front of all the men at the table. But she did her best to muddle through the comment, "We are blessed."

Abigail looked down her nose at Betsey. Betsey's comment seemed to annoy her. "Perhaps you'll have twins!"

"Each child is a gift from God, but about the only thing that runs in our family are girls!" Betsey did her best to counteract Abigail's remark.

Aaron winked at her. "Another girl would be fine."

Betsey wanted to sink under the table. She was embarrassed by Abigail speaking about such a private matter in front of the men, especially John and Horace. She was used to Ambrose and Aaron's various outbursts regarding her female condition.

Diverting the attention away, she whispered to Aaron across the table. "Horace seems a bit off today. Are you sure he's okay?"

"He does seem a bit put-off today." Aaron bit into his chicken leg. "I've never known him to be so quiet."

"I hope he's feeling all right. Keep a watch on him for the fever."

Abigail's demeanor seemed to change on a dime as she mentioned, "They are pesky little things, aren't they Betsey? I've never seen such torment from a little tiny insect." Abigail swished a hand in front of her face as if they were bothering her at that exact moment.

"We've found something that works pretty well to ward them off, but you have to endure quite an odor while wearing it." Betsey grinned at Aaron. Thinking about Abigail wearing the skunk scent made her almost giggle right out loud.

"I've had the opportunity to smell it on Whitmore since spring came. It's repulsive." Abigail wrinkled her small nose.

"Yes, yes, it is. But it does the trick to keep the bugs at bay."

Soon the meal came to an end. Ambrose stood and patted his belly. "Men, let's get back to work. Is everyone finished?"

Horace gave Betsey back his plate. "Thank you, ma'am, that was fine."

Betsey smiled. "You're welcome, Horace. Are you sure you've had enough?"

Horace acted as if even smiling was difficult. "Yes. Plenty. Thank you."

After Betsey put everything back in the basket, she spread a blanket on the ground beside the cabin. She tried to find a shady spot as the afternoon sun pierced even the thinnest of skirts. She wasn't sure how Abigail was comfortable in all of her clothing layers.

"I thought we'd have the opportunity to sit inside the cabin for a bit and not out here on this..." Abigail picked up an edge of the blanket.

"I'm sorry, Abigail, Ambrose doesn't have much furniture yet. He's been working so hard on the outside of his house, he'll need to catch up soon on his furniture building. Besides," Betsey leaned back to watch the men work, "it would be awfully stuffy inside the cabin today."

Abigail huffed, "Well then, we'll have to make do...won't we!"

Betsey wasn't sure how long she could sit here and take the haughty attitude of her sister-in-law.

"Looks to me as if we are finally getting more neighbors in the area. It will be good to attend a tea, or perhaps we could start a literary club. I was able to see Megan today. They stopped by the post this morning."

"How is she?"

"Fine, I guess."

Betsey stifled a comment about Abigail suggesting they start a literary club or have enough time for tea. They might never have time, out here, for the type of things Abigail suggested. Betsey was usually busy from sunup to sundown doing laundry, cleaning her home, harvesting and storing new garden vegetables, caring for Julia. Besides, there were hardly any books to read.

As if she knew Betsey's thoughts, Abigail commented, "Books are for those inclined to learn. Not all of us are cut from the same cloth." Abigail raised her hand to look at her nails. "Some of the women might feel more accustomed to indulging their literary skills."

"Literary skills are important. I agree with you there. But for now, settlers are more interested in building a home, securing their future in the new territory. Planting a garden so there's plenty to eat. Those other things perhaps will come later."

Abigail huffed and looked off toward the edge of Ambrose's property. "I pray that a learned woman will filter into the community soon. Educated company is hard to find here."

Betsey couldn't help it. She rolled her eyes and looked the other way. It was as if this woman was insinuating that Betsey, and those hard-working settlers like her didn't have any use of learning or advancing themselves. The only book Betsey had to read was her Bible. Betsey coughed in her hand.

Abigail lowered her voice to almost a whisper, "And another thing, I wouldn't be caught dead being among men in a condition such as yours without a better way to conceal it. What did you whisper to Aaron? Were you bragging to him that you are with child and I am not?"

Shock filled Betsey's thoughts. "I would never tease another woman about something so sensitive."

"Well," Abigail pulled her skirt down over her protruding shoes, "I'd like to believe that about you, Betsey, but if you can be so upfront about your pregnancy to others, perhaps you'd be forthright about your comments about me."

"I would never, Abigail. I feel sorry that you haven't been able to conceive again. Truly."

It was now Abigail's turn to roll her eyes at Betsey, but instead of turning her head, she made it a point for Betsey to see her.

Betsey placed a hand over her protruding belly. She wanted nothing but to share her joy with Abigail, but it seemed that whatever she would now say might be misconstrued. "It's a bit hard to hide my secret from others. My dress has become a bit threadbare since we arrived. I could use a new dress."

And as fast as the unkind comment had come, Abigail followed with, "I brought many with me. Why don't you stop by someday, and we'll see if I could find something for you to..." Abigail looked up and watched John climb the ladder, "to borrow."

"Borrow? I couldn't borrow a dress from you, Abigail. What if it were to get stains on it, or worse yet, a hole from a wandering spark?"

"I would hope you'd be careful with it. Just wear it for outings, such as these."

Betsey wasn't sure how to feel about the offer. The comment made it clear that Abigail thought her dress was inappropriate, and she was making a fool of herself for wearing it out in public. Sadly, it was Betsey's best dress. This woman didn't realize how affluent she was with her fancy dresses and parasols.

"I'm sorry my dress offends you. You know, I best be getting home soon. Julia will need to eat before she goes down for a nap. I just wanted to be sure the men got a healthy lunch."

"Well, what am I supposed to do while I wait for John?"

The perturbed expression now on Abigail's face made Betsey even more certain she wanted to return to Julia. "It's a beautiful day. Perhaps you can take a walk down the path there. It sure brightened my morning."

Betsey stood to leave. She felt rude but walked to the ladder to tell Aaron and the other men goodbye. She couldn't sit around all afternoon hearing Abigail's complaints or comparisons.

Aaron kissed her cheek, and she found herself back on the delightful path she'd enjoyed just a few hours before. She'd had such high hopes that she and Abigail could one day become friends. A woman her age. Someone in the same stage of life as she was, but that wasn't about to happen. Not with Abigail Swain. Around her, there wasn't anything Betsey could do or say to appease the woman.

As Betsey walked back to her parents' cabin, she thought of the women who'd entered the territory just that spring. She and her parents had done their best to welcome them with the hospitality absent from the unsettled land. After arriving, it wasn't long before the new families became busy hauling water, preparing meals, and planting gardens or crops. A settler's life was hard and hectic during the summer months.

It was odd how, just a year ago, Betsey wouldn't have been brave enough to walk such a deserted path alone. She'd barely thought about the dangers anymore, even though she knew that all around them were things that could harm them.

Thinking back to her fear of the Indians, even that had changed considerably. Of course, they needed to be cautious, but through the summer, they'd not seen any natives close to the cabin as they had the year before.

Nearing her parents' property, she thought about Waussinoodae and how she'd grown accustomed to seeing the woman from time to time. It had been weeks since she'd last seen her. Whitmore believed the new settlers in the area seemed to be driving the Indians north and deeper into the woods.

Perhaps Abigail had a point. A bit more socializing would be helpful for all of them. Maybe even for Abigail herself. She'd soon learn that settling women with different upbringings could be just as refined as she. Betsey admired John for bringing Abigail to the north woods, but she was afraid the woman wouldn't be able to handle much more. She also thanked God for bringing babies into her life so quickly. What a heartache it would be to be barren when all you wanted to do was have a child of your own.

Betsey found Pa outside pounding stakes into the ground. They soon wanted to purchase or trade for a cow, and Pa was preparing a grazing area for one. She saw so many changes in Pa since they'd arrived. The fever sickness had taken a toll on him, just like Ma. He rested more often, and after a long day of work, he fell asleep in a chair long before bedtime.

"Hey Pa!" Betsey called out, waving her hand in the air for him to see her.

"Bit!" Pa stopped pounding a stake and sat down.

"I have one extra slice of bread in this basket. Would you like it?"

A grin widened on her pa's face. "Would I?"

Betsey dug into the basket and pulled out the last bit of bread she'd packed. "Would you like jam on it?"

Pa shook his head and took a large bite. "Got any water?"

"No, Pa. But I can run to the house for some if you need it."

Pa sat down under a large oak tree that graced the edge of his property. He patted the ground beside him. "Come sit with me. Can you do that?"

Betsey sat. It had been quite a while since she and Pa had a chance to chat. "How's the fence coming?"

Pa took a large bite. "I think we'll be able to afford a cow come fall or next spring. Leach has been itchin' for someone to bring a bull into the territory. A few calves would be welcome to many of the newcomers."

Betsey agreed. "I could use some good milk for Julia once the new baby comes."

Pa looked down at her belly. "I know I shouldn't talk about such private things, but when will this one arrive?"

"Right around the end of the year, I believe." Betsey didn't mind answering Pa about such a delicate subject. He was becoming a wonderful grandpa to Julia.

"Perhaps we'll get us a Christmas baby. 'Unto you a child is born, unto you, a son is given.'"

Betsey giggled. "A son would be a nice addition. I know," Betsey pulled her legs up and hugged them. "Aaron would love a son."

"Sons are good, but daughters..."

"Are a burden?"

Pa laughed. "Sometimes. But what I was going to say is, daughters make a man thankful. They bring so much joy to a household with their singing, giggling, and even their squabbling. God knew I needed many women in my life. You've always brought me joy." Pa patted her leg.

After her thoughts about Waussinoodae, Betsey asked. "Have you seen many Indians around lately, Pa?"

"Can't say that I have. I heard from Whitmore that there is some kind of disease infiltrating the tribes."

"Disease?"

"Some kind of cholera. Says it doesn't seem to be infecting the settlers but has taken a toll on the Indians."

Betsey looked off to the edge of the woods. She hoped that it hadn't affected Waussinoodae or any of her tribe.

"Another reason why we need a doctor in these parts. I'd hate for us to have another disease to have to deal with."

"Why do you think none of us have caught it yet?"

"No clue." Pa finished his bread. "Let's hope it continues that way."

Betsey stood and wiped off the back of her dress. "I need to get inside. Julia probably is wondering where her ma ran off to."

"She was a happy girl at lunch. Your ma loves having her around."

"She is a distraction from all the normal frustrations a day can bring."

"Thanks for the snack. Tell Ma I'm going to put a few more poles in the ground and will be in soon. I need some water."

"I'll have Etta or Jillian run some out to you. Don't get too hot." Betsey picked up her basket and headed to the cabin to check on Julia. While walking, she sent up a silent prayer for God to protect them from the illness Whitmore had mentioned to Pa.

CHAPTER TWENTY

As Betsey strolled toward the house, she could hear Jillian and Alexander down by the river, singing as they took turns beating rugs free of dirt. Ma had made rag rugs that winter and placed one beside each bed. The pads felt warm and soft when they stepped on them each morning. Ma had made one for Betsey and Aaron's bedside, too.

Betsey called out and waved. Alexander's voice now rang out as loud as Jillian's. His out-of-tune singing voice made Betsey laugh right out loud. At least he added a new voice to the mix.

As Betsey entered the house, she found Julia and her ma sound asleep in a chair. She tiptoed across the floor, admiring her ma cradling her infant, and her eyes turned moist with emotion. Julia had her soft down-covered head snuggled up close to Ma's neck. Ma startled awake, but Julia didn't stir.

"How is she?" Betsey whispered.

Ma smiled. "Perfect. She got so comfortable I guess I took advantage of this chore and joined her. Is it close to supper?"

"Yes. I need to get home and get mine started."

Ma kissed Julia's forehead. "This baby brings me so much joy. She's pulling herself up on the barrels around the room now. Pretty soon, she'll need scolding for tipping them over, but for now, she seems happy hearing them crash to the floor."

Betsey laughed. "That she is. I've begun telling her no from time to time, but she just looks up at me and smiles. I don't think she understands it yet."

"Oh, she will." Ma shifted the baby from her shoulder position and cradled her. "She's out now. It took me a bit of singing to get her to sleep. The girls and Alexander coming in and out kept waking her." Ma gazed down at the baby as if she were a wonderful treasure to admire. "I didn't think it possible to love someone more than my children, but this blessed experience of holding a grandchild is too much for my heart to hold."

Betsey went to her ma and patted her shoulder. "I think she thinks the same about you, Ma."

"It will be hard on you when you have two little ones underfoot. How are you feeling?"

Betsey sighed, "I'm much better now. The morning sickness seems to be gone. I do find myself eager to get to bed each night, but that's nothing new."

"How was your day? Did the men like their food?"

Betsey relayed how they hooted and hollered upon her arrival. "Horace was helping. He seemed out of sorts today. Do you think he is okay?"

"Was he sick? Not known a time for that boy not to be chattering up a storm."

"No. I asked Aaron about him. He agreed with me that something was amiss."

Betsey placed a light blanket on the table, gently lifted Julia from her ma's arms, and laid her in the middle. The baby didn't stir. "Thanks for watching Julia today." Betsey wrapped her tight to carry her up the ridge. "I hate to wrap her on such a hot day, but the mosquitoes will find her fresh skin too tempting."

"Are you going to use the backboard?"

"I didn't bring it this time. She should sleep well while I walk home."

Betsey left the cabin and headed north. It wouldn't be long before Aaron would return home, and she still had a few chores before supper.

She waved to Alexander and Jillian, now joined by Etta. They were all splashing in the water, cooling off on the hot summer day. As Betsey turned the corner around the barn, she found Caroline mending a chicken fence.

"Caroline. I didn't know you were out here."

Caroline startled. "Oh, Betsey!" She put her hand on her chest. "I didn't hear you coming."

"Just picking up Julia to head home."

"Can I walk with you?"

"Of course," Betsey acknowledged. "You don't think Ma will need you to help with supper?"

Caroline picked up the egg-gathering basket. "I think I can take a break."

Betsey motioned for her to follow. "Well then, let's go."

Caroline took the basket Betsey carried and placed it on her arm.

Her help gave Betsey's arms relief. She thanked her.

"Betsey, can I ask you something?"

"Always." The two sisters headed toward the path that led up to Betsey and Aaron's cabin. A stiff wind came from the west. In the heat of the day, it brought cool relief. "That feels good."

Caroline took a deep breath.

"What's your question?" Betsey knew her job. Her little sisters always had coming-of-age questions for her. She wasn't sure if she answered them to their satisfaction, but usually, they would skip away, seemingly gratified.

"How did you know Aaron was the one for you?"

"Aaron didn't have any competition." Betsey couldn't help but smile at the statement.

Caroline's shoulders drooped. "Betsey! That doesn't help."

"Sorry." Betsey shifted Julia in her arms. "It's true. I didn't have to make a choice. Aaron was and will always be the only one for me."

"Okay. Let's try this. What if someone else had come along right before you married Aaron? Someone so very nice, handsome, and hard-working..."

"I think you've answered your question."

Caroline stopped walking, raising her hands in question. "How?"

Betsey stopped and turned to her sister. "Caroline, listen. If Horace is turning your thoughts away from how you feel about Billie, then that's your answer."

Caroline lowered her head as if she didn't want Betsey to know her true feelings.

"You have to be honest, Caroline. To your thoughts, to Billie, to yourself." Betsey turned and continued up the hill. "This sleeping baby is heavy, Caroline. We have to keep walking."

Caroline rushed after her. "But Betsey, how in the world am I supposed to tell Billie? He came all this way for nothing."

"Nothing? What if God has bigger or better plans for him instead of marrying you?"

Caroline stopped again. "What?"

Betsey's arms began to ache and she motioned for Caroline to keep walking. "Caroline. What if God has different plans for you? And Billie?"

"I never thought about that." Caroline rushed to keep up.

"Sometimes, our best dreams aren't God's plans. Not sometimes, but more often than we'd want to believe. I would have never imagined Aaron and I being here in this new part of the country just two years ago. And now look—I'm having another baby within a year. And to top it all off, I walked from Ambrose's house today, and I wasn't afraid that an Indian would cross my path. I was almost disappointed that I didn't see one. What all of this means is—we often find ourselves on journeys that only God could create.

"Think of men in the Bible like Joseph, David—even Mary, the mother of Jesus. I'm sure Mary never planned to become pregnant without a husband. Joseph never planned to be thrown in prison after denying Potipher's wife's seductive attempts. Think of their thoughts. We can read the end of their stories and see what God was doing in their lives. We don't know the end of our stories. Why did he allow Horace to come into your life right before Billie arrived?"

Caroline gave her a skeptical look. "I don't know."

"Because if he would have come after Billie, would you have paid him any attention?"

Caroline moaned.

Betsey stopped now. Caroline's head was down and nearly bumped right into her but stopped short.

"Caroline. If God wants Horace in your life as more than just a friend, perhaps He is showing you that. And if Billie is to marry someone else, that will be okay. How do you feel about that?"

"Oh, I don't know." Tears sprung to Caroline's eyes. "I just don't know." All of a sudden, Caroline looked past her and pointed to something. With trepidation in her voice, she whispered. "Betsey, look."

As Betsey turned to see what Caroline was pointing at, she glanced toward the woods behind her cabin.

An Indian man, on a horse, was pulling a travois toward them. Caroline remembered him as the Indian who had released Alexander from the curse. On the travois laid a body.

Caroline and Betsey stood still, but neither could deny the delicate body outline on the makeshift traveling bed. The white moccasins and beaded skirt—it had to be only one person.

Betsey murmured, "Waussinoodae."

CHAPTER TWENTY-ONE

Betsey handed Julia off to Caroline and headed toward the Indian on the horse. He shouted out something to Betsey. As she neared the horse, the man shouted it again, *"Noogise!"* This time he held up his hand.

Betsey stopped.

"Innapine." The Indian got off his horse and motioned to the person on the travois.

As Betsey hedged closer, he shouted again, *"Noogise!"*

Betsey shook her head. "I'm sorry, I don't understand."

The man put his finger into his throat and made a guttural sound. *"Innapine,"* and then pointed to the body wrapped tight on a sled made of two poles connected by a frame and pulled by the Indian's horse.

Betsey kneeled beside the travois. Waussinoodae appeared very ill. Betsey whispered a quick prayer that somehow she'd understand what the Indian needed.

"Innapine."

The Indian stared. His black eyes were expressionless, yet he appeared frightened.

Waussinoodae didn't move. She was wrapped tightly but appeared asleep, her face gaunt with black circles shadowing her eyes. "Sick. Is she sick?"

The Indian's eyes lit up.

"Okay." Betsey could hear Caroline approach from behind her. She turned quickly. "Caroline, don't bring Julia close. Take her into the cabin."

Caroline didn't ask questions but carried the now-whimpering baby into Betsey's cabin.

"How can I help you?"

The Indian spoke again. *"Wiidookaw."*

"I'm sorry, I don't understand."

Another man approached from out of the woods. Betsey stood. She recognized him. It wasn't Nibi, Ambrose's friend. Soon a dog appeared beside the tall man. Instantly, Betsey knew who he was. Her heart pounded, and she clutched a fist to her chest. He was the Indian who'd stopped them on the trail last year while traveling to their new home. He pointed to Waussinoodae and spewed off commands.

The Indian beside the travois got down on one knee.

Betsey didn't know what to do, but as the large man approached her, she took two steps toward her home. The dog began to bark until the Indian shouted at him. The dog whimpered but sat down and stopped barking.

Betsey didn't know if she should run to the cabin or stand her ground. She stiffened as a new fear crept into her heart, and despite the heat, it caused her to shiver. She stepped back farther. If it weren't Waussinoodae on the travois, she would have run for her home.

"I don't know what you need from me." Betsey motioned toward the cabin. "I have a baby. I don't want her to get sick, too."

The tall Indian again shouted out what seemed like commands. Betsey wished Whitmore was here. He'd know what they needed. They didn't appear to be trying to harm Betsey or the family, but they wanted something from her. She put her finger to her mouth. "Do you need medicine?"

The Indian, still kneeling, looked up. Betsey wished Alexander was there to help her understand.

"I don't have medicine here, but my ma has something that might help." Betsey pointed down the path. Out of the corner of her eye, she saw Caroline creep out of the cabin and dash down the more direct route to home.

"Baker cabin. Down this way." Betsey motioned for them to head down the path.

The Indian on the ground took one leap onto his horse. Using his heels, he kicked the horse's sides as the travois swayed down the path where Caroline and she had just walked. Betsey bowed her head to the large Indian who shouted a command to the dog. They made their way down the path to her parents' cabin. As she watched them, she prayed Caroline would get there in time to warn her parents regarding the approaching need.

Betsey rushed inside to find Julia on a blanket in the middle of the floor. Blankets surrounded her on each side. Blowing bubbles, she produced a drooling grin when she saw Betsey.

Her legs felt unstable. Creeping to the nearest chair, she sat down to slow her breathing. Gripping the table's edge, she shivered. It wasn't long before her fear gave way to concern for her Indian friend. She quickly said a prayer for Waussinoodae and her parents.

Caroline was out of breath by the time she made it within shouting distance of her home. Seeing Pa in the field, she screamed at him. He soon came running. Ma came outside, too.

"Indians, Ma. They're bringing Waussinoodae. I think they need medicine."

"Where are they?"

Caroline stopped running, bent over, and tried to catch her breath. "At Betsey's house." She felt her hair, now loose from its bun, flutter into her face. She tucked it behind her ears.

"Land sakes! Did you leave Betsey alone?"

"She told them to head here. It was hard to understand what they wanted." Caroline took a deep breath.

Billie approached her from behind. He'd been finally able to get outside for a walk from time to time.

Pa came around the edge of the cabin, "What's wrong?"

"Indians. They stopped at Betsey's. They need something. I took Julia into the cabin while Betsey tried to help them, but once I made sure Julia was safe, I headed down here to warn you."

Ma wrung her hands on her apron. "Hosea, you need to go. Help Betsey."

Pa headed into the cabin and came out with his rifle.

"You can't take that. They'll fight back." Ma took hold of the butt of the rifle.

"I'm just going to load it. If they need something other than help, I need it close." Pa leaned the rifle against the cabin. "You know how to use it, Caroline."

Caroline stood erect. "Yes, Pa."

"Okay then. Which way are they coming, Caroline?"

"Down the path. They have Waussinoodae on a travois. Behind a horse."

Pa headed down the path. "I'll head that direction, but you both stay here. Billie, why don't you come with me? Don't be afraid to use that rifle if you need to, Caroline." He then turned to Ma. "Start praying we know how to help."

"I wish Ambrose were here. He can often figure out the words we need to understand." Ma pulled Caroline close as Etta, Jillian, and Alexander came running up from the river.

Pa pointed to Alexander. "We have him. He'll do the translating for us."

Etta asked, "What's happening, Ma? We heard Caroline screaming." All three of the children gathered around Caroline.

"I don't know." Ma pulled the girls close but then saw Alexander with them. "Alexander, please go with Hosea. You will understand what they are saying."

Alexander's English was now almost better than his Ojibwa. "I'll go." He rushed off after Pa on the path leading to Betsey's cabin.

With Alexander's help, the Indians explained that they had run out of ways to cure their people. Some kind of illness was taking many lives. They needed some 'white man' medicine to help.

Ma did her best to care for Waussinoodae, yet the woman appeared overly weak. It seemed as if she needed water for every drop they gave her. She guzzled down what was offered. Once Ambrose came for supper, he headed south with the Indian who had pulled Waussinoodae's travois. Together, they'd try and see if Whitmore knew what to do.

Before Ambrose left, he explained that the tall Indian was the chief of the tribe who lived close. Nibi had brought him to see Ambrose before and had explained who the man was and that Waussinoodae was the chief's wife.

He stood outside as Pa gave him some food from their evening meal to eat. He ate without sharing it with the man on the horse. Alexander brought the Indian water and nodded as he spoke, seeming to obey his commands.

Pa praised the boy for being so helpful in the situation. Pa also knew, without a doubt, that the Indian now seated beside him was the same one who had stopped them on their path to the new territory and raided their wagons. Yet now, the Indians needed their help. Pa knew what the scriptures commanded when it came to taking care of our enemies.

Whitmore, Ambrose, and the Indian on the horse came back to the cabin the next day.

"It's cholera," Whitmore told Hosea. "It's affecting many in the tribes around here. I've never seen such an outbreak. I'm seeing men, women, and even a few children stop by the post. None of their medicines are working. They must think that we have a magical cure."

Whitmore went in and examined Waussinoodae. Sally was doing everything she knew to help her. She'd spent most of the night trying her best to urge Waussinoodae to drink. Quinine worked on ague; perhaps it could help with cholera, too. "Continue giving her that good water from your source, Sally. For some reason, I'm beginning to wonder if it is a waterborne illness. The Indians drink regularly from the river, and now, with all the settlers here, perhaps the water isn't as pure as it once was."

Sally continued to spoon-feed water to Waussinoodae. The patient took the water heartily and drank as much as someone would give her. The only other symptom seemed to be horrible pain. Sally gave her a bit of quinine, too.

"Thank you for helping them." Whitmore took the Indian chief away from the cabin and talked to him. The Indian nodded, and soon, with the other man who'd left with Ambrose, they headed back up the ridge toward where they'd come.

Whitmore approached Hosea. "I told the chief that Waussinoodae was in good hands. He seems satisfied that she is and has headed back to his village. He will be back, or he will send another Indian to check on her. I also told him that Sally isn't a medicine woman. She's trying hard to help Waussinoodae, but she may die anyway. This truth was good to tell the chief. He often thinks when he demands something, and if it doesn't work, he retaliates. Waussinoodae is his squaw. I made sure he knows you're doing all you can."

Hosea coughed into his fist. "Thanks for that. Sally does good work, but you're right; she's not a real doctor. We'll also pray that whatever she does will help."

Whitmore slapped Hosea on the back. "They do appreciate your help. They often don't know how to show that, but they do see your efforts as helping. If nothing else, if she lives, you will be admired by the chief, as a forever ally and not an enemy."

CHAPTER TWENTY-TWO

Billie found Caroline by the barn, sprinkling seed to the chickens. He wanted nothing more than to talk to her. Alone. As he approached her from behind, he wondered why she wasn't singing, or even humming for that matter.

Stepping closer, he watched her scatter the seeds. She did so with a force that seemed to portray a reflection of her recent demeanor. He needed to find out why she was angry and frustrated with the world.

"Caroline," he said softly, so as to not startle her.

She turned and pasted the same frozen smile she'd given him since he'd recovered from the ague.

She didn't say anything but just went back to flinging the seed.

"You better be careful. I'm afraid those chickens will have dents instead of food for their bellies." Billie stood beside the young woman he'd come all this way to see.

Caroline sighed. "I don't think I'm hurting them."

"Caroline." Billie held her hand that had been scattering seed. "We need to talk."

Caroline's chin dropped to her chest. "About?"

"About...," Billie so wanted to ask her outright what was wrong. Why did she walk around with what appeared to be a thundercloud over her head? Was he the only one seeing it? He hesitated but knew the wall between them wouldn't disappear on its own. "What's been bothering you?"

"Bothering me?" Caroline didn't look up but sifted seed through her fingers.

Billie let out a long breath. "Why do you seem so upset?"

Caroline wouldn't look at him. It was as if he wasn't standing there at all.

Billie nudged her chin up, so she had to look at him. "Caroline. Are you mad that I have come?"

Caroline shook her head, but tears began to form.

Billie dropped his hold on her chin, and she again looked away. "Have I done somethin' to hurt your feelings?"

Again, she shook her head.

Billie raised his hands in surrender. "I'm tryin' to get well enough to start working. If that's what you're worried about. That ague, though, put me way behind. I had it all planned. As soon as I arrived, I wanted to get with your pa and find out where I could work and earn me some money. I've been talking to Ambrose and Aaron. They said I could help your pa with his plans for the sawmill. Did you know that?"

Caroline went back to throwing seeds.

"I figure...as soon as I have enough money to build us a cabin, we can start to plan our wedding. It might take a few months, or even into next year, but hopefully, by then, I'll have enough to get our cabin built. I'm sure Ambrose and Aaron will help, too."

Caroline looked up. A smile crept over her face. It seemed genuine this time. "That sounds fine, Billie."

Despite the smile, the tone in her voice seemed as if she said it with reservation. Hesitation. But Billie continued, "We'll make it here, I know it. I'm glad I came. It's a beautiful place to start our lives together."

Caroline acted like she was going to say something but then stopped herself.

Billie wanted to take her into his arms and kiss her to seal the deal, but for some reason, it just didn't feel right. "Okay." He walked away from her, fairly certain that whatever was bothering Caroline—it appeared not to be something that would halt their plans to be married.

Caroline walked to Betsey's house that afternoon to give her a report on Waussinoodae and her condition. Ma had advised Betsey not to visit while the Indian woman was there and ill. Betsey needed to protect Julia as well as her unborn child, yet she'd asked Ma to report to her often on her friend's condition.

When Ma asked Jillian to head to Betsey's to give her a report, Caroline had stepped up to do it. She needed to walk but also to talk to Betsey.

The heat from the past two months gave way to a cool breeze that morning. It was just a week away from September. Soon the weather would turn cooler, and another long winter would be ahead. It felt good for Caroline to get away to think. Billie's plans to build them a house had come as a surprise. How could she thwart him?

She still needed to tell Billie her thoughts. Horace hadn't been around since she'd told him Billie's intentions. While he stayed away, Caroline began to miss him. Knowing what she needed to do, she couldn't seem to build up enough courage to tell him how she was feeling. Especially her doubts. It didn't seem fair to say she was questioning their future.

What would Billie do when he found out he'd come all this way for nothing? Would he leave her? The territory?

As she approached Betsey's place, she could hear Julia fussing. She hurried a bit faster to see what was wrong with her niece.

Betsey came out of the cabin and nearly threw a bucket of dirty water onto her. Caroline stepped back and yelled, "Betsey! Don't!"

Betsey caught the bucket's motion, just in time. "Oh, Caroline! You startled me." Both girls burst into laughter.

"That would have been awful, but I guess maybe I deserve a bucket of dirty water thrown on me."

"What are you doing up here? Doesn't Ma have you making jam or some other chore today?" Betsey took the bucket out away from the house and tossed the water there.

"Ma wanted me to come and let you know that Waussinoodae seems to be doing better. The more water Ma gives her, the better she is beginning to feel."

Betsey rubbed her forehead with the back of her hand, pushing loose tendrils of hair away from her face. "That is good news."

Caroline pushed Betsey's cabin door. "What's wrong with Julia?" The baby sounded like she was working up to a good cry.

"I had to clean the floor, and she wanted nothing else but my full attention."

Caroline caught sight of her niece, who was trying hard to maneuver herself over the stack of blankets Betsey had piled around her. Her chubby hands came above the piles, and soon Caroline could see her sad eyes peering over the edge to find Betsey. When she caught sight of Caroline, the tears diminished, and she squealed in excitement. Caroline picked her up. The baby put both hands on Caroline's cheeks and mouthed her cheek with a baby kiss.

"Aww, Julia. Are you happy to see me?"

"You little stinker." Betsey placed the empty bucket near the door and put her hands on her hips. "I knew those tears were just to garner sympathy."

The baby laughed as Caroline kissed her cheek. "She just missed me, didn't you?"

"Has Ma continued to give Waussinoodae the quinine?"

Caroline danced around with her niece. Giggles from the child filled the air. "I think she's still giving it to her, especially at night. I've been so busy, I don't know for sure."

Betsey began pushing her furniture back into its original places on the damp floor. "I wish I could come down and help you."

"I don't think Ma will let you."

Betsey brought two of her chairs to the table. "I know, but I feel awful helpless here."

"I'll bring you some berries. You can make jam instead of me."

"I will help if you need me to."

Caroline twirled again with the baby in her arms. Julia's baby giggles helped to ease her mind. "Billie and I talked this morning."

Betsey stopped her work. "You did. What did you tell him?"

"Not much."

Betsey pointed to a chair. "Not much. Did you tell him you are in love with Horace?"

Caroline sat down. She placed Julia's hands on the table, then mimicked how to hit the table with her own hands to make a noise. Julia patted the table, too. "Billie said he'll plan to work with Pa at the sawmill, and as soon as he has enough money, he'll start building us a home."

Betsey pulled out a chair and sat. "Caroline! You didn't tell him the truth?"

"How could I? I don't even know the truth myself."

Betsey leaned into the table. "Of course you do."

Caroline shot a glare at her sister, "Maybe I do. Besides," Caroline patted the table again for Julia to mimic, "I think it's better this way."

Betsey shook her head. "The truth is always better. You're too afraid to tell him. That will only lead to more heartache. Billie deserves better, Caroline."

Caroline grew quiet. She knew her sister was right. She always was. "I can't believe that I would ever find a husband here in the new territory, and now look, I have two wonderful choices." She sighed. "I'll tell him."

"When?"

"Soon." Caroline stood and placed Julia in her sister's arms. "I better be getting back. Ma will need me."

That night as Caroline lay in front of the hearth, she prayed about her next step. She needed to open up to Billie and tell him the truth. A wolf howl pierced the air. They'd been having all kinds of trouble keeping the chickens safe each night. They found two dead over the past two weeks; come morning, all they found were feathers.

She wondered if Pa heard the commotion out by the barn. As soon as she sat up, another howl pierced the silent room. Pa stirred in his bed.

She whispered toward her parents' bed, "Pa? Did you hear that?"

She saw Pa get up from his bed and pull on his pants. "I got it, Carrie girl. Go back to sleep."

"I'm awake. I can go if you want."

Pa reached up for the rifle above the fireplace. "I'll take care of it. I hope I can get out there before they rob another one of your chickens."

Caroline lay back down. "I hope so, too."

Another howl caused her to flinch, despite her knowing that Pa could handle a wolf disturbing their flock. Pa loaded his rifle and headed out into the darkness.

A cool breeze drifted across the floor as the door opened and closed. Perhaps they could expect rain today. It had been over a week since the last shower.

She held her breath for a moment to see if she could hear Pa shoot. Sure enough, within just a few minutes, a shot interrupted the quiet night. Within seconds, another shot followed the last. Caroline sat up. Two shots was unusual. Typically, it took only one shot to send the menacing animals back into the wilds.

She listened for Pa's footsteps outside the cabin. Soon he opened the door and rushed inside.

"Did you shoot one, Pa?"

"Sure did. Kinda spooked me a bit." Pa placed the rifle on the kitchen table and went for the ammunition box left on the mantle. "I'll load the gun. Might not be the last howl we hear tonight.

Those beasts were causing quite the commotion among the flock. They seemed more than just agitated tonight."

"Did the wolves kill any chickens?"

"No. The hens had hurried into the hen house before I even came upon them, but they were still a squawkin' inside the house. Somethin' was riling them up good."

Caroline lay down. "Are you sure it was just wolves?"

Pa placed the loaded rifle on the studs above the mantle. "What else could it have been?"

CHAPTER TWENTY-THREE

Jillian's screams interrupted breakfast. Her voice echoed in the still morning air and grew louder as she approached the cabin. Hosea was trying to finish up the eggs on his plate. He stood to go out to see what could be the matter with his youngest daughter, who'd gone outside to fetch the morning eggs.

As he came around the front of the cabin, Jillian plowed into him at breakneck speed. He took her by the arms. "Jillian! For goodness sake, what's the problem?"

"Pa! You gotta come see." Jillian grabbed his hand and began pulling him toward the barn. "You killed a dog!"

"I did what?" Hosea followed Jillian to the coop.

As they approached the hen house, Hosea stopped dead in his tracks. Right outside the fence was a dog. Hosea knew he must have shot it the night before, for the wound on his side had fresh blood.

"Isn't that the Indian chief's dog?" Jillian pulled Hosea closer, and as they stared down at the animal, Hosea knew Jillian was right. It was the chief's dog. The only tame animal they'd seen since coming into the territory.

Caroline and Etta must have followed them outside, for soon, they all stood around staring at the dead animal.

Etta began to cry as she knelt and patted the hindquarters of the pet. "Pa, what have you done?"

Hosea didn't know what to say, but he knew, without a doubt, this wouldn't go over well with their Indian friends. And of all the animals in these parts, why did he have to kill the chief's companion?

Sally saw the faces of her daughters as they entered the cabin. She knew by their expressions, something was wrong. No one said a word to her but went back to finishing up their morning meal.

Hosea gave her an eye that meant "we need to talk." He motioned for her to follow him outside.

Sally followed. Once outdoors, she couldn't contain her curiosity. "Hosea, for land's sake, what's the matter?"

Hosea closed the door as gently as he could, pushed back his hair, and took a deep breath. "There's something dead out back."

"A wolf, I hope." Sally crossed her arms.

"No. It's the chief's dog."

Sally's arms dropped to her sides. "What dog?"

"I've seen him. Always by the chief's side. You know which one I mean!"

"Don't get riled up. Perhaps it's just a stray. A different dog."

Hosea shook his head. "Nope. It's the one. That's why I brought you out here to tell you. Haven't seen any other pet dog in these parts, have you?" Hosea pointed back toward the door of their cabin. "I don't want Waussinoodae to hear. She's probably as fond of it as the chief!" Hosea began to pace in front of the cabin. "What in the world am I gonna do?"

Sally stopped her husband's pacing. "Now listen. It was an accident. You were protecting the chickens. You just need to tell him the truth."

Hosea raised his hands as if in surrender. "How do you know that an Indian is going to believe the truth?"

Sally crossed her arms again, "We don't. But he knows we mean no harm. Look!" Sally pointed to the door. "We're nursing his wife back to health. Surely, he'll believe you."

"We need Whitmore." Hosea continued pacing. "That's all I know to do. I need to move the carcass into the barn until we can get Whitmore here to help us. Or fetch Alexander. We can't communicate well with an Indian, especially a possible angry one."

Pa sent Billie to Ambrose's house, where Alexander had spent the night, to let him know the news. He was to send Ambrose to Whitmore and bring Alexander back to the cabin. At least there would be one person on the Baker property who could communicate with the chief if he were to show up looking for his dog.

Billie left the barn on Ambrose's horse at a swift gallop. There was no time to waste.

Caroline had never seen Pa so agitated. He couldn't concentrate on any of his chores for very long. He went from one job to the next, keeping an eye to the edge of the woods for any sign of the Indian chief.

Caroline wondered how long it would take for the chief to notice his dog was missing. Indians didn't prize their animals as trusted pets, but they'd rarely saw the chief without the brown-and-white dog by his side. Surely, he would notice it wasn't there.

It was hard for Caroline to see her pa so nervous. What would happen? Surely after telling the chief about the incident, he'd understand.

Soon Caroline could hear a horse galloping onto the property from the direction of Ambrose's cabin. It was Ambrose, not Billie. The horse skidded to a stop.

"Pa. What happened?" Pa took Ambrose by the shoulder and directed him toward the barn.

Caroline could see her pa's animated conversation as they approached the building where they'd hidden the dog. Her brother and Pa stood outside, probably discussing what their next move should be. She edged as close as she could without drawing attention to herself.

"...I didn't see it. I was too busy trying to get a good aim on a wolf, not a dog. It was too dark," Pa said, with a shaky voice. He reached up now and pulled on his beard.

"I'm sure he'll understand. But—I've never had this kind of encounter with an Indian. Perhaps he'll retaliate before thinking clearly."

"Dear God. I hope not." Pa pulled off his hat and scratched his head. "'Who can understand his errors? Cleanse Thou me from secret faults.'"

"Pa, I don't think quoting scripture will help here."

"Just trying to calm my racing heart. It's always worked for me." Pa slapped Ambrose on the back. "C'mon. Let's eat some lunch. For some reason, I'm starving."

"There you go. It might be a while before the chief notices his dog is missing."

Pa shook his head, "I doubt it. The only thing we got going for us is his wife. I hope Sally's prayers and her doctorin' do the trick to make her well. I don't want to think about what will happen to us if I've killed his dog and his wife doesn't survive either."

Each member of the family kept checking the edge of the woods as they worked throughout the day. Ma, the girls, and now

Alexander were told to warn Pa or Ambrose if they saw movement or Indians come onto the property.

Aaron had arrived from Ambrose's house and immediately proceeded up the ridge to check on Betsey. He didn't believe the Indian would retaliate, but it was better to stick close to home until Whitmore arrived and gave them plausible suggestions on what to do.

As he sat down to eat his lunch, he acknowledged Betsey's concerns. "We need law enforcement. And soon. The territory is filling up fast with newcomers. So far, each of our neighbors has been friendly, but all it will take is one incident to trigger either a disagreement or an incident that the settlers won't solve peaceably. It's just a matter of time before someone breaks the law."

"Are you saying that Pa broke the law by shooting the Indian's dog?" Betsey placed a plate of food in front of her husband.

"Not at all. I'm just saying. I'm getting tired of building homes. You know what I'm meant to do here, Betsey. I need to figure out how best to fulfill my life's ambition. I've been ready since we arrived to establish law and order here."

Betsey sat down and they thanked God for their food. She heard little of the prayer, and as soon as Aaron said amen, her questions poured out like water from the spring. "What can you do? What would law enforcement do in a case such as this?"

"We need to use good and fair judgment on garnering the truth. That's the object of the law. Find out who is breaking the law or find out who might break it in upholding their own rule of law instead of having a fair trial."

"But this wasn't Pa's fault. He's gone outside thousands of times to check on the chickens. It could have been Caroline who'd shot the dog."

"I agree. But perhaps the Indians won't care about all that. They might retaliate, no matter what."

Betsey leaned her elbows on the table, cupping her chin with her left hand. "Poor Pa. This is quite the fix he's gotten himself into."

"We all know he didn't do anything on purpose, but as the territory fills up, there will be even more instances like this. I need to give my credentials to Whitmore and see if I need to step up to uphold the law."

"Perhaps you should. Maybe when Waussinoodae starts to feel better she can be a witness to how good Ma and Pa have been to her."

CHAPTER TWENTY-FOUR

Sally brushed the cool towel over Waussinoodae's hot forehead. The fever had come back like a sudden thunderstorm on an otherwise calm day. The Indian woman moaned as her limbs hung limply beside her emaciated body.

"Is she worse?" Hosea came up from behind her.

"Yes. I believe her fever is high."

Hosea placed his hand on Sally's shoulder, motioning for her to talk away from Waussinoodae's hearing, moving her closer to the door. "This isn't good. Now that I'm guilty of killing the man's dog, we can't possibly allow his wife to die, too."

"Hosea." Sally whispered, "You're as innocent of killing that dog as much as not guilty of this woman dying in our home. You know that." Sally returned to the bedside, but kept her voice low. Hosea followed her.

"Perhaps, but you and the girls should head to Ambrose's house to live for a bit. Until all this blows over."

Sally turned back after dipping her cloth in the nearby bowl of cool water, "I'm not going anywhere. This woman needs me, and she shouldn't be moved."

"Let's at least send the girls to Betsey's. I fear for their safety."

Sally wiped the woman's brow. "God will protect us just as He has over the past year and a half. You know that. And I'll do my best to get Waussinoodae through this. When Whitmore gets here, he'll know how to communicate with the Indians."

"I can speak for you." Hosea and Sally turned to find Alexander standing at the foot of his Indian mother's bed. "This used to be my *omaamaamimaa*. That means my mother. I can tell the Chief you are not a bad man."

By the surprised look on Hosea's face, he hadn't realized the boy had followed him to the woman's bedside.

"Is she still very sick?" Alexander asked Sally.

Sally didn't try to hide her concern from Alexander. "Yes. She's fighting hard, but it might beat her yet."

Alexander approached his Indian mother's side and took her hand. "She was good to me. She..." There were moments when Alexander had a hard time coming up with the right English word for what he wanted to say. It appeared to be the case now. "—kept watch over me. Always."

Sally smiled at the young boy and patted his hand. "I'm sure she protected you, Alexander. I would even think that, in the beginning, she might have been the one to save you when you were a tiny baby and alone."

"Please help her, Ma."

"I'm trying, honey. I really am."

Alexander's eyes welled up with tears. "I will speak for you, Pa. I will tell them it was not an act you wanted to do. That you thought Maemaeketchewunk's dog was a wolf."

"Thank you, son. But I don't know that an angry man will listen to a young lad like you." Hosea went to stand by Alexander. He ruffled his hair, pulling him into a sideways hug.

"I don't know. I will try." Alexander spoke to Hosea without taking his eyes off Waussinoodae. "I want her to become well. I love her. She was a good mother."

Hosea pulled his son closer to his side. "We're doing all we can."

Hosea kept his eye to the south of the property for any sight of Whitmore. As darkness approached, he knew there must be some reason why Billie hadn't returned with the fur trader. Ambrose stood guard for any sign of the Indians coming from the north. Tall, elongated tree shadows began to cover the property as night descended.

Hosea went to check on Ambrose. They'd sent Caroline, Jillian, and Etta to Betsey's cabin. He'd suggested to Aaron to stay close and guard them. Aaron had wholeheartedly agreed. "See anyone?"

Ambrose shook his head and leaned his rifle against the cabin wall. "Nothing. Any sign of Whitmore?"

Hosea removed his hat and scratched his head. "Nope."

"I doubt that they will come looking for a pup. What would make them even assume the dog is here?"

"Would seem odd, wouldn't it? But I gotta tell you..."

"What, Pa?"

"I don't think I'll bury the dog until I can be honest and tell them what happened. No matter what they do to me."

"Are you sure?"

Hosea nodded. "The girls are safe. I do worry about your Ma, but she insists on staying here to care for Waussinoodae."

"That has to count for something, Pa."

Hosea placed his hat back on his head. "We'd hope."

Both men stood in the silence. A brilliant sun, complete with rays of red, lit up the approaching evening sky.

"The darkness is coming faster. Hard to believe that fall is close again."

Ambrose cocked his head. "Do you hear that?"

Hosea stopped moving and looked north. "Whip-poor-will?"

"Sounds to be."

Both men stood still to listen. It wouldn't be long before all the bird sounds would grow silent as the heat of summer gave way to the chills of winter. The long slow buzzes of the locusts filled the approaching night.

Again they heard the call of a whip-poor-will.

Standing still, Hosea squinted as he scanned the edge of the woods. "I hope that's a bird making that call."

Alexander came out of the cabin, carrying two plates of food. "Sit." He motioned for the men to sit down, and then he handed them each a plate of food. "Eat."

Both men chuckled at the demands of the boy. Leaning against the cabin wall, both men shimmied down the wall to sit as Alexander placed plates into their hands.

"Sounds like a direct command from Sally's lips." Pa chuckled at the boy's recitation.

"Did you eat, Alexander?"

"Yes. I watch now."

Again the sound of the whip-poor-will pierced the darkness.

"Wait." Alexander lifted his hand for the men not to make a sound. "That's Nibi."

Hosea placed his plate beside him and stood. Ambrose followed his lead and took up his rifle.

"Are you sure, Alexander?"

The boy pointed to the field beside the house. "He's coming."

Before they could say any more, Nibi approached them from the backside of the barn. Four Indians followed him.

Hosea didn't think he was afraid until he watched the men approach them. The men's towering shadows reached the cabin before they did. Hosea could feel a trickle of sweat drip down between his shoulder blades. Ambrose didn't raise his gun, but Hosea knew he'd use it if he had to. Alexander stood right beside them until Hosea took his shoulder and tucked the boy behind him. If they didn't need him to translate, Hosea would have nudged him toward the cabin.

Nibi called out to Ambrose, "Friend, we come in peace."

Relief filled Hosea as Ambrose lowered his gun, the butt resting on the ground beside him. He didn't lean it against the cabin but held on to the barrel. "Welcome, Nibi."

Nibi held up his hand and then motioned to Alexander. "The boy now speaks."

Hosea put his hand on the boy's shoulder. "Yes."

Nibi spoke Ojibwa to the boy. Alexander answered. A terse conversation with short clipped sentences went back and forth until Alexander told Hosea, "They want to know how the chief's wife is doing."

Hosea felt his shoulders relax a bit. "She's had a rough day. Fever is high."

Alexander added, "That's what I told him."

"Tell him we're caring for her."

Alexander translated the words for Hosea.

Nibi crossed his arms and stood taller, speaking to Alexander again.

He asked Hosea, "Will she be well?"

Alexander watched Hosea shake his head. "We don't know, Nibi. Sally, my wife, is doing all she can."

Nibi motioned for Alexander to interpret what Hosea said.

"They said they would tell the chief. He is worried."

Hosea sighed. "Tell him, so are we."

Alexander repeated what Hosea said.

At that moment, the assembly of men heard a horse approaching from the south side of the property. The men all went to the front of the cabin to see who was coming in at a gallop. The horse stopped beside them. Billie slid to the ground from off the horse.

"Whitmore isn't at the post. He's been gone for a week, and they don't know when he'll return."

Decisions haunted Hosea. Should he tell the Indians what had happened? Ambrose seemed to have the same thoughts as he looked inquisitively at him.

The words of Solomon filtered through Hosea's thoughts, *Lying lips are an abomination to the Lord, but they that deal truly are His delight.* Hosea pulled Alexander closer to him. "I need you to tell Nibi what happened."

Alexander shook his head. "Are you sure, Pa?"

Hosea pointed to Nibi. "Yes. Tell him."

The Ojibwa conversation seemed to stir something in Nibi. He glanced at Hosea with questioning eyes. Hosea didn't know what else to do but nod.

Nibi came closer. "Is this truth?" He pointed to Alexander.

Hosea purposefully looked Nibi in the eyes. "Yes," he stammered. "I—I'm very sorry."

Words came from all the Indians now. Two of the men placed their hands on the tomahawks that hung from their breeches. Hosea watched as Ambrose's hand went down the butt of his rifle, and his finger went into the trigger guard.

"Watch out, Hosea. I don't think they're happy about what they've just heard." Billie announced as he tied the horse's rein to a nearby stationary pole.

"It's okay." Hosea held up his hands. "I'm guilty."

Nibi shouted a few words at Alexander, who quickly turned to Hosea. "They plan to tell chief. As soon as they return to the village."

Hosea placed his hands on his hips. "I reckon they will. Tell them I understand. I will face whatever retribution the chief deems fair."

Alexander said a few more words as the Indians backed away and then dashed into the dark woods.

"What will they do to Pa?" Jillian glanced up from her sewing to ask Betsey.

"I don't know. It is...just an animal, and above all, Pa didn't mean to shoot it." Betsey stopped her stitching to look at her youngest sister. "I'm sure it will be fine. You're safe here with us."

"They know where we all live, Betsey. If the chief gets mad enough, he could wipe us all out." Caroline never was one to hold back her opinion.

"I'm here, girls. I won't leave you until this is all settled." Aaron's presence had added a bit of bravery to Betsey's heart. She acknowledged his attempt to calm her sisters.

"I wonder how Waussinoodae is today." Etta put down the book she was reading.

"Your ma is working tirelessly." Betsey gazed down at the tiny hem she was making on a new baby nappy. She would need more of them once the addition to the family arrived in December. Julia would still need them.

Aaron chopped kindling pieces off a hunk of wood beside the fire. "Whitmore says the disease running through the Indian villages is bad. Many have died."

"Why is that?" Caroline shifted in her chair. Betsey knew Caroline was having a hard time staying inside all day. Autumn was just a week away, and much of the garden tools from summer needed put up and stored for winter. They'd tried hard to keep everyone as close to the cabin as they could for safety's sake.

"I believe it has something to do with the outsiders coming into the territory." Aaron carried the pieces of kindling to the pile just outside the door.

A cool breeze drifted in through the open door. "So, we're bringing the diseases to the Indians." Jillian pulled her leg up and under her.

"Possibly. The Indians aren't accustomed to the same diseases we are. We've had many diseases as children. It seems that we can fight off more of them than the Indians can. Just as new settlers brought us new diseases when they arrived from Europe, we're doing the same thing to the Indians now." Betsey put in two more stitches.

"I hope Waussinoodae doesn't die." Jillian wiped a tear off her cheek. "It would make Alexander very sad."

"Pa's right. We need a doctor. And soon." Caroline used her teeth to pinch off a piece of thread from her needle.

CHAPTER TWENTY-FIVE

It had been a week since Alexander interpreted to the Indians what Pa had done to the chief's dog. Fear was still a concern but also replaced by harvests and preparations for the upcoming winter. Ma needed Betsey's younger sisters at home to help while she cared for Waussinoodae.

"I want to head to the outpost to see Whitmore today. All this upheaval with your pa and the Indians has me wondering if we need law enforcement here. I want to ask him if he'll allow me the opportunity to start being in charge of such things." Aaron took a large spoonful of the stew from the pot Betsey had just made and put it into his bowl.

"I knew this was coming." Betsey wiped her hands down the front of her apron, revealing her growing belly. This child seems much more active than Julia ever was. The kicks were growing strong as her time to give birth quickly approached.

Aaron glanced up at her. "Are you okay with my decision?"

She knew Aaron had been itching to get back into law enforcement from the moment they'd set foot on the property nearly eighteen months before. It was time. Something about Pa's situation made her believe it was probably for the best. "Yes."

"I'll head out once I finish my lunch. Should make it there and back before nightfall."

"I'll wrap you up something to eat while you're gone. I have some fresh preserves. Perhaps you could give them to John and Abigail while you are there."

Aaron took the first bite of Betsey's stew. "That's right friendly of you, Betsey. I'd be happy to." Despite how Abigail continued to treat her, she did her best to repay her accusations with as much kindness as she could muster. She remembered the verse Pa often quoted: *Therefore if thine enemy hunger, feed him; if he thirst, give him drink: for in so doing thou shalt heap coals of fire on his head.* She would obey the first part of that verse, but the second half helped encourage her willingness. But she also knew that God knew Abigail's heart, and He should be the one to judge, not her.

Whitmore was exchanging money for furs with an unfamiliar white man when Aaron approached them from the north. He waited his turn to have a word with Whitmore.

The post was busy. Indians lingered close to Whitmore's establishment more as the days grew shorter and the nights cooler. As autumn would soon usher in the snows of a Michigan winter, the natives seemed content to stay close to the trading post. Occasionally, one would look over Whitmore's shoulder to see what was being traded. Whitmore had these transactions down. He'd examine the furs for texture and holes. Often, he'd nudge another trader, visiting the post, to come to have a look at the hides, too. The larger the animal fur, the more curious the young Indian men seemed. Whitmore would shoo them away with his hand if they started to disrupt the transaction, or he'd firmly speak to them in their native tongue.

Aaron began to wonder if he could keep any semblance of order when it came to a disgruntled warrior. Perhaps Alexander could help him with some Ojibwa words. Aaron would roam the country alone to keep the peace between the settlers and the indigenous people. He might not have another officer for miles if he ever needed help. Yet, that didn't hinder Aaron from his mission on this particular day.

As Whitmore continued with the trading, Aaron decided to look around a bit to see if he could find John. They hadn't seen him nor Abigail since they'd visited them while he'd been working on Ambrose's cabin. He wondered how they were faring.

He wandered into the large building that John had helped to build for Whitmore, found the room where his brother had been staying, and knocked on the door. There was no answer. He tried again. Putting his ear to the door, he heard no one stirring inside.

After warming himself a bit by the fire and checking Whitmore's kettle for a bit of coffee, he wandered back to where Whitmore stood. He outstretched his hand to the trader. "Good afternoon, Whitmore. It looks like you've had a busy morning."

Whitmore wiped his hand down his trousers and then reached out to shake Aaron's. "Aaron. How are things at the Baker cabins? Harvest good?"

"Hosea is busy. We feel a bit more ready for the upcoming winter than last year." Aaron smiled at the trader.

"Of course, and next year will be even better. Proud to have you and your in-laws here. You've been a great and helpful addition to the territory."

Aaron fought off the jittery nerves he was feeling about approaching the supposed man-in-charge of their growing community. "I've got a proposition for you."

Whitmore crossed his arms. "Let's hear it."

"I'm not sure if you've heard, and I don't want to be out of turn to tell you..." Aaron stopped and took a deep breath. "I feel it will help you to understand the reason I traveled here today."

Aaron explained the issue Hosea was currently having with the local Indians. He said that Hosea had been honest with the chief's men. Hosea desired for the chief to understand the motivation behind the incident.

Whitmore nodded in agreement. "I've heard about this. The Chief has expressed his anger to others, and I've overheard. He has come to me with his thoughts of what he should do next. And to tell you the truth, Aaron, I'm grateful for Hosea's honesty. Honesty seems to go well with the tribe here. They feel a man's integrity is clear—by his honesty."

"Hosea wouldn't have it any other way."

"But what does this have to do with you coming all this way to speak to me today? I aim to help Hosea any way I can, but the only thing I can do is communicate with the tribe. I can't change how they'll react. It wasn't a big deal that he shot an Indian's dog, but it was Chief Maemaeketchewunk's dog which, unfortunately, makes it a bigger deal. The chief was mighty fond of that animal."

Aaron forged ahead. "It's a partial reason why I've come today. I do believe that we need some law enforcement in these here parts and soon." Aaron motioned around him. "More and more people are settling in the area each day. Once winter hits, issues may arise that will require a mediator or a negotiator. You can't be in all places at once and still keep your business running. As friendly as we believe the community now to be, at times, situations will unfold where folks will need a lawman."

Whitmore pulled at his beard. "I agree. Are you applyin' for the position?"

Aaron took a deep breath. "Yes, sir." He went on to tell Whitmore about his law enforcement experience back in Pennsylvania.

"Funny you should bring this up now. I was thinking about the same thing in the last month or two. I've been feeling mighty stretched as of late. I say you're the right man for the job." Whitmore sat down on a nearby tree stump. "No doubt about that."

Aaron breathed a sigh of relief. "I would be much obliged if you'd consider me for the job, even though in the past, no one was in a similar position. Perhaps I could help you in settlin' of the peace from time to time."

Whitmore straightened his hat. "I'd be mighty happy to have you to help out, young man. Thank you for your willingness to serve."

"I'm honored." Aaron put his hat on his head.

"Perhaps in the spring, I'll make it official with the governor of our new-and-upcoming state. What would you say to an election and have the new neighbors approve of you being in this kind of position?"

"Sounds fair."

"I'll be more than willing to put in a good word for you, but let's see..." Whitmore came closer to Aaron and put his hand on his shoulder. "There is one thing I need to tell you. It could be your first act of duty."

Aaron jutted out his chin and leaned in. "Anything."

Whitmore raised an eyebrow. "I need you to bring Hosea in. To be fair, he needs to stand before the chief. We need to settle this dispute now, for their sake, but more importantly, for everyone's safety."

Aaron stepped back. He knew Whitmore was right, but he never thought his first step toward a new career here in Michigan Territory would be to bring his father-in-law in for questioning. He reluctantly put his hat back on his head but told Whitmore, "Right away," then took two steps back and mounted his horse.

Then Aaron remembered and turned back. "Whitmore, have you seen my brother? I didn't find him or Abigail in their room."

Whitmore pointed out to the west of the post. "They've taken over the Smeed cabin, which sits a bit to the west of here. I think Mrs. Swain got a bit too tired of a hotel room." Whitmore smiled. "It was she who told me about Hosea's troubles."

As Aaron settled into his saddle for the ride home, he wondered how that woman knew everyone's business.

The only thing Aaron knew about the Smeed family was that they'd come early in the spring and soon the entire clan came down with ague. With no one to sow a crop or till the land, they barely made it through the summer. They'd built a part of a shack out west of the trading post. Aaron wasn't sure why John felt it an appropriate place to live, but he knew Abigail was unhappy where they'd lived all summer.

Coming up on the shack, Aaron yelled for his brother. He heard someone chopping wood nearby and went around the small building to find his brother seeming to take out his aggression on a stump nearby. Slivers of split wood shot out in every direction as the man's ax cut into the large stump.

"John!" he called, and his brother stopped his ax in mid-air to look up.

"Aaron. When did you get here?"

"Just now. Everything okay?"

John stumbled over his words, as if casting about to come up with an excuse for his angry chops. He turned and sat down on the stump, dropping the ax as he did. He wouldn't look up but gazed down at his boots.

"John?"

His brother didn't look up or answer.

Aaron slid off his horse to sit down near the stump. "Can I help?"

John shook his head.

"When did you move out here?"

John finally answered but didn't look at him. He picked up another small piece of wood to chop into kindling. "Last week. I thought it might be better to move Abigail. Someplace that could be ours. Out of that crazy room which kept her just going—" He stopped talking, picked his ax up, and felt the edge.

A nearby frog erupted his late afternoon announcement that the evening was drawing nigh. Aaron knew he only had a few more minutes of daylight to get back to their property. He needed to be bold. "Is it Abigail, then?"

John sighed. "There isn't anywhere here that she's happy. Everything upsets her. She wants to go back East. And now—"

More silence. Aaron remembered how his father had struggled with a cantankerous wife. He hated to think that of Abigail, but everyone around him knew the truth. Perhaps admitting it to himself would allow him to help John.

"It's a hard country here. Hard for our womenfolk. Look around. Indians, wild animals, small homes—and sickness, too. They struggle. I've watched Betsey..."

"Abigail is nothing like Betsey!" John stood up and pitched his ax hard into a log, splitting it into several pieces.

"You need to let me finish."

John sighed.

"Betsey's a strong woman. Not all women have that kind of constitution."

Putting both hands on his hips, he looked at Aaron as if he were an enemy. "Don't you think I know that, Aaron?" He laid his ax down. "I never intended us to be here this long. I never thought I'd lose all my money." John threw caution to the wind with a swat to the air. "Then getting here, I thought I could change her mind about it. Perhaps she'd change into a woman who could handle hardships better. But no, that's not my wife. Yours maybe, but not mine."

Aaron didn't know what to say. He knew his brother was fighting anger, so he remained silent.

"I don't know what to do. Look," John pointed to a nearby tree ablaze with red leaves. "It's nearly winter. This tiny, one-room cabin isn't any place to keep a woman. It's overrun by mice. Last night I saw a rat come from out from under it and scamper into the woods." John started walking around in a circle, his hand ruffling his hair. "The roof leaks. I planned to head back into civilization before the season changes, but now—she's ill. So ill, I couldn't move her if I even had the resources to do so. I came here to see you. Start a life with a new wife, and all we've had is heartache and frustrations. All I brought with me went into putting Abigail up at the hotel in Detroit. I thought she'd grow used to it. But even that's better than here."

John stopped his pacing. "What can I do? I don't believe Abigail will be happy until I give up here and head home. To New York. Back to her family. But Aaron, I don't have enough funds to do that."

Aaron shook his head. "Neither do I. If I did, I'd loan it to you."

John crossed his arms. "I know, and thanks, I appreciate the gesture."

Aaron stood, "I'll bring Betsey to help—" Before he could finish, he knew that wouldn't be possible. Betsey didn't need to be around a sick woman in her condition. "I'm sorry, John. Betsey won't be much help either, I'm afraid."

"My wife is sick, Aaron. Sicker than I've ever seen her. We need a doctor, but there isn't one."

Tears began to brim in his brother's eyes. "I want," he fought back his emotions, "to help my wife."

"I understand. Let me see if I can find someone who will come out here and help you. Claire Leach lives close. She's always willing to be of assistance. Let me talk to her tomorrow and see what she can do to help you."

Aaron went back to his horse, and John followed from behind. "I know Abigail has been unkind to you and Betsey's family. She's high-strung, frustrating at times. I know this. I apologize for her. But this! It isn't how I planned any of this to turn out. I thought we could get a fresh start here. Be closer to you and Betsey, especially after Father passed away. Now I'm just sorry we ever came here."

"Believe it or not, John, I'm not. You're right. We need family close. I'm happy you're here with me." Aaron mounted. "I'm sorry Abigail is sick, John. We'll do our best to help her—and you." Aaron turned his horse around and headed back toward home. At that moment, he remembered Betsey's preserves.

Turning his horse around, he found Abigail standing in the doorway of the decrepit home. Her nightgown draped over her gaunt figure, appearing like a ghost standing inside the entrance. Aaron pretended not to see her and scooted his horse around to the back of the cabin again.

John had commenced his wood chopping chore. He was startled to see Aaron back.

"Sorry to bother you again, but Betsey sent these preserves for you." He handed the parcel down to John, who took it reluctantly.

As Aaron again turned his horse around, he saw Abigail coming around the outside of the house, heading right toward them.

John noticed her. "Abigail, what are you doing out here?"

Aaron tipped his hat to the woman but knew it wasn't proper to stop and talk or even acknowledge she was there. He kicked the sides of his horse to spur him into a gallop. Darkness was descending fast.

Abigail took the parcel Aaron had just given him and looked inside.

"Why are you out here? In nothing but your nightgown." If John had been wearing a coat, he could have wrapped it around his wife's shoulders. But as in life, all he had to offer her was a damp, sweat-soaked shirt. He had nothing to satisfy her.

Abigail took Betsey's gift and held it close to her chest. "You're never going to admit they hate us, are you?"

John approached his wife. "Because it isn't true."

"It is true. No one here likes us. We're too refined for the likes of those who live here."

John sighed. Why did his wife refuse to be kind to Aaron's family, but especially Betsey? Even her kind gestures seemed futile. He wondered if anyone could appease his wife. He hated thinking this way, but he'd grown tired of the frustration. "Come on, Abigail. Let's get you back to bed."

CHAPTER TWENTY-SIX

The next morning, Hosea went out to see how the overnight rain had affected his progress in getting all the corn husked and ready for winter. The dampness made him believe it would take a day or two more of warm sun to dry it thoroughly. A horse came out of the trees from the south. The morning sun pointed the rider out with a light beam, reflecting the shimmer of orange leaves from a nearby tree.

He came to a stop just short of Hosea. "Good morning, sir. Lovely morning."

Hosea took off his hat and scratched his head. "Good morning. Yes, it is. Good rain last night."

The man dismounted. "That it was. My small tent didn't do much to shield me."

"Can I help you?" Hosea didn't want to appear too busy for the man, but he did realize the days were shorter than ever before, and he needed to check the corn sooner than later.

"My name is Frederick." Frederick held out his hand.

Hosea took it and smiled. "Nice to meet a new friend, Frederick. My name's Hosea."

"Well, not sure I'll be your friend for long."

Hosea was taken aback by the comment. "How so?"

"I'm here to collect taxes on your property."

Hosea scowled. "Taxes?"

"Yes, sir."

"I've just been here a year and a few months. Not heard they were collectin' taxes round these parts."

Frederick pulled out a book from his horse pack and wet the tip of his finger with his tongue. "Let's see here. Are you not Hosea Baker from Pennsylvania?"

"That's correct."

"And did you not file a claim for 600 acres here on the Shiawassee River?"

Hosea realized that if this stranger knew that much of his business, he must be genuine in his task.

"Yup. Your tax bill will be seventeen dollars and fifty cents."

Hosea couldn't help but give the man a shocked expression. He coughed. "That's a mighty high price for taxes."

"That's less than two cents an acre."

"Unless you have six-hundred acres!" Hosea shifted his hat on his head. "I have to be honest with you, Frederick. I don't have that kind of money."

"Well then. You will have a grace period to figure out how to pay the taxes. But come spring, I'll be back." Frederick licked a pencil and jotted a note in his book. "This is your notice, and I've marked it as such."

Hosea knew only to do the one thing he'd done for a dozen other newcomers. "I can offer you a nice lunch. My wife is a good cook, and we try to be hospitable to all."

Frederick smiled and tipped his hat. "Why, thank you, sir. I know I'm not always a welcome person to see, but I have a job to do for the government. I appreciate your hospitality."

Hosea headed back toward the cabin. "Let's see what Sally has prepared for lunch."

Hosea could barely swallow his lunch. The taxman had piled another enormous burden onto him, adding to his getting crops in before winter and his problems with the nearby Chippewa chief. Since arriving from Pennsylvania, Hosea felt overwhelmed.

It wasn't Frederick's fault that he was in charge of collecting the tax, but it became evident to Hosea that the community would soon need government officials. They needed to warn the incoming settlers of the cost of living in the territory. Yes, it was cheap land, but somehow he knew the government would inevitably tax the new residents for it.

"What will the government do with this here tax money they'd be collecting from us?" Hosea asked Frederick before he left his farm.

"From what I'm told, they want to start educating the settler's children. You'll need roads, not just forged trails. We have to pay the elected government officials who will govern the new land here. Just to name a few."

Hosea took his hat off and scratched his head, "I see. Much of that will be needed. Will a teacher be provided?"

Frederick mounted his horse. "Hopefully. We also want to give the Indian children schoolin' as well. They need to become adept at living as educated citizens and not the heathen we all believe them to be."

"Indians are unlearned, yes, but not heathens. They don't know our ways nor God's ways until someone shows them. Many, around these parts, have been nothing but helpers to us. Yeah, we've had our upcoming with a few, but most are just wanting to live peaceably."

Frederick took the reins of his horse and turned it. "And law enforcers to keep our properties peaceable. You understand that, too, don't you?"

"I assume so." Hosea picked up the shovel he'd dropped on the way into the house for dinner. "I'm sure we'll be able to come up with our tax money come spring. Thanks for a bit of a grace period to raise funds."

"Have a good day, sir, and thanks for the meal." Frederick headed out toward the Leach farm.

Hosea used the shovel as a cane as he headed toward his field. Looking out over his crops from their second year, he knew it would be just enough to keep them through the winter. He had no means of selling his crops just yet. The entire harvest fed his family, Betsey's, and those who came onto the property just starting a place of their own. He'd been as generous as possible. He remembered the promise of God. To sustain him, provide for him, but most importantly—to save him.

There was only one thing Hosea knew to do. He bent down on one knee and asked God for help. It wasn't his first prayer for relief, and Hosea felt confident it wouldn't be his last. What would be the next step for him to keep his family on this land? After asking God for what he needed that day, he rose and headed for the cornfield. Looking out and across the property he'd worked so hard to till, he gazed past and into the woods surrounding it. The only other crop he could produce was lumber. His beloved timber would keep him here.

Trees were shining a bright reflection of fall now. The red, orange, and yellow leaves of the season brought a different beauty to the land he now called his own. As much as he loved the majesty of their protection and shields, he knew they were the answer to his prayers.

His idea for a sawmill, only just imagined that spring as a business venture, now became a necessity to continue living at the new homestead. He needed to talk to Ambrose about the prospect and begin planning a way to make it happen.

Horace found Caroline leading the oxen out of the barn and out toward the place where the grass remained green and where the large animals could munch away their day. Horace had brought Mrs. Baker the herbs she'd asked Ambrose to find for her as she cared for Waussinoodae. Ambrose had asked Horace to bring them, so he could finish off his roof before the western winds ushered in the approaching winter. He'd agreed, only because he hadn't seen Caroline in months and was missing her. It was better to keep his distance and see her from afar. But who was he kidding? He hoped to have a chance to talk to her as well. He missed her. Horribly.

Standing at the edge of the woods, he watched her put two stakes into the ground with a post maul. She was such a small girl but with the strength of a strong young man. She seemed to fear little. It only made Horace love her more. He wanted someone with a reliable determination to live out her life with him here in the new territory. Didn't all men?

As she turned to head back to the barn, she must have seen him. She stopped, slowly raising her hand to wave. He felt embarrassed to think she was waving at someone else. He took one step and then another. Looking around, Horace didn't see anyone else.

"Hello, Horace." Caroline's face flushed a bit. Horace was pretty sure it was because of her recent chore. The September sun had returned to make it a warmer-than-usual fall day.

"Hello, Caroline."

They stood gazing at one another for a moment. Horace didn't have a clue what to say next. He waited for her to speak, but she didn't.

After what seemed like longer than a few seconds, they both talked at once.

"Horace, I—"

"How have you—"

"Oh, go ahead." Caroline stopped talking.

Now Horace couldn't remember what he was going to say.

Silence again ensued.

"Were you going to ask me something?" Caroline's look made his heart race. He took off his hat, struggling to figure out what he had wanted to ask her.

"Horace?"

"I brought these for your ma." Horace took the pouch of herbs from his pocket and handed them to her. "They're from Ambrose. He found them for her, and he's busy working today and asked me to bring them to you." Horace stammered. "Not you! But your ma." Horace shifted his weight to his other foot. "For the Indian woman."

Caroline took the pouch. "Thank you for bringing them."

Horace didn't know what else to say. He wanted to tell her how pretty she looked and ask how she had been doing. He even thought about pulling her close and kissing her again but knew he better not. The only thing he knew to do was to leave her alone. Quickly. "I guess I better get back."

Caroline stepped closer. "Won't you stay for supper? I made cornbread and bean soup. It's almost ready."

Horace backed away more. "Naw. I need to get back before dark."

Caroline continued toward him, narrowing the space between them. Horace knew if he didn't turn away now, he'd have to take her into his arms. As he turned, he came face to face with Billie.

"Caroline. Did you take those oxen into the grazing field all alone?" As Billie drew closer, the couple stepped away from each other. "Oh hey, Horace. I thought you were off helping Ambrose."

"I was," Horace stammered, "I am." He hated to think that Billie could read his thoughts. Billie was the one Caroline had chosen. Not him.

"I did take the oxen out. I've done it many times, Billie. I'll probably end up bringing them back in, as well."

Was that a bit of sarcasm in Caroline's voice?

"Your pa said that was a chore I needed to start doing. Don't you remember?"

Caroline stepped back. "I need to get back to finishing up supper. You're more than welcome to stay, Horace. We have plenty." She smiled at him, and if she would be marrying Billie, the gesture was enough to fill Horace's heart with joy. He was glad he'd approached her and not avoided her as he'd done over the past few months.

Both young men watched Caroline head back to the cabin. The only sound came from the oxen now ripping the grass from the ground and chewing it with gusto. Billie was the first to break the silence. "Well, are you going to stay or not?"

"No. I need to be back before dark. We're putting in floors soon."

"You stayin' with Ambrose?"

"Yes. I'm renting a room from him until I get a place of my own."

"Seems odd that a man your age isn't on his own yet."

Horace stood his ground. "What business of that is yours?"

"It's not. I just wondered is all."

Both men stared the other down. Horace knew he shouldn't get into an altercation with a fellow he barely knew, except Billie had something he wanted. A woman he'd do anything for, even though it was evident that Caroline had made her choice. What more could he do? He turned on his heel and walked back the way he'd come.

Caroline handed the herb pouch to her ma. Ma had been fighting to lower Waussinoodae's temperature again. The woman seemed to rally, and then, as evening approached, her fever came back with a vengeance. Caroline, Etta, and Jillian had taken over preserving the flourishing garden vegetables and hanging the herbs to dry.

"Who brought this? Is Ambrose here?" Ma asked, as she opened the pouch and smelled the contents.

"No. Horace brought them."

"Horace? We haven't seen him around here in a while."

Caroline bit her bottom lip.

"This will help with the poultice I've made for Waussinoodae. She seems to struggle so much with pain. I thought applying this on her forearms and legs would help."

"Is she worse?"

"It's how it goes with all of us. We think we're over the worst, and then the fever returns. It seems as if God uses fevers to fight disease. Yet, who knows for sure? I'm just a farmer's wife, not a doctor."

Caroline folded the cloth she'd just used to wash her hands. "I need to get supper on. Pa will be in soon."

"Caroline." Ma stepped closer. "Has Billie said anything to you about marriage yet? Have you made any plans?"

"Um..." Caroline didn't quite know how to tell her ma that she'd been avoiding being around Billie alone. He seemed much more enamored with Jillian as of late. Jillian loved the attention, flirting and giggling whenever he was near. Despite her young age,

Billie seemed to enjoy her company much more than Caroline's—as of late.

"What is it, Caroline? What are you hesitant about?"

Caroline knew she couldn't hold much back from her ma. She seemed to know her daughters better than they knew themselves.

"Be honest with me, child."

Caroline sighed. "I don't think I like Billie in a..." Caroline didn't know quite how to put it, but she forged ahead. "You know, in a romantic way. Every time I look at him, I see that young boy from ten years ago who stole my slate and helped me learn how to toss a ball like a boy. He doesn't seem to like me in the same way anymore, either."

"How so?" Ma sat down at the table and patted the place across from her.

Caroline obliged.

"I don't know. I remember every single thing we did like it was yesterday. We were always the best of friends. But that was it. I never felt—" Caroline didn't know how to tell her ma that she'd kissed Horace and felt something she'd never felt for Billie. Ever.

"Does this mean you're changing your mind about marrying Billie?"

Caroline tugged at her blouse around her neck. In the last few months, she knew she needed to separate the buttons at her neck as they'd been feeling tighter. And as she talked about Billie with her ma, they felt even more constricting. "I don't know, Ma."

"There you have it." Ma sat back in the chair and crossed her arms.

"What?" Caroline found a dried piece of dough stuck to the wood and began to dig at it with her fingernail.

"You've fallen in love with Horace, haven't you?"

"No! I mean, how could I have done that? I've waited for Billie for an entire year. I loved reading his letters and remembering all my friends from back in Meadville. It kept me abreast of all the happenings. But Ma, he would often say things about getting married and settling down when he arrived, but he doesn't seem all that interested in me anymore. He complains about how I take care of the oxen, and whenever I pick up a rifle, he seems intimidated by that. Maybe I'm imagining it all, but I don't think he likes me in a—you know—a romantic way."

Ma slapped the table. "Daughter, you do beat all. A boy comes from as far away as Pennsylvania for you, and now you're in love with someone else."

"What do you mean? I don't think I'm in love with Horace." Caroline felt her face flush.

"What happens every time you see him? Do you wish it were Billie showing you attention or Horace? And—if you're that interested in Billie, why do you keep avoiding him?"

Caroline looked at her well-worn hands. Despite her age, the summer sun and hard work had made them rough and as brown as the skin of the Indian woman lying in her bed. "Does it show that much?"

"Yes. To everyone, it seems, but Billie."

Ma scooted her chair back. "Now let's get supper on the table before your pa gets in from the garden. That bean soup smells amazing." Pushing down her apron, she turned back to Caroline. "And young lady, if you aren't interested in Billie anymore, I think you need to tell him sooner rather than later."

Caroline moaned as she lowered her forehead down and onto the table. Her life was not going how she'd imagined it would once Billie arrived. Her plans seemed to be unraveling just like a misplaced knitting stitch in a winter mitten.

CHAPTER TWENTY-SEVEN

"I have to take your pa to Whitmore!"

Betsey didn't take her eyes off her husband, who stood by the barrel of water near the front door. He took out the scoop and took a long drink.

"What did you say?"

"My first job as the county law enforcement officer. I have to take your pa to Whitmore for questioning. To be tried."

Betsey couldn't believe what she was hearing. *Why would Whitmore ask Aaron to do such a thing?* "Why you? Why can't someone else do it?"

"It's now my job. Whitmore agreed to allow me to uphold the law in our community until the community has a fair election. He's been communicating with the Indians over this whole affair with your pa. Chief Maemaeketchewunk is asking for retribution. Pa killed his dog. Despite it being an animal, he's the chief."

Betsey folded her arms over her large belly. She was pretty sure that Pa couldn't go to jail over killing an Indian's dog.

"And there's more."

"More?" Betsey let her arms fall to her side.

"Abigail's sick, Betsey. She's got the ague. John's at his wit's end about what to do for her. They're living in that ol' cabin left by the Smeed family."

"Aaron, that's not a cabin; it's a shack."

"I know. It's bad. John wanted to fix it up and make a home for Abigail, but time is running short. Winter's coming. Abigail persuaded him to move her out of the trading post, and now she's sick."

"She's not with child?"

"I don't think so. I think it's just ague, by the way he talked."

"I'll get some supplies together and get out there as soon as I can."

"I don't think that's wise. You're going to have a baby soon. I don't want you to go through what you did when Julia was born. That was brutal."

Betsey sighed. Aaron was right. She didn't want to be sick giving birth again.

"What can we do for them?"

"I'm going to go help John put up a better frame around the house. Something stronger than what's there now. Ambrose has Horace to help him." Aaron strode to the table and sat down. "John hasn't any money to return to New York. He has to stay here with Abigail, at least through the winter. If we can get their home at least somewhat stable before the winter winds hit, they should make it through. They'll need food. I'll hunt up a deer or two, and perhaps we can get it smoked for them before the first snow flies."

Betsey went to the pot over the fireplace and stirred the porridge she was preparing for their upcoming breakfasts that week. "Poor John. I know he's had such a time with Abigail since they've arrived."

"He never should have brought her here."

Julia wobbled to his side and patted his knee. "How's my little girl?" He lifted Julia and seated her on the table, with her chubby legs dangling over the edge. She patted his cheeks with her small hands and made all kinds of sounds without words. Aaron answered as if she'd said something recognizable. "Is that so?"

"But what about Pa, Aaron? What will you tell him about needing to bring him to Whitmore for questioning?"

Aaron kissed the cheek of his tiny, toddling daughter. "The only thing I can. Whitmore wants to talk to him. It's not like he's under arrest or anything. Whitmore has a very upset Indian on his hands. I think he only wants to get to the bottom of what happened." Aaron leaned back in his chair. "It's just protocol, Betsey. Your pa is innocent. We all know that, but it's better this way than to have the chief come and try to settle the matter on his own. We need to uphold the law, and it should start soon."

Julia chattered at Aaron, wanting his attention. He buried his head into her chest and let the baby pull his dark, curly hair.

Betsey loved watching Aaron and Julia interact. Aaron was a wonderful father. He'd even changed a diaper or two when Betsey suffered the worst of morning sickness, making it much harder for her to do it herself.

"Can we have more of these?"

"What do you think I'm doing?" Betsey arched her back to show off the round impression of new life around her middle.

Her husband kissed Julia's neck, making a sound that sent Julia into a fit of giggles. Each time he stopped, Julia put her neck up to him to do it again. Betsey wasn't sure who laughed more, Aaron or the toddler.

"You're probably right about the community needing law enforcement. I just hate to think that Pa has to be the first person you take in for questioning."

Julia giggled again. Betsey knew if she didn't distract the child, Aaron would have to blow slobbery kisses all day. Betsey handed Julia a hard biscuit to chew on. Aaron put Julia on the floor, and away she scampered to a spot in the corner where she loved to sit and play.

Aaron went to his wife, pulling her into his arms and patting her round belly. "Is this one a boy?"

Betsey had heard Aaron ask this question multiple times since the day she'd realized she was with child again. She gave him the same look every time. "Only God knows that, silly man." She kissed her husband, and then he buried his head in her neck and gave her the same slobbery kisses he'd been giving Julia.

"Aaron, stop it!" Betsey giggled, but pulled away. "I'm not as big of a fan of that kind of kiss as your daughter seems to be." She used her apron to wipe off the spit he'd left behind. "Stop being so silly."

Aaron laughed, then turned to leave. "I'll go ask Claire if she can call on Abigail, then go talk to your pa. I'll try to be back by supper."

Caroline could hear Pa yell from outside. Ma touched her sleeve. "Better go see what's up, Caroline."

They'd been rolling out dough for a pie. Caroline wiped her flour covered hands down her apron and headed for the door. When she turned the corner at the front of the cabin, she saw Pa struggling to pull out a stump. Alexander was straining at pulling on the rope with him.

Pa called out again, "Caroline. Please help. Bring Etta, too."

Caroline hung her apron on a hook close by the back door lean-to. She hustled to Pa and Alexander, kicking up her skirts as she ran. As soon as she was close enough, she called out to her pa, "Etta is down by the river washin' up some bedding. I'll have to be your help." She hurried to grab the rope behind Alexander.

"Where are the other men I feed around here?"

"Billie has gone to help Ambrose this afternoon."

"What about Horace?"

"They're all with Ambrose."

Pa spit. "Well then, young'un. It's up to us."

Alexander was growing stronger, but as soon as Caroline took hold of the rope, the branches began to rip free at the tree's base.

"Good job, Carrie. That's my girl!" Pa shouted as he continued to dig and then pull on another rope, from a different angle, close by. "Try again. One more time."

As soon as they had it almost clear of the hole, Billie rode up on his horse. "Hold on, let me help." He took the rope from Caroline and continued the strong pull. More roots ripped out of the ground.

Caroline went to latch on to Pa's rope, and soon the roots were free and the stump removed from the hard soil around it. Caroline stood back, wiped off her forehead with her sleeve, then brushed her hands together to remove the dirt. Both hands tingled from the rope's roughness. No wonder her hands didn't have a lady-like look. "That one was a tough one, Pa."

"That it was, Carrie. That it was." Pa turned his head and spit. "Only four more to go!"

The group laughed.

"I can help you now, Hosea. Caroline or the girls don't have to be out here helping us."

Caroline put her hands on her hips. "We were doing just fine before you showed up." As the words slipped from her tongue, Caroline knew it had probably have been better not to say anything and slink back inside. But she was starting to get more irritated by how Billie wanted her in the kitchen and not anyplace else. Nothing brought her more joy than helping Pa with the farming chores.

She'd been doing it in Pennsylvania and also much more here, on their new property. Caroline never shrunk from getting her hands dirty. If she were going to be Billie's wife soon, did he expect her only in the kitchen doing household chores?

Billie's face revealed what he thought of her outburst.

"It's okay, Billie. Carrie is a big help to me around the farm. If it wasn't for her, there are many things that I would have to do all by myself or with just Alexander's help. Soon he'll be a strapping young man to help me, but right now, the girls are about all I have. I don't know what I'd do without their help."

Billie backed off, taking off his hat. "I'm sorry, sir. Caroline is a young woman, and I want to give her the respect due to a fine lady."

"Well, that's mighty honorable of you. I expect all my girlfolk to receive such courtesy, but I appreciate her out here helping me turn out a stump, rather than in the kitchen turning out a fine loaf of bread. Out here," Pa took off his hat and circled it above his head, "I need all the help I can get." And at that, Pa picked up the ax and began chopping the stump roots into fine slivers of wood.

"I need to get back to my bakin'." Caroline turned to head back to her housework.

"Thanks for your help, Carrie girl," Pa shouted out as he lifted the ax in the air to come down again.

"Sure, Pa." As she stepped away, she didn't give Billie another glance.

Hosea seemed to be finishing up cleaning an area around a recent stump removal when Aaron rode up in his wagon. Pulling back on the reigns, he set the brake and jumped off to greet Hosea.

"Hosea, how's the stump-removing business going?"

Both men laughed. Hosea leaned on the butt of the ax. "Mighty hard work, it surely is."

Aaron removed his hat. "Yes, sir, I believe you."

"What are you doing out and about today?"

"Just came from Leach's house. I had to ask Claire if she would get over to check on Abigail. Abigail has the ague."

Hosea shook his head. "Hits us all, one time or another. It seems to lessen after we get a good frost. Thankfully fall is on its way."

Aaron shaped his hat, turning it from one side to the other to turn up the brim better. "I didn't want Betsey going over there and getting it again. Not this close to giving birth."

Hosea took off his hat and scratched his head. "That's for sure. She had it bad enough last time."

"Claire is also much closer to John and Abigail's place."

"They are?"

"John's moved them to the old Smeed place."

"That place is a shack."

Aaron put his now shapely hat back on his head. "Your daughter said the same thing. It is a run-down place to live. John felt it best to get Abigail into a new place, instead of just a room at Whitmore's post."

"Well, I can understand that, but the Smeed place needs lots of work, and with winter comin'..."

Aaron held up a hand, "That's exactly what I told John. He agreed. He thought he could get it fixed up proper before winter, but now that Abigail is sick, he hasn't had much time to get anything done. And just between you and me, I think they are running out of funds."

"We'll have to help 'em out."

"Thank you. Everyone has been kind to my brother and Abigail since they arrived. Sometimes I wonder..."

"That's what we do here. Neighbor helpin' neighbor. None of us can do it all alone out here."

Aaron hesitated, not wanting to even tell Hosea how he believed his brother had been wrong to bring Abigail here. Aaron took a deep breath. "Hosea. Yesterday I went to Whitmore and asked him if I could become a law enforcement officer here."

"What'd he say? Not sure he has that kind of authority to give you the go-ahead or not."

"That's what he said." Aaron propped his foot on the leftover stump from the tree. "But he did say that if I wanted to give it a try, I could. Until a larger community council is formed and a vote cast."

Hosea nodded. "Sound advice."

"But there's something I need to talk to you about."

Hosea stopped surveying his work to look at Aaron. "What's that?"

"You see—" Aaron hesitated.

Hosea tilted his head to one side. "What is it?"

"I have to bring a resident in for questioning."

"Well, there you go. Best get to it!"

"It's you, Hosea. Whitmore wants to question you."

Hosea stood erect and stepped back. "What?"

Aaron held up his hands. "Hear me out. As you know, the dog you killed belongs to Chief Maemaeketchewunk, it's Waussinoodae's husband."

"I know all of that. Did you tell Whitmore what happened?"

"I didn't have a chance. It isn't like I'm taking you into custody or anything like that, but he wants to question you. If he doesn't, there could be bigger problems if the chief takes it into his own hands. I guess his dog was quite special to him."

Hosea sighed. "I'm mighty busy, Aaron. With winter comin'. I got crops to get in. I was just going to head out and get some hunting and fishing in before the winter snows come."

"It's not like you're going to have to stay at the post—nothing like that. We just need to diffuse this situation with the Indians. Before it gets out of control."

Hosea seemed to understand the situation. Aaron was sure that not having a choice about heading to the post probably didn't sit well with his father-in-law.

"Aaron. This whole thing doesn't have to do with what happened last year. With Betsey and all. Leaving her and the womenfolk alone to go purchase the land."

Aaron couldn't believe what Hosea was insinuating. "Hosea, don't misunderstand me. You're the last person I want to haul in, but you and I both know that we might have an even bigger problem on our hands if this situation doesn't get resolved. You're out here with lots of women. I'd hate to think some of the Indians would take out what you accidentally did on any of them, would you?"

"No, sir. No way. I wouldn't want that to happen."

"So let's get it resolved in a civilized manner. Where everyone, even you," Aaron pointed at Hosea's chest, "are safe and not put in a harmful situation."

Hosea knew Aaron was right, and he hoped the confrontation didn't put a wedge between them. Hosea almost wished that it had been Whitmore to tell him himself. He'd thought Aaron had forgiven him, but there had always been a bit of turmoil between the two men after he'd returned last August.

"When should I go in?"

"That's the thing. I don't plan to haul you in like a prisoner. But I think you need to make the trip soon."

Hosea agreed. "Let's go tomorrow."

Caroline couldn't get over the comments made by Billie that afternoon. What kind of marriage would they have if he was always questioning her ability to help? She loved helping her pa. She loved bringing in the oxen before dark and securing them in the barn. Sure, it wasn't precisely lady's work, but what did that entail way out here in the wilderness? Women had to help. It was as simple as that.

As she set the table, she contemplated the situation.

"Caroline! Why are you slamming the silverware down on the table like that?" Etta took the rest of the silver from her and began doing it herself.

Caroline realized the other women had picked up on her annoyance. She went back to helping Ma cut up the freshly baked cornbread and put it in a tin to place on the table. She must have slammed that down, too, because this time, Ma gave her a look. "What's wrong with everyone?"

"I don't think it's us who have an issue." Etta glanced at Caroline with raised eyebrows.

"I'm sorry." Caroline sat down. "It's just..."

Before she could answer, Pa and Aaron came through the door.

"Sally, we need to talk."

Sally wiped her hands off and greeted Aaron with a pat on his arm. "Is something wrong, Hosea?"

"Let's go outside."

Ma went out the front door, followed by the men.

Caroline looked at Etta, who in turn glanced at Jillian. "Something has to be wrong." Alexander shrugged his shoulders and continued to move chairs toward the table.

"Do you think it's Betsey?" Jillian said in a quiet, shaky voice.

"Why wouldn't they want us to know about a problem Betsey might have?" Etta said in a whisper.

Caroline held up her hand. "Shh. Let's see if we can hear." Although they strained to hear, they could only distinguish mumbles.

It wasn't long before Ma and Pa came in from outside. Pa went to his place at the table and sat down. Ma got busy putting the meal on the table. She handed the plates to the girls and motioned to them to sit down.

"Isn't Aaron staying for dinner?" Etta asked, still in a whisper.

Pa took off his hat and bowed his head to pray. They all did the same.

"Dear Precious Father. We thank Thee, this day, for the provisions You have given us. We pray for those who are hurting, that You will mend their hearts. We pray for those who need healing, especially Waussinoodae and Abigail."

At this portion, Caroline eyed Etta looking back at her as well. Caroline quickly shut her eyes again.

"Please protect us from all harm. Help those who feel harmed to get the restitution they deserve and need. I pray You will be with this family and in our future here in this new land. Help us always to be grateful for all that we have. In Thy precious Name, amen."

Everyone added their usual acknowledgments to Pa's prayer.

Silence reigned as they all began to eat. The only sounds made were the scraping of a plate with a utensil or the slurps from soup spoons. Caroline didn't want to be the first to speak, and she was reasonably sure her younger sisters felt the same way. Alexander seemed a bit concerned, but eating usually held his undivided attention.

Thankfully, Ma broke the silence, "We've just found out that Abigail is sick. She has the fever, as we've all had from time to time. She's doing poorly."

Caroline slowly let out a sigh of relief. Is that all that was wrong? She felt terrible that Abigail was sick, but surely that couldn't be the only reason that Aaron was here. And why so secretive? "Do you need me to go help her?"

"No." Ma shook her head. "I need you here. Aaron has asked Claire Leach to go and see if she can be of service."

Caroline took a bite of her biscuit.

Pa was just too quiet. He finished only half a portion of his dinner and didn't say another word. Something else was the matter. But what could it be?

CHAPTER TWENTY-EIGHT

A soft moaning startled Caroline awake. Blinking, she realized it came from Waussinoodae. Removing her warm covering, she rose to see if there was something she could do to help the suffering woman. Ma had been doing everything in her power to keep her comfortable, but the illness continued to take a toll on the petite, frail, Indian woman.

Tiptoeing to her bedside, she discovered the woman's body covered in sweat. Droplets beaded on the woman's forehead and above her upper lip. The moaning sounded sorrowful and deep. Caroline knew she needed to wake Ma.

As she went for a bowl of cool water from the barrel, she saw Ma approach Waussinoodae's bedside.

Caroline returned with a cloth and the cool water. "Ma, she seems to be doing worse." Caroline placed the bowl of water near the bed as she dipped the cloth and wrung it out.

"Wipe her down the best you can. I'm going to try another ointment I made yesterday."

The two women set to work to cool the Indian woman down, but the fever raged on. She'd been through so much in the last few weeks. Her body was exhausted from the effort to heal. Despite their attempts, Waussinoodae's eyes rolled, and her movements became erratic.

"She's having a fit." Ma did her best to hold the woman's arms down and instructed Caroline to hold her legs. "We need to protect her from harming herself further."

The look in the sick woman's eyes made Caroline shiver with fear. Ma and Caroline tried to prevent the woman from falling out of bed or cracking her head on the bed frame as the convulsion subsided. The woman's eyes shut. Her breathing became shallow and labored.

"This isn't good, Caroline. I think you'd better go wake Pa." Ma put her fist to her mouth as tears threatened to spill from her eyes.

Caroline hadn't seen Ma this distraught since Betsey's difficult birth with Julia. She went to wake her pa. As she did, Alexander stirred awake and jumped up from off the floor. Glancing back, Caroline watched the young boy approach his first mother's bedside.

As soon as Pa was awake and getting out of bed, Caroline returned. She watched as Alexander took Waussinoodae's frail, shaky hand into his own. He tenderly stroked it. The fit had stopped; the woman lay almost lifeless on the bed. Alexander looked toward Ma. "Can't you help her, Ma?"

Ma stood, rubbing the small of her back with her fist. Caring for the sick woman had begun to take a toll on her. "I'm doing the best I can, Alexander. Your mother is very sick."

The young man got on his knees and placed his head on the edge of the bed. "Thank you for trying, Ma. It makes me sad to see her like this. She's always been good to me."

Ma smoothed down the hair of the boy she'd also come to love as a son, "She raised you well, Alexander."

Betsey fed Julia and then boiled a few eggs to put on fresh bread for Aaron. Today he'd have to go with Hosea to see Whitmore. Betsey trembled at the thought. Pa was guilty of killing the chief's dog, but what would be his punishment? Would the Indians be fair in their accusations?

Julia got off Betsey's lap and toddled away to play with a doll that Betsey had made her out of scraps of cloth. She'd sewn on buttons for eyes, and dark thread formed a smile on the smooth fabric of the doll's face. Julia loved it and would drag it around with her through the house and outside. It was dirty and worn by love.

Betsey watched her toddler hug the toy. The scene brought a little spark of contentment to an otherwise strange, frustrating day. Betsey prayed that Julia would give her new sibling the same kind of attention when he or she arrived.

She pointed to Aaron to watch his daughter as she worked hard to take care of the tiny doll. They both sat and watched her try to wrap the cloth child into a small rag Betsey used to wipe down the table from time to time.

"Hard to believe a child so young knows how to nurture and care for a child of her own."

Aaron kissed the top of Betsey's head. "She's just mimicking you. She has a perfect example of a good mother."

Betsey smiled up at him and took his hand. "What do you think will happen to Pa today?"

Aaron took the kettle from off the fire and poured himself a cup of coffee. "Nothing will happen, Betsey. Whitmore will probably just ask him what happened. How the animal was killed."

"I hope they understand."

"Whitmore?"

"No. The Indian chief. Pa meant no harm."

"Whitmore knows that, Betsey. Amicably settling this incident is imperative. You know that."

"Do you think money will be exchanged?"

Aaron shrugged. "I don't know. If your Pa has some animal pelts left from the summer hunts, he might be able to appease them with those."

"I just pray things will go well. Ma has tried so hard to help Waussinoodae. But even a few days ago, Waussinoodae was struggling so. I'm not sure she's strong enough to stay alive."

Aaron took a hesitating sip from his cup. "That does worry me. I pray she continues to heal. It would help Hosea's cause if she were to rally and return to her village well."

The couple didn't have much to say as they ate their breakfast. Julia jabbered in the corner.

"It won't be long before there is much more commotion in this cabin. Two babies to care for." Betsey smiled at Aaron. "I feel so blessed."

"It is hard to believe—"

A hard rapping knock on their door filled the room. "Betsey! Aaron! Please wake up. Pa and Ma need you!"

Aaron gave Betsey a look of distress as he stood and went to unlatch the door. Standing just outside was Caroline, still in her nightgown, with her hair in rags. She pulled her thin coat together as she stepped through the door.

Betsey stood. "Caroline, what's wrong?"

Caroline went to the hearth. Betsey wasn't sure if it was from the cool morning or something else. "I have bad news!"

Aaron placed his mug on the table. "What's wrong?"

Caroline seemed to be fighting back tears. "Waussinoodae didn't make it through the night."

Betsey covered her mouth with her hand. "Oh no!" Tears welled up in her eyes as she thought about the sweet friend she'd made here in the new territory.

Aaron just stood still. He didn't say anything.

"We woke in the middle of the night. She just couldn't hold on. But Aaron," Caroline looked up. "Pa's really worried now. He needs you to come down to the cabin to figure out what we should do. He's worried that the chief will think the whole thing happened on purpose."

Aaron took down his rifle, and went for his coat. "You stay here with Betsey and Julia. If you need to, get my other rifle from the loft." He gave Caroline a deep stare. "You know how to use it, right?"

Caroline rubbed the back of her arms, then nodded.

CHAPTER TWENTY-NINE

When Aaron pulled his horse up, Hosea was pacing in front of the Baker cabin. Aaron wrapped the horse's reins several times around a post near the door.

"Aaron." Hosea's eyes showed fear. "I don't know what to do. If any Indians show up today, I fear what they'll do to us. I've killed the chief's dog, and now this!" Hosea took off his hat, and instead of his standard scratch to his head, he slapped the hat on his knee. "We're in for it now!"

"We need Ambrose. Billie and Horace as well. They can be here to protect the womenfolk until we can ask Whitmore what our next move should be. You and I need to go see Whitmore."

Hosea put his hat back on his head. "I hope everyone will be safe until we can get this all worked out. I don't think we should be telling anyone what's happened to Waussinoodae."

"I agree. Let's send Alexander for the other men. As soon as they arrive, we'll head to the trading post."

Hosea took a long, deep breath.

"Instead of taking care of the body now, let's keep it in the cabin. Will the womenfolk be okay with that?"

"I don't think we have any choice." Hosea took a deep breath, shaking his head.

Aaron patted Hosea on the back. "I agree. We'll figure out something that Ambrose and the others can tell any Indians or settlers who show up to check on Waussinoodae. We need everyone to be of one mind and clear on how to answer anyone who asks about her."

Hosea bowed his head. "May God protect us all." As he uttered the prayer, Alexander came out of the cabin with a bucket. The boy wouldn't look at Aaron. Pa stooped down to Alexander's level and pulled the boy into a hug. "I'm sorry, son. All will be well."

Aaron did the same as Hosea, stooping to look the child in the eyes. "Alexander, I'm sorry about your mother. She was a fine, kind woman."

Alexander's red eyes pooled with tears.

"We need you to do something."

Alexander gazed back at Aaron. He wiped the tears now flowing down his cheeks with the end of his sleeve.

"We need you to go get the other men. Get Ambrose, Billie, and Horace, too. Can you do that?"

Alexander set down the bucket and reached out for Hosea who pulled him close into a firm embrace.

Aaron untied his horse and handed the reins to Alexander. "You need to hurry. Tell them to hurry."

Alexander nodded. "I will."

Aaron picked up the boy and placed him on the horse. "Hurry now." As soon as Alexander gripped the reins with a tight fist, Aaron slapped the horse. "Giddy up, boy!"

Alexander's legs tightened on the horse's ribs as it galloped toward the trail to Ambrose's house.

"He's takin' this mighty hard. I hope he'll be okay."

Hosea nodded. "If I know our Alexander, he'll be fine."

Sally gently wiped down the Indian woman's body. Using her lavender water from the summer's harvest, she placed a clean nightgown beside her on the bed. Her hands began to shake and her mind to wander. What would happen to her family if the chief were to find out that she didn't save his wife?

But as she worked, she did the only thing she knew how to do well. The one thing that always brought her peace in a fear-filled situation. She began to pray. As she wiped down Waussinoodae's sallow face, she thanked God for how the woman had cared for Alexander after finding him, as a tiny baby, in the arms of a dead mother.

She thanked God that she had seen fit to care for the child from infancy to the little boy that Sally now held dear. She thanked God that Waussinoodae had loved their orphaned child.

As she toweled off the dark skin, she thanked God that despite the difference in their skin color, Sally had learned to love her instead of fearing her, as she once had done. God allowed her to be near her in the end. That Waussinoodae wasn't alone nor having to fight this disease without the care of others who loved her.

Pulling socks on the woman, she prayed for the grief that now Alexander would bear. She prayed that he would understand God's ways and accept the early demise of someone he had always known and loved. Sally prayed for those of her household that would mourn the loss of such an amazing woman.

As she put on the white moccasins that Waussinoodae had worn into their home, she laced and tightened them onto her feet. Sally would always try to use her feet to treat others as Waussinoodae had treated Alexander and her family. She remembered the moment when Waussinoodae had barged into the cabin to help Betsey as she struggled through birthing Julia. She prayed that she could, one day, be a blessing and follow Waussinoodae's example of how to love. Unconditionally.

As she slipped the thin yet clean white nightgown over her head and down over her shoulders, she prayed for Hosea's safety and that the chief would show forgiveness toward her husband. She prayed for wisdom for Whitmore and Aaron as they upheld the law.

As she tucked a clean quilt over Waussinoodae, she prayed that she would be an example of Christ to all the Indians they encountered here. She needed to practice gracious, kind, and loving reactions despite what might happen in the approaching days.

They'd come such a long way in relating to the natives of their new home; she hated to see a dispute ruin the peace that had ensued.

She patted the dark skin of the woman who lay in her daughters' bed, and she carefully braided the long, jet-black, hair of the Indian chief's wife. Smoothing back the strands of hair that once stuck to the sides of the sweaty, dying woman, Sally gently put the quilt over Waussinoodae's head.

Claire was out in her garden picking the final tomatoes from the bushes. She heard Alexander's horse before she saw the boy gallop onto Ambrose's property. As the horse rushed by her, she stood, cupped her hand over her eyes, and took in what appeared to be an urgent situation.

Claire wondered if something was wrong with Betsey or the other women at the Baker home. She rushed toward Alexander, animatedly explaining something to Ambrose and Horace.

As she neared, she caught bits of the conversation. "Pa needs you. He told me to bring you both home. Please come. Quickly."

Claire watched Ambrose mount the horse and pull Alexander up in front of him to head north. She reached the horse just before he was about to spur him to move. "Ambrose! What's wrong? Is everything okay? Does your family need help?"

Ambrose shook his head. "I don't know. It sounds like someone has died, from what Alexander is trying to tell us."

"Died!" Claire covered her mouth. "I need to tell Henry."

As she skirted out of the way of the horse, Horace mounted another horse, and both took off for the Baker home.

A hard knock made Betsey and Caroline both jump.

From the other side of the door, they heard Horace say, "It's me. Horace. I've come to stay with you both."

Betsey went to the door, opening it for Horace. He was breathing heavily, and his eyes darted around the room as if trying to find someone.

"Your pa and Aaron sent me. I'm to sit with you. Guard the house." Horace spoke right to Caroline, not taking his eyes off her.

Caroline pulled her thin coat around her tighter. She felt a bit uncomfortable being in her nightgown in front of Horace.

Betsey motioned to Horace. "Come. Sit down." She put a cup in front of him and poured him some water. "Catch your breath."

His attempts at controlling himself seemed to work once he sat down. "I'm sorry. I came up here as fast as I could."

Betsey nodded. "We're happy to have you. Have you eaten this morning?"

Horace shook his head. "No, ma'am."

"Let me stir up a few eggs."

"Much obliged." Horace wrapped his fingers around the cup and drank. "I am a bit thirsty." He then smiled up at Caroline. "I'm hungry, too."

"Well, let's get some food into you."

Betsey took the rifle out of his grasp, leaning it against the door of the cabin. "Caroline has Aaron's other rifle loaded and ready. We did that before you arrived."

Horace glanced up again at Caroline. "Good. That's good."

Caroline felt her face flush. She wasn't sure why Horace always had this effect on her. She swallowed but couldn't seem to move or even sit back down. Betsey must have noticed.

"Caroline. Why don't you go up into the loft, and I'll get you a dress to put on over your nightclothes. I'm sure that will make you feel more comfortable."

Caroline felt herself blush even more, but she left Horace and Betsey, hurrying up the ladder and into the loft.

It wasn't long before she heard Betsey at the top of the ladder. She held out a dress. "Put this on. It might be a bit big, but it is the dress I wore before I grew out of it." She winked at Caroline. "Hurry up, and then you can help me get Horace some breakfast."

Caroline went to the far side of the loft to put the dress on. It was a bit big for her, but it was better than standing around in her nightclothes, especially in front of Horace.

Caroline could faintly hear Betsey and Horace's conversation. Betsey asked him how he liked his eggs cooked, then she asked him if he wanted bread slices, too. Horace's words included a mere, "Yes, ma'am" or "No thank you, ma'am."

Soon Caroline made her way back downstairs. She asked Betsey if she had a brush she could borrow. Betsey pointed to the small table beside her bed. Caroline undid her braid and quickly weaved it back together in a more becoming way than how it appeared after caring for Waussinoodae all night.

"Would you like a bit of coffee, Horace?"

Caroline could overhear the conversation quite clearly now that she was on the lower level of the house. Horace seemed so nervous to be in Betsey's presence. He never appeared as timid when he had been with only Caroline.

As soon as she felt a bit more presentable, Caroline walked back to the table. Julia waddled up to her, holding her arms up for Caroline to pick her up. When she did, Caroline planted a kiss on the small child's cheek. Julia smiled, put her arms around Caroline's neck, and pulled her close.

Caroline sat down and placed Julia on her lap. "What's happening down at the cabin, Horace?"

Horace had just filled his mouth with a fresh spoonful of eggs, but he swallowed. "Everyone's fine. Billie and Ambrose are there, and they sent me here to keep an eye out for Indians."

"And Aaron? Pa?" Caroline asked.

"They've gone to see Whitmore. They think it might be best if we don't tell anyone about Waussinoodae's death. Until they talk to Whitmore."

Betsey picked up her mug of coffee. "I agree."

"But how long can we keep it a secret, Betsey? It won't be long before the chief sends his men to check on her again. They've been here twice this week."

"Just until Aaron and your pa see Whitmore and find out what the next step should be."

"How's Alexander doing?" Caroline felt sorry for the young boy. He'd probably take the death much harder than the rest of them.

"He seemed to want to go with your pa and Aaron, but Ambrose thought it best he stay at the cabin. Just in case the Indians came to see how Waussinoodae is fairing today. They told Alexander not to tell them that she'd died but that she was having a hard day and they didn't want anyone disturbing her."

"Alexander would be the only one to be able to communicate that to them." Betsey tapped the table. "This sure puts Pa in quite the predicament. How did he seem?"

Horace sat back. "A bit nervous, but hopefully, with Whitmore's help, they can figure out what to do."

Caroline stood and handed Julia over to Betsey. "I think it best if we stay outside a bit this morning. It will be better to watch the property instead of sitting inside."

Horace shoveled the last of his bread into his mouth and stood. "Good idea. I'll come with you."

Taking the guns with them, Caroline and Horace made their way outside. Caroline searched the edge of the property around

Betsey and Aaron's house. Everything seemed quiet, except for the falling of an occasional leaf and the scampering of a few squirrels through the dry leaves.

Caroline ventured near the ridge, looking out over the Shiawassee River for any signs of the Indians along the water. Horace soon joined her. He looked toward the north as she looked south.

"See anything?" Picking a long stem of river grass, Horace rubbed it between his fingers. A few stems, filled with seeds, floated from his fingers to the ground.

"I don't. Do you?" Caroline scanned the back edge of the property.

"You're so brave."

The comment caught Caroline off guard. "What?"

"Most girls wouldn't be caught dead having to guard a house, let alone pick up a gun. You're not intimidated by it at all. You're a fearless woman, Caroline Baker."

Caroline felt her face grow warm. His compliment made her stand up straighter. "You have to be out here."

"No, you don't. I've been working close to the shack where John and Abigail are living. That woman couldn't catch a mouse, or even think of chasing off a coyote. But you..."

"I hope I'm not anything like Mrs. Swain."

Horace folded his arms and sat down under a tree. "You're nothing like that. I don't know a single woman as brave or strong as you. You pull those oxen into the barn each night as if they're a couple of horses. You don't flinch to go out, in the darkest of night, to hunt down a wolf."

Caroline laughed. "I soon learned, when we arrived here, that being afraid would do nothing but make a person feel helpless. I don't want to feel that way. We've lived through lots of things out here in the wilderness of Michigan, and sitting around being afraid does not help any situation."

"That you have." Horace smiled at her, and for some reason, Caroline couldn't avert her eyes from staring. Soon she was smiling back.

"What are you afraid of?" Horace patted the ground beside him.

Caroline couldn't tell him. Could she? Just the opportunity to sit close beside him scared her to death. She slowly made her way toward him and sat down.

"At this vantage point, we'll be able to scan the entire property together. If you see anything, let me know, and I'll do the same for you."

Caroline could feel his muscular shoulder up against her own. She wasn't sure why but it felt like lightning traversed through his shoulder and into her own.

"So?"

Caroline responded, "What?"

"What are you afraid of, Caroline Baker? What makes you afraid? What causes you to lie awake at night and not be able to sleep?"

She wanted to tell him. It's you. Every fiber of her being did. She longed to say it as his gaze bore into her soul. She lay awake at night dreaming of him. His smiles made her knees feel like they would buckle. Whenever he said her name, her heart skipped a beat. She wanted to tell him that each time they were alone, she relived the moment his lips touched hers. Those real encounters were better than any dream. That she wanted to be his girl.

But what would he say? How did he feel? Could she handle a rejection without falling to pieces in front of him? If only he knew, really knew. She wasn't all that brave.

"I want to tell you something." Horace waved the stick he'd picked up. "I truly admire you for your courage. It's a beautiful thing."

Caroline held her breath.

He continued as he peeled the bark off the stick. "You're a beautiful thing, Caroline Baker. I don't know if you realize it or not, but I've fallen in love with you. I know I'm not the man you have set your heart on marrying, but for me, that doesn't change how I feel about you."

Caroline turned to look at the man sitting beside her. "Do you mean that?"

Horace smiled. "Of course I do. I just wasn't sure you felt the same way. I mean, Billie's a nice guy. He is. And he came all this way to be with you. That's a very admirable thing to do."

Caroline choked, "Yes." She cleared her throat. "It is."

"So, who do you love, Caroline Baker? Me—or Billie? Cause I have a feeling, you aren't all that certain anymore."

Caroline couldn't answer. She needed to tell Billie first. That was the only kind and truthful thing to do.

Horace seemed to sense her anxiety. "I want you to know that soon I'll be building my home. Soon we'll finish Ambrose's house. And if you're interested in me at all, I want you there to help me make decisions, 'cause you'll be the one cleaning it."

Before she could answer, Horace stood and walked away. As he left, she knew, without any further doubts, that she wanted the house to be exactly like Betsey's. She also knew that all the plans she'd created before Billie arrived would not be her future.

Taking a deep breath, she realized perhaps God's plans seemed to hold much more than she'd ever imagined. Pa was right. God did make crooked paths straight. She just needed to trust God, for He knew her heart better than even she did.

CHAPTER THIRTY

Aaron pulled on Whitmore's sleeve, taking him away from the closeness of the Indian warriors around him.

Whitmore fussed a bit at the intrusion. He'd been making an excellent trade for some highly valued Michigan wolverine pelts.

"What's this all about?" He pulled his sleeve away from Aaron.

"We need to tell you something. Away from the ears of the Indians," Hosea added, as they steered him close to the hearth in the other room.

Whitmore laughed. "Fine. Make a man a lawman and look what happens. He's more important than makin' a dollar."

But Hosea and Aaron didn't laugh with him.

"Whitmore. Something's happened at Hosea's cabin this morning. Something bad."

Whitmore crossed his arms. "Tell me."

Aaron whispered. "Waussinoodae passed away."

Whitmore stepped back. "Chief Maemaeketchewunk's wife?"

Hosea answered, "Yes. I think she had cholera. My wife did her best to nurse her, but she wasn't strong enough. She lost her battle this morning."

Whitmore sighed. "Now I understand your concern."

"What do we do? I've killed his dog, and now, maybe to the chief, it looks like I've done the same thing to his wife. We're concerned for our family's safety."

Turning his back on them, Whitmore added. "I understand, and for good reasons." He turned back to Aaron and Hosea. "Have you told anyone?"

"Only Ambrose and the two boys who have been staying with us. They're back at the cabins watching for any sign of the Indians."

"Good. That's good." Whitmore picked up a log close to the fire and threw it on. "Let's keep this quiet. As long as we can." He then propped his foot upon a stump near the fire. "I need a bit of time to think this one through." Whitmore pulled at his beard. "I know it seems hopeless, but I need time to come up with a good plan. I haven't seen the chief in days. I'll head out and see if I can find him around the post. I'll tell him that we have an issue to solve about his dog. He's been waiting for a chance to talk to you. Are you still willing to meet with him, Hosea?"

"Of course. But do you think it's a good idea not to tell him about Waussinoodae? Shouldn't he know?"

"Yes. And we will. But we need to be very careful how we go about it. There are things Indians want to do to bury their loved ones. We need to honor that for them."

"What can we do in the meantime?" Aaron asked.

Whitmore put his hand on Hosea's shoulder. "If you'll stay here, I'll search for Maemaeketchewunk. I've heard from his warriors that he's close by. He does know she's with you but probably won't be asking about her every day."

"That's true. The warriors have only come about twice a week."

"When was the last time they were there?"

"We told them the woman wasn't doing well. It was the morning after I killed the dog."

"Okay. Hosea, you stay here. If anyone asks you anything, pretend you don't understand them. Let's fetch Alexander and take him with us, Aaron. He'll be a good distraction from Maemaeketchewunk asking about Waussinoodae. He loves seeing the boy. Believe it or not, he is very fond of the boy, despite how it looks to you."

"Hosea, help yourself to anything here. If trouble starts, head back to my quarters at the back of the building. If anyone seems agitated or upset, hide there."

Hosea nodded.

"Don't worry. We have to go about this in a careful, deliberate way. We all have to work together." Whitmore picked up his rifle and headed outside, with Aaron following close behind.

Sitting by the fireplace made Hosea nervous. He had his back to the door. If someone were to come inside looking for him, they'd find him alone and unarmed. But he desired nothing more than solitude and praying time.

He walked to the back of the post and entered Whitmore's quarters. Closing the door behind him, he made his way to a nearby window to peek outside. The place was crowded with Indians. He didn't doubt Whitmore's wisdom on how best to help him, but he had uncertainties, thinking that here was the best place for him.

Could he have handled the events differently? Was he hiding from his problems? What if the Indians harmed his family while he sat at the post, unable to protect them? Folding his arms, he began to pace back and forth in the tiny room. While his steps increased, so did his faith and prayers. God had never failed him. Despite his wandering soul, even when he would imagine the worst scenario, he could always count on God to listen to his words. Help him by heeding whatever scriptures came to mind. And at that moment, Bible verses flooded his thoughts like the flow of the Shiawassee River.

When I am afraid, I will trust in You. Be strong and courageous for the Lord your God goes before you. Seek ye first the kingdom of God and all His righteousness. My present help in the day of trouble. My rock, my shield, my protector.

Despite all of God's promises in scripture, sometimes the best thing to do was take the matter to God and leave it at His feet. Claim the promises of scripture that He is our shield, our very present help in trouble. Hosea found himself in a situation that was not of his doing. He was innocent. He could have been more careful as to what he had shot the night he'd accidentally killed Maemaeketchewunk's dog, but in a wilderness full of predators, sometimes it was best to shoot before thinking. Wolves were not only a menace but dangerous. Hesitation could cause a man to lose his life.

Turning on his heel, he walked another lap. This time he began quoting scripture out loud. For some reason, the words pouring out of his mouth and soul brought him more comfort than the compounding trepidation in his heart. He wasn't quiet but quoted the scripture right out loud like an evangelist at a camp meeting.

"'He that dwelleth in the secret place of the Most High shall abide under the shadow of the Almighty. I will say of the Lord; He is my refuge and my fortress: my God; in Him will I trust.'" Hosea paced some more. "'Surely He shall deliver thee from the snare of the fowler, and the noisome pestilence. He shall cover thee with his feathers, and under His wings shalt thou trust: His truth shall be thy shield and buckler.'"

Hosea stopped a moment and looked up at the dark ceiling above him. "'Thou shalt not be afraid for the terror by night; nor for the arrow that flieth by day; nor for the pestilence that walketh in darkness; nor for the destruction that wasteth at noonday.'"

He continued to pace, now looking down at the floor with his hands folded behind him. "'A thousand shall fall at thy side, and ten thousand at thy right hand; but it shall not come nigh thee.'" Hosea stopped a moment, took off his hat and scratched his head, then continued. "'For He shall give His angels charge over thee, to keep thee in all thy ways. They shall bear thee up in their hands, lest thou dash thy foot against a stone.'"

Hosea's heart began to rest in the assurance of the God who had been with him through many scary moments. The older he grew, the more he knew that God's promises were true. God's ways were sometimes hard to fully comprehend, but each one continued to give Hosea confidence and strength even in his weakest times.

Hosea felt his shoulders relax, but he knew he needed to continue for a bit more. At least until the end of Psalm 91. "'Because He hath set His love upon me, therefore I will deliver him: I will set him on high because he hath known My Name. He shall call upon Me, and I will answer him: I will be with him in trouble; I will deliver him, and honor him. With long life will I satisfy him, and show him my salvation.'" And with that last word, Hosea saw Whitmore's bed in a far corner. He suddenly felt exhausted.

"Everyone here hates me." Abigail felt a cold, wet cloth cover her forehead.

"Shush now, Abigail. You need to rest."

Abigail wasn't sure who was talking to her, but the cloth gave her hot forehead relief. She moaned.

"Everyone hates me. There isn't one person here who cares whether I live or die."

Again, Abigail heard the comforting words of what sounded like a woman attempting to relieve her distress.

"Hate's a strong word, Abigail."

Abigail didn't care. It didn't matter what she said nor to whom she was speaking. Her body ached, her head throbbed, her entire being felt on fire. For a moment, she thought she was all alone with the stranger comforting her, but then she heard John's voice.

"How is she?"

The woman answered, "Not well. Her fever has been raging throughout the night. I'm not altogether sure how long a person can hold on with this illness. It has killed a few of the settlers, including the Indian woman at the Baker cabin."

"She died?" Abigail could make out John's voice. Loud and clear.

"Yes. I believe yesterday morning."

Abigail searched her memory. Who were they talking about? And what did the Baker family do to a woman? She'd always been skeptical of the Baker family, but killing an Indian woman? That sounded a bit off. Perhaps it was a good thing. Indians frightened her.

John came close to her ear. "Abigail, I'm here. It's me, John. I'm sorry you're so sick. Claire and I are doing all we can to help you get well."

Abigail felt him kiss her cheek. She wanted to reach out and pull him close, but she couldn't even lift her arms. "John. Who passed away?"

"The chief's wife. Waussinoodae. Do you remember Sally speaking of her?"

Abigail shook her head.

"It's nothing for you to worry about, sweetheart. Save your strength to get better. Give your body time to fight this disease. As soon as you do, we'll leave and head back to New York. I promise. I was a fool to make you come here. Please, just get well."

Would she be next? Did she have the same disease as the Indian woman? Abigail wanted to ask a dozen questions, but for some reason, she couldn't speak out loud anymore. The effort was too great. What had John said about taking her back to New York? Would he do that for her? Even after all the manipulation and lies she'd started?

Abigail wanted to thank him. She tried to lift her arms to touch John, but exhaustion wouldn't even let her open her eyes. Her very last thought before drifting out of consciousness was that she deserved to die. She'd been awful to John and the Baker family. And now, she'd never have the opportunity to make it right.

Soon everything went silent.

"Will you leave us?" Claire asked the man now leaning against the outside wall of his home.

"I should have never brought her here." John ran his fingers through his hair. "I thought she'd get used to it, somehow. Would start to see how new and exciting this new territory could be. I was stupid to think Abigail could manage in a place like this."

Claire touched his shoulder. "We all want what's best for our spouses." Turning her head and looking out in the forest, Claire shared her heart. "I didn't want to come here, either."

John eyed her. "You didn't?"

Claire shook her head. "No. I especially didn't want my children growing up without proper schooling. If I needed supplies, I wanted the opportunity to run to a store in town." The woman smiled. "I was a typical young wife with small children. My mother lived close when we were back in Ohio. My sisters, too. I loved that most. Here—" Claire pointed to the surrounding forests, "I felt so alone. That is until we met the Bakers. We were cold—freezing, actually." Claire snickered, "Oh, I was so angry with Henry. Not only were we going to catch ourselves ague like the others, but we were also nearly starving. Then we came upon the Baker cabin, and everything changed. That family was placed in the proper place, at the right time. If it hadn't been for their kindness, I don't know where Henry and I would be right now." Claire kneaded her hands together. "They gave us hope. Hope that if they could make a go of it in this godforsaken land, so could others.

"Abigail is a lot like I used to be. Bitter because you've brought her here. She's left everything she knew to be home, just like me. It might take a few months or even years for her to understand your need to be here, close to your brother. She may not ever become accustomed to having to skin a deer or plant a garden, but perhaps she just needs time. Time to figure out her place here."

"Claire, can I ask you something?"

Claire smiled, "Of course."

"Do you think everyone around here hates her so?" John sighed. "I know she's been difficult, but I truly hope that others will keep reaching out to her. I know they've tried, but I pray they don't stop trying. I, more than anyone, know how cantankerous she can be, but I also know the warmth and goodness that sometimes bubbles up from her heart. It's there, but for now—bitterness is shrouding it. Every community needs a party planner like her. A woman to have extravagant teas and social events. Don't you think?"

Claire smiled. "Yes, we'll need that, too. I see a glimmer of hope every time I come to help. She does need others, just as much as I needed friends. I will continue to help because so many others have helped me." Claire picked up the basket she'd brought supplies in and headed down the path.

Claire's confession surprised John. If Abigail did survive, perhaps she and Claire could be good friends. He envisioned Abigail planning social events and having daily visitors for tea. Leaning against his home, John prayed for Abigail's health, and that soon she'd come to love this place and the people who'd settled here, as he did.

He knew the kindness of the Baker family. They'd done everything feasible to make their beginning here as carefree and easy as possible. If Abigail were to survive, he was sure they'd give her a second chance, too.

CHAPTER THIRTY-ONE

Alexander saw them coming from the direction of Whitmore's post. At the same time, he saw the Indian warriors coming onto the property from the north. They appeared angry and agitated. Aaron and Whitmore had arrived, just in time. He hurried toward them, pointing out the small band of Maemaeketchewunk's men now heading toward the Baker cabin.

Whitmore tapped his heels into the side of his horse and beat the Indians to the front door. Aaron followed right behind him.

Alexander turned around as the warriors came to a halt and dismounted from their horses. Speaking out to them in Ojibwa, he told them to listen to Whitmore. The Indians pushed past the young boy and went directly to stand in front of Whitmore, who'd just tied his horse's reins to the post. He held up his hands and spoke.

Thankfully, Alexander could decipher every word of the conversation.

"Hello, brave warriors." Whitmore pointed to the Baker cabin. "I'm sure you are here to find out about Waussinoodae."

The man warrior stomped his foot, then slapped his chest, "She is our queen. We need to take back a report to Maemaeketchewunk."

"I understand. Yes. Let me go in first to ask how Waussinoodae is. Give me a minute." Whitmore ducked into the cabin.

One of the younger warriors glared at Alexander. Alexander remembered him as a wild, young teen from the tribe. He'd only come into contact with him a few times, but he knew him to be easily angered. He knew not to stare back would show he was afraid, so Alexander stood erect and stared right back.

It wasn't long before Whitmore came out of the cabin with a sad expression.

Alexander wondered whether he'd be honest or continue to shroud the truth from the tribe's warriors.

"Warriors. I need you to know that the news is not good today."

The warriors looked to Whitmore for his news. "I'm afraid Waussinoodae has passed on."

Alexander watched the faces of the men before him. Their shoulders slumped, their countenances seemed pained and their eyes showed alarm.

"The chief will not be happy with this turn of events. We will report the news to him. Please allow us time to do that. We will return for her body soon." Without any further hesitation, the Indians mounted their horses and returned into the part of the woods from whence they came.

"What will they do?" Aaron was the first to speak up.

"I didn't think it fair not to allow them their death rituals. We will release the body to them when they return. They will probably come back with the chief. We'll assure them that Mrs. Baker did everything she could to make her well. She's taken great care to clean up the body, and there is no sign of foul play at all. I believe the chief will see that and know she did try to help his wife get well." Whitmore turned and picked up the reins of his horse. "Alexander, take this horse to the barn. It might be a while before they return. I will not leave any of you until Waussinoodae has left your home. Communication is key here."

"Do you think telling them the truth was a good idea?" Aaron asked.

Whitmore handed the reins of his horse to Alexander. "I do. Sally has cared well for the body. It will show by the clothes she wears and the braiding of her hair. I do believe telling the truth is better than trying to keep it a secret any longer."

Alexander knew that lying was a sin. He also knew that being dishonest with an Indian was not wise. He trusted Whitmore. The older man knew the Indians far better than anyone. They had men there to fight the Indians if they came back armed and ready for a battle.

Alexander considered the Indians as much his brothers as the sisters he now had in the Baker family. He felt pulled as to how to feel. He would mourn the death of his Indian mother as much as he would mourn the death of his white mother. Both were loving women who had done nothing but care for him. He pulled on the reins of the horse as it sauntered behind him and to the barn.

Aaron decided to check on Caroline, Betsey, Julia, and Horace instead of staying longer at the Baker farm. Whitmore would stay with Sally, Etta, and Jillian until the Indians returned for the body of Waussinoodae. He'd asked Aaron to return that evening to help keep watch through the night.

Once up the hill, Aaron dismounted from his horse. He found Caroline and Horace out on the ridge above the river. Heading in their direction, he heard them whispering but couldn't make out what they were saying.

Looking back at the cabin, he saw no movement, so he headed out to the couple. "Hey there. How's everything here?"

The two young people startled and then turned quickly. Caroline nearly dropped the rifle as she stood up. "Aaron, I didn't hear you!"

Horace seemed as startled and out of sorts as Caroline. "I guess we weren't watching as carefully as we should. Forgive me, Aaron."

"Has it been quiet here?" Aaron took off his gloves and threw them on a nearby stump.

"Yes. We did see the Indians head back into the woods. Is everything okay?"

Aaron nodded. "Whitmore is here now. He told them about Waussinoodae. I need to head back down to the farm to spend the night there. Will you stay here, Horace? To keep watch?"

Horace answered, "Yes, sir. I'd be happy to do that."

"Caroline. Stay here another night. Your ma and sisters are safe with Whitmore and me."

"Where's Pa?"

"He's back at the post. Due to the involvement with the dog and now Waussinoodae, Whitmore felt it safer for him."

"Does Whitmore think Pa is in danger?"

"He believes we can solve all of this in a peaceful, calm way. We need to be honest with the Indians and then follow their lead. Hopefully, it will prove the best option."

"Are you sure we're safe? You'll be safe?" Betsey tugged her husband closer and hugged him.

"I hope so. Whitmore has been dealing with the Indians for a long time. I'm sure he knows just what to do not to get the Indians more upset."

"What about Pa?" Betsey looked into his eyes.

"I don't know. Whitmore may have to meet with the chief first. The grief of losing his wife will be hard. Perhaps this will overshadow the issue with his dog. Who knows?"

Betsey shivered a bit. Aaron must have felt her, for he put his strong arms around her and held her close. "It will be okay. I'm sure we'll have a few bumps to deal with, but for now, I think everyone is safe."

Horace, Caroline, and now Billie came through the front door as Betsey and Aaron pulled away from each other. Betsey wiped her eyes with her apron.

"Are you okay?" Caroline went to her sister.

Betsey nodded.

"I'm here also, Aaron. Where do you want me?" Billie came in behind Horace. "I'd be more than happy to stay here and protect these women."

"I need you at the farm, Billie. For now."

This time it was Billie's countenance that dropped. "Are you sure? Horace is only one man and—"

"He has Caroline. She's a good shot. I think we'll need you down at the farm. You can guard the barn."

Billie stepped back a bit. "Okay. Wherever you think."

"I'm sure you'd rather be here with Caroline. I apologize for not thinking of that. I guess it's up to you two to decide."

Horace glanced at Billie; Billie looked to Caroline. Caroline gave Horace a fleeting glimpse. Silence followed.

Betsey came out from behind Aaron. "Caroline. Why don't you take Billie outside and explain things to him?"

Caroline stared back at Betsey, her face almost as white as the apron she'd borrowed from Betsey.

Betsey took the rifle from Caroline. "It's okay." Betsey winked and motioned her to the door.

Horace nodded. "I'll stay inside. Give you privacy."

The only person who appeared utterly confused was Billie. The look on his face showed frustration, then confusion. "What do you need to explain?"

Caroline sighed. "Quite a bit. Do you mind?" She pointed to the door.

Billie followed Caroline to the door.

CHAPTER THIRTY-TWO

"What is it, Caroline?" Billie was sitting in the same spot as Horace had sat all day. With him in Horace's place, it gave Caroline more confidence to be honest with Billie as she'd been with Horace all afternoon.

"Billie. I need to tell you something."

Billie held up his hands. "You know what, Caroline. I'm pretty sure I know what you're going to say."

As Caroline took his hand, memories came one by one. Billie was the one she'd spent years getting to know before they'd moved to Michigan. Their desks were always pushed close together back at the Meadville School. They'd gone fishing together on many a Saturday afternoon. Her sisters had convinced her that, without a doubt, he'd be the one she'd marry someday. But as she gazed at the young man seated on a stump close to her, she knew that from this day forward, it wouldn't be Billie by her side. But how could she tell him that?

"Well, what is it?" Billie seemed resigned and defeated before she'd even begun telling him her thoughts.

"I'm sorry. I didn't mean for any of this to happen."

Billie picked up a stick and began writing in the dirt. It appeared as if he was trying to write out her name. "I came all this way to be with you. I wanted to be your husband. To start a family with the girl who has had my heart since we were just little kids."

Caroline bowed her head but watched Billie write her name in the dirt. "I know. And up until this spring, I was sure you would be the person I would spend the rest of my life with. You have to know that by the letters I wrote you."

"I only got two. Remember?"

"I know. It wasn't like I didn't write you a million letters—in my head. Paper is hard to come by here."

Billie finished out her name in the dirt and threw the stick over the ridge. They listened as it caught on a few branches and then splashed into the river below.

"I didn't mean to fall in love with someone else."

Billie's head snapped up. "You're in love with that guy?" He pointed back at the cabin.

Caroline knew now was the time to get her true feelings out in the open. "Yes."

Billie stood. "That's just dandy!"

Caroline stood as well. "Please understand. I want you to be happy, and I don't think I'm the one to give you that. I love you, Billie, but not in the same romantic way I love Horace. I didn't know the difference until I met him."

"I'm going to head back to the farm now." Billie turned to leave. "I hope you know what you're doing, and I hope he doesn't break your heart as you've broken mine!"

"Billie! Wait!" Caroline called after him.

Billie turned back. "Why?"

"Don't go alone. Wait for Aaron to go back with you. It might not be safe to head back by yourself."

"I'll be fine. If not, it will be one less person for you to worry about."

The words struck Caroline's heart. She knew he'd be upset, but he was also angry, which was hard for Caroline to swallow. She watched Billie head down the trail behind the Swain house. Alone. She rushed into Betsey's cabin. "Aaron. You need to go with Billie. He isn't happy and now he's angry. I don't want him alone. It's not safe."

Aaron didn't budge. Betsey had just placed a plate of food in front of him. "I think, Miss Caroline, that boy might be just mad enough to fight off any Indian he finds along the path."

Caroline's eyes pleaded with Horace, too, but he sat down to eat as well.

"I think Aaron's right. After what you've just told him, I don't think anyone will want to get close to him right now."

Caroline sat down, put her hands over her face, and sobbed.

Billie wasn't sure what his next move would be. As he stomped down the path leading to the Baker cabin, he decided his best option was to find another area to settle. He couldn't imagine being close to Caroline daily or watching her continue to fall in love with a stranger.

Picking up a stick, Billie tossed it at a nearby tree. The sound shattered the otherwise silent forest. Darkness was descending; the autumn days were growing shorter.

He couldn't help but feel cheated. How could a woman disregard years of friendship for someone else so quickly? What did Horace possess that Billie didn't? Was he smarter? More confident in himself? It couldn't be his appearance. Billie stood up straighter, assured that it wasn't that.

Maybe he should rule out women in all areas of his life. Be a bachelor like Ambrose. Sighing, he knew that wouldn't be the path he desired. He wanted to be a husband. A father. He wanted to provide for a woman and be everything to her. Perhaps Caroline's choice was a better one. She couldn't go through life married to one man but often wonder what had become of the other. The thought pierced his heart.

Looking down the path, he saw Jillian scurry to the barn to gather eggs laid during the day. It was an evening ritual for her. Jillian didn't carry the same confident spirit as Caroline. She was timid, weak, and often frittered around like something was after her. This simple chore was no different. She scanned the property as she slipped into the fence housing the chickens near their coop.

He couldn't leave the Baker family now. He needed to be a man and stay with them. At least until Hosea settled his differences with the tribe. Glancing again at the open barn door, he knew he could be useful in helping them through the danger. Despite Caroline's rejection, he loved the Baker family and would hate to think that him leaving now would cause them further harm.

Getting close to the barn door, he peeked inside to see Jillian quickly gathering the last of the eggs and placing them in a basket that hung on her arm. Despite the anguish in his heart, he loved seeing her simplicity and innocence.

"Hey, Jilly!"

Jillian turned, and when she did, an egg flew out of her hand and landed right on Billie's foot. It broke open and dripped over the tip of his boot.

Jillian put her hand over her mouth, and her eyes grew wide. "Billie, you scared me. I'm so sorry."

Billie only knew one thing to do. He could allow the conversation with Caroline to make things worse, or he could laugh at the antics of a younger Baker sister. He tipped his head back and took a deep breath. "It's okay, Jillian. No harm done. It's just not my day."

As night emerged over the Baker cabin, everyone grew more tense and cautious. Aaron had returned from spending the evening with Betsey, Caroline, and Horace to help Ambrose, Whitmore, and Billie keep watch over Sally and the girls.

Aaron was surprised to find Billie guarding the backside of the barn. He removed his hat. He felt sorry for the young man who'd come from Pennsylvania to date and marry Caroline, but he also saw how much Caroline respected and admired Horace. "Thanks for helping us tonight, Billie. I heard about your bad news, and I appreciate you sticking it out with us."

Billie bowed his head. "I will until all of this is over with Mr. Baker." He seemed embarrassed and ashamed that Aaron knew what Caroline had told him.

"We appreciate your loyalty, Billie."

Billie's eyes appeared red and watery. Aaron left the young man to head to the Baker cabin. He'd probably appreciate the solitude.

"What do you think the Indians' next step will be?" Aaron asked Whitmore, seated at the table finishing up his supper.

"They'll come for the body. Probably sooner than later."

"Should we post someone in the barn to keep watch? Out of sight?" Aaron pulled out a chair and sat down.

"Would you like a plate, Aaron?" Sally placed a cup of water at the top of Whitmore's plate.

Aaron waved off Sally. "I ate with Betsey. Thank you."

"I think putting Billie and Ambrose out in the barn tonight will probably be a good idea. They can be watching for the Indians and also give us a bit more protection."

Ambrose stood. "We'll keep our guns loaded and watch. I've finished eating."

He loaded his rifle before heading outside.

"You take the first shift tonight and in the middle of the night...Aaron and I will come out to relieve you." Whitmore took a large bite of his supper. He scooted corn around on his plate with a finger. "I imagine they'll not wait until morning to return for her. They have their rituals and beliefs about the bodies of their dead. It will just take them a bit longer to get back to their camp to alert Maemaeketchewunk that his wife has passed. He'll come!"

As Ambrose opened the front door, the entire family could hear a horse galloping onto the property from the south. Aaron motioned for all the women and Alexander to get toward the back of the cabin. Ambrose picked up his gun as Whitmore and Aaron reached for their own.

"Can you see who it is, Ambrose?" Whitmore whispered.

Ambrose carefully put his head out the door to take a look. "It's not an Indian. It's someone coming from the south. Appears to be..."

Everyone held their breath.

"It's Pa!"

CHAPTER THIRTY-THREE

"Blue blazes!" Whitmore shouted out a few more expletives and then turned back toward Sally, Alexander, and the girls. "My apologies." He then went for the door. "—But what in tarnation does that man think he's doing?"

Just then, Billie shouted from behind the barn. "They're coming. From the backside of the property."

"Stay inside here!" Whitmore told Sally and the children. "Don't come out unless we call for you. When the Indians come in for the body, you do everything they say. Do you understand?"

Sally nodded, pushing the children behind her as she stood as tall as her tiny frame could manage. Alexander nudged past Jillian and stood beside her.

Once outside, Whitmore went to Pa as his horse skidded to a stop in front of the cabin. "Why didn't you stay where you were?"

Hosea came around the horse to stand before Whitmore. "I'm sorry, Whitmore. I know you told me to stay put, but I can't just leave my family out here to manage my problems for me. I will stand and face whatever the Indians deem best for me, but I can't sit at your place and allow them to harm anyone here because of me."

Whitmore pulled down on his beard. "For whatever it's worth, I commend you for your attitude, but now they're coming. Be prepared to do whatever I tell you."

Hosea took off his hat. "I'll face whatever they feel I have comin'. But not without the Almighty God facin' it with me."

At that moment, a band of eight Indians came toward the house on horses. Behind them, they were dragging a travois, just like they'd brought Waussinoodae on the day they'd asked for Sally's help. Each Indian was wailing, their heart-piercing cries shattering the otherwise, quiet night air.

It wasn't a sight Whitmore hadn't seen before. The Indians wailed whenever a death occurred. He knew the significance of Waussinoodae to the tribe, and as the Indians approached the group, Whitmore could see that mourning was the agenda of the tribe tonight, not war.

He bowed his head as they came closer. As the small band of men stopped, Whitmore raised his hands and began to speak Ojibwa.

He could hear Alexander translating the words for Sally.

"We are sorrowful for you. This family," Whitmore used his hand to point out everyone around him, "is sad for your chief and your tribe. Sally Baker did the best she could to nurse your chief's wife back to health, but it wasn't enough. You know this disease, as it has been rampant in your tribe all summer. She succumbed to the disease, and we are sorry for your loss."

One of the Indians at the front of the group dismounted and then bowed his head. "Our loss is great. Waussinoodae was a special squaw to our people. We thank you for your goodness to her. She made us promise that we would not harm this family if something like this were to happen. We abide by her wishes."

Whitmore sighed. The woman had again saved the lives of the early settlers by the river. She'd had enough sense to warn her tribe before they ever brought her here. No one could take her place. He bowed his head and pointed to the cabin. "You will find her body there."

The men took a small hide from the travois and went into the Baker cabin, followed by Whitmore. Whitmore put a finger to his lips before going inside and then motioned to Aaron, Ambrose, Billie, and Hosea not to come into the cabin. They acknowledged his request with nods.

Sally felt a chill as the eight Indian men crossed the threshold. She had edged her way to a wall and pinned the children behind her. Alexander stepped in front of her and folded his arms. Jillian and Etta crowded close to her from behind. The men didn't seem to take notice of her or the children standing in the back corner.

The Indians went to Waussinoodae's bed and gently wrapped the woman in the animal skin. One of the warriors fussed a bit about something they were seeing. Whitmore approached the bed and spoke to them. They nodded, then one large Indian picked up the body and carried it outside. The other Indians followed. Except for one. He seemed to be the one in charge. He exchanged Ojibwa words with Whitmore, who seemed agitated and frustrated with what the Indian was telling him. The tall Indian's chin jutted out, and he spat back the words with force. Whatever he was demanding, Whitmore seemed to be doing his best to counteract. Sally hoped it wasn't about Hosea.

Alexander moved toward the two men. Sally reached out to grab his arm, but he pulled free and went to stand by the arguing men.

As the Ojibwa heated conversation continued, Whitmore put his hand on Alexander's shoulder and drew him close. He said something to Alexander, and the boy nodded.

Sally grew fearful. Why were they including Alexander in this conversation? Why should he be involved at all?

Whitmore seemed to be pleading for something. The other Indian wasn't backing down. Soon Whitmore took Alexander by the shoulders, turned him to face him, and spoke to him in English. When he did, Pa came inside the doorway.

"Do you understand what the chief's son is asking you?"

Alexander nodded.

"We won't let them take you. We'll fight these men, but I'm afraid if we try something now—they may take their anger out on the Bakers."

Sally wasn't sure what was happening, but she listened as carefully as she could.

Alexander backed up from Whitmore and went toward the Indian chief's son, answering his sharp requests in Ojibwa.

Alexander followed the chief's son out of the cabin, pushing past Hosea. Sally wasn't sure, but it appeared that Alexander was required to go with them. But why? She tried to rush toward the door, but Whitmore held her back. "Do as I say! Stay here. In the cabin."

"But Alexander!" Sally pleaded to know why he was going with them.

"He'll be okay. He's going of his own free will."

Hosea watched as the men brought out the chief's wife's body. They carefully lowered her onto the cot behind the horse and then wrapped her tightly with ropes. The wailing began again.

Without realizing what was happening, Hosea watched the Indians mount their horses, and turn to leave. Before he could stop him, Alexander sprang up onto the last Indian's horse and held onto the man in front of him. Hosea stepped toward the horse.

"No, Hosea." Whitmore came out of the cabin before Hosea could take a step forward.

"What's happening? Is Alexander going with them?"

"Yes," Whitmore answered, "You need to allow him to go."

"Go where?" Hosea's heart raced. He began to sweat profusely.

"They're requiring him to go with them. They say it, as you say, 'An eye for an eye, a tooth for a tooth.'"

"But why? The boy hasn't done anything wrong!" Hosea grew more agitated as Sally came to stand near him in the doorway.

"It is official. A demand from the chief. Waussinoodae's life for Alexander's."

Hosea clung to Sally. "What do you mean? What will they do to him? Will they harm him?"

"I don't know." Whitmore put his arm out to keep Hosea and Sally from dashing toward the horse to retrieve the boy. "Don't react. Just let them go." Whitmore glanced around at Ambrose and Billie. "No one cock their gun. Do you understand?" The men around Hosea and Sally stood still.

"But I can't," Hosea pleaded. "This boy has done nothing wrong. Stop them, Whitmore. Convince them to take me instead."

Whitmore held Hosea's arm tight. "Alexander decided to go with them. It's best to allow it to happen."

"But no. Not this!" Tears now streamed down Hosea's face. Sally whimpered into her apron. "Don't they know? Can't they see? He's my son now!"

They all watched as the wailing continued and the Indians disappeared back into the forest the way they had come.

CHAPTER THIRTY-FOUR

"Why are you allowing this?" Hosea choked back tears. He wanted to wail just as the Indians had been doing as they made their way off the property.

"I'm not allowing anything to happen that could not change in the future. But for now, you have to understand. We can't go against a demand from the chief, or there will be trouble. Don't you see? Allowing the boy to go is the best way to protect you and your family." Whitmore kicked the ground with the tip of his shoe. "Their ways are not our ways! They're grieving for their chief's wife. The queen of their tribe. Whatever they say must happen, or they will harm you, your family, or even other settlers in the area." Whitmore rubbed down his beard again with his hand. "I'm sorry, Hosea. I know what that boy means to you."

All Hosea could think about was Alexander's safety. Nothing else mattered. He choked out the words, "Tell me the truth. Will they kill him?"

Whitmore hesitated, as if he had to think through what he was about to say. "I think you better pray to that God who is all-important to you. Pray for the boy's safety. I don't believe they'd harm him, but I don't know for sure."

"Oh, God, no!" Sally collapsed to the ground. Etta and Jillian rushed to her from behind. Picking her up, they helped her back inside.

Hosea left the group and stumbled out to the river.

Ambrose, Whitmore and the rest of the men knew better than to follow him.

Ambrose motioned to Whitmore as they watched Hosea walk away. "Do you really believe they might harm Alexander?"

Whitmore seemed at a loss as to what to say. "I don't know, Ambrose. They have their ways. Their customs. Perhaps they'll take his life to appease the gods for Waussinoodae. Or perhaps they'll allow him to live in exchange for Waussinoodae's life. It's all up to them. I hate to be the bearer of bad news, but there is nothing we as newcomers to this land can do. We need to allow them the rights they have to do what they deem best." Whitmore bowed his head. "I'm sorry. I wish I could do more."

Ambrose watched his father make his way to the river beside the house. He'd never seen the man so broken. He could hear his ma crying from inside the cabin. "Is there anything the law would be able to do in a situation like this?"

"Like I said. We need to abide by the Indian wishes. And if Hosea's faith in God's protection is true, we need it now more than ever."

Ambrose went to stand by his sisters near the doorway. They were both crying. Everyone at the Baker home loved Alexander as one of their own. They'd watched the young lad grow, learn to speak English, and become a Baker son. And now this. The Indians had lost Waussinoodae, but now, they were in mourning as well.

"Oh, God!" Hosea went to the edge of the river that seemed just as agitated as his soul. The strong current was rushing close to the banks after the last few nights of heavy rain. He glanced at the mirror of the rising moon now reflecting off the water. Ripples of its light shined bright as darkness encompassed the land. "What have I done? I've put Alexander's life in danger. I never meant for this to happen. You know my heart. It is desperately wicked. But You, oh God, know that I would never want harm to come to Alexander."

Hosea put his hands over his face and sobbed, "Oh God, protect our boy!"

Hosea's heart felt raw. He was but a mere human losing a son. Visions and precious memories flooded Hosea's heart. Watching the little boy follow behind him everywhere he went. Remembering the feeling of Alexander's hand in his. Looking out over the river, he thought back to the day that he and Alexander had fished together on a hot summer day, both falling into the water in the excitement of catching a few fish. His tears grew heavier.

"What would You have me do?" Hosea bowed his head and let the tears drip down his cheeks, wetting his shirt collar. "Should I go to the Indians and give them my own life? Is that what You'd require me to do? If it will bring the boy back, I will, Lord. You know I will."

At that moment, as the grief of losing Alexander penetrated his heart, Hosea gained a glimpse of the God he served. He knew God understood this deep grief he was feeling. He'd given His son, Jesus. Jesus was sent to earth on a mission to save Hosea's soul. The souls of all men. Is this how God felt when he allowed that to happen?

Alexander wasn't a son from Hosea's loins, but a child given to him as a gift. Yet now, God was allowing Hosea an opportunity to understand the Father's gift fully. The sacrifice of Jesus and all He'd done for him on the cross. He was now sharing similar grief. The loss of Alexander was unbearable. Yet, at that moment, Hosea felt assurance that God knew Hosea's pain as he stood in an unknown wilderness. Alexander wasn't insignificant in God's eyes. God knew Hosea well, and he understood his grief. Yet in God's sorrow, scripture also said that the act "pleased the Lord to bruise Him."

It did not please Hosea to allow the Indians to take Alexander in exchange for Waussinoodae. Hosea wasn't God. His sorrow was deep, fresh, and hurt him greater than anything he'd had to endure.

Hosea tipped his head back to gaze into the sky. The cool night air chilled his damp cheeks. Just as he did, Hosea saw ripples of color streaming across the sky like waves on the ocean. Swirling and bouncing off the horizon. He'd heard Whitmore call the flashes 'northern lights,' and on occasion, the brilliance of the show had captivated the Baker family with its colorful aura. The night sky's show helped Hosea to remember that God was listening. God heard his cry. At that moment, Hosea knew that he'd never forget this night for as long as he lived as the 'peace that passeth all understanding' filled his sorrowful heart.

He remembered something Whitmore had told him about Waussinoodae. In Ojibwa, the meaning of her name meant, 'northern lights.' Hosea comprehended the grief of the Indian man who had once stolen from him on the trail leading them to Michigan. Hosea had accidentally killed the man's daily companion, and now the man suffered the most tremendous loss that any man on earth could know, the death of a spouse. Grief affected all people the same, at the awareness that death had stolen someone dear. Shock would soon turn into emptiness. It was only the aftermath of it that was different for everyone.

Hosea now knew that his response was to remember that he wasn't the only one grieving. Alexander was a strong child who'd been through more, in his young life, than any of them. And just as

Jesus, he was willing. If God never allowed Hosea to share any more of his life with the young boy, he had brought happiness, salvation, and sheer joy to their family, even if it had been for just a short time.

Hosea bowed his head and thanked God for that. He also prayed again for the safekeeping of the child's life.

Sally didn't know what else to do the next morning but scour the bedroom where Waussinoodae had passed away. She had Jillian and Etta haul water from the river to heat up in the kettle outside the door, and then she used the last of the lye soap to cleanse the area in and around the bed. The girls had also gathered new, fresh grasses to refill the mattress.

On her hands and knees, Sally scrubbed until her hands turned raw from the hot water and soap. Her knees ached, but it helped to lessen the ache in her heart. What would their life be without Alexander? He'd become such a special part of their lives.

She couldn't erase the sadness on her husband's face nor the tears he shed through the night. It only doubled in her heart. The child's laughter was gone. His bright and willing spirit had vanished. The house felt dark and foreboding.

Whitmore had left that morning to return to the post. He wanted to see if he could hear any rumblings or rumors regarding

Waussinoodae's death from the other Indians living near the post. Perhaps someone could get him information about the young boy. He'd told them the night before that he would do everything in his power to find out information but to fight or attempt to retrieve the boy would probably be futile. They'd only start a war they didn't want to have to fight or finish.

As she went to redo a section of the floor, Sally heard the door squeak open. Glancing up, she found Caroline and Betsey holding Julia silhouetted against the bright sunshine outside. She stood and immediately went into Betsey's arms. Baby Julia squealed in excitement to see Sally and wrapped her tiny arms around her grammy's neck. Sally pulled her into her arms and hugged the child almost too tight, as the child grunted in protest. "Oh, Julia! Grammy sure needed to see you today."

Betsey's face was damp with tears. "Ma, I'm so sorry. We couldn't believe it when Ambrose came to tell us."

Sally couldn't speak, but clung tightly to Betsey and the baby. Betsey's large belly was now making that more challenging. "It will be fine. We need to trust God to protect him."

Betsey pulled away. "I can't believe this is happening." She wiped tears off her cheeks. "How's Pa?"

Sally could only give her daughter a look of despair and shake her head. More tears filled Betsey's eyes and slipped down her cheeks.

"Aaron said Whitmore isn't sure what they might do to him. It scares me to death to think they might harm him."

Sally turned away, taking Julia with her to sit down at the table. "We can't think of the possibilities. It will kill me to talk about them right now."

Betsey pulled off her hat and sat down beside her at the table. Caroline sat across from them.

"It seems like we should be able to do something," Caroline pleaded.

Sally explained what Whitmore had told them. It was better to allow the Indians to have their way. Perhaps later, they'd be able to do something, but for now, their only option was to pray for the boy's protection. "Sometimes God allows the impossible things to come into our lives to build our faith. When there isn't anything we can humanly do to change our situation, that's when trust comes." Sally took off Julia's hat.

She grabbed her grammy's cheeks with her chubby hands.

"Mamee," the baby babbled. "Mamee!"

"Did she just call me *Grammy?*" Sally relished in the sparkling eyes of her first grandbaby and grinned, despite her aching heart.

The baby drooled and then clapped her hands. "Mamee!"

"I do believe she's trying to say it." Betsey smiled.

"And not even a year old. Not only are you my granddaughter, but you're as smart as they come!" Sally gushed over the child.

"What do we do now?" Caroline asked her mother.

Sally gazed into the eyes of her second eldest daughter, who seemed on the verge of bursting into tears at the slightest inclination. "We go on living. We live for Waussinoodae and

Alexander. We pray for his safety. We relish in the memories we have of him and her. We need to thank God in all circumstances, even in our deep sadness, but especially when our hearts have no understanding.

CHAPTER THIRTY-FIVE

Aaron had gotten the word from Whitmore that morning. He'd sent one of his employees to find Aaron and summon both him and Hosea to the trading post.

"What do you think will happen?" Betsey paced the floor with Julia, who'd been up most of the night with another budding tooth.

Aaron packed a knapsack with a bit of food for both himself and Hosea. "Sounds like Whitmore has scheduled a hearing of sorts to work all this out with Maemaeketchewunk and Hosea."

"Is that all it is? Will Pa find further trouble for accidentally killing the chief's dog? What more could they take away? What else will they do?"

"I don't know, Betsey. Perhaps this one-on-one meeting will dissolve some of the hard feelings. We can't sit around here living in fear of Indian retaliation for all of it."

"I do trust Whitmore. He knows the Indians better than all of us." Betsey patted the whimpering child that now clung to her. "I wish he could magically solve the achy gum of this child."

Aaron smirked. "If only life were that simple." Aaron pulled Betsey and Julia close, pecking both of them on their cheeks. "I hope you can get some sleep this afternoon while she naps."

With Betsey just weeks away from giving birth, she found it harder and harder to manage Julia. She'd soon need to figure out how best to care for multiple babies.

"Be safe and take care of Pa. He hasn't been the same since they took Alexander."

Aaron flung the knapsack over his right shoulder. "I will. Maybe the chief and he can talk about what's best for Alexander. Perhaps Whitmore can convince the Indians to let us keep the boy. Just pray."

Betsey shifted Julia to her other hip. "You know I will."

Hosea was ready to go with Aaron as soon as he got to the Baker cabin. His horse was ready, and he mounted as soon as Aaron came from the ridge at a gallop.

"Let's go, Aaron. I want to get this behind me."

The trip to the post was a quiet one. Hosea seemed to be uttering prayers all the way, for his lips moved, but he didn't say anything out loud.

As they entered through the door of the post, Whitmore greeted them. Behind him stood a band of younger, warrior-type men. Among them—Chief Maemaeketchewunk. He was taller than the other men, and appeared to be just about the same age as Hosea.

Whitmore led Hosea to stand before the chief. The chief stared at Hosea after saying something to Whitmore.

Whitmore turned to Hosea. "Stand tall, don't look at the floor. They'll believe you to be a coward if you do."

Hosea twisted his hat in his hands but did as Whitmore advised him.

"Maemaeketchewunk is the chief of the Fisher tribe."

Whitmore pointed to Aaron and said a few more words to the chief, but the chief's glare didn't leave Hosea.

It seemed to Aaron that Whitmore was merely offering up introductions to who each person was. He then motioned everyone to sit down around the fireplace hearth: Indians on one side, Hosea and Aaron opposite them.

Whitmore interpreted the chief's words to Hosea. "He says...the white man has come to his country and taken their land. They are planting corn on the spot where his home had been. The intruders are shooting his deer, snaring his fish. He's lost his rights and has been left no chance for happiness. And now you have killed his dog!"

The chief's blazing eyes and bronze features showed anger. "On top of this...my wife has died in your presence. The disease has decimated our village. We did not have these kinds of diseases until the white man came to live here."

Aaron could tell Hosea was doing his best to sort out how he would reply. He did not take his eyes off the angry Indian but hesitated for just a moment.

"Hosea, just speak, and I'll interpret."

Hosea stood, "I am not guilty of wantonly destroying your property. I have taken no land from you. The land I claim I purchased from my government. You and your people have been paid for this country and have no longer any right to it. You roam over it still to hunt and fish, but only because my government is generous and allows you to do so. I did not kill your dog to injure you but to protect myself. He destroyed what would have been food for my children, and I killed him to keep him from destroying more." Whitmore interpreted every word for the chief. "As for Waussinoodae. She was a fine woman. A treasure to you, I'm sure. Just as my wife is to me. My wife did her best to restore Waussinoodae's health, but God had other plans. We will cherish her memory.

"You've taken my son, Alexander. Please reconsider this. He is dear to us. We love him and want to continue to show him the ways of our people. His people. Do not take your anger out on him. He is innocent of any wrongdoing. If a sin has been committed in any of these situations, it is mine alone."

Hosea sat down. The chief looked at him with disgust and disdain, his arms folding in defiance. But after Whitmore repeated Hosea's words to him, his shoulders drooped. He glanced around at all the men now seated around him. Standing, he took one step toward Hosea and held out his hand.

Whitmore motioned for Hosea to shake his hand. When he did, the Indians spoke a few words and then stomped out of the room. At the door, the chief turned to Whitmore and shouted a few words. Then he walked out of the building with the other Indian men following him.

"What did he say?" Hosea leaned closer to Whitmore.

"He said we would see him no more."

"What about Alexander?"

Whitmore shrugged. "He didn't say anything about the child. I'm sorry."

"Hosea, what happened?" Sally came outside, wiping her hands on a towel. "I've been praying so hard all afternoon."

The sun cast shadows over Hosea's property. The wind whistled in the trees over their heads. A particular fall breeze made Sally shiver as she stood petting the nose of the horse her husband had ridden onto the property.

"Did you ask about Alexander?"

"Woman, let me get off my horse, and we'll talk about it over dinner."

Sally nodded as the younger girls now streamed out of the cabin to greet their pa and Aaron. Her questions seemed to fall on the deaf ears of her subdued husband.

"I'll take your horses to the barn," Caroline spoke up and took the reins from the men, beckoning and clicking to the horses to follow her.

"Thank you, Carrie." Hosea's arms encircled his wife. "Don't worry, Sally Mae. All is well."

As they all walked into the cabin, the girls scurried around to get Aaron and Hosea plates laden with food. "Sit down and eat with us, Aaron. I'm sure it's way past your dinner at home. Caroline went up to check on Betsey this afternoon, and she was exhausted from walking the floor with Julia. Those teeth!" Sally motioned for Aaron to join them.

"Thank you, Sally." He sat down beside Hosea.

"Will they allow Alexander to come home?" Jillian sat down beside her pa and placed her head on his shoulder. He reached around and pulled her close. "I don't know, Jilly. I pled my case and was honest with the man."

"I just miss him," Jillian moaned.

"We all do, sweetheart. Now let your pa eat." Hosea sat back and took his arm back to grab a spoon.

"We'll pray that they will care for the boy. For now, that's all we can do." Hosea thanked God for the day's affairs and their food, and added another plea for Alexander's safety.

CHAPTER THIRTY-SIX

"Where should we put the hearth?" Horace looked to Caroline standing in the middle of a square he'd drawn out in the dirt surrounding her.

"Oh Horace, it doesn't matter to me."

"Don't go getting' all timid on me now. I can't make all the decisions about this house. You need to be a part of it, too." Horace approached her as she looked deep into his eyes.

"I'm not trying to be timid; I guess it all seems so unreal. You want to spend the rest of your life with me. Billie still not understanding my reasons, and then Alexander—I guess I'm overwhelmed by everything."

He could see tears forming in her deep brown eyes. He pulled her into his arms. "I think we should plan a spring wedding."

Caroline stepped back. "Spring?"

"It will take until then to get the house all finished. We'll be able to start next year with a garden in the backyard and a home all our own. What do you say?"

Caroline put her hands on her hips. "Horace Knapp—are you asking me to marry you?"

Horace felt the heat rise from under his collar. He fiddled with the button at the top of his shirt. "Unless of course, you're not wanting to."

Caroline's shoulders drooped. "I would be honored to be your wife, but are you sure we aren't rushing into this?"

"Well, you did just turn seventeen, and I will be twenty in February. I don't see an issue with it. Unless, of course..."

"What?" Caroline walked into his arms again.

"Have you changed your mind again?"

Caroline smiled up at him. "No. I haven't changed my mind. I know what I want and who I want. I choose you." For the first time in a long time, Horace was convinced by the kiss she now gave him.

"Where have you kids been today?" Pa asked Caroline and Horace that night at the dinner table.

"We've been to the property Horace is thinking about settling on. Just west of Ambrose." Caroline picked up the bowl of potatoes and passed it to Etta.

"That's a tight lot there, don't you think, Horace?"

Horace tried hard to swallow the mouthful he'd just taken to answer Pa. "I've been eyeing it for some time now, sir. I wanted to get Caroline's opinion, too."

"Is her opinion important to you, Horace?"

"Yes, sir." Horace wiped his mouth off with his napkin. "It is."

"Since when?" Something happened under the table because Pa winced. Ma gave him her 'none of your business' suggestion with her eyes.

"Ma. Pa. I know we haven't said all that much, but—I think Horace and I would like to be married."

Pa's fork stopped mid-air. "Married?"

"Yes, sir." Horace pushed his plate forward a bit. Eating his dinner now seemed to become second in importance. "I...I mean, we—have decided that we could schedule a spring wedding. We didn't want to bring it up quite yet because we just discussed it this afternoon, but with your permission, sir—I'd like to ask for Caroline's hand," Horace stuttered, "—in marriage."

"Caroline. Have you shared this information with Billie? I was under the impression..." Pa appeared concerned.

"I have, Pa. Day before Alexander went back to the Indians. When Horace and I were staying with Betsey, Billie came to visit, and I told him I couldn't have a relationship with a man that I didn't love."

It was Pa who now scooted his plate forward. "So, you want to marry my daughter then?"

"Yes." Horace coughed. "Yes, sir, I do."

"Well, I appreciate your honesty, so now I'll give you some of my own."

Silence reigned at the table. No one took a bite of food. All eyes were on Hosea. He didn't say a word but looked at Ma with wide eyes.

"What took you so long, son?"

Everyone stared at Pa and then glanced at Caroline.

Ma laughed right out loud. "Hosea. Why do you do things like that?"

Laughter seemed to finally cut through the sadness and worry of the last few weeks since Alexander's departure. It felt good to have good news to share.

"Welcome to our family, son!"

Horace's shoulders sagged. "Thank you, sir."

"I have one other thing to mention." Pa took a large gulp from his coffee mug. "I have a bit of property to the east of here. It's right on a corner, and it is a part of the six hundred acres I own here. I'd like for you and Caroline to head over to see it. See if it might suit you well, and if it does, it will be yours as soon as I can get the deed arranged. Our wedding present to you both. If there is another piece on my land that you'd like better, come see me. We'll work something out."

"Thank you, Pa." Caroline blushed at the thought of her parents now knowing that she and Horace were serious.

"What's happened to Billie?" Jillian asked it so innocently it was almost hard to hear what she said.

"I told him the truth. I don't know what his plans will be now, but I felt it important to tell him the truth." Caroline's matter-of-fact tone seemed to appease Jillian because she smiled at the comment.

Hosea raised his fork. "There is one thing, though. I need to tell you. If you do take the land I'm offering you, you'll need to pay a portion of the taxes owed come spring. Do you have a problem with that?"

Horace knew the gift of the land was worth much more than what he'd have to pay for the property taxes. He answered. "No, sir."

"If you pay a portion, so will Ambrose and Betsey. That way, we can manage to still be together. On our land." Hosea shifted in his seat. "I'd be mighty obliged for the help in getting those taxes paid."

"Thank you, sir." Horace smiled.

Hosea sighed. Sally could hear him from her side of the bed. The man had been tossing and turning in his sleep ever since Alexander left them. It seemed the night was the time he worried about the boy the most. He just worked harder during the day, and Sally was sure it was because it took his mind off what might have happened to the child.

They all missed Alexander. Sally was sure Hosea didn't know how much Alexander helped until he was gone. Hosea would often have him run to the barn for a tool or head up to Betsey's house to fetch Aaron. Each chore now was again on Hosea's shoulders. He wasn't an old man, yet he began to struggle with all the efforts it took to run the farm.

"Hosea?"

"Hmmm?"

"Are you awake?"

Hosea turned to face his wife. "Yes."

"Are you okay?"

Hosea pulled his arm up over his head, using it to prop his head up. "I don't know, Sally Mae. Some days I'm fine and other days—I struggle and worry about the boy so much."

Sally snuggled closer to her husband. "We have to believe that God knows what's best for him."

"We do. I agree." Hosea pulled the covers up to his chin. "I just pray that his life is easy, and they aren't too hard on him. He's an obedient, willing child. I hope they don't take advantage of that."

Sally cuddled closer. She could feel Hosea's whiskers against her cheek. "I love you, Hosea."

He kissed her forehead. "I love you, Sally Mae."

"There's somethin' else I've been thinking about. I think we need to shift the way we support ourselves, Sally. We'll need to pay the taxes on our portion of the land this spring, and I would like to start a gristmill, in addition to the sawmill, soon. We can manage to build it ourselves. I'd have to get millstones to grind the wheat. Bring them up from down south. Ambrose will work for me, but I'm hoping I can hire Horace on, too. We may have to see if the community is ready for it. Borrow a bit of money from each of the neighbors, making it community-owned. What do you think?"

"I trust you, Hosea. You've always known what's best for our family."

"Always?" Hosea pulled her away and looked into her eyes. "That's a change of heart."

"I didn't think so when you moved us from Pennsylvania to Michigan Territory, but I do believe now, it was a good move. Look at the children. They're thriving here. I do wish Etta and Jillian could be in school, but that will start soon enough. I like it here. It feels like home."

"Despite the Indians all around us and all the hardships we've endured?"

"It's strengthened all of our faith. We trust God now and not just ourselves. I will trust you that you will ask God and move forward as both of you see fit for this family."

Hosea kissed Sally's cheek. "Thank you, Sally. I appreciate your confidence in my decisions. She will do him good and not evil all the days of her life."

The quote from a Bible passage about being a virtuous wife made Sally smile as she drifted off to sleep.

As the crops finished coming in for their second year in the new territory, the jars on the shelves began to stack up, and produce filled the barn to overflowing. It had been a good year for their second year on the farm. Sally was thankful to have Betsey and the other girls help get food stored away for another Michigan winter.

Soon they would celebrate a new year and endure their second snowy season. The birth of another grandchild gave the family something to look forward to.

This time Betsey gave birth before even Sally could arrive to help her.

Baby Richard Swain came into the world on December 15, 1834, with a loud, blustery cry. Betsey declared to the family a week after his birth that if her window and door had been open, they would have heard his greeting at the Baker cabin.

Julia adored her little brother and toddled around getting him a nappy or a blanket whenever Betsey asked for her help. Both children kept Betsey home during the days preceding the coming new year.

One warmer than usual afternoon, Sally headed to check on Betsey and the children as Aaron left to go north of their area to scout out some criminal activity at a nearby town. Word of his law enforcement talent spread throughout the territory quickly as he roamed the country to fulfill his duties.

As Sally approached the cabin, she saw a glimpse of someone watching her from the edge of the property. They hadn't seen any Indians on the property since the day the Indians had come to take

Waussinoodae and Alexander from them. Sally stopped but then rushed toward Betsey's cabin as she suspected that an Indian was close. Her trust in their actions had waned a bit since Hosea's issues a few months back.

As she rushed around the front to get to Betsey's door, she saw someone dart across the yard toward her. As she reached for the door handle to push open the door, she realized who was running toward her. She stopped, and placed the basket she was carrying on the snowy ground as Alexander flung himself into her arms.

"Alexander!" Sally grasped the boy by the shoulders. He wore the same pants she'd hemmed a dozen times while he was living with her, but a heavy cloak of deer hide hung over his shoulders. His hair was dirt-filled and scraggly, but his face smiled up at her as she hugged him.

"Ma!"

His smell was awful, and it took all Sally could do to cuddle the child and hold him close. She pushed him a bit away from her. "Alexander!" She wiped back his scraggly hair. "Are you okay?"

"Yes, Ma. I am fine. They have treated me well. I can only stay a little while. I wanted to see you or Pa so you know I'm okay." The boy did seem healthy, other than needing a good bath. "I miss you."

"Oh child, we miss you!" Sally knew she'd have to scrub hard to get the smell off her coat, but she didn't care. It was Alexander, and he was in her arms.

Betsey opened the door. She must have heard the commotion, and when she saw Alexander, she handed her ma the baby and pulled him close. "Alexander! Oh, child. Let me look at you."

Alexander stepped away from Betsey. "I do not smell good."

Both women giggled. "You're right about that, but we do feel blessed to be able to hold you again."

"I need to stay with the tribe. I can't believe the warriors allowed me the opportunity to go hunting today, but they are finding it hard to find game to eat. The camp is north of here." Alexander pointed toward the forest beyond Betsey's cabin.

Sally hesitated, but she needed to know for sure. "Alexander, will they allow you to return to us?"

The boy's head dropped. "I do not think so. The chief never wanted me to return to live with the white man. He fought my mother for many days when she insisted that I go to live with you. He thought I would tell Indian secrets to you and then made me promise not to say anything. He told me, if I did, he would kill my mother.

"As you know, I believed him. So that is why I never spoke." Alexander waved his hand, "Anything." Alexander sighed. "Now that my Indian mother is gone, he says he cannot trust me anymore. I need to live with him. Forever! My life in exchange for my mother's." Alexander lifted his head in determination. "I will fulfill the duty."

"Oh, my dear boy." Sally grabbed Alexander's hands. "You are a wonder, you are!"

"I need to return. Find food. Tell Pa I miss him, but I will make him proud of me."

Sally pulled him close again. "He already is, Alexander. He already is."

Alexander put his hand to his chest and pounded it. He then turned around and dashed back into the woods as it swallowed him within it.

Winter descended in the territory strong and fierce. The pine branches dipping low to the ground with the burden of heavy, white snow, glistened in the forest.

Horace and Caroline had inspected the property that her pa had asked them to choose. They loved the area and decided that Horace would have the help from Ambrose and John to build a home during the winter months. They were planning a spring wedding.

During the cold months, everyone worked together to help Caroline prepare for the wedding and have a house of her own. Jillian and Etta learned how to crochet with thread that Claire had shared with them. Soon they were making Caroline hot pads for her kitchen and a doily for her table.

Caroline began piecing together a wedding dress out of material Horace had purchased for her from a Pontiac store. He'd gone there earlier to buy some needed building materials for their home. It was beautiful cloth, and Caroline was excited to wear something so pretty and new for her special day. Even after the wedding, the dress could be worn for special occasions.

One afternoon, Ma dug through her memory barrel for the veil she'd packed in Pennsylvania. Its age made it delicate, and any quick movement would tear the fragile fabric, so when she handed it to Caroline, she placed it across her lap.

"Ma, what's this?"

"It's my wedding veil. I've saved it for one of my girls to wear on their wedding day. I'd forgotten all about it when Betsey got married. Will you be the first?"

Caroline rubbed the beautiful lace veil in her fingers. "Oh, Ma, it's beautiful. Thank you for saving it for me."

Jillian and Etta jumped from their chairs to look at the veil.

"Can I wear it, too? When it's my turn?" Jillian jumped up and down beside Caroline's chair.

"You all may wear it if you wish." Ma then took it from Caroline. "It's so delicate; I'll place it back in the barrel until your special day. I'd hate for anything to happen to it now."

"Ma, do you think the lilacs will be out and ready for the wedding?" Caroline called after her mother, who was placing the veil back into the barrel.

"They usually come out in May. My bush beside the house should have its first blooms by then."

"I love the smell of lilacs. It's been such a long time since we've seen them." Caroline tipped her head back as if to sniff the air for the imaginary scent.

"Lilacs would make a beautiful bouquet." Etta beamed.

"How is Horace progressing on your home, Caroline?" Ma returned to the hearth where they'd circled their chairs to be close to the fire.

"It's coming. John Swain is very good at carpentry. Not only is it being built faster than even Ambrose could do it, but he's teaching Horace carpentry skills as well." Caroline started again on the stitches of her wedding dress.

"John is a talented man. I feel so badly that he is still dealing with Abigail's sickness. She hasn't been doing well since last fall. Claire says she seems to have just given up. She hates it here, and without the will to fight, she lies in bed all day. I feel so badly for John. He tries hard to help her, but enough is never enough." Ma examined Jillian's crocheting and pointed out a stitch she'd missed.

"I tried to go see her the other day with Claire." Caroline gathered more thread for her needle. "But Abigail told Claire she didn't want visitors. I can't imagine lying in that cabin day in and day out. I'd go crazy."

"I've never been able to understand that young woman. She has a wonderful husband. She could make her home look nice and gain many friends, but it's not what she wants. It will be interesting to see what happens to the couple once spring comes."

Pa burst through the door. His face was pink from the outside cold. "Looky here! All my girls busy with their sewin'."

"Shut the door, Hosea!" Ma pulled her sweater up tighter around her shoulders.

Hosea dropped the two buckets he'd brought from the spring, then shut the door. "I think we'll need to find us a window come spring. I hate not being able to see the sunshine on a winter day. It's makin' the ground just sparkle right now, like a million tiny gems reflecting off the sun." Hosea squinted. "But the darkness of this cabin makes it hard for a man to get his eyes adjusted."

"Did you get to see Ambrose and the boys this morning?" Caroline asked her pa, who now dumped the buckets of water into the barrel by the door. A few large chunks of ice made the water splash onto the floor.

"Hosea! My floor!" Ma stood up to fetch a rag to wipe up the mess.

"I did. Things are coming along nicely. It will be a fine house soon." Hosea stripped out of his heavy winter coat and whistled as he took off his gloves. "It's mighty pretty out there, but boy, it's cold!"

Soon the family gathered around the supper table as Pa bowed his head to bless the food. He thanked the Lord for the beauty of the land. He also praised Him for His loving protection and grace. Before finishing up the prayer, he prayed for Alexander's safety and health through the cold winter. There wasn't a day that went by that he didn't add Alexander to the prayer despite what Sally had told him about the boy's visit. Hosea's demeanor appeared to have changed for the better after finding out that the tribe hadn't harmed Alexander.

It still felt odd to be a small family of five now. Horace and Ambrose now lived at Ambrose's new house on the south of the property. Betsey was busy with her two babies, and Aaron was often traveling and enforcing the law.

"Talked to Henry Leach and Josiah Pierce today about the gristmill. They seem eager to get something like that started. They also suggest we get a few members of the community together to start a township of sorts. Find someone to represent us all if the government decides to make this area a state." Pa took a scoop of beets out of a bowl near him. "They've asked me to be the township president. Come spring of this year, they suggested we all meet and name our community."

All the women at the table exclaimed their excitement.

"Oh, Pa, that's wonderful!"

"It's about time, Hosea. We need a name for our home. Any thoughts on one yet?"

Hosea shook his head as he dug into his food. "None yet. Any ideas from you girls?"

"We could call it Meadville." Jillian passed a bowl of potatoes to Etta.

"We can't call it Meadville." Etta passed the same bowl to Caroline. "It needs to be a different name. Something creative."

"We could use an Indian name of some kind. In honor of their establishing this land and all."

"That's a fine idea, Caroline." Pa stood and placed another log on the fire. Perhaps before the upcomin' meeting, you all could sit down and think over a few options. We'll combine them with what others deem appropriate and see what we come up with."

"There should be the word *new* in it somehow, don't you think, Pa?" Etta was often the last to suggest something, so Pa took notice as he sat back down.

"You might be right, Etta. It is a new place to live. The start of a community. I agree. We'll put that at the top of the list."

Ma leaned back on her chair, "It's hard to believe we've been here now almost two years. Although," she smiled at Pa, "it feels like a whole lot more than just two years. Look what we've accomplished. We have a fine farm, and now Betsey, Ambrose, and soon Caroline will have places of their own, too. I have two beautiful, new grandbabies." Ma folded her arms and smiled.

"But we've also lost, too." Pa stopped eating for a minute.

"We'll always miss Alexander, but even the Indians can't take him from our hearts." Ma patted Pa's arm.

"I sure do miss that boy." Breathing in deep, he added, "The lesson of gaining trust is crucial during our short years on earth. We need to solidify that reliance in our hearts to know how to respond in desperate situations. As hard as it is to learn, the joys of feeling complete trust in God is strong and mighty. We do have much for which to be grateful. It's been a hard year, but also a lot to be thankful for."

CHAPTER THIRTY-SEVEN

Caroline picked up the purple bouquet that Betsey had placed at the foot of the bed. There weren't many lilacs on the tree Pa had planted for Ma the first year he'd come upon the Michigan Territory, but it was enough to make a pretty addition to her wedding day.

Smoothing down the bright blue fabric in her new dress, Caroline nervously attempted to wipe out the wrinkles. Yet her heart gushed with gladness. She would soon be a new wife to Horace. Horace had finished the house on the hill just to the west of Pa and Ma's cabin. They'd all have their own homes soon. In August of this year, Caroline would turn eighteen. She was younger than Betsey was when she got married, but Caroline never felt more prepared than she did today to become a wife.

Etta and Jillian burst through the door. "Caroline, are you ready?"

Caroline answered, "I think so. Do I look okay?" She did a turn in the corner of the cabin.

Both girls squealed and giggled in excitement. "You look beautiful!"

As Caroline made her way to the doorway of her Michigan Territory home, Jillian skipped to the door to open it for her. "Everyone is ready to begin."

Jillian opened the door, and the darkness disappeared as the warm breeze and sunshine from a beautiful May afternoon filled the room. Caroline wanted to cherish each moment of her wedding day. She knew that it would go quickly, and soon she and Horace would get on his horse and arrive at their new home together as husband and wife. If she didn't carefully savor each memory, she'd fail to remember it, so she hesitated a bit and turned to look back into the cabin where it had all began.

She remembered the first day Ambrose brought Horace home for supper. He was handsome. It had been such a long time since they'd seen boys their age. She recalled how Etta and even Jillian had giggled over his presence at their dinner table.

She then gazed over the small cabin and thought of how they'd adapted and creatively made it into a comfortable dwelling.

As she went over the door's threshold, and before her eyes could focus in the light, she heard baby Julia squeal her name. Soon all the people that had come to celebrate with them came into focus.

On one side stood all of her family. Betsey holding baby Richard, Ma carrying Julia. Jillian and Etta had scooted out the door ahead of her and now stood giggling and smiling beside Ma. Pa stood at the right of the door, and soon he held out his arm to her. Caroline took hold and gripped it hard. Oh, how she'd miss her daily adventures with her pa and sharing the work on their farm. She'd never known a day without them.

On the other side of the gathering were Henry and Claire Leach, Megan Pierce and Jacob and Susan Wilkinson with their children. For the first time, many new settlers were coming together to interact and exchange ideas on how to survive in the new territory. When Pa went around to invite everyone to the wedding, they'd all agreed to come. It had been a long time since a celebration of this sort had happened.

Caroline then saw Horace standing close to Aaron at the front of the crowd. He wore a suit he'd borrowed from John Swain. It was a bit big on him, but he still looked handsome in it. Caroline bowed her head and smiled. She suddenly felt very embarrassed to be the center of attention. She steadied her hand holding up the bouquet to avoid shaking the blossoms off the twigs.

As Pa led her closer to Horace, she saw Aaron there, ready to do the ceremony. A pastor of some sort would have been better, but Aaron was the only one legally able to perform a wedding ceremony due to his law enforcement job. John Swain had also offered, but at the last minute, Abigail had experienced another health setback.

The crowd now turned to the couple at the front as Pa took Caroline's hand and handed it to the man who would soon be his son-in-law. Horace's hand felt moist and cold, but soon it grew warm with Caroline's touch.

The ceremony was short and concise. Pa had insisted that Aaron use a bit of scripture and had quickly offered his favorite marriage verses. Caroline wasn't sure who was shaking more: her, Horace, or Aaron as he stumbled through the official words to unite a man to his wife.

Soon the "I do's" were said, and the prayer to start a new married life was over. Aaron winked at Horace. "Horace, you may now kiss your bride."

Horace turned to Caroline and lifted the veil off her face. He pulled her close, and their lips touched. Caroline would never forget this moment. As he pulled away, he winked at her.

Cheers erupted from the families surrounding the couple as Aaron pronounced them husband and wife.

As Caroline turned to face the crowd and exchange hugs with her family and friends, she couldn't believe the difference a year had made in her life. She'd had it all planned just seventeen short months before. The plans included everything she thought would make her happy. Bring her joy. But she'd also learned that when we attempt to plan our paths, God sometimes interrupts our arrangements to bring us something so much better.

Caroline still loved Billie, but as a friend instead of a potential soulmate. She was sure that she'd be seeing him in their new community. Perhaps soon, he'd find someone to love him as much as Horace loved her. She hoped so.

As Betsey approached her with baby Richard in her arms, she wondered how long it would be before she'd be able to give Horace children, and her parents more grandchildren. But for now, she was content to be Mrs. Horace Knapp. Their community would grow with each wedding that would take place. More and more families were even now driving their wagons into the area to take up residence along the banks of the Shiawassee River.

What would another two years bring? What would be God's plans for the community?

Horace came back to Caroline and took her hand. Smiling down at her, he kissed her forehead. Caroline knew that whatever God's plans, it didn't matter—as long as Horace was beside her.

Note from the Author

Crooked Paths Straight continues the saga of the Hosea Baker family as they establish the village of North Newburg in Shiawassee County, Michigan.

I'm sure you are curious as to which part is fiction or fact. As I write the story I often to begin to wonder that myself. As in *The Year the Stars Fell*, I use true facts about the Territory, the Baker family, but embellish much of it—from my imagination.

Betsey Baker-Swain is one of the main characters in this book again and indeed she did become pregnant shortly after giving birth to her first daughter, Julia Swain born October 28, 1833. Richard was born in 1834, but records have it near the beginning of the year. Betsey is an amazing woman, but I don't think she could have given birth in just a few short months after Julia. Somewhere in the records of Richard's birth, someone must have recorded the wrong date. I decided he needed to share the birthdate of my son, Ethan Paul Wehman of December 15 giving Betsey a full nine months to birth another child.

The story of Caroline's love interests did come from my imagination. Another walk through the Newburg Cemetery after publishing *The Year the Stars Fell* resulted in finding her grave and her last name was engraved as Knapp. Buried directly beside her was Horace. I had previously named her beau to be Billie and he would come from Pennsylvania to meet back up with her, but upon finding her real husband's grave I realized I needed to alter that part of my story. The struggle of whether to marry Billie or Horace came from my imagination.

Some of the accurate accounts of the Baker's adventures in this book include: John Ferrar Swain did arrive after the Baker family. At first I thought he was Aaron's father but since writing *The Year the Stars Fell* I realized his recorded age was too young to be Aaron's father. I then realized it had to be a brother or possibly a cousin. This is why Aaron's father never arrived in Michigan. His passing away before he could join Aaron in Michigan was my attempt to fix that misinformation.

John Ferrar was a carpenter and he did help build some of the buildings near Knagg's Bridge. He will stay in the Territory but his life will be a hard one. You'll have to read book three in the series to find out what his trade actually turns out to be to the residents of North Newburg.

It is vague but it does look like Hosea decided to start a sawmill on the Shiawassee River. I hope to put a bit more research into the establishing of the mill and highlight this in my third book.

Asiatic cholera and smallpox affected much of the Indian population from 1834 through 1836. The cholera was suspected to be caused by the settlers infecting the river which had been a source of water for the natives. Smallpox came later and nearly decimated much of the Indian population that remained. Indians disappeared deeper into the woods of Michigan to escape the diseases and increasing population, but disease still reduced their numbers.

The tax collector did come to Hosea and the property owners. The amount of the tax is pretty accurate for the amount of property Hosea owned. He did have his children pay their share on the property he had gifted to them. It is recorded that each one received 80 acres from Hosea as gifts.

Writing his doctor friend, Nicholas Harder was fiction, but soon Harder will come on the scene in book three. He was significant in the forming of North Newburg.

Alexander Stevens is noted in my research as living with the Baker family during their first few years in the Territory, but I have been unable to find any record of his death or a grave in any of the local cemeteries. His being taken back into the Indian fold is from my imagination. He needed to disappear as he has in my research and this is how I solved this.

Hosea did mistakenly kill the Chief's dog. Hosea had received piglets as a trade from a neighbor and the dog must have been trying to find bacon for a meal. He did have to go to the post and meet with Whitmore Knaggs and Chief Maemaeketchewunk to solve the issue. The words he used to defend himself are the exact words I have written.

Whitmore Knaggs was especially loved and admired by the natives in the area. He did probably settle many disputes among the Indians and the settlers coming into the Territory.

Waussinoodae has been created by my imagination. Her name does mean, "Northern Lights." The Baker family was so hospitable to all the new settlers coming into the Territory that I assumed they would also have been kind to the natives. With the lack of bright cities and in the darkness of the Michigan Territory, I'm sure the northern light shows were spectacular. Hopefully, they could have seen them beyond the trees.

The governor of the Michigan Territory at that time was the young twenty-two year old Stevens T. Mason. He has gone down in the books of history as the youngest governor ever to serve in the United States. He was serving as Governor when the Michigan Territory came into statehood in 1837.

Aaron did become a law enforcement officer in the new Territory. He was said to have a huge knowledge of, not only North Newburg, but also the surrounding villages and cities of Michigan. Whenever someone wanted to know about an area, they would seek out Aaron Swain to get directions.

Not to give anything away regarding the final book in the series, but we will watch as more settlers move into the small village by the river. They'll set up a township and begin to make laws for how they'll live and interact. Hosea will still have a main part in establishing the small village by the Shiawassee River called North Newburg.

I hope you enjoyed the second book in the Newburg Chronicles series.

~Elizabeth

About the Author

Elizabeth's first book titled *Under the Windowsill,* is a coming-of-age story about a young woman named Kenna who runs away to Mackinac Island in search of a better life.

Elizabeth's second book titled *Promise at Daybreak,* has a Durand, Michigan setting and is about two elderly sisters who are forced together due to illness. They meet again to fulfill a pact they made at their mother's grave.

Elizabeth's third book titled *Just a Train Ride,* highlights a love story from the 1940s. An elderly woman recalls her love story for a frustrated fellow passenger on a train from Chicago to Michigan.

A sequel to Just a Train Ride is Elizabeth's fourth book, is *Mere Reflection.* It is the continuing story of Blaine, the young girl on the train. What kind of life got Blaine to the place she is now and why is Callie's help so important?

The first book in the Newburg Chronicles series is *The Year the Stars Fell.* It covers the first nine months of the adventures of the Hosea Baker family as they embark on the mission to settle in the Michigan Territory.

For more information on where to find Wehman's books, check out her website at www.elizabethwehman.com or like her on Facebook at Elizabeth Wehman/Author for new and upcoming books. Also, become a fan of Elizabeth's historical series by joining the *North Newburg Chronicles* page on Facebook.

Elizabeth lives in Owosso, Michigan with her husband. You may email her at elizabethwehman@yahoo.com.

Made in the USA
Monee, IL
04 June 2021

69460292R00236